OXFORD WORLD'S CLASSICS

FRANKENSTEIN

MARY WOLLSTONECRAFT SHELLEY was born in 1797, the only daughter of William Godwin, author of *Political Justice* and *Caleb Williams*, and Mary Wollstonecraft, author of *Vindication of the Rights of Woman*, who died a few days after her daughter's birth.

Mary was courted by the poet Percy Bysshe Shelley (who was already married) in the summer of 1814. They eloped to the Continent in July. In 1816 they spent the summer with Lord Byron near Geneva, during which time *Frankenstein* was begun. Shelley's wife committed suicide later that year, and he married Mary. Their two small children died in 1818 and 1819, and in 1822 Shelley himself was drowned. Mary was heart-broken, as her diaries show, and in 1823 she returned to England with her younger son. She had little money, but, largely supporting herself by writing, she managed to send her son to Harrow and Cambridge. Between 1840 and 1843 she and her son travelled abroad. In 1844 Shelley's father died, leaving Mary in better circumstances. She died in 1851 and was buried at Bournemouth near her son's home.

MARILYN BUTLER is Rector of Exeter College, Oxford, and was, until recently, King Edward VII Professor of English Literature at Cambridge University. Her books on the Romantic period include *Jane Austen and the War of Ideas* (1975), and *Romantics, Rebels and Reactionaries* (1981). She has edited a selection of prose texts, *Burke, Paine, Godwin and the Revolution Controversy* (1984); Maria Edgeworth's *Castle Rackrent* and *Ennui* (1992); and, with Janet Todd, the Pickering Masters *Works of Mary Wollstonecraft* (1989).

OXFORD WORLD'S CLASSICS

———

MARY SHELLEY

Frankenstein

OR

The Modern Prometheus

THE 1818 TEXT

———

Edited with an Introduction and Notes by
MARILYN BUTLER

OXFORD
UNIVERSITY PRESS

OXFORD
UNIVERSITY PRESS

Great Clarendon Street, Oxford OX2 6DP

Oxford University Press is a department of the University of Oxford.
It furthers the University's objective of excellence in research, scholarship,
and education by publishing worldwide in

Oxford New York

Athens Auckland Bangkok Bogotá Buenos Aires Calcutta
Cape Town Chennai Dar es Salaam Delhi Florence Hong Kong Istanbul
Karachi Kuala Lumpur Madrid Melbourne Mexico City Mumbai
Nairobi Paris São Paulo Singapore Taipei Tokyo Toronto Warsaw

with associated companies in Berlin Ibadan

Oxford is a registered trade mark of Oxford University Press
in the UK and in certain other countries

Published in the United States
by Oxford University Press Inc., New York

Introduction, Note on the Text, Select Bibliography, Explanatory Notes
© Marilyn Butler 1993
Chronology © Oxford University Press 1969

Database right Oxford University Press (maker)

First published as a World's Classics paperback 1994
Reissued as an Oxford World's Classics paperback 1998

British Library Cataloguing in Publication Data

Data available

Library of Congress Cataloging in Publication Data

Data available

ISBN–13: 978–0–19–283366–2
ISBN–10: 0–19–283366–9

10

Printed in Great Britain by
Clays Ltd, St Ives plc

ACKNOWLEDGEMENTS

All editors owe debts to their predecessors, who begin in this case with the author herself. My main obligation is to James Rieger, thoughtful and careful editor of the first modern edition of the 1818 text, though I have also benefited from the more recent version in the *Mary Shelley Reader*, edited by Betty T. Bennett and Charles E. Robinson. The different editors of the 1831 text, on whom we once had perforce to rely both as teachers and writers, have assembled a body of scholarship on which we continue to draw. I am aware of debts at a number of points to Maurice Hindle's stimulating edition from Penguin (1988).

Though most critical and scholarly debts are acknowledged in the Introduction and notes as they occur, I am conscious that piecemeal annotation does not reflect the light thrown on Mary Shelley during the 1980s by editors of some of her other writings—the letters, edited by Betty T. Bennett, and the journals, by Paula Feldman and Diana Scott-Kilvert. I owe immeasurably to the efficiency and goodwill of the staffs of six of the great institutions of the English-speaking learned world—the British Library, Cambridge University Library, the Bodleian and Radcliffe Science Library, Oxford, the Library of Congress, and the Regenstein Library of the University of Chicago.

Like all university teachers, I learn from students and colleagues, proportionately more when the book is one that demands to be argued over. The Introduction started into life with a paper given in January 1992 to an interdisciplinary Cambridge University seminar on Intellectual History, held for the last six years at King's College. My thanks are due to my fellow-convenors, Stefan Collini, Anthony Pagden and Simon Schaffer; to particular insights from Jim Secord, Marianne Jeanneret, John Forrester, Nigel Leask, and Naomi Segal; and to the stimulus provided over the years by the student and faculty members from the Department of the History and Philosophy of Science. Also in Britain, I benefited from conversations with Timothy Morton, Dr Baruch Blumberg, the Master of Balliol College Oxford, and Dr Jane Blumberg.

Finally, in three richly dialoguic months in the USA, I tested yet again *Frankenstein*'s reputation as the most protean and disputable of even Romantic texts. My thanks for special insights go first to colleagues and students of the University of Chicago, where I was lucky enough to hold a Schaffner Fellowship, notably James Chandler, Jay Schleusener, Paul Hunter, Elizabeth Helsinger, Lawrence Rothfield, and Katie Trumpener; and, for generously sharing their knowledge with a visiting speaker, to Richard Nash, Lee Sterrenburg, Catherine Gallagher, Anne Mellor, George Rousseau, Esther Schor, and Neil Fraistat. It is no mere convention of thanking to say that large ideas emerge from groups. Incidental mistakes and wrong inferences are (as Frankenstein found) the responsibility of solitary authors.

CONTENTS

INTRODUCTION

Beginnings

Mary Shelley inherited fame and even notoriety. She was the baby born on 30 August 1797 to the leading English theorist of the French Revolution, William Godwin, and to his wife Mary Wollstonecraft, after their marriage on 29 March 1797. Though strongly attached to one another, the couple were both embarrassed by Wollstonecraft's pregnancy. Godwin had made a celebrated attack on marriage as an institution in the closing section of his great work *Political Justice*, 1793. Wollstonecraft in *Vindication of the Rights of Woman* (1792) had accepted its necessity for women. But she by now had a 3-year-old daughter, Fanny, by the American trader Gilbert Imlay, and the marriage to Godwin showed everyone who had met her as 'Mrs Imlay' that she had not in fact married him. Wollstonecraft died on 10 September 1797 from complications following the birth of this second daughter, Mary. The story of her life, loves and death was revealed by Godwin the following year, in the frank, touching *Memoir* he issued with his wife's *Posthumous Works*.

After the scandal this publication aroused, the resoundingly named Mary Wollstonecraft Godwin and her elder half-sister Fanny Imlay were persons of note. In 1801 Godwin married his neighbour, Mary Jane Clairmont, who had two children of her own, Charles and Clara Jane Clairmont, and later bore Godwin a son, William. From 1807 a new family home in Skinner Street, Holborn, also served as the offices of a struggling publishing business in the name of M. J. Godwin. Though energetic in business and in Godwin's view a good wife, the temperamental Mary Jane Clairmont had uneven relationships with her stepdaughters, and seems to have been jealous of the clever Mary, her rival for Godwin's attention. Godwin's partly autobiographical mature novels, all narrated in the first person, suggest a merciless self-analyst, a secular product of the profoundly inward Puritan tradition. On the page he showed remarkable psychological insight; but, like his protagonists Fleetwood (1805) and especially Mandeville (1817), he seems to have been awkward in relationships and conversation. Mary then grew up in conditions of some emotional deprivation, and shared her father's inhibitions.

Godwin himself educated her at home, by giving her access to his many books, directing her reading, and in due course taking her to public lectures. He encouraged her literary abilities, in 1808 publishing her light verses *Mounseer Nongtongpaw; or the Discoveries of John Bull in a trip to Paris* in the Godwin Juvenile Library.[1] Godwin, and Mary herself, expected her to become a writer, like both her parents. As she grew up he let her stay in the room when he talked with his intellectual friends, who included Coleridge, Holcroft, Lamb, and Hazlitt, listening rather than speaking herself.

Mary met the 20-year-old poet Percy Shelley, an admirer of her father, when he and his wife Harriet came to dine in Skinner Street on 11 November 1812. During the next two years she was away from home for two periods of several months, staying not far from Dundee in the home of two sisters near her own age, Isabel and Christy Baxter; the tension between Mary and her stepmother is a likely reason for sending her away so long. In Scotland she read, thought, and communed with nature. Back home in May 1814 she met Shelley again. She was now nearly 17, susceptible and at an age when a budding intellectual moves over on to the fast track, if not on it already.

Mary must have been powerfully attracted to Percy Shelley, a young man as much in love as she herself with the idea of both her parents in their youth. A published radical writer, who shared both Godwin's 1790s theorized republicanism and the advanced scientific interests of some of the family's

---

A greatly expanded version of Charles Dibdin's comic song of the same name, Mary Shelley's song achieved a 4th edn. by 1812, and was reissued, illustrated by Robert Cruikshank, in 1830. The English chauvinist John Bull visits Paris, and is driven to enquire, in English, who owns all the impressive things he sees. The reply is always 'Je vous n'entends pas', which John Bull takes for the name of a very great man

current friends, Shelley was also literary and imaginative, like
Wollstonecraft. He was drawn to Mary by her pale good looks,
her name, her intellectual interests (well beyond Harriet's
range), and her habit of retiring to read on her mother's
grave in St Pancras Churchyard.

The couple's elopement on 28 July 1814 to a France suffering from the hardships of military defeat proved far from
romantic. (Mary's journal of the trip later became the basis of
her second publication, *History of a Six Weeks' Tour through a
part of France, Switzerland, Germany and Holland* (London: T.
Hookham & C. and J. Ollier, 1817).) The homecoming was
worse. Percy Shelley's outraged father Sir Timothy cut down
his son's allowance, so that creditors closed in on them.
Godwin's anger hurt both of the couple more; he felt particularly betrayed by Shelley, his avowed disciple, but continued
to ask him for money. Another distressing rebuff was dealt by
David Booth, now husband of Mary's best friend Isabel
Baxter, who refused to let their correspondence continue.
Hurried from one lodging to another to avoid the creditors,
oppressed by the company of Percy's student-style male peer-
group (Thomas Jefferson Hogg and Thomas Love Peacock),
Mary also had to put up with the presence in the household
of her stepmother's daughter, by now calling herself Claire
Clairmont. Hogg spelt trouble because Percy Shelley wanted
him to establish a romantic though apparently not physical
relationship with Mary; Peacock because he sided with Percy's
wife Harriet, who bore Percy's second child, Charles, that
November; Claire because Mary never liked her much, and
soon suspected her and Percy of one of the latter's romantic
liaisons.

To make matters worse Mary was herself pregnant, and
intermittently unwell. On 22 February 1815 she gave birth to
a premature daughter, Clara, who, to her great distress, died
on 6 March. That spring, probably too soon to adjust emotionally, she again became pregnant again with her son,
William, born 24 January 1816. To add to the strains of a
desolating year, Percy became convinced he had syphilis and
was likely to die. In the winter of 1814 and summer of 1815
he consulted a fellow-member of Godwin's circle, the able

young surgeon and physiologist William Lawrence—who has
a significant, previously unnoted part to play in the gestation
of *Frankenstein*. Thanks to Lawrence's treatment Percy announced a partial recovery in late August,[2] and in early September, during a heatwave, he, Mary and Charles Clairmont
allowed Peacock to lead them on a voyage up the Thames.
Along with the Bodleian library and the Clarendon Press,
they visited, in the words of Charles's report to his sister
Claire, 'the very rooms where the two most noted infidels,
Shelley and Hogg ... pored, with the incessant and unwearied application of the alchymist, over the certified and natural boundaries of human knowledge.'[3] Richard Holmes
is right to point out an obvious prompt for the ghost story
Mary Shelley was to tell less than a year later. The tourist trip
to Oxford also figures in the completed novel as an episode
in Frankenstein's trip to Britain in order to make a female
Monster.

Percy Shelley's more stable health, and the couple's temporary retirement to Bishopsgate near Windsor, enabled them
to settle down in the last quarter of 1815 to a somewhat
calmer, more scholarly life. They read steadily in the classics
and, no doubt with the benefit of advice from Lawrence,
developed the reading-programme in the physical sciences
on which Percy had embarked in 1813.[4] In the summer of
1816 they prepared for another Continental trip, this time
with the baby William and Claire Clairmont. It was Claire who
steered the group to Geneva, in pursuit of Byron, whom the
Shelleys had never met. Claire had recently introduced herself to the poet by letter, initially as a budding dramatist, and
as part of her campaign had interested him in Shelley's work.
By the time Byron left England in April, driven out by the

[2] *Letters of P. B. Shelley*, ed. F. L. Jones, 2 vols. (Oxford: Oxford University Press),
1964, i. 429.
[3] Edward Dowden, *Life of P. B. Shelley* (1866), quoted R. Holmes, *Shelley: The
Pursuit* (London: Weidenfeld and Nicolson, 1974), 291.
[4] P. B. Shelley to T. J. Hogg, 26 November 1813; *Letters of P. B. Shelley*, i. 250. For
Shelley's awareness, probably from Lawrence, of German physiologists, see his
Preface to *Frankenstein*, text and n. 3.

scandal which followed his wife's departure from home, Claire was pregnant by him.

Among the tumultuous events of Mary Shelley's life from 17 to 19, its emotional stresses must have had subtle, powerful effects on the shaping of *Frankenstein*, her first and best novel. Her thwarted but longed-for dialogue over the years with her father (which she afterwards described in a letter as 'an excessive & romantic attachment'[5]) was interrupted, to be replaced by a richer but almost equally problematic relationship with her lover Shelley. In the four and a half years from 1815 to mid-1819 she was to lose the first three of her four children. Her suffering over their deaths was complicated by her own sense of guilt, probably dating back to her first realization that her own birth had caused the death of her mother. Mary's capacity for guilt must have been further exercised by two pathetic and from her point of view reproachful suicides in the autumn of 1816: those of Fanny Imlay, Mary's half-sister, on 9 October, and of Harriet (Westbrook) Shelley, Percy's wife, in November–December.

Percy Shelley should have helped his young wife to cope, but he resembled her father in offering support that was intellectually superb, emotionally inadequate; unintentionally he even contributed to the death of her second daughter, another Clara, in September 1818, by ordering Mary to travel across Italy with the sick child in the Italian summer heat. After each bereavement, William Godwin wrote her letters which briskly recommended as little mourning as possible. To the extent that *Frankenstein* is a family drama, centred on parental nurture (or the lack of it), on the failure of communication and mutual support, and on the death of its gentlest, most vulnerable members, it reads like the imaginative reworking of experience.

But novels must be written in a language readers understand and largely know. At first sight it seems astonishing that this quite inexperienced writer should have devised and

---

[5] *Letters of Mary Wollstonecraft Shelley*, ed. Betty T. Bennett, 3 vols. (Baltimore: Johns Hopkins University Press, 1980, 1983, 1988), ii. 215.

executed so powerful a book. But there were advantages as well as deprivations in Mary Shelley's upbringing. Her father trained her in a programme of reading that was deeply and intelligently historical, in the tradition of Enlightenment cultural comparativism, getting her for instance to distinguish between primitive and advanced, ancient and modern cultures. Her brisk whittling down of the so-called Monster's education in history and sociology to four books, Volney's *Ruins: a Survey of the Revolutions of Empire*, Milton's *Paradise Lost*, Plutarch's *Lives* and Goethe's *Sorrows of Young Werther* is both an economical literary device and a wry tribute to her father's powers of reducing intellectual history to essentials.

Godwin thought like a moralist, historian, and social critic, but he also wrote six excellent novels, some of the most original and certainly technically ingenious of the day:[6] Mary was in effect trained in the creative writing that most attracted her, at a time when no such formal training was available. She acknowledges her artistic debt by dedicating *Frankenstein* to her father, and by echoing his titles: *Frankenstein, or the Modern Prometheus* belongs to the same series as his *Fleetwood, or the New Man of Feeling* (1805). From *Caleb Williams* (1794), each novel by Godwin has a tragic action narrated in the first person by an isolated intellectual, a vulnerable, unreliable interpreter, whose unreliability becomes a large part of the novel's interest. As far as the treatment of Frankenstein and Walton goes, any of Godwin's first four novels, even the almost contemporaneous *Mandeville* (1817), could have served as a model for *Frankenstein*. In fact *Mandeville* resembles *Caleb Williams*, and also *Frankenstein*, in basing its plot upon the enmity between two powerful characters, who represent antithetical social and ideological forces, and pursue each other in a complex, shifting chase. But Mary's greatest debt intellectually and emotionally is probably to *St Leon* (1799), which anticipates *Frankenstein*'s themes of science and gender, its

---

[6] See M. Butler and M. Philp, 'General Introduction', in Mark Philp (ed.), *William Godwin's Works: The Novels*, 7 vols. (London: Pickering and Chatto, 1992). i. 7–46.

plot, and its central figure: in both novels, a selfish intellectual trades domestic happiness and marital love for the chimaeras of scientific knowledge, success, and power.

This achievement was in the future, if only a year off; Mary Shelley went to Switzerland with her husband in June 1816 with no immediate ideas of writing a novel. Their family group soon joined forces with a Byron moodily recovering from the scandal of his wife's proceedings against him. He had taken the Villa Diodati at Cologny, on the southern shores of Lake Léman; soon the Shelleys were walking there most days from the smaller Maison Chapuis at nearby Montalègre. It was at the Villa Diodati on the evening of 15 June that Percy Shelley was involved in a conversation about science, and that on 16 June three members of the group each agreed to write a ghost story. Between the talk on science and the talk of a ghost-story contest there is as it happens not merely temporal closeness but a causal connection.

The Shelleys and Radical Science

While Mary Shelley had points to teach her husband about novel-writing, he had a start over her with science. His interest dates back, as is well known, from preparatory-school days at Syon House, and the inspiration of an unorthodox scientist and brilliant itinerant teacher, Adam Walker (1731–1821). Shelley became fascinated by major scientific topics of the day, the solar system, microscopy, magnetism, and electricity. First at Eton, afterwards at University College, Oxford, he was noted for his interest in chemical and electrical experiments. He told his cousin Thomas Medwin that when his career as an Oxford undergraduate, 1810–11, was brought abruptly to an end because of his share in the pamphlet *The Necessity of Atheism*, he began a professional training as a surgeon; that, together with his cousin Charles Grove, he 'walked the wards' of Bart's (St Bartholomew's) Hospital, and attended the London anatomy lectures of a senior surgeon whose notions and writings afterwards figure in *Frankenstein*: John Abernethy (1764–1831). Shelley's visit or visits to Bart's may however have dated from 1813–14, when he was getting to know

Abernethy's demonstrator and former pupil, William Lawrence (1783–1867), who was soon to become Abernethy's professional antagonist, and one of the most publicized scientists of the day.[7] It is in fact hard to date Shelley's early meetings with Lawrence, because of Lawrence's membership of the Godwin circle—to which another avant-garde scientist important to Percy Shelley at this time, John Frank Newton, also belonged.

Whether or not Percy Shelley contemplated the professional training, his industry in reading science is well documented.[8] A long reading list for the years 1813–17 can be culled from Percy's letters, the footnotes to annotated works like *Queen Mab*, and Mary Shelley's *Journal*; it organizes itself into the pursuit of Enlightenment scepticism (Hume, Voltaire, Volney), anthropology (Buffon, Rousseau, Monboddo), and the so-called French materialists, Holbach as author of *The System of Nature*, and from the French-revolutionary period Condorcet, Cabanis, and Laplace. This litany has appeared over time in a number of studies of the science in *Frankenstein*, notably for instance by Samuel Holmes Vasbinder and Anne Mellor.[9] But, though a useful outline sketch to the modern reader otherwise ignorant of late-Enlightenment science, the litany alone will not necessarily serve as a guide to what Mary Shelley was able or willing to incorporate in her novels. In pre-professional times readers' knowledge of so specialized a discourse could not be assumed. The academic reading-list needs qualifying or replacing with a form of newspaper and journal-talk which *could* be thought of as current language, to which Lawrence, who was known to both Shelleys, conspicuously contributed.

[7] For pathbreaking work on P. B. Shelley's education and scientific contacts, esp. William Lawrence, see Hugh J. Luke jun., 'Sir William Lawrence, Physician to Shelley and Mary', *Papers on English Language and Literature*, i (1965), 141–52 and N. Crook and D. Guiton, *Shelley's Venomed Melody* (Cambridge: Cambridge University Press, 1986).

[8] See above, n. 2.

[9] For recent discussions of whether the novel is science fiction, anti-scientific, or in line with a mainstream that includes Davy, see Bibliography, entries on Aldiss, Crouch, Easlea, Friedman, Keller, Scholes, Sharrock, Sherwin, Spector, Vasbinder. Anne K. Mellor also devotes a chapter to the generalized scientific background.

What is more, there is good and bad evidence when we come to explore the growth of a particular idea in an author's imagination. Lawrence was a high-flying professional who could have guided the couple's reading in the physical sciences from the time they became partners in 1814 to the moment of the novel's emergence, some four years later. But we have arrived at a new, much more particularized insight when we find in the Shelley circle's letters of August–September 1815, when Lawrence was playing a particularly important role as Percy Shelley's physician, a cluster of words, ideas, events which surely recur in *Frankenstein*. Facts Mary Shelley learnt of during the trip up the Thames have been cited— Shelley's use of his rooms when an undergraduate for a non-curricular and potentially threatening form of science, and at the same time, his challenge to religion. But there seems to be another bridge which may connect Lawrence to *Frankenstein*: Percy Shelley's train of thought on returning to Bishopsgate reinvigorated in September 1815, when he shows a new interest in keeping records of the processes of his own mind, notably his early thinking and his dreams. Later that autumn he began work on a stylized poetic biography, which is also autobiography, *Alastor*.

The fragment which records and reflects on some of his dreams or fantasies is datable from 1815. Mary Shelley afterwards claimed to have been present when this was written, and grouped it with other fragments on 'Metaphysics', 'Mind', and the germ of a 'little treatise' on 'morals'. While they still draw on Shelley's reading in Berkeley and Hume, these writings sound a distinctive note when they resolve to 'contemplate facts. Let us . . . compel the mind to a rigid consideration of itself . . . by caution, by strict scepticism concerning all assertions'. If someone could give 'a faithful history of his being from the earliest epoch of his recollection', including 'the passage from sensation to reflection—from a state of passive perception to voluntary contemplation', 'a picture would be presented such as the world has never contemplated before' (Clark, 184–6). When Percy Shelley talked with Lawrence, different traditions of thinking about mind plainly converged. The consultations must also have focused on Shelley's nervous condition, his suggestibility and his dreams, those presentations of the non-rational. Like *Alastor* (1816), *Frankenstein* can be read as the testimonies of three deliberately differentiated autobiographers, who together bear witness to a story of universal significance. Thanks to the dialogue set up with Lawrence, such 'records' not only mimic, but imaginatively contribute to current 'science of mind'. Meanwhile almost all Lawrence's own publications in the vitalist and evolutionary field fall into the years of the conceiving and writing of *Frankenstein*. The dialogue continues, embraces the novel, becomes its essential context and at times its text.

It was in 1814 that a schism in the life-sciences between strict materialists and those willing to share a vocabulary with the religious came out into the open in Britain. (For some of the principal books and pamphlets contributing to the so-called vitalist controversy at this time, see Appendix C.) Edinburgh, long Britain's leading university for medicine, was situated in a powerfully theological culture. As President of London's Royal College of Surgeons, the Scottish-trained John Abernethy chose the College and the public occasion of the Hunterian lectures, named after his own old teacher John Hunter, to make a conciliatory move in an issue which threatened to bring believers into collision with outright materialists: the origin and ultimate nature of what afterwards became known as the life-principle.[10] Abernethy attributed his 'Theory of Life' broadly to Hunter, Humphry Davy, and other notables, a modest and diplomatic move. As a moderate willing to conform to religious scruples, he conceded that the modern catchwords 'organization', 'function', 'matter' could not *explain* what was distinctively life-giving. Life, that which vitalized, had to be thought of as something independent. Attributing the view to Hunter, Abernethy declared that a 'superadded' element was needed, some 'subtile, mobile, invisible substance', perhaps a superfine fluid 'analogous to

---

[10] John Abernethy, *An Enquiry into the Probability and Rationality of Mr Hunter's 'Theory of Life'* (London: Longman, etc., 1814), 48, 52.

electricity', which would appear as a correlative to or confirmation of the idea of an (immortal) Soul. Scientists would
be free to pursue their enquiries, so long as these did not
necessarily entail a major victory over religion.

The secular-minded *Edinburgh Review* wittily contested
Abernethy's conclusions. But the issue became a notable professional quarrel, waged in public, only after Abernethy's
former pupil William Lawrence was appointed in 1815 as a
second Professor at the Royal College of Surgeons. In March
1816 Lawrence gave two public inaugural lectures on Abernethy's topic. The first, an introduction to comparative
anatomy (21 March), described work currently being done in
France, with a comprehensiveness no doubt aimed to convey
to his student audience that he was a more fully qualified
professional than Abernethy. Lawrence's second lecture, 'On
Life', by contrast focuses rigorously on the issue as physiology
and anatomy (but no other specialism) can explicate it, in the
spirit and avant-garde medical terminology of M. F. X. Bichat
(1771–1802), who had brought new standards of precision to
French physiology.[11] For biologists (a word Lawrence allegedly introduced to Britain), life is the 'assemblage of all the
functions' a living body can perform. We have done what we
can, Lawrence says, to find origins and 'to observe living
bodies in the moment of their formation . . . when matter
may be supposed to receive the stamp of life. . . . Hitherto,
however, we have not been able to catch nature in the fact.'
On the contrary, what we can observe of animals is that
'all have participated in the existence of other living
beings . . . the motion proper to living bodies, or in one word,
life, has its origin in that of their parents.'[12] The power
that animates animals resists abstraction from matter; for the
materialist thinker, an abstracted approach to Life yields
nothing.

[11] Cf. Lawrence's Advertisement, *An Introduction to Comparative Anatomy, being two
introductory lectures delivered at the Royal College of Surgeons* (London, 1816): 'in several
parts of the second lecture the views correspond with those which have been
entertained and published on the same subjects by Cuvier and Bichat.'

[12] Ibid. 140–2.

Lawrence made an outright attack on Abernethy a year later, in 1817, when, for the first time, he named his colleague and President as his adversary. There he unmistakably ridiculed the argument that electricity, or 'something analogous' to it, could do duty for the soul—'For subtle matter is still matter; and if this fine stuff can possess vital properties, surely they may reside in a fabric which differs only in being a little coarser.'[13] But even in the more guarded 1816 lectures there was an offensive tone of superiority in (for instance) the demand that the Life question should be left to the real professionals; that would mean, on this issue, excluding chemists: 'Organised bodies must be treated differently from those which have inorganic matter for their object . . . the reference to gravity, to attraction, to chemical affinity, to electricity and galvanism, can only serve to perpetuate false notes in philosophy.' Lawrence then gravely suggests that the great John Hunter, after whom his and Abernethy's lectures are named, would have taken the Lawrence side on the question of method:

He did not attempt to explain life by . . . *a priori* speculations, or by the illusory analogies of other sciences . . he sought to discover its nature in the only way, which can possibly lead to any useful and satisfactory result; that is, by a patient examination of the fabric, and close observation of the actions of living creatures.[14]

Mary and Percy Shelley, Lawrence's friends, were living near London in that March of 1816, when Lawrence's materialist case against spiritualized vitalism was first sketched out. It would not be surprising, then, if Mary's contribution to the ghost-story competition to some degree acts out the debate between Abernethy and Lawrence, in a form close enough for those who knew the debate to recognize. Frankenstein the blundering experimenter, still working with superseded notions, shadows the intellectual position of Abernethy, who proposes that the superadded life-element is analogous to

---

[13] W. Lawrence, *Lectures on Physiology, Zoology and the Natural History of Man* (London: Callow, 1819), Lecture 3 [1817], 84.

[14] Id., *Introduction to Comparative Anatomy* (1816), 161–3.

electricity. Lawrence's sceptical commentary on that position finds its echo in Mary Shelley's equally detached, serio-comic representation—though the connection between her satire and Lawrence's is masked by her use of a comic analogy out of the folk tradition, concerning the over-reacher who gets more than he bargains for.

The Ghost-story Contest

The *Diary* of John William Polidori, Byron's doctor, records that at the villa Diodati, near Geneva, on 15 June 1816, the night before the ghost-story project was launched, he and Percy Shelley had a conversation 'about principles—whether man was to be thought merely an instrument'.[15] In her Preface to the third edition, 1831 (given below as Appendix A), Mary Shelley speaks of many conversations between Shelley and Byron, to which she was 'a devout but nearly silent listener'. One of these, which she dates some days after Byron's proposal to hold a ghost-story contest (probably 16 June), concerned 'the nature of the principle of life, and whether there was any probability of its ever being discovered and communicated'. She claims the conversation took in three contemporary scientific proposals to tackle the vitalist problem pragmatically or experimentally—one by Erasmus Darwin, presumably showing that single-cell parasites generate spontaneously, one by reanimating a corpse electrically, using a galvanic battery, and the third, the most notional, the reconstruction of a body which would then also be reanimated. According to Mary Shelley's narrative of fifteen years later, this conversation gave her the sleepless night and waking nightmare which generated her famous novel, about a hideous, transgressive experiment, 'a supremely frightful . . . human endeavour to mock the stupendous mechanism of the Creator of the world'.

[15] (Ed.) W. M. Rossetti, *Diary of J. W. Polidori, 1816* (1911), quoted James Rieger (ed.), 'Introduction', *Frankenstein, or the Modern Prometheus: The 1818 Text* (Chicago: University of Chicago Press, 1982), p xvii.

James Rieger, the first modern scholarly editor of the 1818 edition, points out that there are discrepancies between Mary Shelley's account and Polidori's, and that his contemporaneous one has a certain authority hers lacks. Presumably Polidori was present at the conversation on 15 June; Mary could have been too, because if she was silent he need not have named her as a participant. But if that is the conversation she means, she is then mistaken to say the protagonists were Shelley and *Byron*—Polidori the recently qualified doctor is of course more likely to be familiar with the controversy—and she also has the date wrong. We should however give her more of the benefit of the doubt than Rieger does, and allow that if there were really several conversations in this general area, Shelley may have resumed the topic several nights later with Byron, and perhaps only then moved from the general theory to the more popular, sensational level of 'experiments' staged for the public as semi-theatrical demonstrations.

Rieger does not connect the conversation or conversations with the vitalist controversy, nor is he aware of the Shelleys' significant friendship with Lawrence. He grants that Mary Shelley 'knew something of Sir Humphry Davy's chemistry, Erasmus Darwin's botany, and perhaps Galvani's physics', but believes 'little of this got into her book. Frankenstein's chemistry is switched-on magic, souped-up alchemy, the electrification of Agrippa and Paracelsus.'[16] He does not therefore notice the most interesting discrepancy between Polidori and Mary Shelley as recorders of conversations on the vitalist issue—a three-way split in their ways of defining the problem.

Polidori, Edinburgh-trained, frames the question in a theologically-sensitive way like Abernethy's, by using a word associated pejoratively with materialism—is man to be thought merely an instrument? Mary Shelley in her initial summary of the conversation inclines to the materialist perspective of Lawrence. Her phrase 'the nature of the principle of life' is neutral, but the next sentences convey, and develop,

---

[16] Rieger, 'Introduction', p. xxvii.

Lawrence's scepticism whether a problem framed this way could ever be satisfactorily resolved, least of all by way of experiment.

Within a page, however, her tone changes markedly—and this, significantly, is the moment when she switches from her attempt to remember what others said to put a palpably more subjective, interpretative gloss on what she herself did by way of her creative imagination. The so-called waking dream is conveniently self-promoting and novel-promoting, and may well be lifted from Coleridge's equally creative description, seventeen or nineteen years after the events it claims to describe, of the dream-origins of 'Kubla Khan'. One possible motive for the dubious tale is a professional author's instinct to make her book exciting and accessible, for the purposes of a popular edition and a period attuned to melodrama. Another is the reasonable fear that *Frankenstein* would be contaminated by its thinly covered associations with Lawrence's brand of materialism. Like Coleridge, and like Godwin in 1832, when he in turn came to package *Caleb Williams* for a new cheap edition, Mary Shelley deflected attention from the historical sources and implications of her text by introducing an exaggerated, sensationalized diversion concerning its psychic origins.

Mary Shelley's tale does not survive in its ghost-story format. She says in the 1831 Preface that the tale began with the words 'It was on a dreary night in November . . .'—in the novel, the point at which the Creature is about to come to life, that is the beginning of Volume I, Ch. III in the 1818 edition. Perhaps it is reasonable to speculate that the tale had one more episode, dated some time later, in which the Creature horrifically reappears, to avenge his abandonment either on Frankenstein or on members of his family. Only one of the remaining stories seems to be in its authentic 1816 state: Byron's 'A Fragment' of 2,000 words, which appeared dated 17 June 1816 with the author's poem *Mazeppa* (1819). Byron published it reluctantly ('I have . . . a personal dislike to Vampires, and the little I know of them would by no means induce me to divulge their secrets'), because a 9,000-word version

The Vampyre, claiming to be his, but illicitly altered by Polidori, was published in the April 1819 number of Henry Colburn's *New Monthly Review*. It is in fact an ingenious ingrafting on to the vampire tale of the scurrilous amorous biography of Byron which his ex-mistress Lady Caroline Lamb gave the world in her novel *Glenarvon* (1816): Byron lampooned as his own vampire. As for Polidori's actual contribution to the ghost-story contest, Mary Shelley mockingly remembers this in her 1831 Preface as the story of a woman struck blind as a punishment for peeping through a keyhole. Polidori, however, published a novel in 1819 which he said was developed from the contest: *Ernestus Berchtold: or the Modern Oedipus*, the title of which pays a kind of tribute to *Frankenstein, or the Modern Prometheus*.

Polidori milked the contest twice over, and in the process helped to mystify its actual nature. All the same it is still possible to make out what a sociable event it was, genuinely collaborative in that the four stories or versions of stories we have (to include both those attributed to Polidori) represent variations on the same two themes. One is the punishment ironically but justly visited on the protagonist for his or her transgression, another the idea that the Eastern-European or Near-Eastern figure of the vampire is specifically the bearer of such a punishment.

Behind the four plots are two related ones. In 1831, Mary Shelley recalls that the party read and discussed a volume translated from the German by a Frenchman, Jean-Baptiste Benoit Eyriès, and called *Fantasmagoriana, ou Recueil d'Histories de Spectres, Revenans, Fantômes, etc; traduit de l'allemand, par un Amateur* (Paris, 1812). The title page of this book betrays some sympathy with Illuminism, the late eighteenth-century avant-garde quest for a means of communicating with the dead for which the University of Ingolstadt (where Frankenstein's experiment takes place) was a well-known centre. From the plot of 'La Morte Fiancée', which she misremembers as 'The History of the Inconstant Lover', Mary Shelley calls up the scene when the protagonist tries to clasp his live mistress, only to find himself embracing the corpse of the woman he previously abandoned. In 'Les

Portraits de Famille', 'the sinful founder of his race' is
doomed to return as a vampire to suck the blood of his
descendants.

Both themes are touched on fleetingly in *Frankenstein*, the
first on the night of the experiment, when Frankenstein
dreams of embracing his bride Elizabeth only to find the
corpse of his mother in his arms, and the second early in
Volume III, when he wonders if he has unwittingly released
his own family vampire. By adapting the story of *Oedipus*, a
man doomed to destroy his own family, Polidori perceptively
recognizes that there is in that tightest of dramatic plots a
variation on the legend of the vampire as a vengeful emanation of a guilty individual. Byron himself had already used the
myth in this, its most powerful and ironic form, in the Turkish
fisherman's curse in *The Giaour* (1813), where the prophetic
description of the fresh young girl doomed to die from her
ancestor's bite also sounds like 'Les Portraits de Famille', and
Mary Shelley's recollection of it:

> Thy victims ere they yet expire
> Shall know the daemon for their sire,
> As cursing thee, thou cursing them,
> Thy flowers are wither'd on the stem.
> But one that for thy crime must fall
> The youngest—most belov'd of all,
> Shall bless thee with a *father's* name—
> That word shall wrap thy heart in flame! (ll. 763–71)

Like the Shelleys, Byron already had experience of Gothic,
even a degree of expertise—though his interest may have
been somewhat more antiquarian and scholarly than theirs,
more associated with the attempt to imitate Middle-Eastern
culture, beliefs, and literary forms, which he had demonstrated in *Childe Harold II*, *The Giaour*, and the *Hebrew Melodies*
(1815). Some commentators on the contest have treated it as
Ken Russell does in his film *Gothic*, as the frolic of a group of
bored sophisticates indulging themselves with cruel, macabre
fantasies. A rather older view took literally the various anec-
dotes about Percy Shelley which represent him as seriously
frightened by his own nightmarish 'visions' (including one in

which he saw an eye in Mary's breast). Yet the best evidence about what happened at the villa suggests that the talk was sophisticated in a different way—disengaged from Gothic 'superstition', intrigued by religious unorthodoxy, and actively interested in the formal components of these narratives, what technically makes them work.

For, apart from Byron's 'A Fragment', which lacks much plot at all, both the German/French volume of tales and its various Genevan derivatives have strong plots with an ironic twist, whereby retribution is unexpectedly delivered. But the participants explicitly distance themselves from 'superstition': Byron in his joke on vampires, Mary Shelley in her light 1831 summary of everyone else's stories, Percy Shelley in his anonymous Preface to the 1818 edition. Here he attributes the ghost-story contest in which *Frankenstein* originated to 'a playful desire of imitation', while he adds that 'a mere tale of spectres or enchantment' would not have been worth imitating, without something more serious to impart. Belying the emphasis of the last paragraphs of the Preface of 1831 on the terribleness of 'my hideous progeny', Mary Shelley has to contend with many signs that her text originated in sophisticated, satirical conversations, which treated the Gothic historically, as a symptom of the feudal mentality and thus the occasion for a modern critical appropriation. Above all, her action turns on the classically comic motive of the protagonist's incompetence—a feature which re-emerges in the novel's many emanations as a play or a film.[17]

Late eighteenth-century Gothic and orientalist fiction is often serio-comic, an unstable blend of allegory, satire, and pastiche. While colourful remote periods make worlds of pleasurable fantasy, they also mirror the displeasing vestiges of medievalism in the present day: religion appears as superstition and magic, court power as arbitrary despotism imposed on a gullible populace. Beckford's *Vathek* (1787) and

---

[17] Commentators on modern adaptations of *Frankenstein* have sometimes wondered why the films are often comic, while they take the novel to be tragic. But the comic or serio-comic tradition goes back at least as far as the two stage adaptations of 1823 (for which see Elizabeth Nitchie's chapter, 'Stage History', in *Mary Shelley, Author of 'Frankenstein'* (Westport, Conn., 1953)), is native to the popular strand of Romantic Gothic fed by both ballads and stage melodrama, and in its own day gave the style much of its political change.

Lewis's *The Monk* (1795), in their decades two of the most
influential prose examples of this mixed genre, are each
scurrilous, serio-comic, topically suggestive and ultimately satirical. The most prolific versifier in the Gothic vein in the last
years of the eighteenth century, Robert Southey, specialized
in fairly faithful reconstructions of the type of grimly humor-
ous ballad in which some notable sinner gets his or her just
reward; and Southey, along with Lewis, surely interpreted this
style of comedy as a genuine strain in folk culture, partly
subversive of a more uniformly 'terrific' state religion. In one
of the best of the ballads Southey wrote in the late 1790s,
Bishop Hatto burns the population in a barn for being 'rats
that consume the corn', and is devoured himself next day by
a plague of rats which swarms into the tower where he has
taken refuge.

A less well-known 'metrical tale' Southey first published in
1799, 'Cornelius Agrippa', offers a more direct analogue to
Frankenstein; its topic is even late-medieval necromancy as
practised by one of Frankenstein's boyhood mentors. Southey
imitates the format of the chapbook ballad—'very pithy and
profitable'—down to the clip-clop rhythms, forced rhymes,
homely epigraph and sententious moral. One day the wizard
goes out, leaving his wife with strict instructions not to let
anyone into his study:

> There lived a young man in the house, who in vain
> Access to that Study had sought to obtain;
> And he begg'd and pray'd the books to see,
> Till the foolish woman gave him the key.
>
> On the Study-table a book there lay,
> Which Agrippa himself had been reading that day;
> The letters were written with blood therein,
> And the leaves were made of dead men's skin;
>
> And these horrible leaves of magic between
> Were the ugliest pictures that ever were seen,
> The likeness of things so foul to behold,
> That what they were is not fit to be told.

The young man feels impelled to read, and soon hears a
knocking at the door, which grows louder and louder until
the Devil breaks in:

Two hideous horns on his head he had got,
Like iron heated nine times red-hot;
The breath of his nostrils was brimstone blue
And his tail like a fiery serpent grew.

'What wouldst thou with me?' the Wicked One cried,
But not a word the young man replied;
Every hair on his head was standing upright,
And his limbs like a palsy shook with affright.

'What wouldst thou with me?' cried the Author of ill;
But the wretched young man was silent still;
Not a word had his lips the power to say,
And his marrow seem'd to be melting away.

'What wouldst thou with me?' the third time he cries,
And a flash of lightning came from his eyes,
And he lifted his griffin claw in the air,
And the young man had not strength for a prayer.

His eyes red fire and fury dart
As out he tore the young man's heart;
He grinn'd a horrible grin at his prey,
And in a clap of thunder vanish'd away.

THE MORAL
Henceforth let all young men take heed
How in a Conjuror's books they read.

The parallels between Southey's retelling of 'The Sorcerer's Apprentice' and Mary Shelley's version are still apparent in *Frankenstein* the novel, particularly in the first volume, with its poorly explained preoccupation with Renaissance alchemy, and its partly German location in an old university town. It seems likely that the tale unselfconsciously retained the historical dating, around 1500; in the frontispiece to the 1831 edition the characters are dressed in early sixteenth-century clothes, and the stage and film adaptations tend to use a 'period' setting. A metrical tale like Southey's was the kind of verse children knew, perhaps by heart; no doubt someone was able to throw it into the Gothic stockpot at the villa Diodati along with the translated German tales. It was thus still in the air when Byron in August 1816 began work on his verse drama set in Switzerland, *Manfred* (1817), in the opening scene of which his Faustian hero calls up seven supernatural spirits to aid him. In three cases they ask versions of the traditional question Southey's Devil asks—'And what with me wouldst thou?', 'What wouldst thou, Child of Clay, with me?', and finally, together, 'What wouldst thou with us, son of mortals, say?'[18]

In rewriting the story of 'The Sorcerer's Apprentice' more formally, both Byron and Mary Shelley raised it to the dignity of tragedy and high-cultural myth. In doing so they shifted the focus somewhat from the scientific experiments which, according to the 1831 Preface, set the story going in the author's mind. Yet key passages in the novel encode these experiments, if we look at them carefully, and phrases identifiable with other living experimenters and theorists are introduced, in a form for even general readers to pick up. Mary Shelley seems to me to allude to books of science relatively little, and to draw more on spectator-orientated demonstration, perhaps known about at second hand—such as lectures, given from 1800 in centres such as London to audiences as large as a thousand at a time, and afterwards reported in newspapers and journals:

... I pursued nature to her hiding places. Who shall conceive the horrors of my secret toil, as I dabbled among the unhallowed damps of the grave, or tortured the living animal to animate the lifeless clay? ... I collected bones from charnel houses; and disturbed, with profane fingers, the tremendous secrets of the human frame. In a solitary chamber ... separated from all the other apartments ... I kept my workshop of filthy creation; my eyeballs were starting from their sockets in attending to the details of my employment. The dissecting-room and the slaughter-house furnished many of my materials; and often did my human nature turn with loathing from my occupation, whilst ... I brought my work near to a conclusion. (p. 36)

Probably no paragraph in the book has been more influential in promoting the widely held view that the novel is anti-

---

[18] *Manfred* (1817), I. i. 75, 131, 135.

scientific, even anti-intellectual.[19] But modern readers take this to be the case because of our very different assumptions about experiment. It has become the feature distinguishing Enlightenment laboratory-science from the pre-professional medieval–Renaissance science. Where the latter was personal, secretive, implicated in dangerous magic, the former works in a public, officially sanctioned space, before witnesses: experiment has become central to the process whereby the scientific community circulates knowledge and collectively vets it.[20] But around 1800 few members of even the educated public could have had access to a laboratory, and the collage of impressions they could have put together from newspaper cuttings, review articles and public demonstration-lectures is roughly what they find in Mary Shelley's novel. Frankenstein's 'instruments of life' capable of infusing the 'spark of being' suggest the galvanic battery used in real life to try to bring a poisoned cat or hanged criminal back to life[21]—a sensational way of packaging aspects of the vitalist question for the multitude. In the passage just quoted, Frankenstein's activities seem equally topical and tendentious, since they involve both grave-robbing and vivisection.

Where science was concerned, Mary Shelley was necessarily a populist: she had to use what the public knew, and what moreover they knew with their emotions as well as their intellects. The anatomy lecture, a compulsory part of a student's training, in which human bodies were publicly dissected, was

[19] 'Science in *Frankenstein* is of course pseudo-science', U. C. Knoepflmacher, in Levine and Knoepflmacher (eds.), *The Endurance of Frankenstein* (Berkeley: University of California Press, 1979), 317. Cf. 'Introduction', p. xxi and n. 16 for Rieger's similar view.

[20] Steven Shapin and Simon Schaffer, *Leviathan and the Air-Pump: Hobbes, Boyle and the Experimental Life* (Princeton: Princeton University Press, 1985), esp. ch. 2, 'Seeing and Believing', 22–79.

[21] See Bibliography, Aldini, Crouch, and Davy, for some of the more spectacular public experiments, and for an overview, Jan Golinski, *Science as Public Culture: Chemistry and Enlightenment in Britain, 1760–1820* (Cambridge: Cambridge University Press, 1992). Benjamin Brodie (1783–1862), anatomist, surgeon, lifelong friend of Lawrence, investigated the brain, heart, and muscles, but also intermittently appears in contemporary letters (and in Peacock's *Crotchet Castle*, as Mr Henbane) for his public experiments using live animals. The writer Joanna Baillie adopted as a pet a cat which Brodie poisoned and publicly brought to life. See Butler, *Peacock Displayed* (London: Routledge, 1979), 334 n. 2.

a practice arousing much discussion and deep animosity through most of the eighteenth century in the mass of the populace—for it was the poor's dead that were at most risk of being dissected.[22] By the late eighteenth century humanitarian middle-class sentiment was also aroused by the deliberate infliction of pain on animals. Rather than aiming narrowly at satire or critique, however, Mary Shelley was perhaps bent on an impressionistic and composite group-portrait of the established science of the day as her readers knew it, a scene in which a Humphry Davy achieved dazzling social success and fame, while the knowledge he and others dealt in often seemed to have deeply disturbing implications. This was a paradox publicity-minded scientific performers had themselves learnt to exploit, by adopting a distinctly Romantic vocabulary. Davy's French opposite number, the zoologist and palaeontologist Georges Cuvier, conveyed the excitement of his work on fossils by coining a description of himself that would also do for Frankenstein, 'the magician of the charnel-house'.[23]

Even readers of the first edition might well have remained unaware of its exploitation of the Abernethy–Lawrence debate; it was masked by so many fleeting references to science at a more popular, less specialized and generally less controversial level. When in the autumn of 1816 Mary Shelley expands the story into a novel, the experiment, which refers directly to the vitalist controversy, plays a smaller part in the whole. Yet, as the narrative expands, its field of reference in the physical sciences expands too, and if Abernethy ceases to enjoy the limelight Lawrence does not.

[22] For the series of London riots prompted by the anatomists' claims to the bodies of hanged criminals, see Peter Linebaugh, 'The Tyburn Riots against the Surgeons', in D. Hay, P. Linebaugh, J. G. Rule, E. P. Thompson, and C. Winslow (eds.), *Albion's Fatal Tree: Crime and Society in Eighteenth-century England* (London: Penguin Books, 1975).

[23] Georges Cuvier (1769–1832), was from 1804 a convinced religionist and royalist, who disputed with the more radical Lamarck and Geoffroy St-Hilaire through most of his career. His striking catastrophe-theory was necessary if he was to avoid disputing the chronology of Genesis, his popular palaeontology a triumph of imaginative presentation. See *Edinburgh Review*, 20 (1812), 382, and Loren Eiseley, *Darwin's Century*, 84.

Where the first volume has employed little more of Lawrence than his critique of Abernethy, the second and third use other parts of Lawrence's work, drawing strength from his impressive intellectual range. The socio-historical dimension to Lawrence's science was from the outset the common factor, ultimately an ideological factor, which brought Lawrence into the ambience of Godwin, and the two Shelleys into a fruitful co-operation with him. His interest in the German physiologist and pioneer ethnologist J. F. Blumenbach gave him a broad perspective on human beings as they lived worldwide in different societies, and as they had evidently evolved over time. Though politically out of sympathy with Cuvier, he admired him, characteristically, for relating geology to anatomy in his work with fossils. It is in a lecture of March 1817 that Lawrence praises Blumenbach and Cuvier in these terms: and it is not fanciful to suppose that when Mary Shelley uses the voice of the Creature to convey an impression of human life lived in time, she has noted Lawrence's view of what contemporary science does at its best.

As the daughter of Godwin and Wollstonecraft, Britain's leading theoretical sympathizers with the Revolution, Mary, like her husband, had to come to terms with life in the period of France's defeat. Revolutionary political theory had temporarily become virtually unwritable; but an alternative historical narrative might still be provided by the natural sciences, materialist and especially evolutionary. If revolution were to be put in a new, much grander frame, and redefined as evolution, it could be represented as natural, even inevitable. Percy Shelley put his new reading in the physical sciences to just such a politicized use in his long visionary poem *Queen Mab* (1813). It is a significant factor in the post-publication history of *Frankenstein* that *Queen Mab*, virtually unread on its first appearance, first became popular after it was pirated in 1821. For the next generation it served as a popular handbook in scientific politics and politicized science.

Mary Shelley's novel is neither so didactic, nor so copiously informative, as the prose annotations to Percy Shelley's poem. Since the first edition of *Frankenstein* appeared anonymously in 1818, it aroused suspicion rather than outright denunciation in the conservative press. But after 1820, when Lawrence's most important work was taken over by radical publishers, and even more after 1821, when Percy Shelley's most comparable performance emerged from the same source, the scientific dimensions of the novel must have become more readily decodable. Far from being covered over by the tale's translation into a novel, the novel's commitment to the physical sciences grows more explicit after the first volume, once the story escapes the narrow constraints of the oral tale. The second and third volumes must be largely new, and in them the writing becomes freer, maturer, more expressive of the author. For many modern interpreters it also becomes more sincere, reflective, femininely domestic. In fact we shall see that the story's intellectual horizons expand as the author discovers her natural medium: an apparently domestic drama moves through space and time with an ease probably unmatched in any previous novel.

The Novel, 1: Walton and the Creature

In order to make a novel Mary Shelley must have felt she needed at least eighty-thousand new words—while retaining what was probably from the outset an effective thriller-type plot, with everything that has to happen already in place. The problems were largely technical, and her father's novels showed her ways to solve them. *Caleb Williams* supplies the ideological positioning of the two main protagonists, one high prestige and one low, and the cleverly-worked device of the chase in which first one is the hunter, then the other. *St Leon* (1799) brings in many more ideas, most linked to gender, and associated for Mary Shelley with her mother's later thinking. By the mid-1790s, hopes were fading that France or America could supply some progressive utopia, even on the scale of a model community. For first Wollstonecraft, then more tentatively Godwin, private life, the family, a few chosen friends, became the best remaining hope. The De Lacey family establish a precarious idyll in their Swiss rural refuge, based on the household Marguerite creates for St Leon. But this feminized model of sociability and co-operation in the private sphere breaks down after their disastrous face-to-face encounter with the Creature. Till now, they have taught the

Creature to aspire to a feminized life. After this point, he becomes masculine, combative, masterful, the emanation of the selfish ambitious side of his creator Frankenstein.

Much of the bulk Mary Shelley needs she cleverly provides by using not one narrator but three, who in effect go over some of the same narrative ground. Their different viewpoints might well have dispersed the novel's unusual effect of coherence, had it not been for the most important factor they share—they are all three explorers, investigators of the human race and/or its environment. A new character, Walton the polar explorer, shares the narration with Frankenstein, and as an adventurer in state-subsidized or big science provides some variation on the latter's role as an inventor working alone. Walton's project is also eyecatching, real-life and up-to-the-minute, as Frankenstein's seemingly archaic, idiosyncratic enterprise is not. In 1776 Captain James Cook was driven back from his attempt to circumnavigate North America from the Pacific. His British and French successors were delayed for over a generation by the twenty-two-year French-revolutionary wars. When in 1815 Napoleon's final defeat reopened the seas, the prizes awaiting great voyagers were obvious—glory for their own nation and an advantage over its competitors, shorter trade routes to the east, the discovery and capture of new markets, a headstart in the scramble for Asian, African, and Pacific colonies. In 1817 and 1818 the *Quarterly Review* devotes two long articles to Arctic exploration; even its review of *Frankenstein* contributes to the topic, by highlighting the scientific topicality of the novel's Arctic subplot. In an article devoted to a *Memoir* by Captain James Burney, who sailed on Cook's voyage through the Bering Straits, the reviewer (John Barrow) gives a compelling picture of the personal prestige the explorer stood to gain, a place in the line which has Columbus at its head:

Who could imagine that the power of the magnet . . . would lead to the discovery of a new world? and who can tell what further advantages mankind may derive from the magnetical influence, so very remarkable, so very little understood? or pretend to limit the discoveries to which electricity and galvanism may yet open the way? Had any one thirty years ago been bold enough to assert that he would light up our shops and houses . . . with a bolder flame than anyone had yet produced . . . he would at once have been set down as a madman or imposter . . . Both expeditions [about to set out for the North Pole] may fail in the main object of the arduous enterprise; but they can scarcely fail in being the means of extending the sphere of human knowledge . . . 'Knowledge is power'; and we may safely commit to the stream of time the beneficial results of its irresistible influence.[24]

It is as clear a statement as one can find of the rhetoric which before and after 1800 gave science a notional central place in British as in other western cultures. Science's publicists now put in place a glorious narrative, begun in the Renaissance, by which thought rather than action had led the West or North to its conquest of the known world. In the early nineteenth century, at the beginning of the age of Europe's most massive colonial expropriations, exploration held out very material and publicly acknowledged rewards, yet still needed this idealizing rhetoric to justify them. But while the *Quarterly's* reviewer revels at the thought of such glory, Mary Shelley's approach to her discoverer Walton is unmistakably sardonic. She portrays him as a spoilt young egotist who complains continuously to the patient sister he has left behind, and all along risks the lives of the family men who make up his crew. Mary Shelley's reaction to science of this kind has some similarities to that of the modern physicist Brian Easlea, as he examines the psychic investments and public policy behind the twentieth-century arms race. 'Modern science is basically a masculine endeavour, and in a world of competing nation states and blocs serves to fuel the fires of human conflict rather than to quench them.'[25]

For all their superficial differences, the novel's acknowledged scientists are two of a kind—a fact signalled by Walton's immature admiration for Frankenstein, and by his yearning to follow his last, bad advice, to sacrifice the lives of

[24] [Barrow], 'Capt. Burney, *Memoir* . *on Question whether Asia and America are Contiguous*', *Quarterly Review*, 18 (1818), 457–8.

[25] Brian Easlea, *Fathering the Unthinkable* (1983), 5.

the crew in a push to the North Pole (p. 183).[26] These two enter an admiring compact which is in fact an expression of each man's narcissism. Appropriately enough, Frankenstein's last gift to Walton is his feud with the Creature.

Compared with the professional qualifications of the other two, the Creature has no prior claim to his place as the third narrator, which is in fact the heart of the novel. Just as he owes his very existence to an anomaly, a unique process, he defies probability, and surmounts his parentless situation, in learning language at all. Nevertheless the Creature speaks impressively, with the dignity, even authority, appropriate to a witness brought back from the remote past—another phrase the great showman Cuvier used to describe the fossils he patiently reconstructed into lifelike animals.[27] He is eloquent and persuasive in the two conversations with Frankenstein that introduce and end their meeting. But his stature ultimately depends on his life-history, an exercise in self-observation, gradually supplemented with social observation, always accompanied by retrospective analysis. He tracks his own maturation, from a solitary to a social animal. It is he, not Frankenstein, who follows through Frankenstein's technological achievement in a scientific spirit.

He begins his narration on the night of the experiment, at once challenging Frankenstein, who as the experiment's author has already provided what seemed to be the definitive account. Still unable to focus his eyes, the Creature blundered round Frankenstein's lodgings in the big Ingolstadt rooming house, before finding himself, very cold, out in the woods near the town. His visual impressions were still unclear, but he now began to make the distinction between light and dark. He might have died of hunger and exposure had he not found berries he instinctively ate, water to drink, and a cloak in which to wrap himself. He struggles for the words to tell how he responded, pleasurably, to moonlight and birds when still unable to name them, let alone classify 'the little winged

[26] See Explanatory Notes.

[27] 'My key, my principle, will enable us to restore the appearance of these long-vanished beasts and relate them to the life of the present.' Cuvier, *Essay on the Theory of the Earth* (Edinburgh, 1815).

animals who had often intercepted the light from my eyes'. (p. 81)

In this chapter (II. iii) Mary Shelley employs language experimentally and imaginatively, in a way rare in her own or indeed anyone's prose fiction before the twentieth century: William Golding performs a similar feat in *The Inheritors*, when his Neanderthal narrator describes his first encounters with *homo sapiens*. But the content of the Creature's narrative would be familiar to a reader of eighteenth-century natural science, specifically to readers of the literature on Wild Boys and Girls who had supposedly grown·up among wild animals, or at any rate isolated from humanity. Already in his *System of Nature* (1735), Linnaeus speaks of *homo ferus* as a distinct human species, 'four-footed, mute and hairy', and lists ten recorded instances from 1544. The most famous case of Mary Shelley's day was the Wild Boy of Aveyron, whose discovery came to light in Paris in 1799. Considered medically, for what it reveals of early human physical and cognitive development, this remains a classic instance, thanks to the devoted teaching and careful reporting (1801, 1807) of the young physician of the Paris institution for deaf-mutes, Jean-Marc-Gaspard Itard. The opening sentences of Itard's Preface have a humanity and personal sympathy for these deprived, isolated creatures that may well be reflected in Mary Shelley's Volume II:

Cast upon this globe without physical strength or innate ideas, incapable in himself of obeying the fundamental laws of his nature which call him to the supreme place in the universe, it is only in the heart of society that man can attain the pre-eminent position which is his natural destiny. Without the aid of civilisation he would be one of the feeblest and least intelligent of animals.[28]

In beginning with this reflection, Itard shows he is not merely the empirical scientist, studying the particulars of his case: he is an ideologue, that is a philosopher who subjects to special scrutiny the features unique to human experience—language, and 'civilization'.

But the speculative general issue, whether the wild man is a sub-species, and if so how he relates both to advanced man

---

[28] Itard, Preface to *The Wild Boy of Aveyron* (New York: Century Books, Appleton-Century-Crofts, 1962), p. xxi.

and to the primates, has a longer history of which educated readers would also be aware. Rousseau in his *Second Discourse: On the Origins of Inequality* (1752) had posited an early historical stage in which man lived wild and alone, a noble condition compared with his later socialized interdependency. Monboddo, accepting the existence of a distinct species of wild men, considered that it supplied the missing link which proved man's membership of the family of primates. Using the best-documented case before Itard's, that of the Hanoverian Wild Boy Peter of Hamelin, who was discovered in the 1720s and afterwards taken to England, first J. F. Blumenbach and later (1819) his disciple William Lawrence argued against generalizing from such cases. Generally there were indications that the child concerned was an idiot, who had easily strayed from home, where not actually cast out. Such children found bodily co-ordination difficult, including walking erect, and language (beyond a handful of words) impossible.[29]

The significant point of Mary Shelley's treatment of the Creature's rearing in isolation from humanity is that it makes none of the common exaggerated claims. The Creature's life in the woods is neither superior, nor even natural; it is not introduced as evidence of the existence of a sub-species, whether now or in the remote past, nor of man's affinity with the primates. Mary Shelley takes a more cautious view, and could even be evading or excluding the evolutionist perspective both Erasmus Darwin and Lamarck had advanced, that all forms of organic life had evolved from single cells.[30] On the other hand, the Creature's life-experience may well draw on

---

[29] Lawrence, *Lectures . . . and Natural History*, 134–40.

[30] The Shelleys knew and admired Erasmus Darwin's poem *The Temple of Nature* (1803), along with its philosophical notes. Darwin's first Additional Note supplies a sound scientific reason why Frankenstein's original experiment was misconceived. Believing in the gradual adaptation of species over time from simple beginnings, Darwin argues that only single-cell organisms should be used for attempts to generate life. Lamarck, whom the Shelleys do not mention, gives a more systematic account which amounts to a description of evolution: 'Life is in simple forms constantly emerging, and through its inner perfecting principle or drive it begins to achieve complexity and to ascend toward higher levels.' Quoted Eiseley, *Darwin's Century*, 50.

the careful observation of Itard and the physiology of Itard's leading contemporary Bichat, in *Traité sur les membranes* (1800), *Recherches physiologiques sur la vie et sur la mort* (1800), and *Anatomie Générale* (1801), works which explore the functions and connecting tissue of the nerves, senses and organs, and give the most accurate account yet of every creature's sensitive interactions with its environment.

In relation to fiction's established conventions, the Creature's career works on two levels, as a survival-story like Robinson Crusoe's, and as an allegorical account of the progress of mankind over aeons of time. His evolutionary adaptations are speeded up, in this wittiest, most optimistic part of the book where, through the unconscious assistance of the idealized family, the De Laceys, he masters in turn speech, reading, and political economy:

I heard of the division of property, of immense wealth and squalid poverty; of rank, descent and noble blood . . . [Without wealth or descent a man] was considered . . . a vagabond and a slave, doomed to waste his powers for the profit of the chosen few. And what was I? . . . I possessed no money, no friends, no kind of property . . . Was I then a monster . . . from which all men fled? . . . sorrow only increased with knowledge. Oh that I had for ever remained in my native wood! (p. 96)

And there's the rub. Just half-way through the action, the ascent of this hero of the species is stopped, by the species itself. The De Laceys have taught the Creature how to be human, through their involuntary lessons in mutual affection, support, and interdependence. But in civilized life it seems that the family, whether called Frankenstein or De Lacey, feels little or no affinity with the human family at large. Driven by modern selfish individualism, the De Laceys acknowledge only those strangers who are, like Safie, as beautiful and polished as themselves. In this Voltairean fable told by the Creature, society's civilized, ethical, and Christian pretensions are all exposed, often by way of a discreet, downplayed style of religious parody.

When Natural Man appears in this family's midst it cannot recognize him, and will not give him room. When he kneels like a guiltless Prodigal Son to the Father he hopes will adopt him, old De Lacey (here acting the parts of both God and Blind Justice) has a kindly impulse to receive him. But his true insight is countermanded by the false perception of his sighted children—that the Creature cannot be part of the human family. Their hidden benefactor, with all his potential to be good, is driven away with blows.

The Novel, 2: Parenting and Breeding

In the third volume Mary Shelley returns the narration to Frankenstein. For all the excellence of Volume II in its stylized mode, most readers now probably find Volume III the most brilliantly imaginative and original part of the book— and from a scientific as well as a literary perspective. Frankenstein's psychological condition is far better established here than in Volume I. Reorientated by the Creature, we now see Frankenstein's viewpoint for what it is, not representative of humanity in any neutral, still less noble way, but typically insensitive and self-absorbed. He is moreover a profoundly unreliable narrator, deceived as well as deceiving, at best a depressive and at worst a hallucinator. He knows his family to be in danger from the Creature, and has only to tell them so. The reason he gives for not telling, that he might be thought mad, is given at a time when he *is* thought mad—so that the reader is cleverly led to see the excuse as itself part of the malady.

But is his malady a personal characteristic, or does it represent a social malaise? If mindful of the lead given by Godwin's novels, we should consider the explanation that this is aristocratic pride of rank—since the Frankensteins are, though republicans, as much élitists as Godwin's Falkland, St Leon, and other narrator-protagonists. Alternatively Frankenstein could be suffering from jealous possessiveness with regard to property, in this case intellectual property. Again, this is a possible description of St Leon's suicidal willingness to guard his fatal secret. Like Frankenstein's refusal to tell all until far too late, secrecy itself symbolizes the greed and competitiveness which for Rousseau was the crime of civilized life.

All these readings should be taken seriously; but Frankenstein must also be considered a character distinctively

Mary's. For one thing, he stands for male arrogance and the impulse to dominate, as this trait is observable domestically. An original motive behind his experiment was indeed a version of the mature man's ambition to found a family, but on a scale truly gigantic—'A new species would bless me as its creator and source . . . No father could claim the gratitude of his child so completely as I should deserve theirs.' (p. 36) William and Clerval die at the Creature's hands, but we are not shown how Frankenstein could have prevented this. By his self-protective silence, abdicating the man's protective role towards the women of the household, he is much more obviously complicit in the deaths of Justine and Elizabeth.

Frankenstein's self-absorption and irresponsibility have to be inferred; Godwin, a little more merciful to the male, allows St Leon, Fleetwood, Mandeville, and Deloraine to acknowledge and to regret bitterly the costs *to themselves* of their egotism. In the 1818 text of Mary Shelley's third volume, the exposé of Frankenstein's solipsism is consistent and severe. For all his cries of concern for the safety of his family, he fails to spot that Elizabeth is bound to be present at the appointment the Creature has made with him—'I will be with you on your wedding night.' As a portrayal of male inattentiveness, this is satirical, in fact comic. Its domestic ordinariness does not prevent Frankenstein from serving as the embodiment of an intellectually ambitious concept, civilized degeneracy.

There are signs by now of a rich literary interaction between the Shelleys and Lawrence, one that flows in both directions. In his polemical 1817 lecture on the Life question, Lawrence seems to stray into Mary Shelley's Gothicized rhythms and vocabulary—'an immaterial and spiritual being could not have been discovered among the blood and filth of the dissecting room.'[31] Volume III of the novel in particular echoes details from different writings by Lawrence, not necessarily contemporaneous. For instance, Lawrence in early 1815 studied a boy born without part of his brain, and had him cared for in his own house. Some of the findings of the resulting academic paper are summarized in Lawrence's contribution of the entry on 'Monsters' to Rees's *Cyclopaedia*:

[31] Lawrence, *Lectures . . . and Natural History*, 7.

The function of generation is not exempt from the operation of disturbing causes . . . Particular bodily formations, particular mental characters, and dispositions to certain diseases, are transmitted to the offspring . . . We ascribe then the aberrations from the usual form and structure of the body, which produce monsters, to an irregular operation of the powers concerned in generation.[32]

Lawrence, then, was interested in human abnormality present from birth, and the interest led at least briefly to his fostering an abnormal child or 'monster'. That piece of fieldwork must surely have helped prompt Mary Shelley's 'hideous phantom'; for, to discount the dramatics of 1831 concerning the 'waking dream', the plot of *Frankenstein* boils down to a scientist who fosters, or fails to foster, a monster. Even more clearly, the Lawrence case supplied the germ for the plot of Peacock's satire *Melincourt* (1817), in which an intellectual called Forester (full form of the name Foster) adopts an orang-utan and tries to teach him to speak. (He fails, but a richly corruptible system enables him to secure his protégé a baronetcy and a seat in Parliament.)

Meanwhile Lawrence was also developing in his lectures themes eventually gathered into his magnum opus, *A Natural History of Man* (1819). This important volume, the product of hitherto unpublished lectures Lawrence gave from 1814, studies the human species as a variety of animal. Probably to fend off theological criticism, its opening section considers the connection between human beings and the primates at some length, and, upholding the arguments of Blumenbach, concludes that the link is relatively remote (compared, that is, with the close relations of all racial types of human beings).

Lawrence then turns to his particular interest, variation within the human species as we presently know it, and the probable reasons for this, such as heredity and environment. It is delicate, dangerous ground, but Lawrence makes few concessions to politeness or diplomacy. The most challenging passages in the book are those that raise the question of

---

[32] Lawrence also contributed entries on 'Cranium', 'Generation', and 'Man' for Rees's *Cyclopaedia* (individual vols. undated, complete by 1819). See Appendix C for the reviewer's description of it as a materialist publication.

sexual selection among human beings, and, in Europe, within the different classes. Here Lawrence becomes at points a social critic, even a satirist—as he is when he accuses the social élite, most notably royalty, of in-breeding, a practice good farmers have learnt to avoid in the stockyard. The result has been, he points out, European royal families which currently exhibit madness and degeneracy (as George III of England has done for the last nine years). With varying degrees of frankness, the topics Lawrence considers in this book have been touched on by Mary Shelley, particularly in the third volume of *Frankenstein*—heredity, fosterage and nurturance, sexual selection, and the perverse adoption of choices which lead to extinction.

The novel's third volume begins by raising the issue of Frankenstein's own marriage. It has long been understood that he will marry his first cousin Elizabeth, who has been brought up in the same house like a sister. (See Appendix B for the steps taken by Shelley in 1831 to remove the implication of incest from Victor Frankenstein's marriage, and to make Alphonse Frankenstein's late marriage look healthier.) Frankenstein's reluctance to marry Elizabeth when the question is raised contrasts with the eagerness of the Creature to have Frankenstein make him a mate. The Creature gives as his reason the need for companionship; but in Frankenstein's heated imagination he is soon breeding, and through his progeny making war on mankind. Frankenstein thus projects on to the Creature his own grandiose fantasy as he embarked on his experiment, of artificially making a sub-species. His long-suppressed sexual emotions seem far more aroused when he dismembers the female Creature, and scatters her body-parts into the sea, than on his own wedding night, when he fatally delays accompanying Elizabeth to bed.

In the event both these heterosexual but otherwise grimly unusual unions are thwarted by the violent deaths of both females before consummation can take place. The remainder of the third volume can be read as a blackly funny homoerotic mime, with man chasing man through a world where the loved women are all dead or far away, and no new ones appear. The three male narrators pair off in every combination. The Creature and Frankenstein stalk each other but never again meet; Walton meets and loves Frankenstein; the Creature is reunited with Frankenstein, as a corpse; the Creature in the last scene meets Walton, and a message, of understanding if not love, passes between them. The plot of the last volume has taken a decisive turn in the direction of failure to breed, or to breed healthily.

When it comes to parenting, Frankenstein is himself a monster. He will not acknowledge his only child, the Being he chooses to call Monster, Fiend, and Demon, though no human father ever played so thorough-going a role in any birth. (The good reasons for the critic to avoid Frankenstein's harshest most unpaternal acts of naming should be apparent.) *Frankenstein* repeatedly illustrates, but ironically, Lawrence's scholarly observations about parenting—the medical mishaps to which the birth-process is subject; the one sure feature of any birth, which is the involvement of at least one parent of the same species. But, if this parent–child relationship after a fashion obeys the rules, the roles of those involved become perversely displaced. After Frankenstein vows to hunt down his 'progeny', the Creature nurtures Frankenstein to keep him alive, feeding him for example with a dead hare: only when killing for Frankenstein does the vegetarian Creature kill for food. He still tries in his way to live by the precept that the child is father to the man—and, anthropologically, primitive man *is* father to sophisticated man. But the Creature has slowly emerged as the dominant partner, though originally he was a dependant, a deformed huge child. Of the two antagonists, he is the stronger and better adapted when in the Arctic the natural conditions turn severe. He shares Frankenstein's fate of extinction, but goes to it voluntarily, and with a consoling apprehension of the natural universe to which even he will return.

Set against the desolate landscape of the world's waste places, the eerie chase has not been any ordinary contest. The Creature is at once all of us, a one-off experiment, and Adam, the classic case of a fictional being without a human parent. Though an upstart by comparison, Frankenstein too has a genealogy which is by conventional standards impressive, and he too embodies transhistorical experience: an aristocratic republicanism going back at least to Machiavelli, a scientific tradition which reaches back beyond Baconian science and the Age of Discovery to the natural magic and so-called necromancy of the later Middle Ages. The war to the death between these two is both the poignant struggle of father and rejected child, and the acting out of mankind's internecine, ultimately suicidal rivalry within the species. Above all it represents the attempt of an over-civilized élite to reject its real past and its membership of a wider animal community.

As a man, Frankenstein ought to be capable of acknowledging kinship—with his low-caste human/animal relations, and with woman. It is easy to see why influential readers of *Frankenstein* such as Sterrenberg, Moretti, and Baldick have developed the argument that his dark Other, the Creature, represents the newly politicized masses; equally, why Mary Jacobus and Gilbert and Gubar are inclined to interpret him as woman. The novel allegorizes the issues both of politics and gender, and, since this is so, we need an explanation which encompasses both terms. Between the advanced and primitive stages of mankind's evolutionary progress there is an inequality not dissimilar from the relationship between the sexes, the classes, the races. The structured representation of social inequality, or rather inequalities, is one of the great themes of fiction and non-fiction of the French Revolutionary period. In women's writing perhaps especially, prejudice's many forms are characteristically considered together, as symptoms of an ethical and cultural crisis, not as an issue of either class or gender alone.

Frankenstein after Lawrence

The novel's first reviews tended to be critical, but not violently so. Though published anonymously, it had a dedicatee, whose name appeared before the title-page, William Godwin. The association with the old radical was probably enough to secure the disapproval of conservative journals such as the *Quarterly Review* and the *Edinburgh Magazine and Literary Miscellany*. The former objected to a second mad narrator-hero, within a year of Godwin's protagonist Mandeville: 'Mr Godwin is the patriarch of a literary family, whose chief skill is in delineating the wanderings of the intellect, and which strangely delights in the most afflicting and humiliating of human miseries.'[33] The same reviewer dwelt disapprovingly on the filthiness of the attempt to make a living creature, his strong language implying that the general public was best left in ignorance of the debate on vitalism, but approved, if grudgingly, the up-to-date detail in the Arctic voyage—'Frankenstein . . . probably had read Mr Daines Barrington and Colonel Beaufoy on the subject'.[34] The *Edinburgh Magazine*'s reviewer also noted the presence of 'favourite projects and passions of the times', without specifying what these were, presumably for fear of lending them a helping hand.[35]

On the other hand Walter Scott, reviewing for *Blackwood's*, showed characteristic generosity to the author's 'uncommon powers of poetic imagination'.[36] These powers may have been a spur to the unusual polemical exercise Scott published in the autumn of 1819 in the *Edinburgh Weekly Journal*: three dream-visions, signed by 'Somnambulus', which satirized radical utopias. In the second the dreamer meets, in a barely recognizable Scotland of the future, a democratic 'ogre' with 'a physiognomy which was brutal rather than human', who could owe something to Frankenstein's Creature.[37] If this is indeed using the novel as an 'awful warning' against innovation, it anticipates the mid- to late nineteenth-century *Punch* cartoons in which a radical intellectual becomes terrorized by his unruly protégé the mob.[38]

---

[33] *Quarterly Review*, 18 (1818), 383.   [34] Ibid. 381.

[35] *Edinburgh Magazine and Literary Miscellany*, 2 (1818), 250.

[36] Scott, *Blackwood's Edinburgh Magazine*, 2 (1817–18), 619.

[37] 'Somnambulus' [Scott], *Edinburgh Weekly Journal*, 8 Dec. 1819; Peter Garside (ed.), *The Visionary*, no. 2, *Regency Reprints I* (Cardiff: University College Cardiff Press, 1984), 33–9.

[38] The so-called Monster regularly lent himself to political appropriation during the 19th cent., as the personification of popular, violent radicalism, while the inept liberal politician who has unleashed this now uncontrollable force lurks helplessly at the edge of the picture: e.g. Meadows on Irish Nationalism and Daniel O'Connell (*Punch*, 1843), Tenniel on the Birmingham or 'Brummagem' worker and John Bright MP (*Punch*, 1866) and Tenniel again on the Irish and Charles Parnell (*Punch*, 1882). All three are reproduced by Baldick, the latter two by Levine and Knoepflmacher: see Bibliography.

Since all three reviews showed respect of a kind, this was a much better reception than might have been feared, and better than Percy Shelley had yet encountered. But the next year Lawrence's *Lectures on Physiology, Zoology and the Natural History of Man* appeared. The volume triggered George D'Oyley's long, virulent and prominently placed denunciation in the *Quarterly Review* of November 1819, an opening article surveying the vitalist controversy over five years which constituted a major event in the public reception of evolution theory (see Appendix C). Encouraged by his editor William Gifford, D'Oyley denounced Lawrence for the materialism of his arguments on the vitalist issue, and showed knowledge of other work such as his specialist paper on the brain, and his summary entries in Rees's *Cyclopaedia*—but omitted overt reference to his treatment of heredity and breeding, possibly out of regard for good taste. D'Oyley's tone is exceptionally harsh in its treatment of Lawrence, especially in its conclusion, which calls on the Royal College of Surgeons to discipline him. On pain of dismissal he should be made to withdraw the offending passages, and to undertake not to write again in the same vein.

The Royal College of Surgeons did indeed suspend Lawrence, and, going a little further than asked, would not reinstate him till he withdrew the book entirely. He did so for fear of losing his appointment as Surgeon to the hospitals of Bridewell and Bethlehem. The result ironically was that during the next few years several publishers[39] pirated the volume, under cover of a ruling of 1817 by the Lord Chancellor, Lord Eldon, that where a book was blasphemous, seditious, or immoral the author should not be protected by the law of copyright. In March 1822, under pressure again from the Royal College, Lawrence tried to claim his copyright, and initially obtained an injunction restraining the firm of J. and C. Smith from selling their edition of his book. The

---

[39] In addition to the 1st edn. by J. Callow (1819), the British Library owns early pirated edns. by W. Benbow (1822), Kaygill & Rice (1822), and J. and C. Smith (1823). There was a further edn. in 1823 by Richard Carlile, publisher of Paine and author of an *Address to the Men of Science* (1821) which singles out Lawrence for praise as a popular radical writer. Carlile dedicated it ironically to Lord Eldon. See O. Temkin, 'Basic Science, Medicine and the Romantic Era', 355.

Smiths' lawyers argued that the work was not protected because of passages 'hostile to natural and revealed religion'. After reading both the book and its reviews, Lord Eldon upheld the publishers, even though the book would in consequence remain in circulation, in cheap popular formats.[40] Lord Byron lost similar cases, also tried before Eldon, in February 1822 and in 1823, involving *Cain* and *Don Juan* respectively.

The pursuit of Lawrence's future career, in the 1820s as a radical writing anonymously for the *Lancet*, from the 1830s as an increasingly fashionable surgeon-physician (who cared for Queen Victoria), does not immediately concern the reader of *Frankenstein*.[41] But the publication of Lawrence's major volume and its subsequent notoriety, disseminated and fuelled by copious media coverage, becomes part of the post-publication history of the novel, since it surely influenced the revision of the text which Mary Shelley undertook in 1831. For the author, her circle, and a significant number of informed readers, whether their sympathies were theological or materialist, the plot of *Frankenstein* was either already associated with Lawrence's style of radical science, or was always in danger of being associated—until, that is, Mary Shelley removed most of the tell-tale signs.

As a scientist Lawrence had been relatively cushioned from reviewing in the non-specialist press: he learnt its hazards the hard way. In high culture and general culture, the 1820s belonged as a whole to the theological party, or to those who could and would make a deal with it. The campaign to regulate 'family reading', ensure the propriety of references especially to religion and sex, guard against messages of political and social disaffection, is not specifically Victorian, but was running full steam in the *Quarterly* and lesser right-wing journals well before 1820. Percy Shelley was caught by it, when he

---

[40] Keeping its eye on the Lawrence story, the *Quarterly Review* published another article on these legal proceedings (27 (April 1822), 123–39), and found fault with Eldon for a judgement so damaging to the public interest. See Bibliography for discussions of this legal case by Goodfield-Toulmin, Temkin, and Wells.

[41] For Lawrence's subsequent career as a covert radical, see Adrian Desmond, *Politics of Evolution,* 'Importing the new Morphology', esp. 25–81

too introduced the theme of incest that radical science was making yet more problematical—though Percy Shelley's intellectual association with Lawrence is in fact better hidden than his wife's. Of his two major works of the *Frankenstein* years featuring incest, the romance *Laon and Cythna* (1817) had to be withdrawn and reissued, modified, as the *Revolt of Islam* (Jan. 1818); the drama *The Cenci* (written 1818) could not be staged in London. Mary Shelley's *Mathilda*, written August 1819 to February 1820, portrays incestuous love between a father and daughter. Godwin prevented its publication, because, it is usually assumed, he feared that reviewers would think the novel autobiographical. By 1820 the mere fact that Mathilda portrayed an incestuous family could well have been reason to suppress it.

In Italy, Mary Shelley (like her husband and Byron) could not fully gauge how frightened moderate English public opinion had been by the violence, radical extremism, and press licence manifest in 1819–20. She pencilled in corrections to her published text of 1818 in a copy of the printed book. Those early afterthoughts, almost all stylistic improvements to some admittedly rough writing, were left behind in Italy with an English friend Mary Shelley met there, a Mrs Thomas.[42] By now merely literary corrections would never be enough. It was to a better-policed culture than she had left that Mary Shelley came home as a widow in 1823.

The first dramatic adaptation of her novel was already playing at the English Opera House, Richard Brinsley Peake's significantly named *Presumption: or the Fate of Frankenstein.* Three changes from the novel are particularly significant. The stage Monster does not speak, and has the mind of an infant. Frankenstein confesses his religious remorse to the audience, 'Oh that I could recall my impious labour, or suddenly extinguish the spark that I have so presumptuously bestowed.' And a comic servant, Fritz, is introduced as Frankenstein's assistant, to reinforce the moral by his fearful talk of raising the Devil—a throwback perhaps to the

---

[42] Mary Shelley's proposed corrections marked in Mrs Thomas's copy are given as variants in Rieger's text.

Southeyan anecdote of the Sorcerer's Apprentice. The cautionary reading was already in place, and was repeated later in 1823 by H. M. Milner in *The Daemon of Switzerland*, though this did not save the theatres concerned from demonstrators urging fathers to take their families home.[43] Before she had implemented her own changes Mary Shelley had lost control over the plot and specifically over its range, that dynamic and original dimension symbolized by the fact the Creature speaks.

Her cuts and rewriting were acts of damage-limitation rather than a reassertion of authority. They could have seemed advisable when surgeons and their experiments became the objects of public hysteria because of the Burke and Hare murders in Edinburgh in the late 1820s. What made them inevitable was that conservatives everywhere now interpreted the plot of *Frankenstein* as they wished to, and knew that their readers agreed. As a writer in *Fraser's Magazine* (November 1830) remarks in passing, 'A State without religion is like a human body without a soul, or rather like a human body of the species of the Frankenstein Monster, without a pure and vivifying principle.'[44] Before Mary Shelley publishes the novel in its strategically changed guise, a journalist already claims it for Abernethy's rather than Lawrence's side in the vitalist issue.

After her return to England Mary Shelley lived on as a respectable woman of letters, the mother to a future baronet she meant should take his place in upper-class society. She had little income except what she could earn, and her best chances of earning related directly or indirectly to *Frankenstein*. For some years she had been hoping Bentley would give her a style of third edition that new publishing technology had made much cheaper. Keeping the book clear of scandal may have been the trade-off the publisher exacted, but Mary Shelley had nothing now to gain by scandal. She

[43] See Baldick, *In Frankenstein's Shadow*, 58–60, and Elizabeth Nitchie, *Mary Shelley, Author of 'Frankenstein'* (Westport, Conn., 1953).

[44] Quoted by Lee Sterrenberg, 'MS's Monster: Politics and Psyche in *Frankenstein'*, in Levine and Knoepflmacher (eds.), 166.

accordingly prepared a very different list of corrections from the stylistic ones she first jotted down in Italy in the Thomas edition.

The fate of Shelley's *Frankenstein* was not in the end wholly dissimilar from the fate of Lawrence's *Lectures on Physiology, Zoology and the Natural History of Man*. Both authors submitted to respectable middle-class opinion, in ways that allowed them to rescue what they could of their intellectual property. The changes to *Frankenstein* detailed in Appendix B throw the similarity into relief, and the probable nature of the external pressure. What Mary Shelley added was usually reverent. What she cut resembled the passages the *Quarterly* explicitly or implicitly wanted excised from Lawrence's book: the materialist line on 'organization'; doubt thrown on a non-material mind or spirit, and a divine Creator; the theme of perverse sexual selection or 'breeding', actively keyed into real-life public morals, health and behaviour.

NOTE ON THE TEXT

This book is reprinted from the first edition published in three volumes in March 1818 by Lackington, Hughes, Harding, Mavor, and Jones of Finsbury Square, London. I have adhered to the spelling and punctuation of the original, but silently corrected misprints, and in two places restored missing words.

It is not the first time the 1818 text has been preferred. In 1974 James Rieger published a fine edition based on it (Indiana: Bobbs-Merrill; repr. University of Chicago Press, 1982), to which students of the novel remain indebted. Since then Betty T. Bennett and Charles E. Robinson have preferred it for their *Mary Shelley Reader* (New York: Oxford University Press, 1990). All the same, the third edition of 1813 remains the conventional choice, as the last edition corrected by the author. Its version of the plot has been the standard one since 1831.

There are three influential reasons for choosing 1831. First, Mary Shelley's substantive corrections were carefully worked out and long meditated: Rieger, acknowledging this, incorporates into his text another series of corrections she embarked on as early as 1818. Second, many of the corrections can be justified from a literary point of view, as deepening the character of Frankenstein, invoking a mythical and spiritual dimension, and smoothing over with polished prose some very awkward writing, in the first chapters especially. Third, a reason that can be summarized not too pejoratively as inertia: the changes of 1831 in fact support the interpretation of the novel to which we have become used. This is for the very good reason that most of the changes *introduce* an element of interpretation into Frankenstein's narrative, where they congregate. (See Appendix B, where the substantive changes are listed and discussed.) For over a century and a half, our understanding of *Frankenstein* as a novel (or play or film) that has a religious moral, and/or an antiscientific one, has rested disproportionately on these very passages.

One good reason for choosing the 1818 text is that it enables the editor to set out the substantive additions in an Appendix as an element well worth separate study. (For a full collation, to which mine is necessarily indebted, consult Rieger's edition.) It is only when the relations between the two versions are expressed this way round that readers can see how much turns on the addition of religious attitudes and judgements, and the cancellation or reinterpretation of the science (in which should be included, for reasons I explain in the Introduction, the catastrophic failure of the Frankensteins to propagate in the normal way). The Introduction also shows how much pressure, direct and indirect, was put upon the author to change the book in the way she did. Both she and the publisher might well have shrunk from reissuing *Frankenstein* in 1831 in its unrevised state.

At the same time I hope I have demonstrated that the 1818 version is the more important and serious book. It is for instance a remarkable pioneering work of science fiction. An instant classic in the genre, it delivers an original, specific, and profound fable about the modern world in conditions of social change, brilliantly worked out through the competition of different scientific specialisms and the polarization of gender. The evidence of the eye—that the changes in 1831 are mainly additions—is misleading; so is the author's claim in her new Preface that most are concerned with style. A weak version of the Faust-myth has been brought in, with none of Goethe's massive investment in reorientating the story to post-Enlightenment circumstances. Pious and in this context sentimental, the implants succeed all too well in their task, of blurring or wishing away the sharper, harder quality of the first edition, the flash of the surgeon's knife.

SELECT BIBLIOGRAPHY

Primary Works

Mounseer Nongtongpaw; or, the Discoveries of John Bull in a Trip to Paris. London: Proprietors of the Juvenile Library [M. J. Godwin & Co.], 1808.

History of a Six Weeks' Tour through a Part of France, Switzerland, Germany, and Holland: With Letters Descriptive of a Sail round the Lake of Geneva, and of the Glaciers of Chamouni. [With Percy Bysshe Shelley.] London: T. Hookham, Jun., and C. and J. Ollier, 1817.

Frankenstein; or, The Modern Prometheus. 3 vols. London: Lackington, Hughes, Harding, Mavor, & Jones, 1818.

Valperga: or, The Life and Adventures of Castruccio, Prince of Lucca. 3 vols. London: G. and W. B. Whittaker, 1823.

The Last Man. 3 vols. London: Henry Colburn, 1826.

The Fortunes of Perkin Warbeck, A Romance. 3 vols. London: Henry Colburn and Richard Bentley, 1830.

Frankenstein; or, The Modern Prometheus. A revised one-volume edition. London: Henry Colburn and Richard Bentley, 1831.

'Proserpine: A Mythological Drama, in Two Acts.' In *The Winter's Wreath for 1832.* London: Whittaker, Treacher, and Arnot [1831], 1–20.

Lodore. 3 vols. London: Richard Bentley, 1835.

Lives of the Most Eminent Literary and Scientific Men of Italy, Spain and Portugal. [With James Montgomery and Sir David Brewster.] 3 vols. (vols. 86–8 of the Cabinet Cyclopædia, ed. Rev. Dionysius Lardner.) London: Longman, Rees, Orme, Brown, Green, & Longman; and John Taylor, 1835, 1837.

Falkner: A Novel. 3 vols. London: Saunders and Otley, 1837.

Lives of the Most Eminent Literary and Scientific Men of France. 2 vols. (vols. 102–3 of the Cabinet Cyclopædia, ed. Rev. Dionysius Lardner.) London: Longman, Orme, Brown, Green, & Longman; and John Taylor, 1838, 1839.

Rambles in Germany and Italy, in 1840, 1842, and 1843. 2 vols. London: Edward Moxon, 1844.

The Choice: A Poem on Shelley's Death. Ed. H. Buxton Forman. London: Privately printed, 1876.

Proserpine & Midas: Two Unpublished Mythological Dramas by Mary Shelley. Ed. A[ndré] Koszul. London: Humphrey Milford 1922.

Mathilda. Ed. Elizabeth Nitchie. Extra Series 3 of *Studies in Philology*. Chapel Hill: The University of North Carolina Press, 1959.

Mary Shelley: Collected Tales and Stories, with Original Engravings. Ed. Charles E. Robinson. Baltimore: The Johns Hopkins University Press, 1976.

Edited Works

Posthumous Poems of Percy Bysshe Shelley. [Ed. Mary W. Shelley.] London: John and Henry Leigh Hunt, 1824.

The Poetical Works of Percy Bysshe Shelley. Ed. Mrs Shelley. 4 vols. London: Edward Moxon, 1839.

The Poetical Works of Percy Bysshe Shelley. Ed. Mrs Shelley. 1-vol. edn. with Postscript added to the Preface. London: Edward Moxon, 1840 [1839].

Essays, Letters from Abroad, Translations and Fragments, By Percy Bysshe Shelley. Ed. Mrs Shelley. 2 vols. London: Edward Moxon, 1840 [1839].

Select Secondary Works

Abernethy, John, *An Enquiry into the Probability & Rationality of Mr Hunter's 'Theory of Life'* (London: Longman, 1814).

Aldini, John, *An Account of the Late Improvements in Galvinism*, with a series of curious and interesting experiments [in Paris and London, with] Appendix, containing the author's Experiments on the body of a Malefactor executed at Newgate (London: Cuthell & Martin and J. Murray, 1803).

Aldiss, Brian, *Trillion Year Spree* (London: Gollancz, 1986).

Baldick, Chris, *In Frankenstein's Shadow: Myth, Monstrosity and Nineteenth-century Writing* (Oxford: Oxford University Press, 1987).

Barclay, John, *An Enquiry into Opinions concerning Life and Organisation* (Edinburgh, 1822).

Bennett, Betty T., *Letters of M. W. Shelley*, 3 vols. (Baltimore: Johns Hopkins University Press, 1980, 1983, 1988). With Charles E. Robinson, *Mary Shelley Reader* (NY: Oxford University Press, 1990).

Bichat, M. F. X., *Traité sur les membranes* (1800), *Recherches physiologiques* (1800), *Anatomie generale* (1801).

Blumenbach, J. F., *Institutions of Physiology* [trans. from Ger. by J. Elliotson] (London: 1814).

Cabanis, P. J. G., *Rapports du physique et du moral de l'homme* (Paris, 1796–7).

Cantor, Paul, *Creature and Creator: Mythmaking and English Romanticism* (NY: Cambridge University Press, 1984).

Clark, D. L. (ed.), *Shelley's Prose* (Albuquerque: University of New Mexico Press, 1954).

Crook, Nora and D. Guiton. *Shelley's Venomed Melody* (Cambridge: Cambridge University Press, 1986).

Crouch, Laura, 'Davy, *A Discourse*: a possible scientific source of *Frankenstein', Keats–Shelley Journal,* 27 (1978), 35–44.

Darwin, Erasmus, *Zoonomia* (1794–6); *The Temple of Nature or the Origin of Society: A Poem, with Philosophical Notes* (London: J. Johnson, 1803).

Davy, Humphry, 'Discourse, Introductory to a Course of Lectures on Chemistry' (London: J. Johnson, 1802); *Chemical Philosophy* (London, 1812).

Desmond, Adrian, *The Politics of Evolution* (Chicago: University of Chicago Press, 1989).

Easlea, Brian, *Fathering the Unthinkable: Masculinity, Science and the Nuclear Arms Race* (London: Pluto Press, 1983).

Eiseley, Loren, *Darwin's Century: Evolution and the Men who discovered it* (Garden City, NY: Doubleday, 1958).

Elshtain, J., *Public Man, Private Woman* (Oxford: Robertson, 1981).

Feldman, Paula R. and D. Scott-Kilvert, *Journals of Mary Shelley, 1814–1844,* 2 vols. (Oxford: Clarendon Press, 1987).

Figlio, K., 'The Metaphor of Organisation', *Hist. Sci.* 14 (1976), 17–53.

Friedman, Lester D., 'Sporting with Life: *Frankenstein* and the Responsibility of Medical Research', *Medical Heritage,* 1 (May–June 1985), 181–5.

Gilbert, Sandra, and S. Gubar, *Madwoman in the Attic* (New Haven, Conn.: Yale University Press, 1979).

Godwin, William, *Political Justice* (1793); *Caleb Williams* (1794); *St Leon* (1799); *Fleetwood* (1805); *Mandeville* (1817); *Complete Novels,* ed. Mark Philp (London: Pickering & Chatto, 1992): Introduction by M. Butler and M. Philp.

Golinski, Jan, *Science as Public Culture: Chemistry and Enlightenment in Britain, 1760–1820* (Cambridge: Cambridge University Press, 1992).

Goodfield-Toulmin, J., 'Some Aspects of English Physiology', *Jnl. Hist. of Biol.* 2 (1969), 283–320.

Itard, Jean, *Of the First Developments of the Young Savage of Aveyron* (Fr. 1801), *Report on the Progress of Victor of Aveyron* (Fr. 1807); modern Eng. translations (New York: Century Books, 1962); with Lucien Malson, *Wolf Children* (London: NLB, 1972).

Jacobus, M., 'Is there a woman in this text?', *NLH* 14 (1982), 117–61.

Jacyna, L. S., 'Immanence or Transcendence: Theories of Organisation in Britain, 1790–1835', *Isis*, 74 (1983), 311–29.

Johnson, Barbara, 'My Monster/My Self', *Diacritics*, 12 (1982), 2–20.

Keller, Evelyn Fox, *Reflections on Gender and Science* (New Haven, Conn.: Yale University Press, 1985).

Lawrence, William, *Two Introductory Lectures . . . at the Royal College of Surgeons . . . 21 & 25 March, 1816* (London [June] 1816); *Lectures on Physiology, Zoology and the Natural History of Man* (London: Callow, 1819).

Lecercle, J.-J., *'Frankenstein': mythe et philosophie* (Presses universitaires de France, 1988).

Levine, G., and Knoepflmacher, U. C., *The Endurance of 'Frankenstein'* (Berkeley: University of California Press, 1979). See chapters by the two eds., Ellen Moers ('Female Gothic') and Lee Sterrenburg ('MS's Monster: Politics & Psyche'). Also includes articles on stage and film versions.

Luke, Hugh J., 'Sir Wm Lawrence, Physician to Shelley and Mary', *Papers on English Language and Literature*, 1 (1965), 141–52.

Mayr, Ernst, *The Growth of Biological Thought* (Cambridge, Mass: Belknap Press, 1982).

Mellor, Anne, *Mary Shelley: Her Life, Her Fiction, Her Monsters* (London: Routledge, 1988).

Merchant, Carolyn, *The Death of Nature: Women, Ecology and the Scientific Revolution* (San Francisco: Harper Row, 1980).

Monboddo, Lord (James Burnett), *Of the Origin and Progress of Language*, 6 vols. (1773–92).

Moretti, Franco, *Signs Taken for Wonders* (London: Verso, 1983), 83–108.

Murray, E. B., 'Shelley's Contributions to Mary's *Frankenstein*', *Keats–Shelley Bulletin*, 29 (1978), 50–60.

Newton, John Frank, *Return to Nature* (London, 1811).

O'Flinn, Paul, 'Production and Reproduction: the Case of *Frankenstein*', *Literature & History* (Aut. 1983), 194–213.

Poovey, Mary, *The Proper Lady and the Woman Writer* (Chicago: University of Chicago Press, 1984).

Rieger, James (ed.), Mary Shelley, *Frankenstein; or, The Modern Prometheus: the 1818 Text* (Indianapolis, 1974; Chicago: University of Chicago Press, 1982).

Scholes, R., and Rabkin, E. S., *Science Fiction: History, Science, Vision* (NY: Oxford University Press, 1977).

Sedgwick, Eve K., *Between Men: English Literature and Male Homosocial Desire* (NY: Columbia University Press, 1985).

Sharrock, R., 'The Chemist and the Poet: Davy and Preface to *Lyrical Ballads*', *Notes and Records of the Royal Society*, 17 (1962), 57.

Sherwin, P., '*Frankenstein:* Creation as Catastrophe', *PMLA* 96 (1981), 883–903.

Spector, Judith A., 'Science Fiction and the Sex War', *Literature and Psychology*, 31 (1981), 21–32.

Temkin, O., 'Basic Science, Medicine and the Romantic Era', *The Double Face of Janus* (Baltimore: Johns Hopkins University Press, 1977), 345–72.

Vasbinder, Samuel H., *Scientific Attitudes in MS's* Frankenstein (Ann Arbor, Mich: UMI Research Press, 1976).

Veeder, Wm., *MS and Frankenstein: the Fate of Androgyny* (Chicago: University of Chicago Press, 1986).

Wells, K. D., 'Lawrence on Heredity and Variation', *J. Hist. Biol.* 4 (1971), 319–61.

A CHRONOLOGY OF
MARY SHELLEY

1797   (30 August) Mary Wollstonecraft Godwin born at The Poly-
gon, Somers Town, daughter of William Godwin and Mary
Wollstonecraft, who dies 10 September

1807   Godwin family move to Skinner Street, Holborn

1812   (June) Goes to stay with the Baxter family at Dundee.
Beginning of friendship between Godwin and Percy Bysshe
Shelley

1814   (May) Returns to Skinner Street; meets Shelley again
(28 July) Mary, accompanied by her stepsister, Claire
Clairmont, elopes with Shelley. Travel through France and
Switzerland, and return to England (August–September)

1815   (February) A girl-child born prematurely to Mary and
Shelley, but dies a few days later
(August) Settled with Shelley at Bishops Gate, Windsor
(September) On the recommendation of Percy's physician,
William Lawrence, the Shelleys take a journey by river to
Oxford

1816   (January) A son, William, born
(May) Mary and Shelley, with Claire Clairmont, leave Eng-
land for Geneva, where they meet Lord Byron (who has
already formed a liaison with Claire) and his physician Dr
Polidori
(June) Mary, Shelley, and Claire settle at the Maison
Chappuis, at Montalègre, close to Byron at the Villa Diodati
at Cologny, near Geneva. *Frankenstein* begun
(July) Expedition to Chamonix and the Mer de Glace
(September) Return to England
(October) Suicide of Fanny Imlay, Mary's half-sister
(December) Suicide of Shelley's first wife, Harriet. Mary
and Shelley married at St Mildred's Church, Bread Street,
London (30 December)

1817   (March) Move to Marlow. Shelley refused custody of his
children by his first marriage
(May) *Frankenstein* completed
(September) Daughter Clara born
History of a Six-Weeks' Tour published

1818   (March) Mary and Shelley, with Claire and the children,
leave for Italy. *Frankenstein* published

(June) Settled for two months at Bagni di Lucca

(September) Move to Este. The baby Clara dies in Venice. Visits to Byron in Venice

(November) Journey south to Rome

(December) Settle in Naples for the winter

1819   (March) Return to Rome, where her son William dies

(June) Departure for Leghorn

(September) Move to Florence for approaching confinement

(November) A son, Percy Florence, born

1820   (January) Move to Pisa and (June) to Leghorn

(August) Move to Bagni di San Giuliano, near Pisa

(October) Driven out of San Giuliano by floods, the Shelleys move to Pisa

1821   (April) Return to Bagni di San Giuliano for the summer

(October) The Shelleys move to Pisa, with Edward and Jane Williams and with Byron as near neighbour

1822   (May) The Shelleys settle with the Williamses at Casa Magni, near Lerici

(July) Shelley and Williams sail to Leghorn to meet Leigh Hunt but are lost at sea on the return journey

(September) Mary joins the Hunts and Byron at Genoa

1823   (February) *Valperga* published

(August) Returns to London

1824   (June) Shelley's *Posthumous Poems* published, but withdrawn on the insistence of Shelley's father, Sir Timothy

1826   (February) *The Last Man* published

(September) Percy Florence becomes heir to the Shelley title and estate on the death of Charles Bysshe, Shelley's son by his first wife Harriet

1830   *Perkin Warbeck* published

1832   (September) Percy Florence entered at Harrow

1835   *Lodore* published

1837   *Falkner*, her last novel, published

(July) Percy Florence entered at Trinity College, Cambridge

1839   Publication of Shelley's *Poetical Works*, with notes partly replacing the unwritten biography

Publication of Shelley's *Essays and Letters*

1840   (June–November) Continental tour with Percy Florence and friends

1841   (February) Percy Florence graduates

1842–3 Another Continental tour

1844   *Rambles in Germany and Italy* published
      (April) Death of Sir Timothy Shelley; Percy Florence succeeds to title and estate
1851   (February) Mary Wollstonecraft Shelley dies at Chester Square, London; buried in Bournemouth churchyard

FRANKENSTEIN

OR

THE MODERN PROMETHEUS

Did I request thee, Maker, from my clay
To mould Me man? Did I solicit thee
From darkness to promote me?—

Paradise Lost (x. 743–5)

TO WILLIAM GODWIN,

Author of Political Justice, Caleb Williams, &c.

These Volumes are respectfully inscribed by

THE AUTHOR.

PREFACE*

The event on which this fiction is founded has been supposed, by Dr Darwin,* and some of the physiological writers of Germany,* as not of impossible occurrence. I shall not be supposed as according the remotest degree of serious faith to such an imagination; yet, in assuming it as the basis of a work of fancy, I have not considered myself as merely weaving a series of supernatural terrors.* The event on which the interest of the story depends is exempt from the disadvantages of a mere tale of spectres or enchantment. It was recommended by the novelty of the situations which it developes; and, however impossible as a physical fact, affords a point of view to the imagination for the delineating of human passions more comprehensive and commanding than any which the ordinary relations of existing events can yield.

I have thus endeavoured to preserve the truth of the elementary principles of human nature, while I have not scrupled to innovate upon their combinations. The *Iliad*, the tragic poetry of Greece,—Shakespeare, in the *Tempest* and *Midsummer Night's Dream*,—and most especially Milton, in *Paradise Lost*, conform to this rule; and the most humble novelist, who seeks to confer or receive amusement from his labours, may, without presumption, apply to prose fiction a licence, or rather a rule, from the adoption of which so many exquisite combinations of human feeling have resulted in the highest specimens of poetry.

The circumstance on which my story rests was suggested in casual conversation.* It was commenced, partly as a source of amusement, and partly as an expedient for exercising any untried resources of mind. Other motives were mingled with these, as the work proceeded. I am by no means indifferent to the manner in which whatever moral tendencies exist in the sentiments or characters it contains shall affect the reader; yet my chief concern in this respect has been limited to the avoiding the enervating effects of the novels of the present day, and to the exhibition of the amiableness of domestic affection, and the excellence of universal virtue. The opinions which naturally spring from the character and situation of the hero are by no means to be conceived as existing always in my own conviction, nor is any inference justly to be drawn from the following pages as prejudicing any philosophical doctrine of whatever kind.*

It is a subject also of additional interest to the author, that this story was begun in the majestic region where the scene is principally laid, and in society which cannot cease to be regretted. I passed the summer of 1816 in the environs of Geneva. The season was cold and rainy, and in the evenings we crowded around a blazing wood fire, and occasionally amused ourselves with some German stories of ghosts,* which happened to fall into our hands. These tales excited in us a playful desire of imitation. Two other friends (a tale from the pen of one of whom would be far more acceptable to the public than any thing I can ever hope to produce) and myself agreed to write each a story,* founded on some supernatural occurrence.

The weather, however, suddenly became serene; and my two friends left me on a journey among the Alps, and lost, in the magnificent scenes which they present, all memory of their ghostly visions. The following tale is the only one which has been completed.

FRANKENSTEIN;
OR, THE MODERN PROMETHEUS.

VOLUME I

LETTER I

To Mrs SAVILLE, *England.*

St Petersburgh, Dec. 11th, 17—.

You will rejoice to hear that no disaster has accompanied the commencement of an enterprise which you have regarded with such evil forebodings. I arrived here yesterday; and my first task is to assure my dear sister of my welfare, and increasing confidence in the success of my undertaking.

I am already far north of London; and as I walk in the streets of Petersburgh, I feel a cold northern breeze play upon my cheeks, which braces my nerves, and fills me with delight. Do you understand this feeling? This breeze, which has travelled from the regions towards which I am advancing, gives me a foretaste of those icy climes. Inspirited by this wind of promise, my day dreams become more fervent and vivid. I try in vain to be persuaded that the pole is the seat of frost and desolation; it ever presents itself to my imagination as the region of beauty and delight. There, Margaret, the sun is for ever visible; its broad disk just skirting the horizon, and diffusing a perpetual splendour. There—for with your leave, my sister, I will put some trust in preceding navigators—there snow and frost are banished; and, sailing over a calm sea, we may be wafted to a land surpassing in wonders and in beauty every region hitherto discovered on the habitable globe. Its productions and features may be without example, as the phænomena of the heavenly bodies undoubtedly are in those undiscovered solitudes. What may not be expected in a country of eternal light? I may there discover the wondrous power which attracts the needle; and may regulate a thousand celestial observations, that require only this voyage to render their seeming eccentricities consistent for ever.* I shall satiate my ardent curiosity with the sight of a part of the world never before visited, and may tread a land never before imprinted by the foot of man. These are my enticements, and they are sufficient to conquer all fear of danger or death, and to induce me to commence this laborious voyage with the joy a child feels when he embarks in a little boat, with his holiday mates, on an expedition of discovery up his native river. But, supposing all these conjectures to be false, you cannot contest the inestimable benefit which I shall confer on all mankind to the last generation, by discovering a passage near the pole to those countries, to reach which at present so many months are requisite; or by ascertaining the secret of the magnet, which, if at all possible, can only be effected by an undertaking such as mine.

These reflections have dispelled the agitation with which I began my letter, and I feel my heart glow with an entnusiasm which elevates me to heaven; for nothing contributes so much to tranquillize the mind as a steady purpose,—a point on which the soul may fix its intellectual eye. This expedition has been the favourite dream of my early years. I have read with ardour the accounts of the various voyages which have been made in the prospect of arriving at the North Pacific Ocean through the seas which surround the pole. You may remember, that a history of all the voyages made for purposes of discovery composed the whole of our good uncle Thomas's library. My education was neglected, yet I was passionately fond of reading. These volumes were my study day and night, and my familiarity with them increased that regret which I had felt, as a child, on learning that my father's dying injunction had forbidden my uncle to allow me to embark in a seafaring life.

These visions faded when I perused, for the first time, those poets whose effusions entranced my soul, and lifted it to heaven. I also became a poet, and for one year lived in a

Paradise of my own creation; I imagined that I also might obtain a niche in the temple where the names of Homer and Shakespeare are consecrated. You are well acquainted with my failure, and how heavily I bore the disappointment. But just at that time I inherited the fortune of my cousin, and my thoughts were turned into the channel of their earlier bent.

Six years have passed since I resolved on my present under-taking. I can, even now, remember the hour from which I dedicated myself to this great enterprise. I commenced by inuring my body to hardship. I accompanied the whale-fishers on several expeditions to the North Sea; I voluntarily endured cold, famine, thirst, and want of sleep; I often worked harder than the common sailors during the day, and devoted my nights to the study of mathematics, the theory of medicine, and those branches of physical science from which a naval adventurer might derive the greatest practical advantage. Twice I actually hired myself as an under-mate in a Greenland whaler, and acquitted myself to admiration. I must own I felt a little proud, when my captain offered me the second dignity in the vessel, and entreated me to remain with the greatest earnestness; so valuable did he consider my services.

And now, dear Margaret, do I not deserve to accomplish some great purpose. My life might have been passed in ease and luxury; but I preferred glory to every enticement that wealth placed in my path. Oh, that some encouraging voice would answer in the affirmative! My courage and my resolution is firm; but my hopes fluctuate, and my spirits are often depressed. I am about to proceed on a long and difficult voyage; the emergencies of which will demand all my forti-tude: I am required not only to raise the spirits of others, but sometimes to sustain my own, when theirs are failing.

This is the most favourable period for travelling in Russia. They fly quickly over the snow in their sledges; the motion is pleasant, and, in my opinion, far more agreeable than that of an English stage-coach. The cold is not excessive, if you are wrapt in furs, a dress which I have already adopted; for there is a great difference between walking the deck and remaining seated motionless for hours, when no exercise prevents the blood from actually freezing in your veins. I have no ambition to lose my life on the post-road between St Petersburgh and Archangel.

I shall depart for the latter town in a fortnight or three weeks; and my intention is to hire a ship there, which can easily be done by paying the insurance for the owner, and to engage as many sailors as I think necessary among those who are accustomed to the whale-fishing. I do not intend to sail until the month of June: and when shall I return? Ah, dear sister, how can I answer this question? If I succeed, many, many months, perhaps years, will pass before you and I may meet. If I fail, you will see me again soon, or never.

Farewell, my dear, excellent, Margaret. Heaven shower down blessings on you, and save me, that I may again and again testify my gratitude for all your love and kindness.

Your affectionate brother,
R. WALTON.

LETTER II

To Mrs SAVILLE, England.

Archangel, 28th March, 17—.
How slowly the time passes here, encompassed as I am by frost and snow; yet a second step is taken towards my enterprise. I have hired a vessel, and am occupied in collecting my sailors; those whom I have already engaged appear to be men on whom I can depend, and are certainly possessed of dauntless courage.

But I have one want which I have never yet been able to satisfy; and the absence of the object of which I now feel as a most severe evil. I have no friend, Margaret: when I am glowing with the enthusiasm of success, there will be none to participate my joy; if I am assailed by disappointment, no one will endeavour to sustain me in dejection. I shall commit my thoughts to paper, it is true; but that is a poor medium for the communication of feeling. I desire the company of a man who could sympathize with me; whose eyes would reply to mine. You may deem me romantic, my dear sister, but I bitterly feel the want of a friend. I have no one near me, gentle yet courageous, possessed of a cultivated as well as of a capacious mind, whose tastes are like my own, to approve or amend my plans. How would such a friend repair the faults of your poor brother! I am too ardent in execution, and too impatient of difficulties. But it is a still greater evil to me that I am self-educated: for the first fourteen years of my life I ran wild on a common, and read nothing but our uncle Thomas's books of voyages. At that age I became acquainted with the celebrated poets of our own country; but it was only when it had ceased to be in my power to derive its most important benefits from such a conviction, that I perceived the necessity of becoming acquainted with more languages than that of my native country. Now I am twenty-eight, and am in reality more illiterate than many school-boys of fifteen. It is true that I have thought more, and that my day dreams are more extended and magnificent; but they want (as the painters call it) *keeping*;* and I greatly need a friend who would have sense enough not to despise me as romantic, and affection enough for me to endeavour to regulate my mind.

Well, these are useless complaints; I shall certainly find no friend on the wide ocean, nor even here in Archangel, among merchants and seamen. Yet some feelings, unallied to the dross of human nature, beat even in these rugged bosoms. My lieutenant, for instance, is a man of wonderful courage and enterprise; he is madly desirous of glory. He is an Englishman, and in the midst of national and professional prejudices, unsoftened by cultivation, retains some of the noblest endowments of humanity. I first became acquainted with him on board a whale vessel: finding that he was unemployed in this city, I easily engaged him to assist in my enterprise.

The master is a person of an excellent disposition, and is remarkable in the ship for his gentleness, and the mildness of his discipline. He is, indeed, of so amiable a nature, that he will not hunt (a favourite, and almost the only amusement here), because he cannot endure to spill blood. He is, moreover, heroically generous. Some years ago he loved a young Russian lady, of moderate fortune; and having amassed a considerable sum in prize-money, the father of the girl con-

sented to the match. He saw his mistress once before the
destined ceremony; but she was bathed in tears, and, throwing herself at his feet, entreated him to spare her, confessing
at the same time that she loved another, but that he was poor,
and that her father would never consent to the union. My
generous friend reassured the suppliant, and on being informed of the name of her lover instantly abandoned his
pursuit. He had already bought a farm with his money, on
which he had designed to pass the remainder of his life; but
he bestowed the whole on his rival, together with the remains
of his prize-money to purchase stock, and then himself solicited the young woman's father to consent to her marriage
with her lover. But the old man decidedly refused, thinking
himself bound in honour to my friend; who, when he found
the father inexorable, quitted his country, nor returned until
he heard that his former mistress was married according to
her inclinations. 'What a noble fellow!' you will exclaim. He is
so; but then he has passed all his life on board a vessel, and
has scarcely an idea beyond the rope and the shroud.

But do not suppose that, because I complain a little, or
because I can conceive a consolation for my toils which I may
never know, that I am wavering in my resolutions. Those are
as fixed as fate; and my voyage is only now delayed until the
weather shall permit my embarkation. The winter has been
dreadfully severe; but the spring promises well, and it is considered as a remarkably early season; so that, perhaps, I may
sail sooner than I expected. I shall do nothing rashly; you
know me sufficiently to confide in my prudence and consid-
erateness whenever the safety of others is committed to my
care.

I cannot describe to you my sensations on the near prospect of my undertaking. It is impossible to communicate to
you a conception of the trembling sensation, half pleasurable
and half fearful, with which I am preparing to depart. I am
going to unexplored regions, to 'the land of mist and snow;'*
but I shall kill no albatross, therefore do not be alarmed for
my safety.

Shall I meet you again, after having traversed immense
seas, and returned by the most southern cape of Africa or
America? I dare not expect such success, yet I cannot bear to

look on the reverse side of the picture. Continue to write to me by every opportunity: I may receive your letters (though the chance is very doubtful) on some occasions when I need them most to support my spirits. I love you very tenderly. Remember me with affection, should you never hear from me again.

Your affectionate brother,
ROBERT WALTON.

LETTER III

To Mrs SAVILLE, *England.*

July 7th, 17—.

MY DEAR SISTER,

I write a few lines in haste, to say that I am safe, and well advanced on my voyage. This letter will reach England by a merchant-man now on its homeward voyage from Archangel; more fortunate than I, who may not see my native land, perhaps, for many years. I am, however, in good spirits: my men are bold, and apparently firm of purpose; nor do the floating sheets of ice that continually pass us, indicating the dangers of the region towards which we are advancing, appear to dismay them. We have already reached a very high latitude; but it is the height of summer, and although not so warm as in England, the southern gales, which blow us speedily towards those shores which I so ardently desire to attain, breathe a degree of renovating warmth which I had not expected.

No incidents have hitherto befallen us, that would make a figure in a letter. One or two stiff gales, and the breaking of a mast, are accidents which experienced navigators scarcely remember to record; and I shall be well content, if nothing worse happen to us during our voyage.

Adieu, my dear Margaret. Be assured, that for my own sake, as well as yours, I will not rashly encounter danger. I will be cool, persevering, and prudent.

Remember me to all my English friends.

Most affectionately yours,
R. W.

LETTER IV

To Mrs SAVILLE, *England.*

August 5th, 17—.

So strange an accident has happened to us, that I cannot forbear recording it, although it is very probable that you will see me before these papers can come into your possession.

Last Monday (July 31st), we were nearly surrounded by ice, which closed in the ship on all sides, scarcely leaving her the sea room in which she floated. Our situation was somewhat dangerous, especially as we were compassed round by a very thick fog. We accordingly lay to, hoping that some change would take place in the atmosphere and weather.

About two o'clock the mist cleared away, and we beheld, stretched out in every direction, vast and irregular plains of ice, which seemed to have no end. Some of my comrades groaned, and my own mind began to grow watchful with anxious thoughts, when a strange sight suddenly attracted our attention, and diverted our solicitude from our own situation. We perceived a low carriage, fixed on a sledge and drawn by dogs, pass on towards the north, at the distance of half a mile: a being which had the shape of a man, but apparently of gigantic stature, sat in the sledge, and guided the dogs. We watched the rapid progress of the traveller with our telescopes, until he was lost among the distant inequalities of the ice.

This appearance excited our unqualified wonder. We were, as we believed, many hundred miles from any land; but this apparition seemed to denote that it was not, in reality, so distant as we had supposed. Shut in, however, by ice, it was impossible to follow his track, which we had observed with the greatest attention.

About two hours after this occurrence, we heard the ground sea,* and before night the ice broke, and freed our ship. We, however, lay to until the morning, fearing to encounter in the dark those large loose masses which float about after the breaking up of the ice. I profited of this time to rest for a few hours.

In the morning, however, as soon as it was light, I went upon deck, and found all the sailors busy on one side of the vessel, apparently talking to some one in the sea. It was, in fact, a sledge, like that we had seen before, which had drifted towards us in the night, on a large fragment of ice. Only one dog remained alive; but there was a human being within it, whom the sailors were persuading to enter the vessel. He was not, as the other traveller seemed to be, a savage inhabitant of some undiscovered island, but an European. When I appeared on deck, the master said, 'Here is our captain, and he will not allow you to perish on the open sea.'

On perceiving me, the stranger addressed me in English, although with a foreign accent. 'Before I come on board your vessel,' said he, 'will you have the kindness to inform me whither you are bound?'

You may conceive my astonishment on hearing such a question addressed to me from a man on the brink of destruction, and to whom I should have supposed that my vessel would have been a resource which he would not have exchanged for the most precious wealth the earth can afford. I replied, however, that we were on a voyage of discovery towards the northern pole.

Upon hearing this he appeared satisfied, and consented to come on board. Good God! Margaret, if you had seen the man who thus capitulated for his safety, your surprise would have been boundless. His limbs were nearly frozen, and his body dreadfully emaciated by fatigue and suffering. I never saw a man in so wretched a condition. We attempted to carry him into the cabin; but as soon as he had quitted the fresh air, he fainted. We accordingly brought him back to the deck, and restored him to animation by rubbing him with brandy, and forcing him to swallow a small quantity. As soon as he shewed signs of life, we wrapped him up in blankets, and placed him near the chimney of the kitchen-stove. By slow degrees he recovered, and ate a little soup, which restored him wonderfully.

Two days passed in this manner before he was able to speak; and I often feared that his sufferings had deprived him of understanding. When he had in some measure recovered,

I removed him to my own cabin, and attended on him as much as my duty would permit. I never saw a more interesting creature: his eyes have generally an expression of wildness, and even madness; but there are moments when, if any one performs an act of kindness towards him, or does him any the most trifling service, his whole countenance is lighted up, as it were, with a beam of benevolence and sweetness that I never saw equalled. But he is generally melancholy and despairing; and sometimes he gnashes his teeth, as if impatient of the weight of woes that oppresses him.

When my guest was a little recovered, I had great trouble to keep off the men, who wished to ask him a thousand questions; but I would not allow him to be tormented by their idle curiosity, in a state of body and mind whose restoration evidently depended upon entire repose. Once, however, the lieutenant asked, Why he had come so far upon the ice in so strange a vehicle?

His countenance instantly assumed an aspect of the deepest gloom; and he replied, 'To seek one who fled from me.'

'And did the man whom you pursued travel in the same fashion?'

'Yes.'

'Then I fancy we have seen him; for, the day before we picked you up, we saw some dogs drawing a sledge, with a man in it, across the ice.'

This aroused the stranger's attention; and he asked a multitude of questions concerning the route which the dæmon, as he called him, had pursued. Soon after, when he was alone with me, he said, 'I have, doubtless, excited your curiosity, as well as that of these good people; but you are too considerate to make inquiries.'

'Certainly; it would indeed be very impertinent and inhuman in me to trouble you with any inquisitiveness of mine.'

'And yet you rescued me from a strange and perilous situation; you have benevolently restored me to life.'

Soon after this he inquired, if I thought that the breaking up of the ice had destroyed the other sledge? I replied, that I could not answer with any degree of certainty; for the ice had not broken until near midnight, and the traveller might have arrived at a place of safety before that time; but of this I could not judge.

From this time the stranger seemed very eager to be upon deck, to watch for the sledge which had before appeared; but I have persuaded him to remain in the cabin, for he is far too weak to sustain the rawness of the atmosphere. But I have promised that some one should watch for him, and give him instant notice if any new object should appear in sight.

Such is my journal of what relates to this strange occurrence up to the present day. The stranger has gradually improved in health, but is very silent, and appears uneasy when any one except myself enters his cabin. Yet his manners are so conciliating and gentle, that the sailors are all interested in him, although they have had very little communication with him. For my own part, I begin to love him as a brother; and his constant and deep grief fills me with sympathy and compassion. He must have been a noble creature in his better days, being even now in wreck so attractive and amiable.

I said in one of my letters, my dear Margaret, that I should find no friend on the wide ocean; yet I have found a man who, before his spirit had been broken by misery, I should have been happy to have possessed as the brother of my heart.

I shall continue my journal concerning the stranger at intervals, should I have any fresh incidents to record.

August 13th, 17—.

My affection for my guest increases every day. He excites at once my admiration and my pity to an astonishing degree. How can I see so noble a creature destroyed by misery without feeling the most poignant grief? He is so gentle, yet so wise; his mind is so cultivated; and when he speaks, although his words are culled with the choicest art, yet they flow with rapidity and unparalleled eloquence.

He is now much recovered from his illness, and is continually on the deck, apparently watching for the sledge that preceded his own. Yet, although unhappy, he is not so utterly occupied by his own misery, but that he interests himself deeply in the employments of others. He has asked me many questions concerning my design; and I have related my little history frankly to him. He appeared pleased with the confidence, and suggested several alterations in my plan, which I shall find exceedingly useful. There is no pedantry in his manner; but all he does appears to spring solely from the interest he instinctively takes in the welfare of those who surround him. He is often overcome by gloom, and then he sits by himself, and tries to overcome all that is sullen or unsocial in his humour. These paroxysms pass from him like a cloud from before the sun, though his dejection never leaves him. I have endeavoured to win his confidence; and I trust that I have succeeded. One day I mentioned to him the desire I had always felt of finding a friend who might sympathize with me, and direct me by his counsel. I said, I did not belong to that class of men who are offended by advice. 'I am self-educated, and perhaps I hardly rely sufficiently upon my own powers. I wish therefore that my companion should be wiser and more experienced than myself, to confirm and support me; nor have I believed it impossible to find a true friend.'

'I agree with you,' replied the stranger, 'in believing that friendship is not only a desirable, but a possible acquisition. I once had a friend, the most noble of human creatures, and am entitled, therefore, to judge respecting friendship. You have hope, and the world before you, and have no cause for despair. But I—I have lost every thing, and cannot begin life anew.'

As he said this, his countenance became expressive of a calm settled grief, that touched me to the heart. But he was silent, and presently retired to his cabin.

Even broken in spirit as he is, no one can feel more deeply than he does the beauties of nature. The starry sky, the sea, and every sight afforded by these wonderful regions, seems still to have the power of elevating his soul from earth. Such a man has a double existence: he may suffer misery, and be overwhelmed by disappointments; yet when he has retired into himself, he will be like a celestial spirit, that has a halo around him, within whose circle no grief or folly ventures.

Will you laugh at the enthusiasm I express concerning this divine wanderer? If you do, you must have certainly lost that simplicity which was once your characteristic charm. Yet, if you will, smile at the warmth of my expressions, while I find every day new causes for repeating them.

August 19th, 17—.

Yesterday the stranger said to me, 'You may easily perceive, Captain Walton, that I have suffered great and unparalleled misfortunes. I had determined, once, that the memory of these evils should die with me; but you have won me to alter my determination. You seek for knowledge and wisdom, as I once did; and I ardently hope that the gratification of your wishes may not be a serpent to sting you, as mine has been. I do not know that the relation of my misfortunes will be useful to you, yet, if you are inclined, listen to my tale. I believe that the strange incidents connected with it will afford a view of nature, which may enlarge your faculties and understanding. You will hear of powers and occurrences, such as you have been accustomed to believe impossible: but I do not doubt that my tale conveys in its series internal evidence of the truth of the events of which it is composed.'

You may easily conceive that I was much gratified by the offered communication; yet I could not endure that he should renew his grief by a recital of his misfortunes. I felt the greatest eagerness to hear the promised narrative, partly from curiosity, and partly from a strong desire to ameliorate his fate, if it were in my power. I expressed these feelings in my answer.

'I thank you,' he replied, 'for your sympathy, but it is useless; my fate is nearly fulfilled. I wait but for one event, and then I shall repose in peace. I understand your feeling,' continued he, perceiving that I wished to interrupt him; 'but you are mistaken, my friend, if thus you will allow me to name you; nothing can alter my destiny: listen to my history, and you will perceive how irrevocably it is determined.'

He then told me, that he would commence his narrative the next day when I should be at leisure. This promise drew from me the warmest thanks. I have resolved every night, when I am not engaged, to record, as nearly as possible in his own words, what he has related during the day. If I should be engaged, I will at least make notes. This manuscript will doubtless afford you the greatest pleasure: but to me, who know him, and who hear it from his own lips, with what interest and sympathy shall I read it in some future day!

CHAPTER I

I am by birth a Genevese; and my family is one of the most distinguished of that republic. My ancestors had been for many years counsellors and syndics;* and my father had filled several public situations with honour and reputation. He was respected by all who knew him for his integrity and indefatigable attention to public business. He passed his younger days perpetually occupied by the affairs of his country; and it was not until the decline of life that he thought of marrying, and bestowing on the state sons who might carry his virtues and his name down to posterity.

As the circumstances of his marriage illustrate his character, I cannot refrain from relating them. One of his most intimate friends was a merchant, who, from a flourishing state, fell, through numerous mischances, into poverty. This man, whose name was Beaufort, was of a proud and unbending disposition, and could not bear to live in poverty and oblivion in the same country where he had formerly been distinguished for his rank and magnificence. Having paid his debts, therefore, in the most honourable manner, he retreated with his daughter to the town of Lucerne, where he lived unknown and in wretchedness. My father loved Beaufort with the truest friendship, and was deeply grieved by his retreat in these unfortunate circumstances. He grieved also for the loss of his society, and resolved to seek him out and endeavour to persuade him to begin the world again through his credit and assistance.

Beaufort had taken effectual measures to conceal himself; and it was ten months before my father discovered his abode.

Overjoyed at this discovery, he hastened to the house, which was situated in a mean street, near the Reuss. But when he entered, misery and despair alone welcomed him. Beaufort had saved but a very small sum of money from the wreck of his fortunes; but it was sufficient to provide him with sustenance for some months, and in the mean time he hoped to procure some respectable employment in a merchant's house. The interval was consequently spent in inaction; his grief only became more deep and rankling, when he had leisure for reflection; and at length it took so fast hold of his mind, that at the end of three months he lay on a bed of sickness, incapable of any exertion.

His daughter attended him with the greatest tenderness; but she saw with despair that their little fund was rapidly decreasing, and that there was no other prospect of support. But Caroline Beaufort possessed a mind of an uncommon mould; and her courage rose to support her in her adversity. She procured plain work; she plaited straw; and by various means contrived to earn a pittance scarcely sufficient to support life.

Several months passed in this manner. Her father grew worse; her time was more entirely occupied in attending him; her means of subsistence decreased; and in the tenth month her father died in her arms, leaving her an orphan and a beggar. This last blow overcame her; and she knelt by Beaufort's coffin, weeping bitterly, when my father entered the chamber. He came like a protecting spirit to the poor girl, who committed herself to his care, and after the interment of his friend he conducted her to Geneva, and placed her under the protection of a relation. Two years after this event Caroline became his wife.

When my father became a husband and a parent, he found his time so occupied by the duties of his new situation, that he relinquished many of his public employments, and devoted himself to the education of his children. Of these I was the eldest, and the destined successor to all his labours and utility. No creature could have more tender parents than mine. My improvement and health were their constant care, especially as I remained for several years their only child. But before I continue my narrative, I must record an incident which took place when I was four years of age.

My father had a sister, whom he tenderly loved, and who had married early in life an Italian gentleman. Soon after her marriage, she had accompanied her husband into his native country, and for some years my father had very little communication with her. About the time I mentioned she died; and a few months afterwards he received a letter from her husband, acquainting him with his intention of marrying an Italian lady, and requesting my father to take charge of the infant Elizabeth, the only child of his deceased sister. 'It is my wish,' he said, 'that you should consider her as your own daughter, and educate her thus. Her mother's fortune is secured to her, the documents of which I will commit to your keeping. Reflect upon this proposition; and decide whether you would prefer educating your niece yourself to her being brought up by a stepmother.'

My father did not hesitate, and immediately went to Italy, that he might accompany the little Elizabeth to her future home. I have often heard my mother say, that she was at that time the most beautiful child she had ever seen, and shewed signs even then of a gentle and affectionate disposition. These indications, and a desire to bind as closely as possible the ties of domestic love, determined my mother to consider Elizabeth as my future wife; a design which she never found reason to repent.

From this time Elizabeth Lavenza became my playfellow, and, as we grew older, my friend. She was docile and good tempered, yet gay and playful as a summer insect. Although she was lively and animated, her feelings were strong and deep, and her disposition uncommonly affectionate. No one could better enjoy liberty, yet no one could submit with more grace than she did to constraint and caprice. Her imagination was luxuriant, yet her capability of application was great. Her person was the image of her mind; her hazel eyes, although as lively as a bird's, possessed an attractive softness. Her figure was light and airy; and, though capable of enduring great fatigue, she appeared the most fragile creature in the world. While I admired her understanding and fancy, I loved to tend on her, as I should on a favourite animal; and I never saw so much grace both of person and mind united to so little pretension.

Every one adored Elizabeth. If the servants had any request to make, it was always through her intercession. We were strangers to any species of disunion and dispute; for although there was a great dissimilitude in our characters, there was an harmony in that very dissimilitude. I was more calm and philosophical than my companion; yet my temper was not so yielding. My application was of longer endurance; but it was not so severe whilst it endured. I delighted in investigating the facts relative to the actual world; she busied herself in following the aërial creations of the poets. The world was to me a secret, which I desired to discover; to her it was a vacancy, which she sought to people with imaginations of her own.

My brothers were considerably younger than myself; but I had a friend in one of my schoolfellows, who compensated for this deficiency. Henry Clerval was the son of a merchant of Geneva, an intimate friend of my father. He was a boy of singular talent and fancy. I remember, when he was nine years old, he wrote a fairy tale, which was the delight and amazement of all his companions. His favourite study consisted in books of chivalry and romance; and when very young, I can remember, that we used to act plays composed by him out of these favourite books, the principal characters of which were Orlando, Robin Hood, Amadis, and St George.*

No youth could have passed more happily than mine. My parents were indulgent, and my companions amiable. Our studies were never forced; and by some means we always had an end placed in view, which excited us to ardour in the prosecution of them. It was by this method, and not by emulation, that we were urged to application. Elizabeth was not incited to apply herself to drawing, that her companions might not outstrip her; but through the desire of pleasing her aunt, by the representation of some favourite scene done by her own hand. We learned Latin and English, that we might read the writings in those languages; and so far from study being made odious to us through punishment, we loved application, and our amusements would have been the labours of other children. Perhaps we did not read so many books, or learn languages so quickly, as those who are disciplined according to the ordinary methods; but what we learned was impressed the more deeply on our memories.

In this description of our domestic circle I include Henry Clerval; for he was constantly with us. He went to school with me, and generally passed the afternoon at our house; for being an only child, and destitute of companions at home, his father was well pleased that he should find associates at our house; and we were never completely happy when Clerval was absent.

I feel pleasure in dwelling on the recollections of childhood, before misfortune had tainted my mind, and changed its bright visions of extensive usefulness into gloomy and narrow reflections upon self. But, in drawing the picture of my early days, I must not omit to record those events which led, by insensible steps to my after tale of misery: for when I would account to myself for the birth of that passion, which afterwards ruled my destiny, I find it arose, like a mountain river, from ignoble and almost forgotten sources; but, swelling as it proceeded, it became the torrent which, in its course, has swept away all my hopes and joys.

Natural philosophy* is the genius that has regulated my fate; I desire therefore, in this narration, to state those facts which led to my predilection for that science. When I was thirteen years of age, we all went on a party of pleasure to the baths near Thonon: the inclemency of the weather obliged us to remain a day confined to the inn. In this house I chanced to find a volume of the works of Cornelius Agrippa.* I opened it with apathy; the theory which he attempts to demonstrate, and the wonderful facts which he relates, soon changed this feeling into enthusiasm. A new light seemed to dawn upon my mind; and, bounding with joy, I communicated my discovery to my father. I cannot help remarking here the many opportunities instructors possess of directing the attention of their pupils to useful knowledge, which they utterly neglect. My father looked carelessly at the title-page of my book, and said,

Ah! Cornelius Agrippa! My dear Victor, do not waste your time upon this; it is sad trash.'

If, instead of this remark, my father had taken the pains to explain to me, that the principles of Agrippa had been entirely exploded, and that a modern system of science had been introduced, which possessed much greater powers than the ancient, because the powers of the latter were chimerical, while those of the former were real and practical; under such circumstances, I should certainly have thrown Agrippa aside, and, with my imagination warmed as it was, should probably have applied myself to the more rational theory of chemistry which has resulted from modern discoveries. It is even possible, that the train of my ideas would never have received the fatal impulse that led to my ruin. But the cursory glance my father had taken of my volume by no means assured me that he was acquainted with its contents; and I continued to read with the greatest avidity.

When I returned home, my first care was to procure the whole works of this author, and afterwards of Paracelsus and Albertus Magnus.* I read and studied the wild fancies of these writers with delight; they appeared to me treasures known to few beside myself; and although I often wished to communicate these secret stores of knowledge to my father, yet his indefinite censure of my favourite Agrippa always withheld me. I disclosed my discoveries to Elizabeth, therefore, under a promise of strict secrecy; but she did not interest herself in the subject, and I was left by her to pursue my studies alone.

It may appear very strange, that a disciple of Albertus Magnus should arise in the eighteenth century; but our family was not scientifical, and I had not attended any of the lectures given at the schools of Geneva. My dreams were therefore undisturbed by reality; and I entered with the greatest diligence into the search of the philosopher's stone and the elixir of life. But the latter obtained my most undivided attention: wealth was an inferior object; but what glory would attend the discovery, if I could banish disease from the human frame, and render man invulnerable to any but a violent death!

Nor were these my only visions. The raising of ghosts or devils* was a promise liberally accorded by my favourite authors, the fulfilment of which I most eagerly sought; and if my incantations were always unsuccessful, I attributed the failure rather to my own inexperience and mistake, than to a want of skill or fidelity in my instructors.

The natural phænomena that take place every day before our eyes did not escape my examinations. Distillation, and the wonderful effects of steam, processes of which my favourite authors were utterly ignorant, excited my astonishment; but my utmost wonder was engaged by some experiments on an airpump, which I saw employed by a gentleman whom we were in the habit of visiting.

The ignorance of the early philosophers on these and several other points served to decrease their credit with me: but I could not entirely throw them aside, before some other system should occupy their place in my mind.

When I was about fifteen years old, we had retired to our house near Belrive, when we witnessed a most violent and terrible thunder-storm. It advanced from behind the mountains of Jura; and the thunder burst at once with frightful loudness from various quarters of the heavens. I remained, while the storm lasted, watching its progress with curiosity and delight. As I stood at the door, on a sudden I beheld a stream of fire issue from an old and beautiful oak, which stood about twenty yards from our house; and so soon as the dazzling light vanished, the oak had disappeared, and nothing remained but a blasted stump. When we visited it the next morning, we found the tree shattered in a singular manner. It was not splintered by the shock, but entirely reduced to thin ribbands of wood. I never beheld any thing so utterly destroyed.

The catastrophe of this tree excited my extreme astonishment; and I eagerly inquired of my father the nature and origin of thunder and lightning. He replied, 'Electricity;' describing at the same time the various effects of that power. He constructed a small electrical machine, and exhibited a few experiments; he made also a kite, with a wire and string, which drew down that fluid from the clouds.*

This last stroke completed the overthrow of Cornelius Agrippa, Albertus Magnus, and Paracelsus, who had so long reigned the lords of my imagination. But by some fatality I did not feel inclined to commence the study of any modern system; and this disinclination was influenced by the following circumstance.

My father expressed a wish that I should attend a course of lectures upon natural philosophy, to which I cheerfully consented. Some accident prevented my attending these lectures until the course was nearly finished. The lecture, being therefore one of the last, was entirely incomprehensible to me. The professor discoursed with the greatest fluency of potassium and boron, of sulphates and oxyds, terms to which I could affix no idea; and I became disgusted with the science of natural philosophy, although I still read Pliny and Buffon* with delight, authors, in my estimation, of nearly equal interest and utility.

My occupations at this age were principally the mathematics, and most of the branches of study appertaining to that science. I was busily employed in learning languages; Latin was already familiar to me, and I began to read some of the easiest Greek authors without the help of a lexicon. I also perfectly understood English and German. This is the list of my accomplishments at the age of seventeen; and you may conceive that my hours were fully employed in acquiring and maintaining a knowledge of this various literature.

Another task also devolved upon me, when I became the instructor of my brothers. Ernest was six years younger than myself, and was my principal pupil. He had been afflicted with ill health from his infancy, through which Elizabeth and I had been his constant nurses: his disposition was gentle, but he was incapable of any severe application. William, the youngest of our family, was yet an infant, and the most beautiful little fellow in the world; his lively blue eyes, dimpled cheeks, and endearing manners, inspired the tenderest affection.

Such was our domestic circle, from which care and pain seemed for ever banished. My father directed our studies, and my mother partook of our enjoyments. Neither of us possessed the slightest pre-eminence over the other; the voice of command was never heard amongst us; but mutual affection engaged us all to comply with and obey the slightest desire of each other.

CHAPTER II

When I had attained the age of seventeen, my parents resolved that I should become a student at the university of Ingolstadt.* I had hitherto attended the schools of Geneva; but my father thought it necessary, for the completion of my education, that I should be made acquainted with other customs than those of my native country. My departure was therefore fixed at an early date; but, before the day resolved upon could arrive, the first misfortune of my life occurred— an omen, as it were, of my future misery.

Elizabeth had caught the scarlet fever; but her illness was not severe, and she quickly recovered. During her confinement, many arguments had been urged to persuade my mother to refrain from attending upon her. She had, at first, yielded to our entreaties; but when she heard that her favourite was recovering, she could no longer debar herself from her society, and entered her chamber long before the danger of infection was past. The consequences of this imprudence were fatal. On the third day my mother sickened; her fever was very malignant, and the looks of her attendants prognosticated the worst event. On her death-bed the fortitude and benignity of this admirable woman did not desert her. She joined the hands of Elizabeth and myself: 'My children,' she said, 'my firmest hopes of future happiness were placed on the prospect of your union. This expectation will now be the consolation of your father. Elizabeth, my love, you must supply my place to your younger cousins. Alas! I regret that I am taken from you; and, happy and beloved as I have been, is it not hard to quit you all? But these are not thoughts befitting me; I will endeavour to resign myself cheerfully to death, and will indulge a hope of meeting you in another world.'

She died calmly; and her countenance expressed affection even in death. I need not describe the feelings of those whose dearest ties are rent by that most irreparable evil, the void that presents itself to the soul, and the despair that is exhibited on the countenance. It is so long before the mind can persuade itself that she, whom we saw every day, and whose very existence appeared a part of our own, can have departed for ever—that the brightness of a beloved eye can have been extinguished, and the sound of a voice so familiar, and dear to the ear, can be hushed, never more to be heard. These are the reflections of the first days; but when the lapse of time proves the reality of the evil, then the actual bitterness of grief commences. Yet from whom has not that rude hand rent away some dear connexion; and why should I describe a sorrow which all have felt, and must feel? The time at length arrives, when grief is rather an indulgence than a necessity; and the smile that plays upon the lips, although it may be deemed a sacrilege, is not banished. My mother was dead, but we had still duties which we ought to perform; we must continue our course with the rest, and learn to think ourselves fortunate, whilst one remains whom the spoiler has not seized.

My journey to Ingolstadt, which had been deferred by these events, was now again determined upon. I obtained from my father a respite of some weeks. This period was spent sadly; my mother's death, and my speedy departure, depressed our spirits; but Elizabeth endeavoured to renew the spirit of cheerfulness in our little society. Since the death of her aunt, her mind had acquired new firmness and vigour. She determined to fulfil her duties with the greatest exactness; and she felt that that most imperious duty, of rendering her uncle and cousins happy, had devolved upon her. She consoled me, amused her uncle, instructed my brothers; and I never beheld her so enchanting as at this time, when she was continually endeavouring to contribute to the happiness of others, entirely forgetful of herself.

The day of my departure at length arrived. I had taken leave of all my friends, excepting Clerval, who spent the last evening with us. He bitterly lamented that he was unable to accompany me: but his father could not be persuaded to part with him, intending that he should become a partner with him in business, in compliance with his favourite theory, that learning was superfluous in the commerce of ordinary life. Henry had a refined mind; he had no desire to be idle, and was well pleased to become his father's partner, but he believed that a man might be a very good trader, and yet possess a cultivated understanding.

We sat late, listening to his complaints, and making many little arrangements for the future. The next morning early I departed. Tears gushed from the eyes of Elizabeth; they proceeded partly from sorrow at my departure, and partly because she reflected that the same journey was to have taken place three months before, when a mother's blessing would have accompanied me.

I threw myself into the chaise that was to convey me away, and indulged in the most melancholy reflections. I, who had ever been surrounded by amiable companions, continually engaged in endeavouring to bestow mutual pleasure, I was now alone. In the university, whither I was going, I must form my own friends, and be my own protector. My life had hitherto been remarkably secluded and domestic; and this had given me invincible repugnance to new countenances. I loved my brothers, Elizabeth, and Clerval; these were 'old familiar faces;'* but I believed myself totally unfitted for the company of strangers. Such were my reflections as I commenced my journey; but as I proceeded, my spirits and hopes rose. I ardently desired the acquisition of knowledge. I had often, when at home, thought it hard to remain during my youth cooped up in one place, and had longed to enter the world, and take my station among other human beings. Now my desires were complied with, and it would, indeed, have been folly to repent.

I had sufficient leisure for these and many other reflections during my journey to Ingolstadt, which was long and fatiguing. At length the high white steeple of the town met my eyes. I alighted, and was conducted to my solitary apartment, to spend the evening as I pleased.

The next morning I delivered my letters of introduction, and paid a visit to some of the principal professors, and

among others to M. Krempe, professor of natural philosophy. He received me with politeness, and asked me several
questions concerning my progress in the different branches of science appertaining to natural philosophy. I mentioned, it is true, with fear and trembling, the only authors I
had ever read upon those subjects. The professor stared:
'Have you,' he said, 'really spent your time in studying such
nonsense?'

I replied in the affirmative. 'Every minute,' continued M.
Krempe with warmth, 'every instant that you have wasted on
those books is utterly and entirely lost. You have burdened
your memory with exploded systems, and useless names.
Good God! in what desert land have you lived, where no one
was kind enough to inform you that these fancies, which you
have so greedily imbibed, are a thousand years old, and as
musty as they are ancient? I little expected in this enlightened
and scientific age to find a disciple of Albertus Magnus and
Paracelsus. My dear Sir, you must begin your studies entirely
anew.'

So saying, he stept aside, and wrote down a list of several
books treating of natural philosophy, which he desired me
to procure, and dismissed me, after mentioning that in the
beginning of the following week he intended to commence
a course of lectures upon natural philosophy in its general relations, and that M. Waldman, a fellow-professor,
would lecture upon chemistry the alternate days that he
missed.

I returned home, not disappointed, for I had long considered those authors useless whom the professor had so
strongly reprobated; but I did not feel much inclined to study
the books which I procured at his recommendation. M.
Krempe was a little squat man, with a gruff voice and repulsive
countenance; the teacher, therefore, did not prepossess me
in favour of his doctrine. Besides, I had a contempt for the
uses of modern natural philosophy. It was very different,
when the masters of the science sought immortality and
power; such views, although futile, were grand: but now the
scene was changed. The ambition of the inquirer seemed to
limit itself to the annihilation of those visions on which my

interest in science was chiefly founded. I was required to exchange chimeras of boundless grandeur for realities of little worth.

Such were my reflections during the first two or three days spent almost in solitude. But as the ensuing week commenced, I thought of the information which M. Krempe had given me concerning the lectures. And although I could not consent to go and hear that little conceited fellow deliver sentences out of a pulpit, I recollected what he had said of M. Waldman, whom I had never seen, as he had hitherto been out of town.

Partly from curiosity, and partly from idleness, I went into the lecturing room, which M. Waldman entered shortly after. This professor was very unlike his colleague. He appeared about fifty years of age, but with an aspect expressive of the greatest benevolence; a few gray hairs covered his temples, but those at the back of his head were nearly black. His person was short, but remarkably erect; and his voice the sweetest I had ever heard. He began his lecture by a recapitulation of the history of chemistry and the various improvements made by different men of learning, pronouncing with fervour the names of the most distinguished discoverers. He then took a cursory view of the present state of the science, and explained many of its elementary terms. After having made a few preparatory experiments, he concluded with a panegyric upon modern chemistry, the terms of which I shall never forget: —

'The ancient teachers of this science,' said he, 'promised impossibilities, and performed nothing. The modern masters promise very little; they know that metals cannot be transmuted, and that the elixir of life is a chimera. But these philosophers, whose hands seem only made to dabble in dirt, and their eyes to pore over the microscope or crucible, have indeed performed miracles. They penetrate into the recesses of nature, and shew how she works in her hiding places. They ascend into the heavens; they have discovered how the blood circulates, and the nature of the air we breathe. They have acquired new and almost unlimited powers; they can command the thunders of heaven, mimic the earthquake, and even mock the invisible world with its own shadows.'

I departed highly pleased with the professor and his lecture, and paid him a visit the same evening. His manners in private were even more mild and attractive than in public; for there was a certain dignity in his mien during his lecture, which in his own house was replaced by the greatest affability and kindness. He heard with attention my little narration concerning my studies, and smiled at the names of Cornelius Agrippa, and Paracelsus, but without the contempt that M. Krempe had exhibited. He said, that 'these were men to whose indefatigable zeal modern philosophers were indebted for most of the foundations of their knowledge. They had left to us, as an easier task, to give new names, and arrange in connected classifications, the facts which they in a great degree had been the instruments of bringing to light. The labours of men of genius, however erroneously directed, scarcely ever fail in ultimately turning to the solid advantage of mankind.' I listened to his statement, which was delivered without any presumption or affectation; and then added, that his lecture had removed my prejudices against modern chemists; and I, at the same time, requested his advice concerning the books I ought to procure.

'I am happy,' said M. Waldman, 'to have gained a disciple; and if your application equals your ability, I have no doubt of your success. Chemistry is that branch of natural philosophy in which the greatest improvements have been and may be made; it is on that account that I have made it my peculiar study; but at the same time I have not neglected the other branches of science. A man would make but a very sorry chemist, if he attended to that department of human knowledge alone. If your wish is to become really a man of science, and not merely a petty experimentalist, I should advise you to apply to every branch of natural philosophy, including mathematics.'

He then took me into his laboratory, and explained to me the uses of his various machines; instructing me as to what I ought to procure, and promising me the use of his own, when I should have advanced far enough in the science not to derange their mechanism. He also gave me the list of books which I had requested; and I took my leave.

Thus ended a day memorable to me; it decided my future destiny.

CHAPTER III

From this day natural philosophy, and particularly chemistry, in the most comprehensive sense of the term, became nearly my sole occupation. I read with ardour those works, so full of genius and discrimination, which modern inquirers have written on these subjects. I attended the lectures, and cultivated the acquaintance, of the men of science of the university; and I found even in M. Krempe a great deal of sound sense and real information, combined, it is true, with a repulsive physiognomy and manners, but not on that account the less valuable. In M. Waldman I found a true friend. His gentleness was never tinged by dogmatism; and his instructions were given with an air of frankness and good nature, that banished every idea of pedantry. It was, perhaps, the amiable character of this man that inclined me more to that branch of natural philosophy which he professed, than an intrinsic love for the science itself. But this state of mind had place only in the first steps towards knowledge: the more fully I entered into the science, the more exclusively I pursued it for its own sake. That application, which at first had been a matter of duty and resolution, now became so ardent and eager, that the stars often disappeared in the light of morning whilst I was yet engaged in my laboratory.

As I applied so closely, it may be easily conceived that I improved rapidly. My ardour was indeed the astonishment of the students; and my proficiency, that of the masters. Professor Krempe often asked me, with a sly smile, how Cornelius Agrippa went on? whilst M. Waldman expressed the most heartfelt exultation in my progress. Two years passed in this manner, during which I paid no visit to Geneva, but was engaged, heart and soul, in the pursuit of some discoveries, which I hoped to make. None but those who have experienced them can conceive of the enticements of science. In other studies you go as far as others have gone before you, and there is nothing more to know; but in a scientific pursuit there is continual food for discovery and wonder. A mind of moderate capacity, which closely pursues one study, must infallibly arrive at great proficiency in that study; and I, who continually sought the attainment of one object of pursuit, and was solely wrapt up in this, improved so rapidly, that, at the end of two years, I made some discoveries in the improvement of some chemical instruments, which procured me great esteem and admiration at the university. When I had arrived at this point, and had become as well acquainted with the theory and practice of natural philosophy as depended on the lessons of any of the professors at Ingolstadt, my residence there being no longer conducive to my improvements, I thought of returning to my friends and my native town, when an incident happened that protracted my stay.

One of the phænomena which had peculiarly attracted my attention was the structure of the human frame, and, indeed, any animal endued with life. Whence, I often asked myself, did the principle of life proceed? It was a bold question, and one which has ever been considered as a mystery; yet with how many things are we upon the brink of becoming acquainted, if cowardice or carelessness did not restrain our inquiries. I revolved these circumstances in my mind, and determined thenceforth to apply myself more particularly to those branches of natural philosophy which relate to physiology. Unless I had been animated by an almost supernatural enthusiasm, my application to this study would have been irksome, and almost intolerable. To examine the causes of life, we must first have recourse to death. I became acquainted with the science of anatomy: but this was not sufficient; I must also observe the natural decay and corruption of the human body. In my education my father had taken the greatest precautions that my mind should be impressed with no supernatural horrors. I do not ever remember to have trembled at a tale of superstition, or to have feared the apparition of a spirit. Darkness had no effect upon my fancy; and a church-yard was to me merely the receptacle of bodies deprived of life, which, from being the seat of beauty and strength, had become food for the worm. Now I was led to examine the cause and progress of this decay, and forced to spend days and nights in vaults and charnel houses. My attention was fixed upon every object the most insupportable to the delicacy of the human feelings. I saw how the fine form of man was degraded and wasted; I beheld the corruption of death succeed to the blooming cheek of life; I saw how the worm inherited the wonders of the eye and brain. I paused, examining and ana-lysing all the minutiæ of causation, as exemplified in the change from life to death, and death to life, until from the midst of this darkness a sudden light broke in upon me—a light so brilliant and wondrous, yet so simple, that while I became dizzy with the immensity of the prospect which it illustrated, I was surprised that among so many men of genius, who had directed their inquiries towards the same science, that I alone should be reserved to discover so astonishing a secret.

Remember, I am not recording the vision of a madman. The sun does not more certainly shine in the heavens, than that which I now affirm is true. Some miracle might have produced it, yet the stages of the discovery were distinct and probable. After days and nights of incredible labour and fatigue, I succeeded in discovering the cause of generation and life; nay, more, I became myself capable of bestowing animation upon lifeless matter.

The astonishment which I had at first experienced on this discovery soon gave place to delight and rapture. After so much time spent in painful labour, to arrive at once at the summit of my desires, was the most gratifying consummation of my toils. But this discovery was so great and overwhelming, that all the steps by which I had been progressively led to it were obliterated, and I beheld only the result. What had been the study and desire of the wisest men since the creation of the world, was now within my grasp. Not that, like a magic scene, it all opened upon me at once: the information I had obtained was of a nature rather to direct my endeavours so soon as I should point them towards the object of my search, than to exhibit that object already accomplished. I was like the Arabian who had been buried with the dead, and found a passage to life aided only by one glimmering, and seemingly ineffectual, light.*

I see by your eagerness, and the wonder and hope which your eyes express, my friend, that you expect to be informed of the secret with which I am acquainted; that cannot be: listen patiently until the end of my story, and you will easily perceive why I am reserved upon that subject. I will not lead you on, unguarded and ardent as I then was, to your destruction and infallible misery. Learn from me, if not by my precepts, at least by my example, how dangerous is the acquirement of knowledge, and how much happier that man is who believes his native town to be the world, than he who aspires to become greater than his nature will allow.

When I found so astonishing a power placed within my hands, I hesitated a long time concerning the manner in which I should employ it. Although I possessed the capacity of bestowing animation, yet to prepare a frame for the reception of it, with all its intricacies of fibres, muscles, and veins, still remained a work of inconceivable difficulty and labour. I doubted at first whether I should attempt the creation of a being like myself or one of simpler organization; but my imagination was too much exalted by my first success to permit me to doubt of my ability to give life to an animal as complex and wonderful as man. The materials at present within my command hardly appeared adequate to so arduous an undertaking; but I doubted not that I should ultimately succeed. I prepared myself for a multitude of reverses; my operations might be incessantly baffled, and at last my work be imperfect: yet, when I considered the improvement which every day takes place in science and mechanics, I was encouraged to hope my present attempts would at least lay the foundations of future success. Nor could I consider the magnitude and complexity of my plan as any argument of its impracticability. It was with these feelings that I began the creation of an human being. As the minuteness of the parts formed a great hindrance to my speed, I resolved, contrary to my first intention, to make the being of a gigantic stature; that is to say, about eight feet in height, and proportionably large. After having formed this determination, and having spent some months in successfully collecting and arranging my materials, I began.

No one can conceive the variety of feelings which bore me onwards, like a hurricane, in the first enthusiasm of success. Life and death appeared to me ideal bounds, which I should first break through, and pour a torrent of light into our dark world. A new species would bless me as its creator and source; many happy and excellent natures would owe their being to me. No father could claim the gratitude of his child so completely as I should deserve theirs. Pursuing these reflections, I thought, that if I could bestow animation upon lifeless matter, I might in process of time (although I now found it impossible) renew life where death had apparently devoted the body to corruption.*

These thoughts supported my spirits, while I pursued my undertaking with unremitting ardour. My cheek had grown pale with study, and my person had become emaciated with confinement. Sometimes, on the very brink of certainty, I failed; yet still I clung to the hope which the next day or the next hour might realize. One secret which I alone possessed was the hope to which I had dedicated myself; and the moon gazed on my midnight labours, while, with unrelaxed and breathless eagerness, I pursued nature to her hiding places. Who shall conceive the horrors of my secret toil, as I dabbled among the unhallowed damps of the grave, or tortured the living animal to animate the lifeless clay? My limbs now tremble, and my eyes swim with the remembrance; but then a resistless, and almost frantic impulse, urged me forward; I seemed to have lost all soul or sensation but for this one pursuit. It was indeed but a passing trance, that only made me feel with renewed acuteness so soon as, the unnatural stimulus ceasing to operate, I had returned to my old habits. I collected bones from charnel houses; and disturbed, with profane fingers, the tremendous secrets of the human frame. In a solitary chamber, or rather cell, at the top of the house, and separated from all the other apartments by a gallery and staircase, I kept my workshop of filthy creation; my eyeballs were starting from their sockets in attending to the details of my employment. The dissecting room and the slaughter-house furnished many of my materials; and often did my human nature turn with loathing from my occupation, whilst, still urged on by an eagerness which perpetually increased, I brought my work near to a conclusion.

The summer months passed while I was thus engaged, heart and soul, in one pursuit. It was a most beautiful season; never did the fields bestow a more plentiful harvest, or the vines yield a more luxuriant vintage: but my eyes were insensible to the charms of nature. And the same feelings which made me neglect the scenes around me caused me also to forget those friends who were so many miles absent, and whom I had not seen for so long a time. I knew my silence disquieted them; and I well remembered the words of my father: 'I know that while you are pleased with yourself, you will think of us with affection, and we shall hear regularly from you. You must pardon me, if I regard any interruption in your correspondence as a proof that your other duties are equally neglected.'

I knew well therefore what would be my father's feelings; but I could not tear my thoughts from my employment, loath-some in itself, but which had taken an irresistible hold of my imagination. I wished, as it were, to procrastinate all that related to my feelings of affection until the great object, which swallowed up every habit of my nature, should be completed.

I then thought that my father would be unjust if he ascribed my neglect to vice, or faultiness on my part; but I am now convinced that he was justified in conceiving that I should not be altogether free from blame. A human being in perfection ought always to preserve a calm and peaceful mind, and never to allow passion or a transitory desire to disturb his tranquil-lity. I do not think that the pursuit of knowledge is an exception to this rule. If the study to which you apply yourself has a tendency to weaken your affections, and to destroy your taste for those simple pleasures in which no alloy can possibly mix, then that study is certainly unlawful, that is to say, not befitting the human mind. If this rule were always observed; if no man allowed any pursuit whatsoever to interfere with the tranquillity of his domestic affections, Greece had not been enslaved; Cæsar would have spared his country; America would have been discovered more gradually; and the empires of Mexico and Peru had not been destroyed.

But I forget that I am moralizing in the most interesting part of my tale: and your looks remind me to proceed.

My father made no reproach in his letters; and only took notice of my silence by inquiring into my occupations more particularly than before. Winter, spring, and summer, passed away during my labours; but I did not watch the blossom or the expanding leaves—sights which before always yielded me supreme delight, so deeply was I engrossed in my occupation. The leaves of that year had withered before my work drew near to a close; and now every day shewed me more plainly how well I had succeeded. But my enthusiasm was checked by my anxiety, and I appeared rather like one doomed by slavery to toil in the mines, or any other unwholesome trade, than an artist occupied by his favourite employment. Every night I was oppressed by a slow fever, and I became nervous to a most painful degree; a disease that I regretted the more because I had hitherto enjoyed most excellent health, and had always boasted of the firmness of my nerves. But I believed that exercise and amusement would soon drive away such symptoms; and I promised myself both of these, when my creation should be complete.

CHAPTER IV

It was on a dreary night of November, that I beheld the accomplishment of my toils. With an anxiety that almost amounted to agony, I collected the instruments of life* around me, that I might infuse a spark of being into the lifeless thing that lay at my feet. It was already one in the morning; the rain pattered dismally against the panes, and my candle was nearly burnt out, when, by the glimmer of the half-extinguished light, I saw the dull yellow eye of the creature open; it breathed hard, and a convulsive motion agitated its limbs.

How can I describe my emotions at this catastrophe, or how delineate the wretch whom with such infinite pains and care I had endeavoured to form? His limbs were in proportion, and I had selected his features as beautiful. Beautiful!—Great God! His yellow skin scarcely covered the work of muscles and arteries beneath; his hair was of a lustrous black, and flowing; his teeth of a pearly whiteness; but these luxuriances only formed a more horrid contrast with his watery eyes, that seemed almost of the same colour as the dun white sockets in which they were set, his shrivelled complexion, and straight black lips.

The different accidents of life are not so changeable as the feelings of human nature. I had worked hard for nearly two years, for the sole purpose of infusing life into an inanimate body. For this I had deprived myself of rest and health. I had desired it with an ardour that far exceeded moderation; but now that I had finished, the beauty of the dream vanished, and breathless horror and disgust filled my heart. Unable to endure the aspect of the being I had created, I rushed out of the room, and continued a long time traversing my bed-chamber, unable to compose my mind to sleep. At length lassitude succeeded to the tumult I had before endured; and I threw myself on the bed in my clothes, endeavouring to seek a few moments of forgetfulness. But it was in vain: I slept indeed, but I was disturbed by the wildest dreams. I thought I saw Elizabeth, in the bloom of health, walking in the streets of Ingolstadt. Delighted and surprised, I embraced her; but as I imprinted the first kiss on her lips, they became livid with the hue of death; her features appeared to change, and I thought that I held the corpse of my dead mother in my arms; a shroud enveloped her form, and I saw the grave-worms crawling in the folds of the flannel. I started from my sleep with horror; a cold dew covered my forehead, my teeth chattered, and every limb became convulsed; when, by the dim and yellow light of the moon, as it forced its way though the window-shutters, I beheld the wretch—the miserable monster whom I had created. He held up the curtain of the bed; and his eyes, if eyes they may be called, were fixed on me. His jaws opened, and he muttered some inarticulate sounds, while a grin wrinkled his cheeks. He might have spoken, but I did not hear; one hand was stretched out, seemingly to detain me, but I escaped, and rushed down stairs. I took refuge in the court-yard belonging to the house which I inhabited; where I remained during the rest of the night, walking up and down in the greatest agitation, listening attentively, catching and fearing each sound as if it were to announce the approach of the demoniacal corpse to which I had so miserably given life.

Oh! no mortal could support the horror of that countenance. A mummy again endued with animation could not be so hideous as that wretch. I had gazed on him while unfinished; he was ugly then; but when those muscles and joints were rendered capable of motion, it became a thing such as even Dante could not have conceived.

I passed the night wretchedly. Sometimes my pulse beat so quickly and hardly, that I felt the palpitation of every artery; at others, I nearly sank to the ground through languor and extreme weakness. Mingled with this horror, I felt the bitterness of disappointment: dreams that had been my food and pleasant rest for so long a space, were now become a hell to me; and the change was so rapid, the overthrow so complete!

Morning, dismal and wet, at length dawned, and discovered to my sleepless and aching eyes the church of Ingolstadt, its white steeple and clock, which indicated the sixth hour. The porter opened the gates of the court, which had that night been my asylum, and I issued into the streets, pacing them with quick steps, as if I sought to avoid the wretch whom I feared every turning of the street would present to my view. I did not dare return to the apartment which I inhabited, but felt impelled to hurry on, although wetted by the rain, which poured from a black and comfortless sky.

I continued walking in this manner for some time, endeavouring, by bodily exercise, to ease the load that weighed upon my mind. I traversed the streets, without any clear conception of where I was, or what I was doing. My heart palpitated in the sickness of fear; and I hurried on with irregular steps, not daring to look about me:

> Like one who, on a lonely road,
>   Doth walk in fear and dread,
> And, having once turn'd round, walks on,
>   And turns no more his head;
> Because he knows a frightful fiend
>   Doth close behind him tread.*

Continuing thus, I came at length opposite to the inn at which the various diligences* and carriages usually stopped. Here I paused, I knew not why; but I remained some minutes with my eyes fixed on a coach that was coming towards me from the other end of the street. As it drew nearer, I observed that it was the Swiss diligence: it stopped just where I was standing; and, on the door being opened, I perceived Henry Clerval, who, on seeing me, instantly sprung out. 'My dear Frankenstein,' exclaimed he, 'how glad I am to see you! how fortunate that you should be here at the very moment of my alighting!'

Nothing could equal my delight on seeing Clerval; his presence brought back to my thoughts my father, Elizabeth, and all those scenes of home so dear to my recollection. I grasped his hand, and in a moment forgot my horror and misfortune; I felt suddenly, and for the first time during many months, calm and serene joy. I welcomed my friend, therefore, in the most cordial manner, and we walked towards my college. Clerval continued talking for some time about our mutual friends, and his own good fortune in being permitted to come to Ingolstadt. 'You may easily believe,' said he, 'how great was the difficulty to persuade my father that it was not absolutely necessary for a merchant not to understand any thing except book-keeping; and, indeed, I believe I left him incredulous to the last, for his constant answer to my unwearied entreaties was the same as that of the Dutch school-master in *The Vicar of Wakefield*:* "I have ten thousand florins a year without Greek, I eat heartily without Greek." But his affection for me at length overcame his dislike of learning, and he has permitted me to undertake a voyage of discovery to the land of knowledge.'

'It gives me the greatest delight to see you; but tell me how you left my father, brothers, and Elizabeth.'

'Very well, and very happy, only a little uneasy that they hear from you so seldom. By the bye, I mean to lecture you a little upon their account myself.—But, my dear Frankenstein,' continued he, stopping short, and gazing full in my face, 'I did not before remark how very ill you appear; so thin and pale; you look as if you had been watching for several nights.'

'You have guessed right; I have lately been so deeply engaged in one occupation, that I have not allowed myself sufficient rest, as you see: but I hope, I sincerely hope, that all these employments are now at an end, and that I am at length free.'

I trembled excessively; I could not endure to think of, and far less to allude to the occurrences of the preceding night. I walked with a quick pace, and we soon arrived at my college. I then reflected, and the thought made me shiver, that the creature whom I had left in my apartment might still be there, alive, and walking about. I dreaded to behold this monster; but I feared still more that Henry should see him. Entreating him therefore to remain a few minutes at the bottom of the stairs, I darted up towards my own room. My hand was already on the lock of the door before I recollected myself. I then paused; and a cold shivering came over me. I threw the door forcibly open, as children are accustomed to do when they expect a spectre to stand in waiting for them on the other side; but nothing appeared. I stepped fearfully in: the apartment was empty; and my bedroom was also freed from its hideous guest. I could hardly believe that so great a good-fortune could have befallen me; but when I became assured that my enemy had indeed fled, I clapped my hands for joy, and ran down to Clerval.

We ascended into my room, and the servant presently brought breakfast; but I was unable to contain myself. It was not joy only that possessed me; I felt my flesh tingle with excess of sensitiveness, and my pulse beat rapidly. I was unable to remain for a single instant in the same place; I jumped over the chairs, clapped my hands, and laughed aloud Clerval at first attributed my unusual spirits to joy on his arrival; but when he observed me more attentively, he saw a wildness in my eyes for which he could not account; and my loud, unrestrained, heartless laughter, frightened and astonished him.

'My dear Victor,' cried he, 'what, for God's sake, is the matter? Do not laugh in that manner. How ill you are! What is the cause of all this?'

'Do not ask me,' cried I, putting my hands before my eyes, for I thought I saw the dreaded spectre glide into the room; '*he* can tell.—Oh, save me! save me!' I imagined that the monster seized me; I struggled furiously, and fell down in a fit.

Poor Clerval! what must have been his feelings? A meeting, which he anticipated with such joy, so strangely turned to bitterness. But I was not the witness of his grief; for I was lifeless, and did not recover my senses for a long, long time.

This was the commencement of a nervous fever, which confined me for several months. During all that time Henry was my only nurse. I afterwards learned that, knowing my father's advanced age, and unfitness for so long a journey, and how wretched my sickness would make Elizabeth, he spared them this grief by concealing the extent of my disorder. He knew that I could not have a more kind and attentive nurse than himself; and, firm in the hope he felt of my recovery, he did not doubt that, instead of doing harm, he performed the kindest action that he could towards them.

But I was in reality very ill; and surely nothing but the unbounded and unremitting attentions of my friend could have restored me to life. The form of the monster on whom I had bestowed existence was for ever before my eyes, and I raved incessantly concerning him. Doubtless my words surprised Henry: he at first believed them to be the wanderings of my disturbed imagination; but the pertinacity with which I continually recurred to the same subject persuaded him that my disorder indeed owed its origin to some uncommon and terrible event.

By very slow degrees, and with frequent relapses, that alarmed and grieved my friend, I recovered. I remember the first time I became capable of observing outward objects with any kind of pleasure, I perceived that the fallen leaves had disappeared, and that the young buds were shooting forth from the trees that shaded my window. It was a divine spring; and the season contributed greatly to my convalescence. I felt also sentiments of joy and affection revive in my bosom; my gloom disappeared, and in a short time I became as cheerful as before I was attacked by the fatal passion.

'Dearest Clerval,' exclaimed I, 'how kind, how very good you are to me. This whole winter, instead of being spent in study, as you promised yourself, has been consumed in my sick room. How shall I ever repay you? I feel the greatest remorse for the disappointment of which I have been the occasion; but you will forgive me.'

'You will repay me entirely, if you do not discompose yourself, but get well as fast as you can; and since you appear in such good spirits, I may speak to you on one subject, may I not?'

I trembled. One subject! what could it be? Could he allude to an object on whom I dared not even think?

'Compose yourself,' said Clerval, who observed my change of colour, 'I will not mention it, if it agitates you; but your father and cousin would be very happy if they received a letter from you in your own hand-writing. They hardly know how ill you have been, and are uneasy at your long silence.'

'Is that all? my dear Henry. How could you suppose that my first thought would not fly towards those dear, dear friends whom I love, and who are so deserving of my love.'

'If this is your present temper, my friend, you will perhaps be glad to see a letter that has been lying here some days for you: it is from your cousin, I believe.'

CHAPTER V

Clerval then put the following letter into my hands.

'*To* V. FRANKENSTEIN.

'MY DEAR COUSIN,

'I cannot describe to you the uneasiness we have all felt concerning your health. We cannot help imagining that your friend Clerval conceals the extent of your disorder: for it is now several months since we have seen your hand-writing; and all this time you have been obliged to dictate your letters to Henry. Surely, Victor, you must have been exceedingly ill; and this makes us all very wretched, as much so nearly as after the death of your dear mother. My uncle was almost persuaded that you were indeed dangerously ill, and could hardly be restrained from undertaking a journey to Ingolstadt. Clerval always writes that you are getting better; I eagerly hope that you will confirm this intelligence soon in your own hand-writing; for indeed, indeed, Victor, we are all very miserable on this account. Relieve us from this fear, and we shall be the happiest creatures in the world. Your father's health is now so vigorous, that he appears ten years younger since last winter. Ernest also is so much improved, that you would hardly know him: he is now nearly sixteen, and has lost that sickly appearance which he had some years ago; he is grown quite robust and active.

'My uncle and I conversed a long time last night about what profession Ernest should follow. His constant illness when young has deprived him of the habits of application; and now that he enjoys good health, he is continually in the open air, climbing the hills, or rowing on the lake. I therefore proposed that he should be a farmer; which you know, Cousin, is a favourite scheme of mine. A farmer's is a very healthy happy life; and the least hurtful, or rather the most beneficial profession of any. My uncle had an idea of his being educated as an advocate, that through his interest he might become a judge. But, besides that he is not at all fitted for such an occupation, it is certainly more creditable to cultivate the earth for the sustenance of man, than to be the confidant, and sometimes the accomplice, of his vices; which is the profession of a lawyer. I said, that the employments of a prosperous farmer, if they were not a more honourable, they were at least a happier species of occupation than that of a judge, whose misfortune it was always to meddle with the dark side of human nature. My uncle smiled, and said, that I ought to be an advocate myself, which put an end to the conversation on that subject.

'And now I must tell you a little story that will please, and perhaps amuse you. Do you not remember Justine Moritz? Probably you do not; I will relate her history, therefore, in a few words. Madame Moritz, her mother, was a widow with four children, of whom Justine was the third. This girl had always been the favourite of her father; but, through a strange perversity, her mother could not endure her, and, after the death of M. Moritz, treated her very ill. My aunt observed this; and, when Justine was twelve years of age, prevailed on her mother to allow her to live at her house. The republican institutions of our country have produced simpler and happier manners than those which prevail in the great monarchies that surround it. Hence there is less distinction between the several classes of its inhabitants; and the lower orders being neither so poor nor so despised, their manners are more refined and moral. A servant in Geneva does not mean the same thing as a servant in France and England. Justine, thus received in our family, learned the duties of a servant; a condition which, in our fortunate country, does not include the idea of ignorance, and a sacrifice of the dignity of a human being.

'After what I have said, I dare say you well remember the heroine of my little tale: for Justine was a great favourite of yours; and I recollect you once remarked, that if you were in an ill humour, one glance from Justine could dissipate it, for the same reason that Ariosto gives concerning the beauty of Angelica*—she looked so frank-hearted and happy. My aunt conceived a great attachment for her, by which she was induced to give her an education superior to that which she had at first intended. This benefit was fully repaid; Justine was the most grateful little creature in the world: I do not mean that she made any professions, I never heard one pass her lips; but you could see by her eyes that she almost adored her protectress. Although her disposition was gay, and in many respects inconsiderate, yet she paid the greatest attention to every gesture of my aunt. She thought her the model of all excellence, and endeavoured to imitate her phraseology and manners, so that even now she often reminds me of her.

'When my dearest aunt died, every one was too much occupied in their own grief to notice poor Justine, who had attended her during her illness with the most anxious affection. Poor Justine was very ill; but other trials were reserved for her.

'One by one, her brothers and sister died; and her mother, with the exception of her neglected daughter, was left childless. The conscience of the woman was troubled; she began to think that the deaths of her favourites was a judgment from heaven to chastise her partiality. She was a Roman Catholic; and I believe her confessor confirmed the idea which she had conceived. Accordingly, a few months after your departure for Ingolstadt, Justine was called home by her repentant mother. Poor girl! she wept when she quitted our house: she was much altered since the death of my aunt; grief had given softness and a winning mildness to her manners, which had before been remarkable for vivacity. Nor was her residence at her mother's house of a nature to restore her gaiety. The poor woman was very vacillating in her repentance. She sometimes begged Justine to forgive her unkindness, but much oftener accused her of having caused the deaths of her brothers and sister. Perpetual fretting at length threw Madame Moritz into a decline, which at first increased her irritability, but she is now at peace for ever. She died on the first approach of cold weather, at the beginning of this last winter. Justine has returned to us; and I assure you I love her tenderly. She is very clever and gentle, and extremely pretty; as I mentioned before, her mien and her expressions continually remind me of my dear aunt.

'I must say also a few words to you, my dear cousin, of little darling William. I wish you could see him; he is very tall of his age, with sweet laughing blue eyes, dark eye-lashes, and curling hair. When he smiles, two little dimples appear on each cheek, which are rosy with health. He has already had one or two little *wives*, but Louisa Biron is his favourite, a pretty little girl of five years of age.

'Now, dear Victor, I dare say you wish to be indulged in a little gossip concerning the good people of Geneva. The pretty Miss Mansfield has already received the congratulatory visits on her approaching marriage with a young Englishman, John Melbourne, Esq. Her ugly sister, Manon, married M. Duvillard, the rich banker, last autumn. Your favourite schoolfellow, Louis Manoir, has suffered several misfortunes since the departure of Clerval from Geneva. But he has already recovered his spirits, and is reported to be on the point of marrying a very lively pretty Frenchwoman, Madame Tavernier. She is a widow, and much older than Manoir; but she is very much admired, and a favourite with every body.

'I have written myself into good spirits, dear cousin; yet I cannot conclude without again anxiously inquiring concerning your health. Dear Victor, if you are not very ill, write yourself, and make your father and all of us happy; or—I cannot bear to think of the other side of the question; my tears already flow. Adieu, my dearest cousin.

'ELIZABETH LAVENZA.
'Geneva, March 18th, 17—.'

'Dear, dear Elizabeth!' I exclaimed when I had read her letter, 'I will write instantly, and relieve them from the anxiety they must feel.' I wrote, and this exertion greatly fatigued me; but my convalescence had commenced, and proceeded regularly. In another fortnight I was able to leave my chamber.

One of my first duties on my recovery was to introduce Clerval to the several professors of the university. In doing this, I underwent a kind of rough usage, ill befitting the wounds that my mind had sustained. Ever since the fatal night, the end of my labours, and the beginning of my misfortunes, I had conceived a violent antipathy even to the name of natural philosophy. When I was otherwise quite restored to health, the sight of a chemical instrument would renew all the agony of my nervous symptoms. Henry saw this, and had removed all my apparatus from my view. He had also changed my apartment; for he perceived that I had acquired a dislike for the room which had previously been my laboratory. But these cares of Clerval were made of no avail when I visited the professors. M. Waldman inflicted torture when he praised, with kindness and warmth, the astonishing progress I had made in the sciences. He soon perceived that I disliked the subject; but, not guessing the real cause, he attributed my feelings to modesty, and changed the subject from my improvement to the science itself, with a desire, as I evidently saw, of drawing me out. What could I do? He meant to please, and he tormented me. I felt as if he had placed carefully, one by one, in my view those instruments which were to be afterwards used in putting me to a slow and cruel death. I writhed under his words, yet dared not exhibit the pain I felt. Clerval, whose eyes and feelings were always quick in discerning the sensations of others, declined the subject, alleging, in excuse, his total ignorance; and the conversation took a more general turn. I thanked my friend from my heart, but I did not speak. I saw plainly that he was surprised, but he never attempted to draw my secret from me; and although I loved him with a mixture of affection and reverence that knew no bounds, yet I could never persuade myself to confide to him that event which was so often present to my recollection, but which I feared the detail to another would only impress more deeply.

M. Krempe was not equally docile; and in my condition at that time, of almost insupportable sensitiveness, his harsh blunt encomiums gave me even more pain than the benevolent approbation of M. Waldman. 'D——n the fellow!' cried he; 'why, M. Clerval, I assure you he has outstript us all. Aye, stare if you please; but it is nevertheless true. A youngster who, but a few years ago, believed Cornelius Agrippa as firmly as the gospel, has now set himself at the head of the university; and if he is not soon pulled down, we shall all be out of countenance.—Aye, aye,' continued he, observing my face expressive of suffering, 'M. Frankenstein is modest; an excellent quality in a young man. Young men should be diffident of themselves, you know, M. Clerval; I was myself when young: but that wears out in a very short time.'

M. Krempe had now commenced an eulogy on himself, which happily turned the conversation from a subject that was so annoying to me.

Clerval was no natural philosopher. His imagination was too vivid for the minutiæ of science. Languages were his principal study; and he sought, by acquiring their elements, to open a field for self-instruction on his return to Geneva.

Persian, Arabic, and Hebrew, gained his attention, after he had made himself perfectly master of Greek and Latin. For my own part, idleness had ever been irksome to me; and now that I wished to fly from reflection, and hated my former studies, I felt great relief in being the fellow-pupil with my friend, and found not only instruction but consolation in the works of the orientalists. Their melancholy is soothing, and their joy elevating to a degree I never experienced in studying the authors of any other country. When you read their writings, life appears to consist in a warm sun and garden of roses,—in the smiles and frowns of a fair enemy, and the fire that consumes your own heart. How different from the manly and heroical poetry of Greece and Rome.

Summer passed away in these occupations, and my return to Geneva was fixed for the latter end of autumn; but being delayed by several accidents, winter and snow arrived, the roads were deemed impassable, and my journey was retarded until the ensuing spring. I felt this delay very bitterly; for I longed to see my native town, and my beloved friends. My return had only been delayed so long from an unwillingness to leave Clerval in a strange place, before he had become acquainted with any of its inhabitants. The winter, however, was spent cheerfully; and although the spring was uncommonly late, when it came, its beauty compensated for its dilatoriness.

The month of May had already commenced, and I expected the letter daily which was to fix the date of my departure, when Henry proposed a pedestrian tour in the environs of Ingolstadt that I might bid a personal farewell to the country I had so long inhabited. I acceded with pleasure to this proposition: I was fond of exercise, and Clerval had always been my favourite companion in the rambles of this nature that I had taken among the scenes of my native country.

We passed a fortnight in these perambulations: my health and spirits had long been restored, and they gained additional strength from the salubrious air I breathed, the natural incidents of our progress, and the conversation of my friend. Study had before secluded me from the intercourse of my fellow-creatures, and rendered me unsocial; but Clerval called forth the better feelings of my heart; he again taught me to love the aspect of nature, and the cheerful faces of children. Excellent friend! how sincerely did you love me, and endeavour to elevate my mind, until it was on a level with your own. A selfish pursuit had cramped and narrowed me, until your gentleness and affection warmed and opened my senses; I became the same happy creature who, a few years ago, loving and beloved by all, had no sorrow or care. When happy, inanimate nature had the power of bestowing on me the most delightful sensations. A serene sky and verdant fields filled me with ecstacy. The present season was indeed divine; the flowers of spring bloomed in the hedges, while those of summer were already in bud: I was undisturbed by thoughts which during the preceding year had pressed upon me, notwithstanding my endeavours to throw them off, with an invincible burden.

Henry rejoiced in my gaiety, and sincerely sympathized in my feelings: he exerted himself to amuse me, while he expressed the sensations that filled his soul. The resources of his mind on this occasion were truly astonishing: his conversation was full of imagination; and very often, in imitation of the Persian and Arabic writers, he invented tales of wonderful fancy and passion. At other times he repeated my favourite poems, or drew me out into arguments, which he supported with great ingenuity.

We returned to our college on a Sunday afternoon: the peasants were dancing, and every one we met appeared gay and happy. My own spirits were high, and I bounded along with feelings of unbridled joy and hilarity.

CHAPTER VI

On my return, I found the following letter from my father:—

'*To* V. FRANKENSTEIN.

'MY DEAR VICTOR,

'You have probably waited impatiently for a letter to fix the date of your return to us; and I was at first tempted to write only a few lines, merely mentioning the day on which I should expect you. But that would be a cruel kindness, and I dare not do it. What would be your surprise, my son, when you expected a happy and gay welcome, to behold, on the contrary, tears and wretchedness? And how, Victor, can I relate our misfortune? Absence cannot have rendered you callous to our joys and griefs; and how shall I inflict pain on an absent child? I wish to prepare you for the woeful news, but I know it is impossible; even now your eye skims over the page, to seek the words which are to convey to you the horrible tidings.

'William is dead!—that sweet child, whose smiles delighted and warmed my heart, who was so gentle, yet so gay! Victor, he is murdered!

'I will not attempt to console you; but will simply relate the circumstances of the transaction.

'Last Thursday (May 7th) I, my niece, and your two brothers, went to walk in Plainpalais. The evening was warm and serene, and we prolonged our walk farther than usual. It was already dusk before we thought of returning; and then we discovered that William and Ernest, who had gone on before, were not to be found. We accordingly rested on a seat until they should return. Presently Ernest came, and inquired if we had seen his brother: he said, that they had been playing together, that William had run away to hide himself, and that he vainly sought for him, and afterwards waited for him a long time, but that he did not return.

'This account rather alarmed us, and we continued to search for him until night fell, when Elizabeth conjectured that he might have returned to the house. He was not there. We returned again, with torches; for I could not rest, when I thought that my sweet boy had lost himself, and was exposed to all the damps and dews of night: Elizabeth also suffered extreme anguish. About five in the morning I discovered my lovely boy, whom the night before I had seen blooming and active in health, stretched on the grass livid and motionless: the print of the murderer's finger was on his neck.

'He was conveyed home, and the anguish that was visible in my countenance betrayed the secret to Elizabeth. She was very earnest to see the corpse. At first I attempted to prevent her; but she persisted, and entering the room where it lay, hastily examined the neck of the victim, and clasping her hands exclaimed, "O God! I have murdered my darling infant!"

'She fainted, and was restored with extreme difficulty. When she again lived, it was only to weep and sigh. She told me, that that same evening William had teazed her to let him wear a very valuable miniature that she possessed of your mother. This picture is gone, and was doubtless the temptation which urged the murderer to the deed. We have no trace of him at present, although our exertions to discover him are unremitted; but they will not restore my beloved William.

'Come, dearest Victor; you alone can console Elizabeth. She weeps continually, and accuses herself unjustly as the cause of his death; her words pierce my heart. We are all unhappy; but will not that be an additional motive for you, my son, to return and be our comforter? Your dear mother! Alas, Victor! I now say, Thank God she did not live to witness the cruel, miserable death of her youngest darling!

'Come, Victor; not brooding thoughts of vengeance against the assassin, but with feelings of peace and gentleness, that will heal, instead of festering the wounds of our minds. Enter the house of mourning, my friend, but with kindness and affection for those who love you, and not with hatred for your enemies.

'Your affectionate and afflicted father,

ALPHONSE FRANKENSTEIN.

'Geneva, May 12th, 17—.'

Clerval, who had watched my countenance as I read this letter, was surprised to observe the despair that succeeded to the joy I at first expressed on receiving news from my friends. I threw the letter on the table, and covered my face with my hands.

'My dear Frankenstein,' exclaimed Henry, when he perceived me weep with bitterness, 'are you always to be unhappy? My dear friend, what has happened?'

I motioned to him to take up the letter, while I walked up and down the room in the extremest agitation. Tears also gushed from the eyes of Clerval, as he read the account of my misfortune.

'I can offer you no consolation, my friend,' said he; 'your disaster is irreparable. What do you intend to do?'

'To go instantly to Geneva: come with me, Henry, to order the horses.'

During our walk, Clerval endeavoured to raise my spirits. He did not do this by common topics of consolation, but by exhibiting the truest sympathy. 'Poor William!' said he, 'that dear child; he now sleeps with his angel mother. His friends mourn and weep, but he is at rest: he does not now feel the murderer's grasp; a sod covers his gentle form, and he knows no pain. He can no longer be a fit subject for pity; the survivors are the greatest sufferers, and for them time is the only consolation. Those maxims of the Stoics, that death was no evil, and that the mind of man ought to be superior to despair on the eternal absence of a beloved object, ought not to be urged. Even Cato wept over the dead body of his brother.'

Clerval spoke thus as we hurried through the streets; the words impressed themselves on my mind, and I remembered them afterwards in solitude. But now, as soon as the horses arrived, I hurried into a cabriole,* and bade farewell to my friend.

My journey was very melancholy. At first I wished to hurry on, for I longed to console and sympathize with my loved and sorrowing friends; but when I drew near my native town, I slackened my progress. I could hardly sustain the multitude of feelings that crowded into my mind. I passed through scenes familiar to my youth, but which I had not seen for nearly six years. How altered every thing might be during that time? One sudden and desolating change had taken place; but a thousand little circumstances might have by degrees worked other alterations, which, although they were done more tranquilly, might not be the less decisive. Fear overcame me; I dared not advance, dreading a thousand nameless evils that made me tremble, although I was unable to define them.

I remained two days at Lausanne, in this painful state of mind. I contemplated the lake: the waters were placid; all around was calm, and the snowy mountains, 'the palaces of nature,'* were not changed. By degrees the calm and heavenly scene restored me, and I continued my journey towards Geneva.

The road ran by the side of the lake, which became narrower as I approached my native town. I discovered more distinctly the black sides of Jura, and the bright summit of Mont Blanc; I wept like a child: 'Dear mountains! my own beautiful lake! how do you welcome your wanderer? Your summits are clear; the sky and lake are blue and placid. Is this to prognosticate peace, or to mock at my unhappiness?'

I fear, my friend, that I shall render myself tedious by dwelling on these preliminary circumstances; but they were days of comparative happiness, and I think of them with pleasure. My country, my beloved country! who but a native can tell the delight I took in again beholding thy streams, thy mountains, and, more than all, thy lovely lake.

Yet, as I drew nearer home, grief and fear again overcame me. Night also closed around; and when I could hardly see the dark mountains, I felt still more gloomily. The picture appeared a vast and dim scene of evil, and I foresaw obscurely that I was destined to become the most wretched of human beings. Alas! I prophesied truly, and failed only in one single circumstance, that in all the misery I imagined and dreaded, I did not conceive the hundredth part of the anguish I was destined to endure.

It was completely dark when I arrived in the environs of Geneva; the gates of the town were already shut; and I was obliged to pass the night at Secheron, a village half a league to the east of the city. The sky was serene; and, as I was unable to rest, I resolved to visit the spot where my poor William had been murdered. As I could not pass through the town, I was obliged to cross the lake in a boat to arrive at Plainpalais. During this short voyage I saw the lightnings playing on the summit of Mont Blanc in the most beautiful figures. The storm appeared to approach rapidly; and, on landing, I ascended a low hill, that I might observe its progress. It advanced; the heavens were clouded, and I soon felt the rain coming slowly in large drops, but its violence quickly increased.

I quitted my seat, and walked on, although the darkness and storm increased every minute, and the thunder burst with a terrific crash over my head. It was echoed from Salêve, the Juras, and the Alps of Savoy; vivid flashes of lightning dazzled my eyes, illuminating the lake, making it appear like a vast sheet of fire; then for an instant every thing seemed of a pitchy darkness, until the eye recovered itself from the preceding flash. The storm, as is often the case in Switzerland, appeared at once in various parts of the heavens. The most violent storm hung exactly north of the town, over that part of the lake which lies between the promontory of Belrive and the village of Copêt. Another storm enlightened Jura with faint flashes; and another darkened and sometimes disclosed the Môle, a peaked mountain to the east of the lake.

While I watched the storm, so beautiful yet terrific, I wandered on with a hasty step. This noble war in the sky elevated my spirits; I clasped my hands, and exclaimed aloud, 'William, dear angel! this is thy funeral, this thy dirge!' As I said these words, I perceived in the gloom a figure which stole from behind a clump of trees near me; I stood fixed, gazing intently: I could not be mistaken. A flash of lightning illuminated the object, and discovered its shape plainly to me; its gigantic stature, and the deformity of its aspect, more hideous than belongs to humanity, instantly informed me that it was the wretch, the filthy dæmon to whom I had given life. What did he there? Could he be (I shuddered at the conception) the murderer of my brother? No sooner did that idea cross my imagination, than I became convinced of its truth; my teeth chattered, and I was forced to lean against a tree for support. The figure passed me quickly, and I lost it in the gloom. Nothing in human shape could have destroyed that fair child. *He* was the murderer! I could not doubt it. The mere presence of the idea was an irresistible proof of the fact. I thought of pursuing the devil; but it would have been in vain, for another flash discovered him to me hanging among the rocks of the nearly perpendicular ascent of Mont Salêve, a hill that bounds Plainpalais on the south. He soon reached the summit, and disappeared.

I remained motionless. The thunder ceased; but the rain still continued, and the scene was enveloped in an impenetrable darkness. I revolved in my mind the events which I had until now sought to forget: the whole train of my progress towards the creation; the appearance of the work of my own hands alive at my bed side; its departure. Two years had now nearly elapsed since the night on which he first received life; and was this his first crime? Alas! I had turned loose into the world a depraved wretch, whose delight was in carnage and misery; had he not murdered my brother?

No one can conceive the anguish I suffered during the remainder of the night, which I spent, cold and wet, in the open air. But I did not feel the inconvenience of the weather; my imagination was busy in scenes of evil and despair. I considered the being whom I had cast among mankind, and endowed with the will and power to effect purposes of horror, such as the deed which he had now done, nearly in the light of my own vampire, my own spirit let loose from the grave, and forced to destroy all that was dear to me.

Day dawned; and I directed my steps towards the town. The gates were open; and I hastened to my father's house. My first thought was to discover what I knew of the murderer, and cause instant pursuit to be made. But I paused when I reflected on the story that I had to tell. A being whom I myself had formed, and endued with life, had met me at midnight among the precipices of an inaccessible mountain. I remembered also the nervous fever with which I had been seized just at the time that I dated my creation, and which would give an air of delirium to a tale otherwise so utterly improbable. I well knew that if any other had communicated such a relation to me, I should have looked upon it as the ravings of insanity. Besides, the strange nature of the animal would elude all pursuit, even if I were so far credited as to persuade my relatives to commence it. Besides, of what use would be pursuit? Who could arrest a creature capable of scaling the overhanging sides of Mont Salêve? These reflections determined me, and I resolved to remain silent.

It was about five in the morning when I entered my father's house. I told the servants not to disturb the family, and went into the library to attend their usual hour of rising.

Six years had elapsed, passed as a dream but for one indelible trace, and I stood in the same place where I had last embraced my father before my departure for Ingolstadt. Beloved and respectable parent! He still remained to me. I gazed on the picture of my mother, which stood over the mantelpiece. It was an historical subject, painted at my father's desire, and represented Caroline Beaufort in an agony of despair, kneeling by the coffin of her dead father. Her garb was rustic, and her cheek pale; but there was an air of dignity and beauty, that hardly permitted the sentiment of pity. Below this picture was a miniature of William; and my tears flowed when I looked upon it. While I was thus engaged, Ernest entered: he had heard me arrive, and hastened to welcome me. He expressed a sorrowful delight to see me: 'Welcome, my dearest Victor,' said he. 'Ah! I wish you had come three months ago, and then you would have found us all joyous and delighted. But we are now unhappy; and, I am afraid, tears instead of smiles will be your welcome. Our father looks so sorrowful: this dreadful event seems to have revived in his mind his grief on the death of Mamma. Poor Elizabeth also is quite inconsolable.' Ernest began to weep as he said these words.

'Do not,' said I, 'welcome me thus; try to be more calm, that I may not be absolutely miserable the moment I enter my father's house after so long an absence. But, tell me, how does my father support his misfortunes? and how is my poor Elizabeth?'

'She indeed requires consolation; she accused herself of having caused the death of my brother, and that made her very wretched. But since the murderer has been discovered—'

'The murderer discovered! Good God! how can that be? who could attempt to pursue him? It is impossible; one might as well try to overtake the winds, or confine a mountain-stream with a straw.'

'I do not know what you mean; but we were all very unhappy when she was discovered. No one would believe it at first; and even now Elizabeth will not be convinced, notwith-standing all the evidence. Indeed, who would credit that Justine Moritz, who was so amiable, and fond of all the family, could all at once become so extremely wicked?'

'Justine Moritz! Poor, poor girl, is she the accused? But it is wrongfully; every one knows that; no one believes it, surely, Ernest?'

'No one did at first; but several circumstances came out, that have almost forced conviction upon us: and her own behaviour has been so confused, as to add to the evidence of facts a weight that, I fear, leaves no hope for doubt. But she will be tried to-day, and you will then hear all.'

He related that, the morning on which the murder of poor William had been discovered, Justine had been taken ill, and confined to her bed; and, after several days, one of the serv-ants, happening to examine the apparel she had worn on the night of the murder, had discovered in her pocket the picture of my mother, which had been judged to be the temptation of the murderer. The servant instantly shewed it to one of the others, who, without saying a word to any of the family, went to a magistrate; and, upon their deposition, Justine was appre-hended. On being charged with the fact, the poor girl con-firmed the suspicion in a great measure by her extreme confusion of manner.

This was a strange tale, but it did not shake my faith; and I replied earnestly, 'You are all mistaken; I know the murderer. Justine, poor, good Justine is innocent.'

At that instant my father entered. I saw unhappiness deeply impressed on his countenance, but he endeavoured to wel-come me cheerfully; and, after we had exchanged our mourn-ful greeting, would have introduced some other topic than that of our disaster, had not Ernest exclaimed, 'Good God, Papa! Victor says that he knows who was the murderer of poor William.'

'We do also, unfortunately,' replied my father; 'for indeed I had rather have been for ever ignorant than have discov-ered so much depravity and ingratitude in one I valued so highly.'

'My dear father, you are mistaken; Justine is innocent.'

'If she is, God forbid that she should suffer as guilty. She is to be tried to-day, and I hope, I sincerely hope, that she will be acquitted.'

This speech calmed me. I was firmly convinced in my own mind that Justine, and indeed every human being, was guiltless of this murder. I had no fear, therefore, that any circumstantial evidence could be brought forward strong enough to convict her; and, in this assurance, I calmed myself, expecting the trial with eagerness, but without prognosticating an evil result.

We were soon joined by Elizabeth. Time had made great alterations in her form since I had last beheld her. Six years before she had been a pretty, good-humoured girl, whom every one loved and caressed. She was now a woman in stature and expression of countenance, which was uncommonly lovely. An open and capacious forehead gave indications of a good understanding, joined to great frankness of disposition. Her eyes were hazel, and expressive of mildness, now through recent affliction allied to sadness. Her hair was of a rich dark auburn, her complexion fair, and her figure slight and graceful. She welcomed me with the greatest affection. 'Your arrival, my dear cousin,' said she, 'fills me with hope. You perhaps will find some means to justify my poor guiltless Justine. Alas! who is safe, if she be convicted of crime? I rely on her innocence as certainly as I do upon my own. Our misfortune is doubly hard to us; we have not only lost that lovely darling boy, but this poor girl, whom I sincerely love, is to be torn away by even a worse fate. If she is condemned, I never shall know joy more. But she will not, I am sure she will not; and then I shall be happy again, even after the sad death of my little William.'

'She is innocent, my Elizabeth,' said I, 'and that shall be proved; fear nothing, but let your spirits be cheered by the assurance of her acquittal.'

'How kind you are! every one else believes in her guilt, and that made me wretched; for I knew that it was impossible: and to see every one else prejudiced in so deadly a manner, rendered me hopeless and despairing.' She wept.

'Sweet niece,' said my father, 'dry your tears. If she is, as you believe, innocent, rely on the justice of our judges, and the activity with which I shall prevent the slightest shadow of partiality.'

CHAPTER VII

We passed a few sad hours, until eleven o'clock, when the trial was to commence. My father and the rest of the family being obliged to attend as witnesses, I accompanied them to the court. During the whole of this wretched mockery of justice, I suffered living torture. It was to be decided, whether the result of my curiosity and lawless devices would cause the death of two of my fellow-beings: one a smiling babe, full of innocence and joy; the other far more dreadfully murdered, with every aggravation of infamy that could make the murder memorable in horror. Justine also was a girl of merit, and possessed qualities which promised to render her life happy: now all was to be obliterated in an ignomini-ous grave; and I the cause! A thousand times rather would I have confessed myself guilty of the crime ascribed to Justine; but I was absent when it was committed, and such a de-claration would have been considered as the ravings of a madman, and would not have exculpated her who suffered through me.

The appearance of Justine was calm. She was dressed in mourning; and her countenance, always engaging, was ren-dered, by the solemnity of her feelings, exquisitely beautiful. Yet she appeared confident in innocence, and did not trem-ble, although gazed on and execrated by thousands; for all the kindness which her beauty might otherwise have excited, was obliterated in the minds of the spectators by the imagina-tion of the enormity she was supposed to have committed. She was tranquil, yet her tranquillity was evidently con-strained; and as her confusion had before been adduced as a proof of her guilt, she worked up her mind to an appearance of courage. When she entered the court, she threw her eyes round it, and quickly discovered where we were seated. A tear seemed to dim her eye when she saw us; but she quickly recovered herself, and a look of sorrowful affection seemed to attest her utter guiltlessness.

The trial began; and after the advocate against her had stated the charge, several witnesses were called. Several strange facts combined against her, which might have staggered any one who had not such proof of her innocence as I had. She had been out the whole of the night on which the murder had been committed, and towards morning had been perceived by a market-woman not far from the spot where the body of the murdered child had been afterwards found. The woman asked her what she did there; but she looked very strangely, and only returned a confused and unintelligible answer. She returned to the house about eight o'clock; and when one inquired where she had passed the night, she replied, that she had been looking for the child, and demanded earnestly, if any thing had been heard concerning him. When shewn the body, she fell into violent hysterics, and kept her bed for several days. The picture was then produced, which the servant had found in her pocket; and when Elizabeth, in a faltering voice, proved that it was the same which, an hour before the child had been missed, she had placed round his neck, a murmur of horror and indignation filled the court.

Justine was called on for her defence. As the trial had proceeded, her countenance had altered. Surprise, horror, and misery, were strongly expressed. Sometimes she struggled with her tears; but when she was desired to plead, she collected her powers, and spoke in an audible although variable voice:—

'God knows,' she said, 'how entirely I am innocent. But I do not pretend that my protestations should acquit me: I rest my innocence on a plain and simple explanation of the facts which have been adduced against me; and I hope the character I have always borne will incline my judges to a favourable interpretation, where any circumstance appears doubtful or suspicious.'

She then related that, by the permission of Elizabeth, she had passed the evening of the night on which the murder had been committed, at the house of an aunt at Chêne, a village situated at about a league from Geneva. On her return, at about nine o'clock, she met a man, who asked her if she had seen any thing of the child who was lost. She was alarmed by this account, and passed several hours in looking for him, when the gates of Geneva were shut, and she was forced to remain several hours of the night in a barn belonging to a cottage, being unwilling to call up the inhabitants, to whom she was well known. Unable to rest or sleep, she quitted her asylum early, that she might again endeavour to find my brother. If she had gone near the spot where his body lay, it was without her knowledge. That she had been bewildered when questioned by the market-woman, was not surprising, since she had passed a sleepless night, and the fate of poor William was yet uncertain. Concerning the picture she could give no account.

'I know,' continued the unhappy victim, 'how heavily and fatally this one circumstance weighs against me, but I have no power of explaining it; and when I have expressed my utter ignorance, I am only left to conjecture concerning the probabilities by which it might have been placed in my pocket. But here also I am checked. I believe that I have no enemy on earth, and none surely would have been so wicked as to destroy me wantonly. Did the murderer place it there? I know of no opportunity afforded him for so doing; or if I had, why should he have stolen the jewel, to part with it again so soon?

'I commit my cause to the justice of my judges, yet I see no room for hope. I beg permission to have a few witnesses examined concerning my character; and if their testimony shall not overweigh my supposed guilt, I must be condemned, although I would pledge my salvation on my innocence.'

Several witnesses were called, who had known her for many years, and they spoke well of her; but fear, and hatred of the crime of which they supposed her guilty, rendered them timorous, and unwilling to come forward. Elizabeth saw even this last resource, her excellent dispositions and irreproachable conduct, about to fail the accused, when, although violently agitated, she desired permission to address the court.

'I am,' said she, 'the cousin of the unhappy child who was murdered, or rather his sister, for I was educated by and have lived with his parents ever since and even long before his birth. It may therefore be judged indecent in me to come forward on this occasion; but when I see a fellow-creature about to perish through the cowardice of her pretended friends, I wish to be allowed to speak, that I may say what I know of her character. I am well acquainted with the accused. I have lived in the same house with her, at one time for five, and at another for nearly two years. During all that period she appeared to me the most amiable and benevolent of human creatures. She nursed Madame Frankenstein, my aunt, in her last illness with the greatest affection and care; and afterwards attended her own mother during a tedious illness, in a manner that excited the admiration of all who knew her. After which she again lived in my uncle's house, where she was beloved by all the family. She was warmly attached to the child who is now dead, and acted towards him like a most affectionate mother. For my own part, I do not hesitate to say, that, notwithstanding all the evidence produced against her, I believe and rely on her perfect innocence. She had no temptation for such an action: as to the bauble on which the chief proof rests, if she had earnestly desired it, I should have willingly given it to her; so much do I esteem and value her.'

Excellent Elizabeth! A murmur of approbation was heard; but it was excited by her generous interference, and not in favour of poor Justine, on whom the public indignation was turned with renewed violence, charging her with the blackest ingratitude. She herself wept as Elizabeth spoke, but she did not answer. My own agitation and anguish was extreme during the whole trial. I believed in her innocence; I knew it. Could the dæmon, who had (I did not for a minute doubt) murdered my brother, also in his hellish sport have betrayed the innocent to death and ignominy. I could not sustain the horror of my situation; and when I perceived that the popular voice, and the countenances of the judges, had already condemned my unhappy victim, I rushed out of the court in agony. The tortures of the accused did not equal mine; she was sustained by innocence, but the fangs of remorse tore my bosom, and would not forego their hold.

I passed a night of unmingled wretchedness. In the morning I went to the court; my lips and throat were parched. I dared not ask the fatal question; but I was known, and the officer guessed the cause of my visit. The ballots had been thrown; they were all black, and Justine was condemned.

I cannot pretend to describe what I then felt. I had before experienced sensations of horror; and I have endeavoured to bestow upon them adequate expressions, but words cannot convey an idea of the heart-sickening despair that I then endured. The person to whom I addressed myself added, that Justine had already confessed her guilt. 'That evidence,' he observed, 'was hardly required in so glaring a case, but I am glad of it; and, indeed, none of our judges like to condemn a criminal upon circumstantial evidence, be it ever so decisive.'

When I returned home, Elizabeth eagerly demanded the result.

'My cousin,' replied I, 'it is decided as you may have expected; all judges had rather that ten innocent should suffer, than that one guilty should escape. But she had confessed.'

This was a dire blow to poor Elizabeth, who had relied with firmness upon Justine's innocence. 'Alas!' said she, 'how shall I ever again believe in human benevolence? Justine, whom I loved and esteemed as my sister, how could she put on those smiles of innocence only to betray; her mild eyes seemed incapable of any severity or ill-humour, and yet she has committed a murder.'

Soon after we heard that the poor victim had expressed a wish to see my cousin. My father wished her not to go; but said, that he left it to her own judgment and feelings to decide. 'Yes,' said Elizabeth, 'I will go, although she is guilty; and you, Victor, shall accompany me: I cannot go alone.' The idea of this visit was torture to me, yet I could not refuse.

We entered the gloomy prison-chamber, and beheld Justine sitting on some straw at the further end; her hands were manacled, and her head rested on her knees. She rose on seeing us enter; and when we were left alone with her, she threw herself at the feet of Elizabeth, weeping bitterly. My cousin wept also.

'Oh, Justine!' said she, 'why did you rob me of my last consolation. I relied on your innocence; and although I was then very wretched, I was not so miserable as I am now.'

'And do you also believe that I am so very, very wicked? Do you also join with my enemies to crush me?' Her voice was suffocated with sobs.

'Rise, my poor girl,' said Elizabeth, 'why do you kneel, if you are innocent? I am not one of your enemies; I believed you guiltless, notwithstanding every evidence, until I heard that you had yourself declared your guilt. That report, you say, is false; and be assured, dear Justine, that nothing can shake my confidence in you for a moment, but your own confession.'

'I did confess; but I confessed a lie. I confessed, that I might obtain absolution; but now that falsehood lies heavier at my heart than all my other sins. The God of heaven forgive me! Ever since I was condemned, my confessor has besieged me; he threatened and menaced, until I almost began to think that I was the monster that he said I was. He threatened excommunication and hell fire in my last moments, if I continued obdurate. Dear lady, I had none to support me; all looked on me as a wretch doomed to ignominy and perdition. What could I do? In an evil hour I subscribed to a lie; and now only am I truly miserable.'

She paused, weeping, and then continued—'I thought with horror, my sweet lady, that you should believe your Justine, whom your blessed aunt had so highly honoured, and whom you loved, was a creature capable of a crime which none but the devil himself could have perpetrated. Dear William! dearest blessed child! I soon shall see you again in heaven, where we shall all be happy; and that consoles me, going as I am to suffer ignominy and death.'

'Oh, Justine! forgive me for having for one moment distrusted you. Why did you confess? But do not mourn, my dear girl; I will every where proclaim your innocence, and force belief. Yet you must die; you, my playfellow, my companion, my more than sister. I never can survive so horrible a misfortune.'

'Dear, sweet Elizabeth, do not weep. You ought to raise me with thoughts of a better life, and elevate me from the petty cares of this world of injustice and strife. Do not you, excellent friend, drive me to despair.'

'I will try to comfort you; but this, I fear, is an evil too deep and poignant to admit of consolation, for there is no hope. Yet heaven bless thee, my dearest Justine, with resignation, and a confidence elevated beyond this world. Oh! how I hate its shews and mockeries! when one creature is murdered, another is immediately deprived of life in a slow torturing manner; then the executioners, their hands yet reeking with the blood of innocence, believe that they have done a great deed. They call this *retribution*. Hateful name! When that word is pronounced, I know greater and more horrid punishments are going to be inflicted than the gloomiest tyrant has ever invented to satiate his utmost revenge. Yet this is not consolation for you, my Justine, unless indeed that you may glory in escaping from so miserable a den. Alas! I would I were in peace with my aunt and my lovely William, escaped from a world which is hateful to me, and the visages of men which I abhor.'

Justine smiled languidly. 'This, dear lady, is despair, and not resignation. I must not learn the lesson that you would teach me. Talk of something else, something that will bring peace, and not increase of misery.'

During this conversation I had retired to a corner of the prison-room, where I could conceal the horrid anguish that possessed me. Despair! Who dared talk of that? The poor victim, who on the morrow was to pass the dreary boundary between life and death, felt not as I did, such deep and bitter agony. I gnashed my teeth, and ground them together, uttering a groan that came from my inmost soul. Justine started. When she saw who it was, she approached me, and said, 'Dear Sir, you are very kind to visit me; you, I hope, do not believe that I am guilty.'

I could not answer. 'No, Justine,' said Elizabeth; 'he is more convinced of your innocence than I was; for even when he heard that you had confessed, he did not credit it.'

'I truly thank him. In these last moments I feel the sincerest gratitude towards those who think of me with kindness. How sweet is the affection of others to such a wretch as I am! It removes more than half my misfortune; and I feel as if I could die in peace, now that my innocence is acknowledged by you, dear lady, and your cousin.'

Thus the poor sufferer tried to comfort others and herself. She indeed gained the resignation she desired. But I, the true murderer, felt the never-dying worm alive in my bosom, which allowed of no hope or consolation. Elizabeth also wept, and was unhappy; but hers also was the misery of innocence, which, like a cloud that passes over the fair moon, for a while hides, but cannot tarnish its brightness. Anguish and despair had penetrated into the core of my heart; I bore a hell within me, which nothing could extinguish. We staid several hours with Justine; and it was with great difficulty that Elizabeth could tear herself away. 'I wish,' cried she, 'that I were to die with you; I cannot live in this world of misery.'

Justine assumed an air of cheerfulness, while she with difficulty repressed her bitter tears. She embraced Elizabeth, and said, in a voice of half-suppressed emotion, 'Farewell, sweet lady, dearest Elizabeth, my beloved and only friend; may heaven in its bounty bless and preserve you; may this be the last misfortune that you will ever suffer. Live, and be happy, and make others so.'

As we returned, Elizabeth said, 'You know not, my dear Victor, how much I am relieved, now that I trust in the innocence of this unfortunate girl. I never could again have known peace, if I had been deceived in my reliance on her. For the moment that I did believe her guilty, I felt an anguish that I could not have long sustained. Now my heart is lightened. The innocent suffers; but she whom I thought amiable and good has not betrayed the trust I reposed in her, and I am consoled.'

Amiable cousin! such were your thoughts, mild and gentle as your own dear eyes and voice. But I—I was a wretch, and none ever conceived of the misery that I then endured.

END OF VOLUME I.

VOLUME II

CHAPTER I

Nothing is more painful to the human mind, than, after the feelings have been worked up by a quick succession of events, the dead calmness of inaction and certainty which follows, and deprives the soul both of hope and fear. Justine died; she rested; and I was alive. The blood flowed freely in my veins, but a weight of despair and remorse pressed on my heart, which nothing could remove. Sleep fled from my eyes; I wandered like an evil spirit, for I had committed deeds of mischief beyond description horrible, and more, much more, (I persuaded myself) was yet behind. Yet my heart overflowed with kindness, and the love of virtue. I had begun life with benevolent intentions, and thirsted for the moment when I should put them in practice, and make myself useful to my fellow-beings. Now all was blasted: instead of that serenity of conscience, which allowed me to look back upon the past with self-satisfaction, and from thence to gather promise of new hopes, I was seized by remorse and the sense of guilt, which hurried me away to a hell of intense tortures, such as no language can describe.

This state of mind preyed upon my health, which had entirely recovered from the first shock it had sustained. I shunned the face of man; all sound of joy or complacency was torture to me; solitude was my only consolation—deep, dark, death-like solitude.

My father observed with pain the alteration perceptible in my disposition and habits, and endeavoured to reason with me on the folly of giving way to immoderate grief. 'Do you think, Victor,' said he, 'that I do not suffer also? No one could love a child more than I loved your brother;' (tears came into his eyes as he spoke); 'but is it not a duty to the survivors, that we should refrain from augmenting their unhappiness by an appearance of immoderate grief? It is also a duty owed to yourself; for excessive sorrow prevents improvement or enjoyment, or even the discharge of daily usefulness, without which no man is fit for society.'

This advice, although good, was totally inapplicable to my case; I should have been the first to hide my grief, and console my friends, if remorse had not mingled its bitterness with my other sensations. Now I could only answer my father with a look of despair, and endeavour to hide myself from his view.

About this time we retired to our house at Belrive.* This change was particularly agreeable to me. The shutting of the gates regularly at ten o'clock, and the impossibility of remaining on the lake after that hour, had rendered our residence within the walls of Geneva very irksome to me. I was now free. Often, after the rest of the family had retired for the night, I took the boat, and passed many hours upon the water. Sometimes, with my sails set, I was carried by the wind; and sometimes, after rowing into the middle of the lake, I left the boat to pursue its own course, and gave way to my own miserable reflections. I was often tempted, when all was at peace around me, and I the only unquiet thing that wandered restless in a scene so beautiful and heavenly, if I except some bat, or the frogs, whose harsh and interrupted croaking was heard only when I approached the shore—often, I say, I was tempted to plunge into the silent lake, that the waters might close over me and my calamities for ever. But I was restrained, when I thought of the heroic and suffering Elizabeth, whom I tenderly loved, and whose existence was bound up in mine. I thought also of my father, and surviving brother: should I by my base desertion leave them exposed and unprotected to the malice of the fiend whom I had let loose among them?

At these moments I wept bitterly, and wished that peace would revisit my mind only that I might afford them consolation and happiness. But that could not be. Remorse extinguished every hope. I had been the author of unalterable evils; and I lived in daily fear, lest the monster whom I had created should perpetrate some new wickedness. I had an obscure feeling that all was not over, and that he would still commit some signal crime, which by its enormity should almost efface the recollection of the past. There was always scope for fear, so long as any thing I loved remained behind.

My abhorrence of this fiend cannot be conceived. When I thought of him, I gnashed my teeth, my eyes became inflamed, and I ardently wished to extinguish that life which I had so thoughtlessly bestowed. When I reflected on his crimes and malice, my hatred and revenge burst all bounds of moderation. I would have made a pilgrimage to the highest peak of the Andes, could I, when there, have precipitated him to their base. I wished to see him again, that I might wreak the utmost extent of anger on his head, and avenge the deaths of William and Justine.

Our house was the house of mourning. My father's health was deeply shaken by the horror of the recent events. Elizabeth was sad and desponding; she no longer took delight in her ordinary occupations; all pleasure seemed to her sacrilege toward the dead; eternal woe and tears she then thought was the just tribute she should pay to innocence so blasted and destroyed. She was no longer that happy creature, who in earlier youth wandered with me on the banks of the lake, and talked with ecstacy of our future prospects. She had become grave, and often conversed of the inconstancy of fortune, and the instability of human life.

'When I reflect, my dear cousin,' said she, 'on the miserable death of Justine Moritz, I no longer see the world and its works as they before appeared to me. Before, I looked upon the accounts of vice and injustice, that I read in books or heard from others, as tales of ancient days, or imaginary evils; at least they were remote, and more familiar to reason than to the imagination; but now misery has come home, and men appear to me as monsters thirsting for each other's blood. Yet I am certainly unjust. Every body believed that poor girl to be guilty; and if she could have committed the crime for which she suffered, assuredly she would have been the most depraved of human creatures. For the sake of a few jewels, to have murdered the son of her benefactor and friend, a child whom she had nursed from its birth, and appeared to love as if it had been her own! I could not consent to the death of any human being; but certainly I should have thought such a creature unfit to remain in the society of men. Yet she was innocent. I know, I feel she was innocent; you are of the same opinion, and that confirms me. Alas! Victor. when falsehood can look so like the truth, who can assure themselves of certain happiness? I feel as if I were walking on the edge of a precipice, towards which thousands are crowding, and endeavouring to plunge me into the abyss. William and Justine were assassinated, and the murderer escapes; he walks about the world free, and perhaps respected. But even if I were condemned to suffer on the scaffold for the same crimes, I would not change places with such a wretch.'

I listened to this discourse with the extremest agony. I, not in deed, but in effect, was the true murderer. Elizabeth read my anguish in my countenance, and kindly taking my hand said, 'My dearest cousin, you must calm yourself. These events have affected me, God knows how deeply; but I am not so wretched as you are. There is an expression of despair, and sometimes of revenge, in your countenance, that makes me tremble. Be calm, my dear Victor; I would sacrifice my life to your peace. We surely shall be happy: quiet in our native country, and not mingling in the world, what can disturb our tranquillity?'

She shed tears as she said this, distrusting the very solace that she gave; but at the same time she smiled, that she might chase away the fiend that lurked in my heart. My father, who saw in the unhappiness that was painted in my face only an exaggeration of that sorrow which I might naturally feel, thought that an amusement suited to my taste would be the best means of restoring to me my wonted serenity. It was from this cause that he had removed to the country; and, induced by the same motive, he now proposed that we should all make an excursion to the valley of Chamounix. I had been there before, but Elizabeth and Ernest never had; and both had often expressed an earnest desire to see the scenery of this place, which had been described to them as so wonderful and sublime. Accordingly we departed from Geneva on this tour about the middle of the month of August, nearly two months after the death of Justine.

The weather was uncommonly fine; and if mine had been a sorrow to be chased away by any fleeting circumstance, this excursion would certainly have had the effect intended by my father. As it was, I was somewhat interested in the scene; it sometimes lulled, although it could not extinguish my grief. During the first day we travelled in a carriage. In the morning we had seen the mountains at a distance, towards which we gradually advanced. We perceived that the valley through which we wound, and which was formed by the river Arve, whose course we followed, closed in upon us by degrees; and when the sun had set, we beheld immense mountains and precipices overhanging us on every side, and heard the sound of the river raging among rocks, and the dashing of waterfalls around.

The next day we pursued our journey upon mules; and as we ascended still higher, the valley assumed a more magnificent and astonishing character. Ruined castles hanging on the precipices of piny mountains; the impetuous Arve, and cottages every here and there peeping forth from among the trees, formed a scene of singular beauty. But it was augmented and rendered sublime by the mighty Alps, whose white and shining pyramids and domes towered above all, as belonging to another earth, the habitations of another race of beings.

We passed the bridge of Pelissier, where the ravine, which the river forms, opened before us, and we began to ascend the mountain that overhangs it. Soon after we entered the valley of Chamounix. This valley is more wonderful and sublime, but not so beautiful and picturesque as that of Servox, through which we had just passed. The high and snowy mountains were its immediate boundaries; but we saw no more ruined castles and fertile fields. Immense glaciers approached the road; we heard the rumbling thunder of the falling avalanche, and marked the smoke of its passage. Mont Blanc, the supreme and magnificent Mont Blanc, raised itself from the surrounding *aiguilles*,* and its tremendous *dome* overlooked the valley.

During this journey, I sometimes joined Elizabeth, and exerted myself to point out to her the various beauties of the scene. I often suffered my mule to lag behind, and indulged in the misery of reflection. At other times I spurred on the animal before my companions, that I might forget them, the world, and, more than all, myself. When at a distance, I alighted, and threw myself on the grass, weighed down by horror and despair. At eight in the evening I arrived at Chamounix. My father and Elizabeth were very much fatigued; Ernest, who accompanied us, was delighted, and in high spirits: the only circumstance that detracted from his pleasure was the south wind, and the rain it seemed to promise for the next day.

We retired early to our apartments, but not to sleep; at least I did not. I remained many hours at the window, watching the pallid lightning that played above Mont Blanc, and listening to the rushing of the Arve, which ran below my window.

CHAPTER II

The next day, contrary to the prognostications of our guides, was fine, although clouded. We visited the source of the Arveiron, and rode about the valley until evening. These sublime and magnificent scenes afforded me the greatest consolation that I was capable of receiving. They elevated me from all littleness of feeling; and although they did not remove my grief, they subdued and tranquillized it. In some degree, also, they diverted my mind from the thoughts over which it had brooded for the last month. I returned in the evening, fatigued, but less unhappy, and conversed with my family with more cheerfulness than had been my custom for some time. My father was pleased, and Elizabeth overjoyed. 'My dear cousin,' said she, 'you see what happiness you diffuse when you are happy; do not relapse again!'

The following morning the rain poured down in torrents, and thick mists hid the summits of the mountains. I rose early, but felt unusually melancholy. The rain depressed me; my old feelings recurred, and I was miserable. I knew how disappointed my father would be at this sudden change, and I wished to avoid him until I had recovered myself so far as to be enabled to conceal those feelings that overpowered me. I knew that they would remain that day at the inn; and as I had ever inured myself to rain, moisture, and cold, I resolved to go alone to the summit of Montanvert. I remembered the effect that the view of the tremendous and ever-moving glacier had produced upon my mind when I first saw it. It had then filled me with a sublime ecstacy that gave wings to the soul, and allowed it to soar from the obscure world to light and joy. The sight of the awful and majestic in nature had indeed always the effect of solemnizing my mind, and causing me to forget the passing cares of life. I determined to go alone, for I was well acquainted with the path, and the presence of another would destroy the solitary grandeur of the scene.

The ascent is precipitous, but the path is cut into continual and short windings, which enable you to surmount the per-pendicularity of the mountain. It is a scene terrifically deso-late. In a thousand spots the traces of the winter avalanche may be perceived, where trees lie broken and strewed on the ground; some entirely destroyed, others bent, leaning upon the jutting rocks of the mountain, or transversely upon other trees. The path, as you ascend higher, is intersected by ravines of snow, down which stones continually roll from above; one of them is particularly dangerous, as the slightest sound, such as even speaking in a loud voice, produces a concussion of air sufficient to draw destruction upon the head of the speaker. The pines are not tall or luxuriant, but they are sombre, and add an air of severity to the scene. I looked on the valley beneath; vast mists were rising from the rivers which ran through it, and curling in thick wreaths around the opposite mountains, whose summits were hid in the uniform clouds, while rain poured from the dark sky, and added to the melan-choly impression I received from the objects around me. Alas! why does man boast of sensibilities superior to those apparent in the brute; it only renders them more necessary* beings. If our impulses were confined to hunger, thirst, and desire, we might be nearly free; but now we are moved by every wind that blows, and a chance word or scene that that word may convey to us.

> We rest; a dream has power to poison sleep.
> We rise; one wand'ring thought pollutes the day.
> We feel, conceive, or reason; laugh, or weep,
> Embrace fond woe, or cast our cares away;
> It is the same: for, be it joy or sorrow,
> The path of its departure still is free.

Man's yesterday may ne'er be like his morrow;
Nought may endure but mutability!*

It was nearly noon when I arrived at the top of the ascent. For some time I sat upon the rock that overlooks the sea of ice. A mist covered both that and the surrounding mountains. Presently a breeze dissipated the cloud, and I descended upon the glacier. The surface is very uneven, rising like the waves of a troubled sea, descending low, and interspersed by rifts that sink deep. The field of ice is almost a league in width, but I spent nearly two hours in crossing it. The opposite mountain is a bare perpendicular rock. From the side where I now stood Montanvert was exactly opposite, at the distance of a league; and above it rose Mont Blanc, in awful majesty. I remained in a recess of rock, gazing on this wonderful and stupendous scene. The sea, or rather the vast river of ice, wound among its dependent mountains, whose aërial summits hung over its recesses. Their icy and glittering peaks shone in the sunlight over the clouds. My heart, which was before sorrowful, now swelled with something like joy; I exclaimed—'Wandering spirits, if indeed ye wander, and do not rest in your narrow beds, allow me this faint happiness, or take me, as your companion, away from the joys of life.'

As I said this, I suddenly beheld the figure of a man, at some distance, advancing towards me with superhuman speed. He bounded over the crevices in the ice, among which I had walked with caution; his stature also, as he approached, seemed to exceed that of man. I was troubled: a mist came over my eyes, and I felt a faintness seize me; but I was quickly restored by the cold gale of the mountains. I perceived, as the shape came nearer, (sight tremendous and abhorred!) that it was the wretch whom I had created. I trembled with rage and horror, resolving to wait his approach, and then close with him in mortal combat. He approached; his countenance bespoke bitter anguish, combined with disdain and malignity, while its unearthly ugliness rendered it almost too horrible for human eyes. But I scarcely observed this; anger and hatred had at first deprived me of utterance, and I recovered only to overwhelm him with words expressive of furious detestation and contempt.

'Devil!' I exclaimed, 'do you dare approach me? and do not you fear the fierce vengeance of my arm wreaked on your miserable head? Begone, vile insect! or rather stay, that I may trample you to dust! and, oh, that I could, with the extinction of your miserable existence, restore those victims whom you have so diabolically murdered!'

'I expected this reception,' said the dæmon. 'All men hate the wretched; how then must I be hated, who am miserable beyond all living things! Yet you, my creator, detest and spurn me, thy creature, to whom thou art bound by ties only dissoluble by the annihilation of one of us. You purpose to kill me. How dare you sport thus with life? Do your duty towards me, and I will do mine towards you and the rest of mankind. If you will comply with my conditions, I will leave them and you at peace; but if you refuse, I will glut the maw of death, until it be satiated with the blood of your remaining friends.'

'Abhorred monster! fiend that thou art! the tortures of hell are too mild a vengeance for thy crimes. Wretched devil! you reproach me with your creation; come on then, that I may extinguish the spark which I so negligently bestowed.'

My rage was without bounds; I sprang on him, impelled by all the feelings which can arm one being against the existence of another.

He easily eluded me, and said,

'Be calm! I entreat you to hear me, before you give vent to your hatred on my devoted head. Have I not suffered enough, that you seek to increase my misery? Life, although it may only be an accumulation of anguish, is dear to me, and I will defend it. Remember, thou hast made me more powerful than thyself; my height is superior to thine; my joints more supple. But I will not be tempted to set myself in opposition to thee. I am thy creature, and I will be even mild and docile to my natural lord and king, if thou wilt also perform thy part, the which thou owest me. Oh, Frankenstein, be not equitable to every other, and trample upon me alone, to whom thy justice, and even thy clemency and affection, is most due. Remember, that I am thy creature: I ought to be thy Adam; but I am rather the fallen angel, whom thou drivest from joy for no misdeed. Every where I see bliss, from which I alone am irrevocably excluded. I was benevolent and good; misery made me a fiend. Make me happy, and I shall again be virtuous.'

'Begone! I will not hear you. There can be no community between you and me; we are enemies. Begone, or let us try our strength in a fight, in which one must fall.'

'How can I move thee? Will no entreaties cause thee to turn a favourable eye upon thy creature, who implores thy goodness and compassion. Believe me, Frankenstein: I was benevolent; my soul glowed with love and humanity: but am I not alone, miserably alone? You, my creator, abhor me; what hope can I gather from your fellow-creatures, who owe me nothing? they spurn and hate me. The desert mountains and dreary glaciers are my refuge. I have wandered here many days; the caves of ice, which I only do not fear, are a dwelling to me, and the only one which man does not grudge. These bleak skies I hail, for they are kinder to me than your fellow-beings. If the multitude of mankind knew of my existence, they would do as you do, and arm themselves for my destruction. Shall I not then hate them who abhor me? I will keep no terms with my enemies. I am miserable, and they shall share my wretchedness. Yet it is in your power to recompense me, and deliver them from an evil which it only remains for you to make so great, that not only you and your family, but thousands of others, shall be swallowed up in the whirlwinds of its rage. Let your compassion be moved, and do not disdain me. Listen to my tale: when you have heard that, abandon or commiserate me, as you shall judge that I deserve. But hear me. The guilty are allowed, by human laws, bloody as they may be, to speak in their own defence before they are condemned. Listen to me, Frankenstein. You accuse me of murder; and yet you would, with a satisfied conscience, destroy your own creature. Oh, praise the eternal justice of man! Yet I ask you not to spare me: listen to me; and then, if you can, and if you will, destroy the work of your hands.'

'Why do you call to my remembrance circumstances of which I shudder to reflect, that I have been the miserable origin and author? Cursed be the day, abhorred devil, in which you first saw light! Cursed (although I curse myself) be the hands that formed you! You have made me wretched beyond expression. You have left me no power to consider whether I am just to you, or not. Begone! relieve me from the sight of your detested form.'

'Thus I relieve thee, my creator,' he said, and placed his hated hands before my eyes, which I flung from me with violence; 'thus I take from thee a sight which you abhor. Still thou canst listen to me, and grant me thy compassion. By the virtues that I once possessed, I demand this from you. Hear my tale; it is long and strange, and the temperature of this place is not fitting to your fine sensations; come to the hut upon the mountain. The sun is yet high in the heavens; before it descends to hide itself behind yon snowy precipices, and illuminate another world, you will have heard my story, and can decide. On you it rests, whether I quit for ever the neighbourhood of man, and lead a harmless life, or become the scourge of your fellow-creatures, and the author of your own speedy ruin.'

As he said this, he led the way across the ice: I followed. My heart was full, and I did not answer him; but, as I proceeded, I weighed the various arguments that he had used, and determined at least to listen to his tale. I was partly urged by curiosity, and compassion confirmed my resolution. I had hitherto supposed him to be the murderer of my brother, and I eagerly sought a confirmation or denial of this opinion. For the first time, also, I felt what the duties of a creator towards his creature were, and that I ought to render him happy before I complained of his wickedness. These motives urged me to comply with his demand. We crossed the ice, therefore, and ascended the opposite rock. The air was cold, and the rain again began to descend: we entered the hut, the fiend with an air of exultation, I with a heavy heart, and depressed spirits. But I consented to listen; and, seating myself by the fire which my odious companion had lighted, he thus began his tale.

CHAPTER III

'It is with considerable difficulty that I remember the original æra of my being: all the events of that period appear confused and indistinct. A strange multiplicity of sensations seized me, and I saw, felt, heard, and smelt, at the same time; and it was, indeed, a long time before I learned to distinguish between the operations of my various senses. By degrees, I remember, a stronger light pressed upon my nerves, so that I was obliged to shut my eyes. Darkness then came over me, and troubled me; but hardly had I felt this, when, by opening my eyes, as I now suppose, the light poured in upon me again. I walked, and, I believe, descended; but I presently found a great alteration in my sensations. Before, dark and opaque bodies had surrounded me, impervious to my touch or sight; but I now found that I could wander on at liberty, with no obstacles which I could not either surmount or avoid. The light became more and more oppressive to me; and, the heat wearying me as I walked, I sought a place where I could receive shade. This was the forest near Ingolstadt; and here I lay by the side of a brook resting from my fatigue, until I felt tormented by hunger and thirst. This roused me from my nearly dormant state, and I ate some berries which I found hanging on the trees, or lying on the ground. I slaked my thirst at the brook; and then lying down, was overcome by sleep.

'It was dark when I awoke; I felt cold also, and half-frightened as it were instinctively, finding myself so desolate. Before I had quitted your apartment, on a sensation of cold, I had covered myself with some clothes; but these were insufficient to secure me from the dews of night. I was a poor, helpless, miserable wretch; I knew, and could distinguish, nothing; but, feeling pain invade me on all sides, I sat down and wept.

'Soon a gentle light stole over the heavens, and gave me a sensation of pleasure. I started up, and beheld a radiant form rise from among the trees. I gazed with a kind of wonder. It moved slowly, but it enlightened my path; and I again went out in search of berries. I was still cold, when under one of the trees I found a huge cloak, with which I covered myself, and sat down upon the ground. No distinct ideas occupied my mind; all was confused. I felt light, and hunger, and thirst, and darkness; innumerable sounds rung in my ears, and on all sides various scents saluted me: the only object that I could distinguish was the bright moon, and I fixed my eyes on that with pleasure.

'Several changes of day and night passed, and the orb of night had greatly lessened when I began to distinguish my sensations from each other. I gradually saw plainly the clear stream that supplied me with drink, and the trees that shaded me with their foliage. I was delighted when I first discovered that a pleasant sound, which often saluted my ears, proceeded from the throats of the little winged animals who had often intercepted the light from my eyes. I began also to observe, with greater accuracy, the forms that surrounded me, and to perceive the boundaries of the radiant roof of light which canopied me. Sometimes I tried to imitate the pleasant songs of the birds, but was unable. Sometimes I wished to express my sensations in my own mode, but the uncouth and inarticulate sounds which broke from me frightened me into silence again.

'The moon had disappeared from the night, and again, with a lessened form, shewed itself, while I still remained in the forest. My sensations had, by this time, become distinct, and my mind received every day additional ideas. My eyes became accustomed to the light, and to perceive objects in their right forms; I distinguished the insect from the herb, and, by degrees, one herb from another. I found that the sparrow uttered none but harsh notes, whilst those of the blackbird and thrush were sweet and enticing.

'One day, when I was oppressed by cold, I found a fire which had been left by some wandering beggars, and was overcome with delight at the warmth I experienced from it. In my joy I thrust my hand into the live embers, but quickly drew it out again with a cry of pain. How strange, I thought, that the same cause should produce such opposite effects! I examined the materials of the fire, and to my joy found it to be composed of wood. I quickly collected some branches; but they were wet, and would not burn. I was pained at this, and sat still watching the operation of the fire. The wet wood which I had placed near the heat dried, and itself became inflamed. I reflected on this; and, by touching the various branches, I discovered the cause, and busied myself in collecting a great quantity of wood, that I might dry it, and have a plentiful supply of fire. When night came on, and brought sleep with it,

I was in the greatest fear lest my fire should be extinguished.
I covered it carefully with dry wood and leaves, and placed wet
branches upon it; and then, spreading my cloak, I lay on the
ground, and sunk into sleep.

'It was morning when I awoke, and my first care was to visit
the fire. I uncovered it, and a gentle breeze quickly fanned it
into a flame. I observed this also, and contrived a fan of
branches, which roused the embers when they were nearly
extinguished. When night came again, I found, with pleasure,
that the fire gave light as well as heat; and that the discovery
of this element was useful to me in my food; for I found some
of the offals that the travellers had left had been roasted, and
tasted much more savoury than the berries I gathered from
the trees. I tried, therefore, to dress my food in the same
manner, placing it on the live embers. I found that the berries
were spoiled by this operation, and the nuts and roots much
improved.

'Food, however, became scarce; and I often spent the whole
day searching in vain for a few acorns to assuage the pangs of
hunger. When I found this, I resolved to quit the place that I
had hitherto inhabited, to seek for one where the few wants I
experienced would be more easily satisfied. In this emigra-
tion, I exceedingly lamented the loss of the fire which I had
obtained through accident, and knew not how to re-produce
it. I gave several hours to the serious consideration of this
difficulty; but I was obliged to relinquish all attempt to supply
it; and, wrapping myself up in my cloak, I struck across the
wood towards the setting sun. I passed three days in these
rambles, and at length discovered the open country. A great
fall of snow had taken place the night before, and the fields
were of one uniform white; the appearance was disconsolate,
and I found my feet chilled by the cold damp substance that
covered the ground.

'It was about seven in the morning, and I longed to obtain
food and shelter; at length I perceived a small hut, on a rising
ground, which had doubtless been built for the convenience
of some shepherd. This was a new sight to me; and I examined the structure with great curiosity. Finding the door
open, I entered. An old man sat in it, near a fire, over which

he was preparing his breakfast. He turned on hearing a noise; and, perceiving me, shrieked loudly, and, quitting the hut, ran across the fields with a speed of which his debilitated form hardly appeared capable. His appearance, different from any I had ever before seen, and his flight, somewhat surprised me. But I was enchanted by the appearance of the hut: here the snow and rain could not penetrate; the ground was dry; and it presented to me then as exquisite and divine a retreat as Pandæmonium appeared to the dæmons of hell after their sufferings in the lake of fire.* I greedily devoured the remnants of the shepherd's breakfast, which consisted of bread, cheese, milk, and wine; the latter, however, I did not like. [Then] overcome by fatigue, I lay down among some straw, and fell asleep.

'It was noon when I awoke; and, allured by the warmth of the sun, which shone brightly on the white ground, I determined to recommence my travels; and, depositing the remains of the peasant's breakfast in a wallet I found, I proceeded across the fields for several hours, until at sunset I arrived at a village. How miraculous did this appear! the huts, the neater cottages, and stately houses, engaged my admiration by turns. The vegetables in the gardens, the milk and cheese that I saw placed at the windows of some of the cottages, allured my appetite. One of the best of these I entered; but I had hardly placed my foot within the door, before the children shrieked, and one of the women fainted. The whole village was roused; some fled, some attacked me, until, grievously bruised by stones and many other kinds of missile weapons, I escaped to the open country, and fearfully took refuge in a low hovel, quite bare, and making a wretched appearance after the palaces I had beheld in the village. This hovel, however, joined a cottage of a neat and pleasant appearance; but, after my late dearly-bought experience, I dared not enter it. My place of refuge was constructed of wood, but so low, that I could with difficulty sit upright in it. No wood, however, was placed on the earth, which formed the floor, but it was dry; and although the wind entered it by innumerable chinks, I found it an agreeable asylum from the snow and rain.

'Here then I retreated, and lay down, happy to have found a shelter, however miserable, from the inclemency of the season, and still more from the barbarity of man.

'As soon as morning dawned, I crept from my kennel, that I might view the adjacent cottage, and discover if I could remain in the habitation I had found. It was situated against the back of the cottage, and surrounded on the sides which were exposed by a pig-stye and a clear pool of water. One part was open, and by that I had crept in; but now I covered every crevice by which I might be perceived with stones and wood, yet in such a manner that I might move them on occasion to pass out: all the light I enjoyed came through the stye, and that was sufficient for me.

'Having thus arranged my dwelling, and carpeted it with clean straw, I retired; for I saw the figure of a man at a distance, and I remembered too well my treatment the night before, to trust myself in his power. I had first, however, provided for my sustenance for that day, by a loaf of coarse bread, which I purloined, and a cup with which I could drink, more conveniently than from my hand, of the pure water which flowed by my retreat. The floor was a little raised, so that it was kept perfectly dry, and by its vicinity to the chimney of the cottage it was tolerably warm.

'Being thus provided, I resolved to reside in this hovel, until something should occur which might alter my determination. It was indeed a paradise, compared to the bleak forest, my former residence, the rain-dropping branches, and dank earth. I ate my breakfast with pleasure, and was about to remove a plank to procure myself a little water, when I heard a step, and, looking through a small chink, I beheld a young creature, with a pail on her head, passing before my hovel. The girl was young and of gentle demeanour, unlike what I have since found cottagers and farm-house servants to be. Yet she was meanly dressed, a coarse blue petticoat and a linen jacket being her only garb; her fair hair was plaited, but not adorned; she looked patient, yet sad. I lost sight of her; and in about a quarter of an hour she returned, bearing the pail, which was now partly filled with milk. As she walked along, seemingly incommoded by the burden, a young man met her, whose countenance expressed a deeper despondence. Uttering a few sounds with an air of melancholy, he took the pail from her head, and bore it to the cottage himself. She followed, and they disappeared. Presently I saw the young man again, with some tools in his hand, cross the field behind the cottage; and the girl was also busied, sometimes in the house, and sometimes in the yard.

'On examining my dwelling, I found that one of the windows of the cottage had formerly occupied a part of it, but the panes had been filled up with wood. In one of these was a small and almost imperceptible chink, through which the eye could just penetrate. Through this crevice, a small room was visible, white-washed and clean, but very bare of furniture. In one corner, near a small fire, sat an old man, leaning his head on his hands in a disconsolate attitude. The young girl was occupied in arranging the cottage; but presently she took something out of a drawer, which employed her hands, and she sat down beside the old man, who, taking up an instrument, began to play, and to produce sounds, sweeter than the voice of the thrush or the nightingale. It was a lovely sight, even to me, poor wretch! who had never beheld aught beautiful before. The silver hair and benevolent countenance of the aged cottager, won my reverence; while the gentle manners of the girl enticed my love. He played a sweet mournful air, which I perceived drew tears from the eyes of his amiable companion, of which the old man took no notice, until she sobbed audibly; he then pronounced a few sounds, and the fair creature, leaving her work, knelt at his feet. He raised her, and smiled with such kindness and affection, that I felt sensations of a peculiar and overpowering nature: they were a mixture of pain and pleasure, such as I had never before experienced, either from hunger or cold, warmth or food; and I withdrew from the window, unable to bear these emotions.

'Soon after this the young man returned, bearing on his shoulders a load of wood. The girl met him at the door, helped to relieve him of his burden, and, taking some of the fuel into the cottage, placed it on the fire; then she and the youth went apart into a nook of the cottage, and he shewed her a large loaf and a piece of cheese. She seemed pleased; and went into the garden for some roots and plants, which she placed in water, and then upon the fire. She afterwards continued her work, whilst the young man went into the garden, and appeared busily employed in digging and pulling up roots. After he had been employed thus about an hour, the young woman joined him, and they entered the cottage together.

'The old man had, in the mean time, been pensive; but, on the appearance of his companions, he assumed a more cheerful air, and they sat down to eat. The meal was quickly dispatched. The young woman was again occupied in arranging the cottage; the old man walked before the cottage in the sun for a few minutes, leaning on the arm of the youth. Nothing could exceed in beauty the contrast between these two excellent creatures. One was old, with silver hairs and a countenance beaming with benevolence and love: the younger was slight and graceful in his figure, and his features were moulded with the finest symmetry; yet his eyes and attitude expressed the utmost sadness and despondency. The old man returned to the cottage; and the youth, with tools different from those he had used in the morning, directed his steps across the fields.

'Night quickly shut in; but, to my extreme wonder, I found that the cottagers had a means of prolonging light, by the use of tapers, and was delighted to find, that the setting of the sun did not put an end to the pleasure I experienced in watching my human neighbours. In the evening, the young girl and her companion were employed in various occupations which I did not understand; and the old man again took up the instrument, which produced the divine sounds that had enchanted me in the morning. So soon as he had finished, the youth began, not to play, but to utter sounds that were monotonous, and neither resembling the harmony of the old man's instrument or the songs of the birds; I since found that he read aloud, but at that time I knew nothing of the science of words or letters.

'The family, after having been thus occupied for a short time, extinguished their lights, and retired, as I conjectured, to rest.

CHAPTER IV

'I lay on my straw, but I could not sleep. I thought of the occurrences of the day. What chiefly struck me was the gentle manners of these people; and I longed to join them, but dared not. I remembered too well the treatment I had suffered the night before from the barbarous villagers, and resolved, whatever course of conduct I might hereafter think it right to pursue, that for the present I would remain quietly in my hovel, watching, and endeavouring to discover the motives which influenced their actions.

'The cottagers arose the next morning before the sun. The young woman arranged the cottage, and prepared the food; and the youth departed after the first meal.

'This day was passed in the same routine as that which preceded it. The young man was constantly employed out of doors, and the girl in various laborious occupations within. The old man, whom I soon perceived to be blind, employed his leisure hours on his instrument, or in contemplation. Nothing could exceed the love and respect which the younger cottagers exhibited towards their venerable companion. They performed towards him every little office of affection and duty with gentleness; and he rewarded them by his benevolent smiles.

'They were not entirely happy. The young man and his companion often went apart, and appeared to weep. I saw no cause for their unhappiness; but I was deeply affected by it. If such lovely creatures were miserable, it was less strange that I, an imperfect and solitary being, should be wretched. Yet why were these gentle beings unhappy? They possessed a delightful house (for such it was in my eyes), and every luxury; they had a fire to warm them when chill, and delicious viands when hungry; they were dressed in excellent clothes; and, still more, they enjoyed one another's company and speech, interchanging each day looks of affection and kindness. What did their tears imply? Did they really express pain? I was at first unable to solve these questions; but perpetual attention, and time, explained to me many appearances which were at first enigmatic.

'A considerable period elapsed before I discovered one of the causes of the uneasiness of this amiable family; it was poverty: and they suffered that evil in a very distressing degree. Their nourishment consisted entirely of the vegetables of their garden, and the milk of one cow, who gave very little during the winter, when its masters could scarcely procure food to support it. They often, I believe, suffered the pangs of hunger very poignantly, especially the two younger cottagers; for several times they placed food before the old man, when they reserved none for themselves.

'This trait of kindness moved me sensibly. I had been accustomed, during the night, to steal a part of their store for my own consumption; but when I found that in doing this I inflicted pain on the cottagers, I abstained, and satisfied myself with berries, nuts, and roots, which I gathered from a neighbouring wood.

'I discovered also another means through which I was enabled to assist their labours. I found that the youth spent a great part of each day in collecting wood for the family fire; and, during the night, I often took his tools, the use of which I quickly discovered, and brought home firing sufficient for the consumption of several days.

'I remember, the first time that I did this, the young woman, when she opened the door in the morning, appeared greatly astonished on seeing a great pile of wood on the outside. She uttered some words in a loud voice, and the youth joined her, who also expressed surprise. I observed, with pleasure, that he did not go to the forest that day, but spent it in repairing the cottage and cultivating the garden.

'By degrees I made a discovery of still greater moment. I found that these people possessed a method of communicating their experience and feelings to one another by articulate sounds. I perceived that the words they spoke sometimes produced pleasure or pain, smiles or sadness, in the minds and countenances of the hearers. This was indeed a godlike science, and I ardently desired to become acquainted with it. But I was baffled in every attempt I made for this purpose. Their pronunciation was quick; and the words they uttered, not having any apparent connexion with visible objects, I was unable to discover any clue by which I could unravel the mystery of their reference. By great application, however, and after having remained during the space of several revolutions of the moon in my hovel, I discovered the names that were given to some of the most familiar objects of discourse: I learned and applied the words *fire, milk, bread,* and *wood.* I learned also the names of the cottagers themselves. The youth and his companion had each of them several names, but the old man had only one, which was *father.* The girl was called *sister,* or *Agatha;* and the youth *Felix, brother,* or *son.* I cannot describe the delight I felt when I learned the ideas appropriated to each of these sounds, and was able to pronounce them. I distinguished several other words, without being able as yet to understand or apply them; such as *good, dearest, unhappy.*

'I spent the winter in this manner. The gentle manners and beauty of the cottagers greatly endeared them to me: when they were unhappy, I felt depressed; when they rejoiced, I sympathized in their joys. I saw few human beings beside them; and if any other happened to enter the cottage, their harsh manners and rude gait only enhanced to me the superior accomplishments of my friends. The old man, I could perceive, often endeavoured to encourage his children, as sometimes I found that he called them, to cast off their melancholy. He would talk in a cheerful accent, with an expression of goodness that bestowed pleasure even upon me. Agatha listened with respect, her eyes sometimes filled with tears, which she endeavoured to wipe away unperceived; but I generally found that her countenance and tone were more cheerful after having listened to the exhortations of her father. It was not thus with Felix. He was always the saddest of the groupe; and, even to my unpractised senses, he appeared to have suffered more deeply than his friends. But if his countenance was more sorrowful, his voice was more cheerful than that of his sister, especially when he addressed the old man.

'I could mention innumerable instances, which, although slight, marked the dispositions of these amiable cottagers. In the midst of poverty and want, Felix carried with pleasure to his sister the first little white flower that peeped out from beneath the snowy ground. Early in the morning before she had risen, he cleared away the snow that obstructed her path to the milk-house, drew water from the well, and brought the wood from the outhouse, where, to his perpetual astonishment, he found his store always replenished by an invisible hand. In the day, I believe, he worked sometimes for a neighbouring farmer, because he often went forth, and did not return until dinner, yet brought no wood with him. At other times he worked in the garden; but, as there was little to do in the frosty season, he read to the old man and Agatha.

'This reading had puzzled me extremely at first; but, by degrees, I discovered that he uttered many of the same sounds when he read as when he talked. I conjectured, therefore, that he found on the paper signs for speech which he understood, and I ardently longed to comprehend these also; but how was that possible, when I did not even understand the sounds for which they stood as signs? I improved, however, sensibly in this science, but not sufficiently to follow up any kind of conversation, although I applied for my whole mind to the endeavour: for I easily perceived that, although I eagerly longed to discover myself to the cottagers, I ought not to make the attempt until I had first become master of their language; which knowledge might enable me to make them overlook the deformity of my figure; for with this also the contrast perpetually presented to my eyes had made me acquainted.

'I had admired the perfect forms of my cottagers—their grace, beauty, and delicate complexions: but how was I terrified, when I viewed myself in a transparent pool! At first I started back, unable to believe that it was indeed I who was reflected in the mirror; and when I became fully convinced that I was in reality the monster that I am, I was filled with the bitterest sensations of despondence and mortification. Alas! I did not yet entirely know the fatal effects of this miserable deformity.

'As the sun became warmer, and the light of day longer, the snow vanished, and I beheld the bare trees and the black earth. From this time Felix was more employed; and the heart-moving indications of impending famine disappeared.

Their food, as I afterwards found, was coarse, but it was wholesome; and they procured a sufficiency of it. Several new kinds of plants sprung up in the garden, which they dressed; and these signs of comfort increased daily as the season advanced.

'The old man, leaning on his son, walked each day at noon, when it did not rain, as I found it was called when the heavens poured forth its waters. This frequently took place; but a high wind quickly dried the earth, and the season became far more pleasant than it had been.

'My mode of life in my hovel was uniform. During the morning I attended the motions of the cottagers; and when they were dispersed in various occupations, I slept: the remainder of the day was spent in observing my friends. When they had retired to rest, if there was any moon, or the night was starlight, I went into the woods, and collected my own food and fuel for the cottage. When I returned, as often as it was necessary, I cleared their path from the snow, and performed those offices that I had seen done by Felix. I afterwards found that these labours, performed by an invisible hand, greatly astonished them; and once or twice I heard them, on these occasions, utter the words *good spirit, wonderful;* but I did not then understand the signification of these terms.

'My thoughts now became more active, and I longed to discover the motives and feelings of these lovely creatures; I was inquisitive to know why Felix appeared so miserable, and Agatha so sad. I thought (foolish wretch!) that it might be in my power to restore happiness to these deserving people. When I slept, or was absent, the forms of the venerable blind father, the gentle Agatha, and the excellent Felix, flitted before me. I looked upon them as superior beings, who would be the arbiters of my future destiny. I formed in my imagination a thousand pictures of presenting myself to them, and their reception of me. I imagined that they would be disgusted, until, by my gentle demeanour and conciliating words, I should first win their favour, and afterwards their love.

'These thoughts exhilarated me, and led me to apply with fresh ardour to the acquiring the art of language. My organs were indeed harsh, but supple; and although my voice was very unlike the soft music of their tones, yet I pronounced such words as I understood with tolerable ease. It was as the ass and the lap-dog;* yet surely the gentle ass, whose intentions were affectionate, although his manners were rude, deserved better treatment than blows and execration.

'The pleasant showers and genial warmth of spring greatly altered the aspect of the earth. Men, who before this change seemed to have been hid in caves, dispersed themselves, and were employed in various arts of cultivation. The birds sang in more cheerful notes, and the leaves began to bud forth on the trees. Happy, happy earth! fit habitation for gods, which, so short a time before, was bleak, damp, and unwholesome. My spirits were elevated by the enchanting appearance of nature; the past was blotted from my memory, the present was tranquil, and the future gilded by bright rays of hope, and anticipations of joy.

CHAPTER V

'I now hasten to the more moving part of my story. I shall relate events that impressed me with feelings which, from what I was, have made me what I am.

'Spring advanced rapidly; the weather became fine, and the skies cloudless. It surprised me, that what before was desert and gloomy should now bloom with the most beautiful flowers and verdure. My senses were gratified and refreshed by a thousand scents of delight, and a thousand sights of beauty.

'It was on one of these days, when my cottagers periodically rested from labour—the old man played on his guitar, and the children listened to him—I observed that the countenance of Felix was melancholy beyond expression: he sighed frequently; and once his father paused in his music, and I conjectured by his manner that he inquired the cause of his son's sorrow. Felix replied in a cheerful accent, and the old man was recommencing his music, when some one tapped at the door.

'It was a lady on horseback, accompanied by a countryman as a guide. The lady was dressed in a dark suit, and covered with a thick black veil. Agatha asked a question; to which the stranger only replied by pronouncing, in a sweet accent, the name of Felix. Her voice was musical, but unlike that of either of my friends. On hearing this word, Felix came up hastily to the lady; who, when she saw him, threw up her veil, and I beheld a countenance of angelic beauty and expression. Her hair of a shining raven black, and curiously braided; her eyes were dark, but gentle, although animated; her features of a regular proportion, and her complexion wondrously fair, each cheek tinged with a lovely pink.

'Felix seemed ravished with delight when he saw her, every trait of sorrow vanished from his face, and it instantly expressed a degree of ecstatic joy, of which I could hardly have believed it capable; his eyes sparkled, as his cheek flushed with pleasure; and at that moment I thought him as beautiful as the stranger. She appeared affected by different feelings; wiping a few tears from her lovely eyes, she held out her hand to Felix, who kissed it rapturously, and called her, as well as I could distinguish, his sweet Arabian. She did not appear to understand him, but smiled. He assisted her to dismount, and, dismissing her guide, conducted her into the cottage. Some conversation took place between him and his father; and the young stranger knelt at the old man's feet, and would have kissed his hand, but he raised her, and embraced her affectionately.

'I soon perceived, that although the stranger uttered articulate sounds, and appeared to have a language of her own, she was neither understood by, or herself understood, the cottagers. They made many signs which I did not comprehend; but I saw that her presence diffused gladness through the cottage, dispelling their sorrow as the sun dissipates the morning mists. Felix seemed peculiarly happy, and with smiles of delight welcomed his Arabian. Agatha, the ever-gentle Agatha, kissed the hands of the lovely stranger; and, pointing to her brother, made signs which appeared to me to mean that he had been sorrowful until she came. Some hours passed thus, while they, by their countenances, expressed joy, the cause of which I did not comprehend. Presently I found, by the frequent recurrence of one sound which the stranger repeated after them, that she was endeavouring to learn their language; and the idea instantly occurred to me, that I should make use of the same instructions to the same end. The stranger learned about twenty words at the first lesson, most of them indeed were those which I had before understood, but I profited by the others.

'As night came on, Agatha and the Arabian retired early. When they separated, Felix kissed the hand of the stranger, and said, "Good night, sweet Safie." He sat up much longer, conversing with his father; and, by the frequent repetition of her name, I conjectured that their lovely guest was the subject of their conversation. I ardently desired to understand them, and bent every faculty towards that purpose, but found it utterly impossible.

'The next morning Felix went out to his work; and, after the usual occupations of Agatha were finished, the Arabian sat at the feet of the old man, and, taking his guitar, played some airs so entrancingly beautiful, that they at once drew tears of sorrow and delight from my eyes. She sang, and her voice flowed in a rich cadence, swelling or dying away, like a nightingale of the woods.

'When she had finished, she gave the guitar to Agatha, who at first declined it. She played a simple air, and her voice accompanied it in sweet accents, but unlike the wondrous strain of the stranger. The old man appeared enraptured, and said some words, which Agatha endeavoured to explain to Safie, and by which he appeared to wish to express that she bestowed on him the greatest delight by her music.

'The days now passed as peaceably as before, with the sole alteration, that joy had taken place of sadness in the countenances of my friends. Safie was always gay and happy; she and I improved rapidly in the knowledge of language, so that in two months I began to comprehend most of the words uttered by my protectors.

'In the meanwhile also the black ground was covered with herbage, and the green banks interspersed with innumerable flowers, sweet to the scent and the eyes, stars of pale radiance among the moonlight woods; the sun became warmer, the nights clear and balmy; and my nocturnal rambles were an extreme pleasure to me, although they were considerably shortened by the late setting and early rising of the sun; for I never ventured abroad during daylight, fearful of meeting with the same treatment as I had formerly endured in the first village which I entered.

'My days were spent in close attention, that I might more speedily master the language; and I may boast that I improved more rapidly than the Arabian, who understood very little, and conversed in broken accents, whilst I comprehended and could imitate almost every word that was spoken.

'While I improved in speech, I also learned the science of letters, as it was taught to the stranger; and this opened before me a wide field for wonder and delight.

'The book from which Felix instructed Safie was Volney's *Ruins of Empires.** I should not have understood the purport of this book, had not Felix, in reading it, given very minute explanations. He had chosen this work, he said, because the declamatory style was framed in imitation of the eastern authors. Through this work I obtained a cursory knowledge of history, and a view of the several empires at present existing in the world; it gave me an insight into the manners, governments, and religions of the different nations of the earth. I heard of the slothful Asiatics; of the stupendous genius and mental activity of the Grecians; of the wars and wonderful virtue of the early Romans—of their subsequent degeneration—of the decline of that mighty empire; of chivalry, christianity, and kings. I heard of the discovery of the American hemisphere, and wept with Safie over the hapless fate of its original inhabitants.

'These wonderful narrations inspired me with strange feelings. Was man, indeed, at once so powerful, so virtuous, and magnificent, yet so vicious and base? He appeared at one time a mere scion of the evil principle, and at another as all that can be conceived of noble and godlike. To be a great and virtuous man appeared the highest honour that can befall a sensitive being; to be base and vicious, as many on record have been, appeared the lowest degradation, a condition more abject than that of the blind mole or harmless worm. For a long time I could not conceive how one man could go forth to murder his fellow, or even why there were laws and governments; but when I heard details of vice and bloodshed, my wonder ceased, and I turned away with disgust and loathing.

'Every conversation of the cottagers now opened new wonders to me. While I listened to the instructions which Felix bestowed upon the Arabian, the strange system of human society was explained to me. I heard of the division of property, of immense wealth and squalid poverty; of rank, descent, and noble blood.

'The words induced me to turn towards myself. I learned that the possessions most esteemed by your fellow-creatures were, high and unsullied descent united with riches. A man might be respected with only one of these acquisitions; but without either he was considered, except in very rare instances, as a vagabond and a slave, doomed to waste his powers for the profit of the chosen few. And what was I? Of my creation and creator I was absolutely ignorant; but I knew that I possessed no money, no friends, no kind of property. I was, besides, endowed with a figure hideously deformed and loathsome; I was not even of the same nature as man. I was more agile than they, and could subsist upon coarser diet; I bore the extremes of heat and cold with less injury to my frame; my stature far exceeded theirs. When I looked around, I saw and heard of none like me. Was I then a monster, a blot upon the earth, from which all men fled, and whom all men disowned?

'I cannot describe to you the agony that these reflections inflicted upon me; I tried to dispel them, but sorrow only increased with knowledge. Oh, that I had for ever remained in my native wood, nor known or felt beyond the sensations of hunger, thirst, and heat!

'Of what a strange nature is knowledge! It clings to the mind, when it has once seized on it, like a lichen on the rock. I wished sometimes to shake off all thought and feeling; but I learned that there was but one means to overcome the sensation of pain, and that was death—a state which I feared yet did not understand. I admired virtue and good feelings, and loved the gentle manners and amiable qualities of my cottagers; but I was shut out from intercourse with them, except through means which I obtained by stealth, when I was unseen and unknown, and which rather increased than satisfied the desire I had of becoming one among my fellows. The gentle words of Agatha, and the animated smiles of the charming Arabian, were not for me. The mild exhortations of the old man, and the lively conversation of the loved Felix, were not for me. Miserable, unhappy wretch!

'Other lessons were impressed upon me even more deeply. I heard of the difference of sexes; of the birth and growth of children; how the father doated on the smiles of the infant, and the lively sallies of the older child; how all the life and cares of the mother were wrapt up in the precious charge; how the mind of youth expanded and gained knowledge; of brother, sister, and all the various relationships which bind one human being to another in mutual bonds.

'But where were my friends and relations? No father had watched my infant days, no mother had blessed me with smiles and caresses; or if they had, all my past life was now a blot, a blind vacancy in which I distinguished nothing. From my earliest remembrance I had been as I then was in height and proportion. I had never yet seen a being resembling me, or who claimed any intercourse with me. What was I? The question again recurred, to be answered only with groans.

'I will soon explain to what these feelings tended; but allow me now to return to the cottagers, whose story excited in me such various feelings of indignation, delight, and wonder, but which all terminated in additional love and reverence for my protectors (for so I loved, in an innocent, half painful self-deceit, to call them).

CHAPTER VI

'Some time elapsed before I learned the history of my friends. It was one which could not fail to impress itself deeply on my mind, unfolding as it did a number of circumstances each interesting and wonderful to one so utterly inexperienced as I was.

'The name of the old man was De Lacey. He was descended from a good family in France, where he had lived for many years in affluence, respected by his superiors, and beloved by his equals. His son was bred in the service of his country; and Agatha had ranked with ladies of the highest distinction. A few months before my arrival, they had lived in a large and luxurious city, called Paris, surrounded by friends, and possessed of every enjoyment which virtue, refinement of intellect, or taste, accompanied by a moderate fortune, could afford.

'The father of Safie had been the cause of their ruin. He was a Turkish merchant, and had inhabited Paris for many years, when, for some reason which I could not learn, he became obnoxious to the government. He was seized and cast into prison the very day that Safie arrived from Constantinople to join him. He was tried, and condemned to death. The injustice of his sentence was very flagrant; all Paris was indignant; and it was judged that his religion and wealth, rather than the crime alleged against him, had been the cause of his condemnation.

'Felix had been present at the trial; his horror and indignation were uncontrollable, when he heard the decision of the court. He made, at that moment, a solemn vow to deliver him, and then looked around for the means. After many fruitless attempts to gain admittance to the prison, he found a strongly grated window in an unguarded part of the building, which lighted the dungeon of the unfortunate Mahometan; who, loaded with chains, waited in despair the execution of the barbarous sentence. Felix visited the grate at night, and made known to the prisoner his intentions in his favour. The Turk, amazed and delighted, endeavoured to kindle the zeal of his deliverer by promises of reward and wealth. Felix rejected his offers with contempt; yet when he saw the lovely Safie, who was allowed to visit her father, and who, by her gestures, expressed her lively gratitude, the youth could not help owning to his own mind, that the captive possessed a treasure which would fully reward his toil and hazard.

'The Turk quickly perceived the impression that his daughter had made on the heart of Felix, and endeavoured to secure him more entirely in his interests by the promise of her hand in marriage, so soon as he should be conveyed to a place of safety. Felix was too delicate to accept this offer; yet he looked forward to the probability of that event as to the consummation of his happiness.

'During the ensuing days, while the preparations were going forward for the escape of the merchant, the zeal of Felix was warmed by several letters that he received from this lovely girl, who found means to express her thoughts in the language of her lover by the aid of an old man, a servant of her father's, who understood French. She thanked him in the most ardent terms for his intended services towards her father; and at the same time she gently deplored her own fate.

'I have copies of these letters; for I found means, during my residence in the hovel, to procure the implements of writing; and the letters were often in the hands of Felix or Agatha. Before I depart, I will give them to you, they will prove the truth of my tale; but at present, as the sun is already far declined, I shall only have time to repeat the substance of them to you.

'Safie related, that her mother was a Christian Arab, seized and made a slave by the Turks; recommended by her beauty, she had won the heart of the father of Safie, who married her. The young girl spoke in high and enthusiastic terms of her mother, who, born in freedom spurned the bondage to which she was now reduced. She instructed her daughter in the tenets of her religion, and taught her to aspire to higher powers of intellect, and an independence of spirit, forbidden to the female followers of Mahomet. This lady died; but her lessons were indelibly impressed on the mind of Safie, who sickened at the prospect of again returning to Asia, and the being immured within the walls of a haram, allowed only to occupy herself with puerile amusements, ill suited to the temper of her soul, now accustomed to grand ideas and a noble emulation for virtue. The prospect of marrying a Christian, and remaining in a country where women were allowed to take a rank in society, was enchanting to her.

'The day for the execution of the Turk was fixed; but, on the night previous to it, he had quitted prison, and before morning was distant many leagues from Paris. Felix had procured passports in the name of his father, sister, and himself. He had previously communicated his plan to the former, who aided the deceit by quitting his house, under the pretence of a journey, and concealed himself, with his daughter, in an obscure part of Paris.

'Felix conducted the fugitives through France to Lyons, and across Mont Cenis to Leghorn, where the merchant had decided to wait a favourable opportunity of passing into some part of the Turkish dominions.

'Safie resolved to remain with her father until the moment of his departure, before which time the Turk renewed his promise that she should be united to his deliverer; and Felix remained with them in expectation of that event; and in the mean time he enjoyed the society of the Arabian, who exhibited towards him the simplest and tenderest affection. They conversed with one another through the means of an interpreter, and sometimes with the interpretation of looks; and Safie sang to him the divine airs of her native country.

'The Turk allowed this intimacy to take place, and encouraged the hopes of the youthful lovers, while in his heart he had formed far other plans. He loathed the idea that his daughter should be united to a Christian; but he feared the resentment of Felix if he should appear lukewarm; for he knew that he was still in the power of his deliverer, if he should choose to betray him to the Italian state which they inhabited. He revolved a thousand plans by which he should be enabled to prolong the deceit until it might be no longer necessary, and secretly to take his daughter with him when he departed. His plans were greatly facilitated by the news which arrived from Paris.

'The government of France were greatly enraged at the escape of their victim, and spared no pains to detect and punish his deliverer. The plot of Felix was quickly discovered, and De Lacey and Agatha were thrown into prison. The news reached Felix, and roused him from his dream of pleasure. His blind and aged father, and his gentle sister, lay in a noisome dungeon, while he enjoyed the free air, and the society of her whom he loved. This idea was torture to him. He quickly arranged with the Turk, that if the latter should find a favourable opportunity for escape before Felix could return to Italy, Safie should remain as a boarder at a convent at Leghorn; and then, quitting the lovely Arabian, he hastened to Paris, and delivered himself up to the vengeance of the law, hoping to free De Lacey and Agatha by this proceeding.

'He did not succeed. They remained confined for five months before the trial took place; the result of which deprived them of their fortune, and condemned them to a perpetual exile from their native country.

'They found a miserable asylum in the cottage in Germany, where I discovered them. Felix soon learned that the treacherous Turk, for whom he and his family endured such unheard-of oppression, on discovering that his deliverer was thus reduced to poverty and impotence, became a traitor to good feeling and honour, and had quitted Italy with his daughter, insultingly sending Felix a pittance of money to aid him, as he said, in some plan of future maintenance.

'Such were the events that preyed on the heart of Felix, and rendered him, when I first saw him, the most miserable of his family. He could have endured poverty, and when this distress had been the meed of his virtue, he would have gloried in it: but the ingratitude of the Turk, and the loss of his beloved Safie, were misfortunes more bitter and irreparable. The arrival of the Arabian now infused new life into his soul.

'When the news reached Leghorn, that Felix was deprived of his wealth and rank, the merchant commanded his daughter to think no more of her lover, but to prepare to return with him to her native country. The generous nature of Safie was outraged by this command; she attempted to expostulate with her father, but he left her angrily, reiterating his tyrannical mandate.

'A few days after, the Turk entered his daughter's apartment, and told her hastily, that he had reason to believe that his residence at Leghorn had been divulged, and that he should speedily be delivered up to the French government; he had, consequently, hired a vessel to convey him to Constantinople, for which city he should sail in a few hours. He intended to leave his daughter under the care of a confidential servant, to follow at her leisure with the greater part of his property, which had not yet arrived at Leghorn.

'When alone, Safie resolved in her own mind the plan of conduct that it would become her to pursue in this emergency. A residence in Turkey was abhorrent to her; her religion and feelings were alike adverse to it. By some papers of her father's, which fell into her hands, she heard of the exile of her lover, and learned the name of the spot where he then resided. She hesitated some time, but at length she formed her determination. Taking with her some jewels that belonged to her, and a small sum of money, she quitted Italy, with an attendant, a native of Leghorn, but who understood the common language of Turkey, and departed for Germany.

'She arrived in safety at a town about twenty leagues from the cottage of De Lacey, when her attendant fell dangerously ill. Safie nursed her with the most devoted affection; but the poor girl died, and the Arabian was left alone, unacquainted with the language of the country, and utterly ignorant of the customs of the world. She fell, however, into good hands. The Italian had mentioned the name of the spot for which they were bound; and, after her death, the woman of the house in which they had lived took care that Safie should arrive in safety at the cottage of her lover.

CHAPTER VII

'Such was the history of my beloved cottagers. It impressed me deeply. I learned, from the views of social life which it developed, to admire their virtues, and to deprecate the vices of mankind.

'As yet I looked upon crime as a distant evil; benevolence and generosity were ever present before me, inciting within me a desire to become an actor in the busy scene where so many admirable qualities were called forth and displayed. But, in giving an account of the progress of my intellect, I must not omit a circumstance which occurred in the beginning of the month of August of the same year.

'One night, during my accustomed visit to the neighbouring wood, where I collected my own food, and brought home firing for my protectors, I found on the ground a leathern portmanteau, containing several articles of dress and some books. I eagerly seized the prize, and returned with it to my hovel. Fortunately the books were written in the language the elements of which I had acquired at the cottage; they consisted of *Paradise Lost*, a volume of *Plutarch's Lives*, and the *Sorrows of Werter*.* The possession of these treasures gave me extreme delight; I now continually studied and exercised my mind upon these histories, whilst my friends were employed in their ordinary occupations.

'I can hardly describe to you the effect of these books. They produced in me an infinity of new images and feelings, that sometimes raised me to ecstacy, but more frequently sunk me into the lowest dejection. In the *Sorrows of Werter*, besides the interest of its simple and affecting story, so many opinions are canvassed, and so many lights thrown upon what had hitherto been to me obscure subjects, that I found in it a never-ending source of speculation and astonishment. The gentle and domestic manners it described, combined with lofty sentiments and feelings, which had for their object something out of self, accorded well with my experience among my protectors, and with the wants which were for ever alive in my own bosom. But I thought Werter himself a more divine being than I had ever beheld or imagined; his character contained no pretension, but it sunk deep. The disquisitions upon death and suicide were calculated to fill me with wonder. I did not pretend to enter into the merits of the case, yet I inclined towards the opinions of the hero, whose extinction I wept, without precisely understanding it.

'As I read, however, I applied much personally to my own feelings and condition. I found myself similar, yet at the same time strangely unlike the beings concerning whom I read, and to whose conversation I was a listener. I sympathized with, and partly understood them, but I was unformed in mind; I was dependent on none, and related to none. "The path of my departure was free;"* and there was none to lament my annihilation. My person was hideous, and my stature gigantic: what did this mean? Who was I? What was I? Whence did I come? What was my destination? These questions continually recurred, but I was unable to solve them.

'The volume of *Plutarch's Lives* which I possessed, contained the histories of the first founders of the ancient republics. This book had a far different effect upon me from the *Sorrows of Werter*. I learned from Werter's imaginations despondency and gloom: but Plutarch taught me high thoughts; he elevated me above the wretched sphere of my own reflections, to admire and love the heroes of past ages. Many things I read surpassed my understanding and experience. I had a very confused knowledge of kingdoms, wide extents of country, mighty rivers, and boundless seas. But I was perfectly unacquainted with towns, and large assemblages of men. The cottage of my protectors had been the only school in which I had studied human nature; but this book developed new and mightier scenes of action. I read of men concerned in public affairs governing or massacring their species. I felt the greatest ardour for virtue rise within me, and abhorrence for vice, as far as I understood the signification of those terms, relative as they were, as I applied them, to pleasure and pain alone. Induced by these feelings, I was of course led to admire peaceable law-givers, Numa, Solon, and Lycurgus, in preference to Romulus and Theseus.* The patriarchal lives of my protectors caused these impressions to take a firm hold on my mind; perhaps, if my first introduction to humanity had been made by a young soldier, burning for glory and slaughter, I should have been imbued with different sensations.

'But *Paradise Lost* excited different and far deeper emotions. I read it, as I had read the other volumes which had fallen into my hands, as a true history. It moved every feeling of wonder and awe, that the picture of an omnipotent God warring with his creatures was capable of exciting. I often referred the several situations, as their similarity struck me, to my own. Like Adam, I was created apparently united by no link to any other being in existence; but his state was far different from mine in every other respect. He had come forth from the hands of God a perfect creature, happy and prosperous, guarded by the especial care of his Creator; he was allowed to converse with, and acquire knowledge from beings of a superior nature: but I was wretched, helpless, and alone. Many times I considered Satan as the fitter emblem of my condition; for often, like him, when I viewed the bliss of my protectors, the bitter gall of envy rose within me.

'Another circumstance strengthened and confirmed these feelings. Soon after my arrival in the hovel, I discovered some papers in the pocket of the dress which I had taken from your laboratory. At first I had neglected them; but now that I was able to decypher the characters in which they were written, I began to study them with diligence. It was your journal of the four months that preceded my creation. You minutely described in these papers every step you took in the progress of your work; this history was mingled with accounts of domestic occurrences. You, doubtless, recollect these papers. Here they are. Every thing is related in them which bears reference to my accursed origin; the whole detail of that series of disgusting circumstances which produced it is set in view; the minutest description of my odious and loathsome person is given, in language which painted your own horrors, and rendered mine ineffaceable. I sickened as I read. "Hateful day when I received life!" I exclaimed in agony. "Cursed creator! Why did you form a monster so hideous that even you turned from me in disgust? God in pity made man beautiful and alluring, after his own image; but my form is a filthy type of yours, more horrid from its very resemblance. Satan had his companions, fellow-devils, to admire and encourage him; but I am solitary and detested."

'These were the reflections of my hours of despondency and solitude; but when I contemplated the virtues of the cottagers, their amiable and benevolent dispositions, I persuaded myself that when they should become acquainted with my admiration of their virtues, they would compassionate me, and overlook my personal deformity. Could they turn from their door one, however monstrous, who solicited their compassion and friendship? I resolved, at least, not to despair, but in every way to fit myself for an interview with them which would decide my fate. I postponed this attempt for some months longer; for the importance attached to its success inspired me with a dread lest I should fail. Besides, I found that my understanding improved so much with every day's experience, that I was unwilling to commence this undertaking until a few more months should have added to my wisdom.

'Several changes, in the mean time, took place in the cottage. The presence of Safie diffused happiness among its inhabitants; and I also found that a greater degree of plenty reigned there. Felix and Agatha spent more time in amusement and conversation, and were assisted in their labours by servants. They did not appear rich, but they were contented and happy; their feelings were serene and peaceful, while mine became every day more tumultuous. Increase of knowledge only discovered to me more clearly what a wretched outcast I was. I cherished hope, it is true; but it vanished, when I beheld my person reflected in water, or my shadow in the moon-shine, even as that frail image and that inconstant shade.

'I endeavoured to crush these fears, and to fortify myself for the trial which in a few months I resolved to undergo; and sometimes I allowed my thoughts, unchecked by reason, to ramble in the fields of Paradise, and dared to fancy amiable and lovely creatures sympathizing with my feelings and cheering my gloom; their angelic countenances breathed smiles of consolation. But it was all a dream: no Eve soothed my sorrows, or shared my thoughts; I was alone. I remembered Adam's supplication to his Creator; but where was mine? he had abandoned me, and, in the bitterness of my heart, I cursed him.

'Autumn passed thus. I saw, with surprise and grief, the leaves decay and fall, and nature again assume the barren and bleak appearance it had worn when I first beheld the woods and the lovely moon. Yet I did not heed the bleakness of the weather; I was better fitted by my conformation for the endurance of cold than heat. But my chief delights were the sight of the flowers, the birds, and all the gay apparel of summer; when those deserted me, I turned with more attention towards the cottagers. Their happiness was not decreased by the absence of summer. They loved, and sympathized with one another; and their joys, depending on each other, were not interrupted by the casualties that took place around them. The more I saw of them, the greater became my desire to claim their protection and kindness; my heart yearned to be known and loved by these amiable creatures: to see their sweet looks turned towards me with affection, was the utmost limit of my ambition. I dared not think that they would turn them from me with disdain and horror. The poor that stopped at their door were never driven away. I asked, it is true, for greater treasures than a little food or rest; I required kindness and sympathy; but I did not believe myself utterly unworthy of it.

'The winter advanced, and an entire revolution of the seasons had taken place since I awoke into life. My attention, at this time, was solely directed towards my plan of introducing myself into the cottage of my protectors. I revolved many projects; but that on which I finally fixed was, to enter the dwelling when the blind old man should be alone. I had sagacity enough to discover, that the unnatural hideousness of my person was the chief object of horror with those who had formerly beheld me. My voice, although harsh, had nothing terrible in it; I thought, therefore, that if, in the absence of his children, I could gain the good-will and mediation of the old De Lacy,* I might, by his means, be tolerated by my younger protectors.

'One day, when the sun shone on the red leaves that strewed the ground, and diffused cheerfulness, although it denied warmth, Safie, Agatha, and Felix, departed on a long country walk, and the old man, at his own desire, was left alone in the cottage. When his children had departed, he took up his guitar, and played several mournful, but sweet airs, more sweet and mournful than I had ever heard him play before. At first his countenance was illuminated with pleasure, but, as he continued, thoughtfulness and sadness succeeded; at length, laying aside the instrument, he sat absorbed in reflection.

'My heart beat quick; this was the hour and moment of trial, which would decide my hopes, or realize my fears. The servants were gone to a neighbouring fair. All was silent in and around the cottage: it was an excellent opportunity; yet, when I proceeded to execute my plan, my limbs failed me, and I sunk to the ground. Again I rose; and, exerting all the firmness of which I was master, removed the planks which I had placed before my hovel to conceal my retreat. The fresh air revived me, and, with renewed determination, I approached the door of their cottage.

'I knocked. "Who is there?" said the old man—"Come in."

'I entered; "Pardon this intrusion," said I, "I am a traveller in want of a little rest; you would greatly oblige me, if you would allow me to remain a few minutes before the fire."

' "Enter," said De Lacy; "and I will try in what manner I can relieve your wants; but, unfortunately, my children are from home, and, as I am blind, I am afraid I shall find it difficult to procure food for you."

' "Do not trouble yourself, my kind host, I have food; it is warmth and rest only that I need."

'I sat down, and a silence ensued. I knew that every minute was precious to me, yet I remained irresolute in what manner to commence the interview; when the old man addressed me—

' "By your language, stranger, I suppose you are my countryman;—are you French?"

' "No; but I was educated by a French family, and understand that language only. I am now going to claim the protection of some friends, whom I sincerely love, and of whose favour I have some hopes."

' "Are these Germans?"

' "No, they are French. But let us change the subject. I am an unfortunate and deserted creature; I look around, and I have no relation or friend upon earth. These amiable people to whom I go have never seen me, and know little of me. I am full of fears; for if I fail there, I am ⌐n outcast in the world for ever."

' "Do not despair. To be friendless is indeed to be unfortunate; but the hearts of men, when unprejudiced by any obvious self-interest, are full of brotherly love and charity. Rely, therefore, on your hopes; and if these friends are good and amiable, do not despair."

' "They are kind—they are the most excellent creatures in the world; but, unfortunately, they are prejudiced against me. I have good dispositions; my life has been hitherto harmless, and, in some degree, beneficial; but a fatal prejudice clouds their eyes, and where they ought to see a feeling and kind friend, they behold only a detestable monster."

' "That is indeed unfortunate; but if you are really blameless, cannot you undeceive them?"

' "I am about to undertake that task; and it is on that account that I feel so many overwhelming terrors. I tenderly love these friends; I have, unknown to them, been for many months in the habits of daily kindness towards them; but they believe that I wish to injure them, and it is that prejudice which I wish to overcome."

' "Where do these friends reside?"

' "Near this spot."

'The old man paused, and then continued, "If you will unreservedly confide to me the particulars of your tale, I perhaps may be of use in undeceiving them. I am blind, and cannot judge of your countenance, but there is something in your words which persuades me that you are sincere. I am poor, and an exile; but it will afford me true pleasure to be in any way serviceable to a human creature."

' "Excellent man! I thank you, and accept your generous offer. You raise me from the dust by this kindness; and I trust that, by your aid, I shall not be driven from the society and sympathy of your fellow-creatures."

' "Heaven forbid! even if you were really criminal; for that can only drive you to desperation, and not instigate you to virtue. I also am unfortunate; I and my family have been condemned, although innocent: judge, therefore, if I do not feel for your misfortunes."

' "How can I thank you, my best and only benefactor? from your lips first have I heard the voice of kindness directed towards me; I shall be for ever grateful; and your present humanity assures me of success with those friends whom I am on the point of meeting."

' "May I know the names and residence of those friends?"

'I paused. This, I thought, was the moment of decision, which was to rob me of, or bestow happiness on me for ever. I struggled vainly for firmness sufficient to answer him, but the effort destroyed all my remaining strength; I sank on the chair, and sobbed aloud. At that moment I heard the steps of my younger protectors. I had not a moment to lose; but, seizing the hand of the old man, I cried, "Now is the time!—save and protect me! You and your family are the friends whom I seek. Do not you desert me in the hour of trial!"

' "Great God!" exclaimed the old man, "who are you?"

'At that instant the cottage door was opened, and Felix, Safie and Agatha entered. Who can describe their horror and consternation on beholding me? Agatha fainted; and Safie, unable to attend to her friend, rushed out of the cottage. Felix darted forward, and with supernatural force tore me from his father, to whose knees I clung: in a transport of fury, he dashed me to the ground, and struck me violently with a stick. I could have torn him limb from limb, as the lion rends the antelope. But my heart sunk within me as with bitter sickness, and I refrained. I saw him on the point of repeating his blow, when, overcome by pain and anguish, I quitted the cottage, and in the general tumult escaped unperceived to my hovel.

CHAPTER VIII

'Cursed, cursed creator! Why did I live? Why, in that instant, did I not extinguish the spark of existence which you had so wantonly bestowed? I know not; despair had not yet taken possession of me; my feelings were those of rage and revenge.

I could with pleasure have destroyed the cottage and its inhabitants, and have glutted myself with their shrieks and misery.

'When night came, I quitted my retreat, and wandered in the wood; and now, no longer restrained by the fear of discovery, I gave vent to my anguish in fearful howlings. I was like a wild beast that had broken the toils; destroying the objects that obstructed me, and ranging through the wood with a stag-like swiftness. Oh! what a miserable night I passed! the cold stars shone in mockery, and the bare trees waved their branches above me: now and then the sweet voice of a bird burst forth amidst the universal stillness. All, save I, were at rest or in enjoyment: I, like the arch fiend, bore a hell within me;* and, finding myself unsympathized with, wished to tear up the trees, spread havoc and destruction around me, and then to have sat down and enjoyed the ruin.

'But this was a luxury of sensation that could not endure; I became fatigued with excess of bodily exertion, and sank on the damp grass in the sick impotence of despair. There was none among the myriads of men that existed who would pity or assist me; and should I feel kindness towards my enemies? No: from that moment I declared everlasting war against the species, and, more than all, against him who had formed me, and sent me forth to this insupportable misery.

'The sun rose; I heard the voices of men, and knew that it was impossible to return to my retreat during that day. Accordingly I hid myself in some thick underwood, determining to devote the ensuing hours to reflection on my situation.

'The pleasant sunshine, and the pure air of day, restored me to some degree of tranquillity; and when I considered what had passed at the cottage, I could not help believing that I had been too hasty in my conclusions. I had certainly acted imprudently. It was apparent that my conversation had interested the father in my behalf, and I was a fool in having exposed my person to the horror of his children. I ought to have familiarized the old De Lacy to me, and by degrees have discovered myself to the rest of his family, when they should have been prepared for my approach. But I did not believe my errors to be irretrievable; and, after much consideration,

I resolved to return to the cottage, seek the old man, and by my representations win him to my party.

'These thoughts calmed me, and in the afternoon I sank into a profound sleep; but the fever of my blood did not allow me to be visited by peaceful dreams. The horrible scene of the preceding day was for ever acting before my eyes; the females were flying, and the enraged Felix tearing me from his father's feet. I awoke exhausted; and, finding that it was already night, I crept forth from my hiding-place, and went in search of food.

'When my hunger was appeased, I directed my steps towards the well-known path that conducted to the cottage. All there was at peace. I crept into my hovel, and remained in silent expectation of the accustomed hour when the family arose. That hour past, the sun mounted high in the heavens, but the cottagers did not appear. I trembled violently, apprehending some dreadful misfortune. The inside of the cottage was dark, and I heard no motion; I cannot describe of the agony of this suspence.

'Presently two countrymen passed by; but, pausing near the cottage, they entered into conversation, using violent gesticulations; but I did not understand what they said, as they spoke the language of the country, which differed from that of my protectors. Soon after, however, Felix approached with another man: I was surprised, as I knew that he had not quitted the cottage that morning, and waited anxiously to discover, from his discourse, the meaning of these unusual appearances.

' "Do you consider," said his companion to him, "that you will be obliged to pay three months' rent, and to lose the produce of your garden? I do not wish to take any unfair advantage, and I beg therefore that you will take some days to consider of your determination."

' "It is utterly useless," replied Felix, "we can never again inhabit your cottage. The life of my father is in the greatest danger, owing to the dreadful circumstance that I have related. My wife and my sister will never recover their horror. I entreat you not to reason with me any more. Take possession of your tenement, and let me fly from this place."

'Felix trembled violently as he said this. He and his companion entered the cottage, in which they remained for a few minutes, and then departed. I never saw any of the family of De Lacy more.

'I continued for the remainder of the day in my hovel in a state of utter and stupid despair. My protectors had departed, and had broken the only link that held me to the world. For the first time the feelings of revenge and hatred filled my bosom, and I did not strive to controul them; but, allowing myself to be borne away by the stream, I bent my mind towards injury and death. When I thought of my friends, of the mild voice of De Lacy, the gentle eyes of Agatha, and the exquisite beauty of the Arabian, these thoughts vanished, and a gush of tears somewhat soothed me. But again, when I reflected that they had spurned and deserted me, anger returned, a rage of anger; and, unable to injure any thing human, I turned my fury towards inanimate objects. As night advanced, I placed a variety of combustibles around the cottage; and, after having destroyed every vestige of cultivation in the garden, I waited with forced impatience until the moon had sunk to commence my operations.

'As the night advanced, a fierce wind arose from the woods, and quickly dispersed the clouds that had loitered in the heavens: the blast tore along like a mighty avalanche, and produced a kind of insanity in my spirits, that burst all bounds of reason and reflection. I lighted the dry branch of a tree, and danced with fury around the devoted cottage, my eyes still fixed on the western horizon, the edge of which the moon nearly touched. A part of its orb was at length hid, and I waved my brand; it sunk, and, with a loud scream, I fired the straw, and heath, and bushes, which I had collected. The wind fanned the fire, and the cottage was quickly enveloped by the flames, which clung to it, and licked it with their forked and destroying tongues.

'As soon as I was convinced that no assistance could save any part of the habitation, I quitted the scene, and sought for refuge in the woods.

'And now, with the world before me, whither should I bend my steps?* I resolved to fly far from the scene of my misfortunes; but to me, hated and despised, every country must be equally horrible. At length the thought of you crossed my mind. I learned from your papers that you were my father, my creator; and to whom could I apply with more fitness than to him who had given me life? Among the lessons that Felix had bestowed upon Safie geography had not been omitted: I had learned from these the relative situations of the different countries of the earth. You had mentioned Geneva as the name of your native town; and towards this place I resolved to proceed.

'But how was I to direct myself? I knew that I must travel in a south-westerly direction to reach my destination; but the sun was my only guide. I did not know the names of the towns that I was to pass through, nor could I ask information from a single human being; but I did not despair. From you only could I hope for succour, although towards you I felt no sentiment but that of hatred. Unfeeling, heartless creator! you had endowed me with perceptions and passions, and then cast me abroad an object for the scorn and horror of mankind. But on you only had I any claim for pity and re- dress, and from you I determined to seek that justice which I vainly attempted to gain from any other being that wore the human form.

'My travels were long, and the sufferings I endured intense. It was late in autumn when I quitted the district where I had so long resided. I travelled only at night, fearful of encounter- ing the visage of a human being. Nature decayed around me, and the sun became heatless; rain and snow poured around me; mighty rivers were frozen; the surface of the earth was hard, and chill, and bare, and I found no shelter. Oh, earth! how often did I imprecate curses on the cause of my being! The mildness of my nature had fled, and all within me was turned to gall and bitterness. The nearer I approached to your habitation, the more deeply did I feel the spirit of re- venge enkindled in my heart. Snow fell, and the waters were hardened, but I rested not. A few incidents now and then directed me, and I possessed a map of the country; but I often wandered wide from my path. The agony of my feelings al- lowed me no respite: no incident occurred from which my

rage and misery could not extract its food; but a circumstance
that happened when I arrived on the confines of Switzerland,
when the sun had recovered its warmth, and the earth again
began to look green, confirmed in an especial manner the
bitterness and horror of my feelings.

'I generally rested during the day, and travelled only when
I was secured by night from the view of man. One morning,
however, finding that my path lay through a deep wood, I
ventured to continue my journey after the sun had risen; the
day, which was one of the first of spring, cheered even me by
the loveliness of its sunshine and the balminess of the air. I
felt emotions of gentleness and pleasure, that had long appeared dead, revive within me. Half surprised by the novelty
of these sensations, I allowed myself to be borne away by
them; and, forgetting my solitude and deformity, dared to be
happy. Soft tears again bedewed my cheeks, and I even raised
my humid eyes with thankfulness towards the blessed sun
which bestowed such joy upon me.

'I continued to wind among the paths of the wood, until I
came to its boundary, which was skirted by a deep and rapid
river, into which many of the trees bent their branches, now
budding with the fresh spring. Here I paused, not exactly
knowing what path to pursue, when I heard the sound of
voices, that induced me to conceal myself under the shade of
a cypress. I was scarcely hid, when a young girl came running
towards the spot where I was concealed, laughing as if she ran
from some one in sport. She continued her course along the
precipitous sides of the river, when suddenly her foot slipt,
and she fell into the rapid stream. I rushed from my hiding-
place, and, with extreme labour from the force of the current,
saved her, and dragged her to shore. She was senseless; and I
endeavoured, by every means in my power, to restore animation, when I was suddenly interrupted by the approach of
a rustic, who was probably the person from whom she had
playfully fled. On seeing me, he darted towards me, and,
tearing the girl from my arms, hastened towards the deeper
parts of the wood. I followed speedily, I hardly knew why;
but when the man saw me draw near, he aimed a gun, which
he carried, at my body, and fired. I sunk to the ground,

and my injurer, with increased swiftness, escaped into the wood.

'This was then the reward of my benevolence! I had saved a human being from destruction, and, as a recompence, I now writhed under the miserable pain of a wound, which shattered the flesh and bone. The feelings of kindness and gentleness, which I had entertained but a few moments before, gave place to hellish rage and gnashing of teeth. Inflamed by pain, I vowed eternal hatred and vengeance to all mankind. But the agony of my wound overcame me; my pulses paused, and I fainted.

'For some weeks I led a miserable life in the woods, endeavouring to cure the wound which I had received. The ball had entered my shoulder, and I knew not whether it had remained there or passed through; at any rate I had no means of extracting it. My sufferings were augmented also by the oppressive sense of the injustice and ingratitude of their infliction. My daily vows rose for revenge—a deep and deadly revenge, such as would alone compensate for the outrages and anguish I had endured.

'After some weeks my wound healed, and I continued my journey. The labours I endured were no longer to be alleviated by the bright sun or gentle breezes of spring; all joy was but a mockery, which insulted my desolate state, and made me feel more painfully that I was not made for the enjoyment of pleasure.

'But my toils now drew near a close; and, two months from this time, I reached the environs of Geneva.

'It was evening when I arrived, and I retired to a hiding-place among the fields that surround it, to meditate in what manner I should apply to you. I was oppressed by fatigue and hunger, and far too unhappy to enjoy the gentle breezes of evening, or the prospect of the sun setting behind the stupendous mountains of Jura.

'At this time a slight sleep relieved me from the pain of reflection, which was disturbed by the approach of a beautiful child, who came running into the recess I had chosen with all the sportiveness of infancy. Suddenly, as I gazed on him, an idea seized me, that this little creature was unprejudiced, and

had lived too short a time to have imbibed a horror of deformity. If, therefore, I could seize him, and educate him as
my companion and friend, I should not be so desolate in this
peopled earth.

'Urged by this impulse, I seized on the boy as he passed,
and drew him towards me. As soon as he beheld my form, he
placed his hands before his eyes, and uttered a shrill scream:
I drew his hand forcibly from his face, and said, "Child, what
is the meaning of this? I do not intend to hurt you; listen to
me."

'He struggled violently; "Let me go," he cried; "monster!
ugly wretch! you wish to eat me, and tear me to pieces—You
are an ogre—Let me go, or I will tell my papa."

' "Boy, you will never see your father again; you must come
with me."

' "Hideous monster! let me go; My papa is a Syndic—he is
M. Frankenstein—he would punish you. You dare not keep
me."

' "Frankenstein! you belong then to my enemy—to him
towards whom I have sworn eternal revenge; you shall be my
first victim."

'The child still struggled, and loaded me with epithets
which carried despair to my heart: I grasped his throat to
silence him, and in a moment he lay dead at my feet.

'I gazed on my victim, and my heart swelled with exultation
and hellish triumph: clapping my hands, I exclaimed, "I, too,
can create desolation; my enemy is not impregnable; this
death will carry despair to him, and a thousand other miseries
shall torment and destroy him."

'As I fixed my eyes on the child, I saw something glittering
on his breast. I took it; it was a portrait of a most lovely
woman. In spite of my malignity, it softened and attracted me.
For a few moments I gazed with delight on her dark eyes
fringed by deep lashes, and her lovely lips; but presently my
rage returned: I remembered that I was for ever deprived of
the delights that such beautiful creatures could bestow; and
that she whose resemblance I contemplated would, in regarding me, have changed that air of divine benignity to one
expressive of disgust and affright.

'Can you wonder that such thoughts transported me with rage? I only wonder that at that moment, instead of venting my sensations in exclamations and agony, I did not rush among mankind, and perish in the attempt to destroy them.

'While I was overcome by these feelings, I left the spot where I had committed the murder, and was seeking a more secluded hiding-place, when I perceived a woman passing near me. She was young, not indeed so beautiful as her whose portrait I held, but of an agreeable aspect, and blooming in the loveliness of youth and health. Here, I thought, is one of those whose smiles are bestowed on all but me; she shall not escape: thanks to the lessons of Felix, and the sanguinary laws of man, I have learned how to work mischief. I approached her unperceived, and placed the portrait securely in one of the folds of her dress.

'For some days I haunted the spot where these scenes had taken place; sometimes wishing to see you, sometimes resolved to quit the world and its miseries for ever. At length I wandered towards these mountains, and have ranged through their immense recesses, consumed by a burning passion which you alone can gratify. We may not part until you have promised to comply with my requisition. I am alone, and miserable; man will not associate with me; but one as deformed and horrible as myself would not deny herself to me. My companion must be of the same species, and have the same defects. This being you must create.'

CHAPTER IX

The being finished speaking, and fixed his looks upon me in expectation of a reply. But I was bewildered, perplexed, and unable to arrange my ideas sufficiently to understand the full extent of his proposition. He continued—

'You must create a female for me, with whom I can live in the interchange of those sympathies necessary for my being. This you alone can do; and I demand it of you as a right which you must not refuse.'

The latter part of his tale had kindled anew in me the anger that had died away while he narrated his peaceful life among the cottagers, and, as he said this, I could no longer suppress the rage that burned within me.

'I do refuse it,' I replied; 'and no torture shall ever extort a consent from me. You may render me the most miserable of men, but you shall never make me base in my own eyes. Shall I create another like yourself, whose joint wickedness might desolate the world. Begone! I have answered you; you may torture me, but I will never consent.'

'You are in the wrong,' replied the fiend; 'and, instead of threatening, I am content to reason with you. I am malicious because I am miserable; am I not shunned and hated by all mankind? You, my creator, would tear me to pieces, and triumph; remember that, and tell me why I should pity man more than he pities me? You would not call it murder, if you could precipitate me into one of those ice-rifts, and destroy my frame, the work of your own hands. Shall I respect man, when he contemns me? Let him live with me in the inter-change of kindness, and, instead of injury, I would bestow every benefit upon him with tears of gratitude at his accept-ance. But that cannot be; the human senses are insurmount-able barriers to our union. Yet mine shall not be the submission of abject slavery. I will revenge my injuries: if I cannot inspire love, I will cause fear; and chiefly towards you my arch-enemy, because my creator, do I swear inextinguish-able hatred. Have a care: I will work at your destruction, nor finish until I desolate your heart, so that you curse the hour of your birth.'

A fiendish rage animated him as he said this; his face was wrinkled into contortions too horrible for human eyes to behold; but presently he calmed himself, and proceeded—

'I intended to reason. This passion is detrimental to me; for you do not reflect that you are the cause of its excess. If any being felt emotions of benevolence towards me, I should return them an hundred and an hundred fold; for that one creature's sake, I would make peace with the whole kind! But I now indulge in dreams of bliss that cannot be realized. What I ask of you is reasonable and moderate; I demand a creature of another sex, but as hideous as myself: the gratification is small, but it is all that I can receive, and it shall content me. It is true, we shall be monsters, cut off from all the world; but on that account we shall be more attached to one another. Our lives will not be happy, but they will be harmless, and free from the misery I now feel. Oh! my creator, make me happy; let me feel gratitude towards you for one benefit! Let me see that I excite the sympathy of some existing thing; do not deny me my request!'

I was moved. I shuddered when I thought of the possible consequences of my consent; but I felt that there was some justice in his argument. His tale, and the feelings he now expressed, proved him to be a creature of fine sensations; and did I not, as his maker, owe him all the portion of happiness that it was in my power to bestow? He saw my change of feeling, and continued—

'If you consent, neither you nor any other human being shall ever see us again: I will go to the vast wilds of South America. My food is not that of man; I do not destroy the lamb and the kid, to glut my appetite; acorns and berries afford me sufficient nourishment. My companion will be of the same nature as myself, and will be content with the same fare. We shall make our bed of dried leaves; the sun will shine on us as on man, and will ripen our food. The picture I present to you is peaceful and human, and you must feel that you could deny it only in the wantonness of power and cruelty. Pitiless as you have been towards me, I now see compassion in your eyes; let me seize the favourable moment, and persuade you to promise what I so ardently desire.'

'You propose,' replied I, 'to fly from the habitations of man, to dwell in those wilds where the beasts of the field will be your only companions. How can you, who long for the love and sympathy of man, persevere in this exile? You will return, and again seek their kindness, and you will meet with their detestation; your evil passions will be renewed, and you will then have a companion to aid you in the task of destruction. This may not be; cease to argue the point, for I cannot consent.'

'How inconstant are your feelings! but a moment ago you were moved by my representations, and why do you again harden yourself to my complaints? I swear to you, by the earth which I inhabit, and by you that made me, that, with the companion you bestow, I will quit the neighbourhood of man, and dwell, as it may chance, in the most savage of places. My evil passions will have fled, for I shall meet with sympathy; my life will flow quietly away, and, in my dying moments, I shall not curse my maker.'

His words had a strange effect upon me. I compassionated him, and sometimes felt a wish to console him; but when I looked upon him, when I saw the filthy mass that moved and talked, my heart sickened, and my feelings were altered to those of horror and hatred. I tried to stifle these sensations; I thought, that as I could not sympathize with him, I had no right to withhold from him the small portion of happiness which was yet in my power to bestow.

'You swear,' I said, 'to be harmless; but have you not already shewn a degree of malice that should reasonably make me distrust you? May not even this be a feint that will increase your triumph by affording a wider scope for your revenge?'

'How is this? I thought I had moved your compassion, and yet you still refuse to bestow on me the only benefit that can soften my heart, and render me harmless. If I have no ties and no affections, hatred and vice must be my portion; the love of another will destroy the cause of my crimes, and I shall become a thing, of whose existence every one will be ignorant. My vices are the children of a forced solitude that I abhor; and my virtues will necessarily arise when I live in communion with an equal. I shall feel the affections of a sensitive being, and become linked to the chain of existence and events, from which I am now excluded.'

I paused some time to reflect on all he had related, and the various arguments which he had employed. I thought of the promise of virtues which he had displayed on the opening of his existence, and the subsequent blight of all kindly feeling by the loathing and scorn which his protectors had manifested towards him. His power and threats were not omitted in my calculations: a creature who could exist in the ice caves of the glaciers, and hide himself from pursuit among the ridges of inaccessible precipices, was a being possessing faculties it would be vain to cope with. After a long pause of reflection, I concluded, that the justice due both to him and my fellow-creatures demanded of me that I should comply with his request. Turning to him, therefore, I said—

'I consent to your demand, on your solemn oath to quit Europe for ever, and every other place in the neighbourhood of man, as soon as I shall deliver into your hands a female who will accompany you in your exile.'

'I swear,' he cried, 'by the sun, and by the blue sky of heaven, that if you grant my prayer, while they exist you shall never behold me again. Depart to your home, and commence your labours: I shall watch their progress with unutterable anxiety; and fear not but that when you are ready I shall appear.'

Saying this, he suddenly quitted me, fearful, perhaps, of any change in my sentiments. I saw him descend the mountain with greater speed than the flight of an eagle, and quickly lost him among the undulations of the sea of ice.

His tale had occupied the whole day; and the sun was upon the verge of the horizon when he departed. I knew that I ought to hasten my descent towards the valley, as I should soon be encompassed in darkness; but my heart was heavy, and my steps slow. The labour of winding among the little paths of the mountains, and fixing my feet firmly as I advanced, perplexed me, occupied as I was by the emotions which the occurrences of the day had produced. Night was far advanced, when I came to the half-way resting-place, and seated myself beside the fountain. The stars shone at intervals, as the clouds passed from over them; the dark pines rose before me, and every here and there a broken tree lay on the ground: it was a scene of wonderful solemnity, and stirred strange thoughts within me. I wept bitterly; and, clasping my hands in agony, I exclaimed, 'Oh! stars, and clouds, and winds, ye are all about to mock me: if ye really pity me, crush sensation and memory; let me become as nought; but if not, depart, depart and leave me in darkness.'

These were wild and miserable thoughts; but I cannot describe to you how the eternal twinkling of the stars weighed upon me, and how I listened to every blast of wind, as if it were a dull ugly siroc on its way to consume me.*

Morning dawned before I arrived at the village of Chamounix; but my presence, so haggard and strange, hardly calmed the fears of my family, who had waited the whole night in anxious expectation of my return.

The following day we returned to Geneva. The intention of my father in coming had been to divert my mind, and to restore me to my lost tranquillity; but the medicine had been fatal. And, unable to account for the excess of misery I appeared to suffer, he hastened to return home, hoping the quiet and monotony of a domestic life would by degrees alleviate my sufferings from whatsoever cause they might spring.

For myself, I was passive in all their arrangements; and the gentle affection of my beloved Elizabeth was inadequate to draw me from the depth of my despair. The promise I had made to the dæmon weighed upon my mind, like Dante's iron cowl on the heads of the hellish hypocrites.* All pleasures of earth and sky passed before me like a dream, and that thought only had to me the reality of life. Can you wonder, that sometimes a kind of insanity possessed me, or that I saw continually about me a multitude of filthy animals inflicting on me incessant torture, that often extorted screams and bitter groans?

By degrees, however, these feelings became calmed. I entered again into the every-day scene of life, if not with interest, at least with some degree of tranquillity.

END OF VOLUME II.

VOLUME III

CHAPTER I

Day after day, week after week, passed away on my return to Geneva; and I could not collect the courage to recommence my work. I feared the vengeance of the disappointed fiend, yet I was unable to overcome my repugnance to the task which was enjoined me. I found that I could not compose a female without again devoting several months to profound study and laborious disquisition. I had heard of some discoveries having been made by an English philosopher, the knowledge of which was material to my success, and I sometimes thought of obtaining my father's consent to visit England for this purpose; but I clung to every pretence of delay, and could not resolve to interrupt my returning tranquillity. My health, which had hitherto declined, was now much restored; and my spirits, when unchecked by the memory of my unhappy promise, rose proportionably. My father saw this change with pleasure, and he turned his thoughts towards the best method of eradicating the remains of my melancholy, which every now and then would return by fits, and with a devouring blackness overcast the approaching sunshine. At these moments I took refuge in the most perfect solitude. I passed whole days on the lake alone in a little boat, watching the clouds, and listening to the rippling of the waves, silent and listless. But the fresh air and bright sun seldom failed to restore me to some degree of composure; and, on my return, I met the salutations of my friends with a readier smile and a more cheerful heart.

It was after my return from one of these rambles that my father, calling me aside, thus addressed me:—

'I am happy to remark, my dear son, that you have resumed your former pleasures, and seem to be returning to yourself. And yet you are still unhappy, and still avoid our society. For some time I was lost in conjecture as to the cause of this; but yesterday an idea struck me, and if it is well founded, I conjure you to avow it. Reserve on such a point would be not only useless, but draw down treble misery on us all.'

I trembled violently at this exordium, and my father continued—

'I confess, my son, that I have always looked forward to your marriage with your cousin as the tie of our domestic comfort, and the stay of my declining years. You were attached to each other from your earliest infancy; you studied together, and appeared, in dispositions and tastes, entirely suited to one another. But so blind is the experience of man, that what I conceived to be the best assistants to my plan may have entirely destroyed it. You, perhaps, regard her as your sister, without any wish that she might become your wife. Nay, you may have met with another whom you may love; and, considering yourself as bound in honour to your cousin, this struggle may occasion the poignant misery which you appear to feel.'

'My dear father, re-assure yourself. I love my cousin tenderly and sincerely. I never saw any woman who excited, as Elizabeth does, my warmest admiration and affection. My future hopes and prospects are entirely bound up in the expectation of our union.'

'The expression of your sentiments on this subject, my dear Victor, gives me more pleasure than I have for some time experienced. If you feel thus, we shall assuredly be happy, however present events may cast a gloom over us. But it is this gloom, which appears to have taken so strong a hold of your mind, that I wish to dissipate. Tell me, therefore, whether you object to an immediate solemnization of the marriage. We have been unfortunate, and recent events have drawn us from that every-day tranquillity befitting my years and infirmities. You are younger; yet I do not suppose, possessed as you are of a competent fortune, that an early marriage would at all interfere with any future plans of honour and utility that you may have formed. Do not suppose, however, that I wish to dictate happiness to you, or that a delay on your part would cause me any serious uneasiness. Interpret my words with candour, and answer me, I conjure you, with confidence and sincerity.'

I listened to my father in silence, and remained for some time incapable of offering any reply. I revolved rapidly in my mind a multitude of thoughts, and endeavoured to arrive at some conclusion. Alas! to me the idea of an immediate union with my cousin was one of horror and dismay. I was bound by a solemn promise, which I had not yet fulfilled, and dared not break; or, if I did, what manifold miseries might not impend over me and my devoted family! Could I enter into a festival with this deadly weight yet hanging round my neck, and bowing me to the ground. I must perform my engagement, and let the monster depart with his mate, before I allowed myself to enjoy the delight of an union from which I expected peace.

I remembered also the necessity imposed upon me of either journeying to England, or entering into a long correspondence with those philosophers of that country, whose knowledge and discoveries were of indispensable use to me in my present undertaking. The latter method of obtaining the desired intelligence was dilatory and unsatisfactory: besides, any variation was agreeable to me, and I was delighted with the idea of spending a year or two in change of scene and variety of occupation, in absence from my family; during which period some event might happen which would restore me to them in peace and happiness: my promise might be fulfilled, and the monster have departed; or some accident might occur to destroy him, and put an end to my slavery for ever.

These feelings dictated my answer to my father. I expressed a wish to visit England; but, concealing the true reasons of this request, I clothed my desires under the guise of wishing to travel and see the world before I sat down for life within the walls of my native town.

I urged my entreaty with earnestness, and my father was easily induced to comply; for a more indulgent and less dictatorial parent did not exist upon earth. Our plan was soon arranged. I should travel to Strasburgh, where Clerval would join me. Some short time would be spent in the towns of Holland, and our principal stay would be in England. We should return by France; and it was agreed that the tour should occupy the space of two years.

My father pleased himself with the reflection, that my union with Elizabeth should take place immediately on my return to Geneva. 'These two years,' said he, 'will pass swiftly, and it will be the last delay that will oppose itself to your happiness. And, indeed, I earnestly desire that period to arrive, when we shall all be united, and neither hopes or fears arise to disturb our domestic calm.'

'I am content,' I replied, 'with your arrangement. By that time we shall both have become wiser, and I hope happier, than we at present are.' I sighed; but my father kindly forbore to question me further concerning the cause of my dejection. He hoped that new scenes, and the amusement of travelling, would restore my tranquillity.

I now made arrangements for my journey; but one feeling haunted me, which filled me with fear and agitation. During my absence I should leave my friends unconscious of the existence of their enemy, and unprotected from his attacks, exasperated as he might be by my departure. But he had promised to follow me wherever I might go; and would he not accompany me to England? This imagination was dreadful in itself, but soothing, inasmuch as it supposed the safety of my friends. I was agonized with the idea of the possibility that the reverse of this might happen. But through the whole period during which I was the slave of my creature, I allowed myself to be governed by the impulses of the moment; and my present sensations strongly intimated that the fiend would follow me, and exempt my family from the danger of his machinations.

It was in the latter end of August that I departed, to pass two years of exile. Elizabeth approved of the reasons of my departure, and only regretted that she had not the same opportunities of enlarging her experience, and cultivating her understanding. She wept, however, as she bade me farewell, and entreated me to return happy and tranquil. 'We all,' said she, 'depend upon you; and if you are miserable, what must be our feelings?'

I threw myself into the carriage that was to convey me away, hardly knowing whither I was going, and careless of what was passing around. I remembered only, and it was with a bitter anguish that I reflected on it, to order that my chemical instruments should be packed to go with me: for I resolved to fulfil my promise while abroad, and return, if possible, a free man. Filled with dreary imaginations, I passed through many beautiful and majestic scenes; but my eyes were fixed and unobserving. I could only think of the bourne of my travels, and the work which was to occupy me whilst they endured.

After some days spent in listless indolence, during which I traversed many leagues, I arrived at Strasburgh, where I waited two days for Clerval. He came. Alas, how great was the contrast between us! He was alive to every new scene; joyful when he saw the beauties of the setting sun, and more happy when he beheld it rise, and recommence a new day. He pointed out to me the shifting colours of the landscape, and the appearances of the sky. 'This is what it is to live;' he cried, 'now I enjoy existence! But you, my dear Frankenstein, wherefore are you desponding and sorrowful?' In truth, I was occupied by gloomy thoughts, and neither saw the descent of the evening star, nor the golden sun-rise reflected in the Rhine.— And you, my friend, would be far more amused with the journal of Clerval, who observed the scenery with an eye of feeling and delight, than to listen to my reflections. I, a miserable wretch, haunted by a curse that shut up every avenue to enjoyment.

We had agreed to descend the Rhine in a boat from Strasburgh to Rotterdam, whence we might take shipping for London. During this voyage, we passed by many willowy islands, and saw several beautiful towns. We staid a day at Manheim, and, on the fifth from our departure from Strasburgh, arrived at Mayence. The course of the Rhine below Mayence becomes much more picturesque. The river descends rapidly, and winds between hills, not high, but steep, and of beautiful forms. We saw many ruined castles standing on the edges of precipices, surrounded by black woods, high and inaccessible. This part of the Rhine, indeed, presents a singularly variegated landscape. In one spot you view rugged hills, ruined castles overlooking tremendous precipices, with the dark Rhine rushing beneath; and, on the sudden turn of a promontory, flourishing vineyards, with green sloping banks, and a meandering river, and populous towns, occupy the scene.

We travelled at the time of the vintage, and heard the song of the labourers, as we glided down the stream. Even I, depressed in mind, and my spirits continually agitated by gloomy feelings, even I was pleased. I lay at the bottom of the boat, and, as I gazed on the cloudless blue sky, I seemed to drink in a tranquillity to which I had long been a stranger. And if these were my sensations, who can describe those of Henry? He felt as if he had been transported to Fairy-land, and enjoyed a happiness seldom tasted by man. 'I have seen,' he said, 'the most beautiful scenes of my own country; I have visited the lakes of Lucerne and Uri, where the snowy mountains descend almost perpendicularly to the water, casting black and impenetrable shades, which would cause a gloomy and mournful appearance, were it not for the most verdant islands that relieve the eye by their gay appearance; I have seen this lake agitated by a tempest, when the wind tore up whirlwinds of water, and gave you an idea of what the waterspout must be on the great ocean, and the waves dash with fury the base of the mountain, where the priest and his mistress were overwhelmed by an avalanche, and where their dying voices are still said to be heard amid the pauses of the nightly wind; I have seen the mountains of La Valais, and the Pays de Vaud: but this country, Victor, pleases me more than all those wonders. The mountains of Switzerland are more majestic and strange; but there is a charm in the banks of this divine river, that I never before saw equalled. Look at that castle which overhangs yon precipice; and that also on the island, almost concealed amongst the foliage of those lovely trees; and now that group of labourers coming from among their vines; and that village half-hid in the recess of the mountain. Oh, surely, the spirit that inhabits and guards this place has a source more in harmony with man, than those who pile the glacier, or retire to the inaccessible peaks of the mountains of our own country.'

Clerval! beloved friend! even now it delights me to record your words, and to dwell on the praise of which you are so eminently deserving. He was a being formed in the 'very poetry of nature.'* His wild and enthusiastic imagination was chastened by the sensibility of his heart. His soul overflowed with ardent affections, and his friendship was of that devoted and wondrous nature that the worldly-minded teach us to look for only in the imagination. But even human sympathies were not sufficient to satisfy his eager mind. The scenery of external nature, which others regard only with admiration, he loved with ardour:.

> ——————'The sounding cataract
> Haunted *him* like a passion: the tall rock,
> The mountain, and the deep and gloomy wood,
> Their colours and their forms, were then to him
> An appetite: a feeling, and a love,
> That had no need of a remoter charm,
> By thought supplied, or any interest
> Unborrowed from the eye.'*

And where does he now exist? Is this gentle and lovely being lost for ever? Has this mind so replete with ideas, imaginations fanciful and magnificent, which formed a world, whose existence depended on the life of its creator; has this mind perished? Does it now only exist in my memory? No, it is not thus; your form so divinely wrought, and beaming with beauty, has decayed, but your spirit still visits and consoles your unhappy friend.

Pardon this gush of sorrow; these ineffectual words are but a slight tribute to the unexampled worth of Henry, but they soothe my heart, overflowing with the anguish which his remembrance creates. I will proceed with my tale.

Beyond Cologne we descended to the plains of Holland; and we resolved to post the remainder of our way; for the wind was contrary, and the stream of the river was too gentle to aid us.

Our journey here lost the interest arising from beautiful scenery; but we arrived in a few days at Rotterdam, whence we proceeded by sea to England. It was on a clear morning, in the latter days of December, that I first saw the white cliffs of

Britain. The banks of the Thames presented a new scene; they were flat, but fertile, and almost every town was marked by the remembrance of some story. We saw Tilbury Fort, and remembered the Spanish armada; Gravesend, Woolwich, and Greenwich, places which I had heard of even in my country.

At length we saw the numerous steeples of London, St Paul's towering above all, and the Tower famed in English history.

CHAPTER II

London was our present point of rest; we determined to remain several months in this wonderful and celebrated city. Clerval desired the intercourse of the men of genius and talent who flourished at this time; but this was with me a secondary object; I was principally occupied with the means of obtaining the information necessary for the completion of my promise, and quickly availed myself of the letters of introduction that I had brought with me, addressed to the most distinguished natural philosophers.

If this journey had taken place during my days of study and happiness, it would have afforded me inexpressible pleasure. But a blight had come over my existence, and I only visited these people for the sake of the information they might give me on the subject in which my interest was so terribly profound. Company was irksome to me; when alone, I could fill my mind with the sights of heaven and earth; the voice of Henry soothed me, and I could thus cheat myself into a transitory peace. But busy uninteresting joyous faces brought back despair to my heart. I saw an insurmountable barrier placed between me and my fellow-men; this barrier was sealed with the blood of William and Justine; and to reflect on the events connected with those names filled my soul with anguish.

But in Clerval I saw the image of my former self; he was inquisitive, and anxious to gain experience and instruction. The difference of manners which he observed was to him an inexhaustible source of instruction and amusement. He was for ever busy; and the only check to his enjoyments was my sorrowful and dejected mien. I tried to conceal this as much as possible, that I might not debar him from the pleasures natural to one who was entering on a new scene of life, undisturbed by any care or bitter recollection. I often refused to accompany him, alleging another engagement, that I might remain alone. I now also began to collect the materials necessary for my new creation, and this was to me like the torture of single drops of water continually falling on the head. Every thought that was devoted to it was an extreme anguish, and every word that I spoke in allusion to it caused my lips to quiver, and my heart to palpitate.

After passing some months in London, we received a letter from a person in Scotland, who had formerly been our visitor at Geneva. He mentioned the beauties of his native country, and asked us if those were not sufficient allurements to induce us to prolong our journey as far north as Perth, where he resided. Clerval eagerly desired to accept this invitation; and I, although I abhorred society, wished to view again mountains and streams, and all the wondrous works with which Nature adorns her chosen dwelling-places.

We had arrived in England at the beginning of October, and it was now February. We accordingly determined to commence our journey towards the north at the expiration of another month. In this expedition we did not intend to follow the great road to Edinburgh, but to visit Windsor, Oxford, Matlock, and the Cumberland lakes, resolving to arrive at the completion of this tour about the end of July. I packed my chemical instruments, and the materials I had collected, resolving to finish my labours in some obscure nook in the northern highlands of Scotland.

We quitted London on the 27th of March, and remained a few days at Windsor, rambling in its beautiful forest. This was a new scene to us mountaineers; the majestic oaks, the quantity of game, and the herds of stately deer, were all novelties to us.

From thence we proceeded to Oxford. As we entered this city, our minds were filled with the remembrance of the events that had been transacted there more than a century and a half before. It was here that Charles I had collected his forces. This city had remained faithful to him, after the whole nation had forsaken his cause to join the standard of parliament and liberty. The memory of that unfortunate king, and his companions, the amiable Falkland,* the insolent Gower,* his queen, and son, gave a peculiar interest to every part of the city, which they might be supposed to have inhabited. The spirit of elder days found a dwelling here, and we delighted to trace its footsteps. If these feelings had not found an imaginary gratification, the appearance of the city had yet in itself sufficient beauty to obtain our admiration. The colleges are ancient and picturesque; the streets are almost magnificent; and the lovely Isis,* which flows beside it through meadows of exquisite verdure, is spread forth into a placid expanse of waters, which reflects its majestic assemblage of towers, and spires, and domes, embosomed among aged trees.

I enjoyed this scene; and yet my enjoyment was embittered both by the memory of the past, and the anticipation of the future. I was formed for peaceful happiness. During my youthful days discontent never visited my mind; and if I was ever overcome by *ennui*,* the sight of what is beautiful in nature, or the study of what is excellent and sublime in the productions of man, could always interest my heart, and communicate elasticity to my spirits. But I am a blasted tree; the bolt has entered my soul; and I felt then that I should survive to exhibit, what I shall soon cease to be—a miserable spectacle of wrecked humanity, pitiable to others, and abhorrent to myself.

We passed a considerable period at Oxford, rambling among its environs, and endeavouring to identify every spot which might relate to the most animating epoch of English history. Our little voyages of discovery were often prolonged by the successive objects that presented themselves. We visited the tomb of the illustrious Hampden, and the field on which that patriot fell.* For a moment my soul was elevated from its debasing and miserable fears to contemplate the divine ideas of liberty and self-sacrifice, of which these sights were the monuments and the remembrancers. For an instant I dared to shake off my chains, and look around me with a free and lofty spirit; but the iron had eaten into my flesh, and I sank again, trembling and hopeless, into my miserable self.

We left Oxford with regret, and proceeded to Matlock, which was our next place of rest. The country in the neighbourhood of this village resembled, to a greater degree, the scenery of Switzerland; but every thing is on a lower scale, and the green hills want the crown of distant white Alps, which always attend on the piny mountains of my native country. We visited the wondrous cave, and the little cabinets of natural history, where the curiosities are disposed in the same manner as in the collections at Servox and Chamounix.* The latter name made me tremble, when pronounced by Henry; and I hastened to quit Matlock, with which that terrible scene was thus associated.

From Derby still journeying northward, we passed two months in Cumberland and Westmoreland. I could now almost fancy myself among the Swiss mountains. The little patches of snow which yet lingered on the northern sides of the mountains, the lakes, and the dashing of the rocky streams, were all familiar and dear sights to me. Here also we made some acquaintances, who almost contrived to cheat me into happiness.* The delight of Clerval was proportionably greater than mine; his mind expanded in the company of men of talent, and he found in his own nature greater capacities and resources than he could have imagined himself to have possessed while he associated with his inferiors. 'I could pass my life here,' said he to me; 'and among these mountains I should scarcely regret Switzerland and the Rhine.'

But he found that a traveller's life is one that includes much pain amidst its enjoyments. His feelings are for ever on the stretch; and when he begins to sink into repose, he finds himself obliged to quit that on which he rests in pleasure for something new, which again engages his attention, and which also he forsakes for other novelties.

We had scarcely visited the various lakes of Cumberland and Westmoreland, and conceived an affection for some of the inhabitants, when the period of our appointment with our Scotch friend approached, and we left them to travel on.

For my own part I was not sorry. I had now neglected my promise for some time, and I feared the effects of the dæmon's disappointment. He might remain in Switzerland, and wreak his vengeance on my relatives. This idea pursued me, and tormented me at every moment from which I might otherwise have snatched repose and peace. I waited for my letters with feverish impatience: if they were delayed, I was miserable, and overcome by a thousand fears; and when they arrived, and I saw the superscription of Elizabeth or my father, I hardly dared to read and ascertain my fate. Sometimes I thought that the fiend followed me, and might expedite my remissness by murdering my companion. When these thoughts possessed me, I would not quit Henry for a moment, but followed him as his shadow, to protect him from the fancied rage of his destroyer. I felt as if I had committed some great crime, the consciousness of which haunted me. I was guiltless, but I had indeed drawn down a horrible curse upon my head, as mortal as that of crime.

I visited Edinburgh with languid eyes and mind; and yet that city might have interested the most unfortunate being. Clerval did not like it so well as Oxford; for the antiquity of the latter city was more pleasing to him. But the beauty and regularity of the new town of Edinburgh, its romantic castle, and its environs, the most delightful in the world, Arthur's Seat, St Bernard's Well, and the Pentland Hills, compensated him for the change, and filled him with cheerfulness and admiration. But I was impatient to arrive at the termination of my journey.

We left Edinburgh in a week, passing through Coupar, St Andrews, and along the banks of the Tay, to Perth, where our friend expected us.* But I was in no mood to laugh and talk with strangers, or enter into their feelings or plans with the good humour expected from a guest; and accordingly I told Clerval that I wished to make the tour of Scotland alone. 'Do you,' said I, 'enjoy yourself, and let this be our rendezvous. I may be absent a month or two; but do not interfere with my motions, I entreat you: leave me to peace and solitude for a short time; and when I return, I hope it will be with a lighter heart, more congenial to your own temper.'

Henry wished to dissuade me; but, seeing me bent on this plan, ceased to remonstrate. He entreated me to write often. 'I had rather be with you,' he said, 'in your solitary rambles, than with these Scotch people, whom I do not know: hasten then, my dear friend, to return, that I may again feel myself somewhat at home, which I cannot do in your absence.'

Having parted from my friend, I determined to visit some remote spot of Scotland, and finish my work in solitude. I did not doubt but that the monster followed me, and would discover himself to me when I should have finished, that he might receive his companion.

With this resolution I traversed the northern highlands, and fixed on one of the remotest of the Orkneys as the scene [of my] labours. It was a place fitted for such a work, being hardly more than a rock, whose high sides were continually beaten upon by the waves. The soil was barren, scarcely affording pasture for a few miserable cows, and oatmeal for its inhabitants, which consisted of five persons, whose gaunt and scraggy limbs gave tokens of their miserable fare. Vegetables and bread, when they indulged in such luxuries, and even fresh water, was to be procured from the main land, which was about five miles distant.

On the whole island there were but three miserable huts, and one of these was vacant when I arrived. This I hired. It contained but two rooms, and these exhibited all the squalidness of the most miserable penury. The thatch had fallen in, the walls were unplastered, and the door was off its hinges. I ordered it to be repaired, bought some furniture, and took possession; an incident which would, doubtless, have occasioned some surprise, had not all the senses of the cottagers been benumbed by want and squalid poverty. As it was, I lived ungazed at and unmolested, hardly thanked for the pittance of food and clothes which I gave; so much does suffering blunt even the coarsest sensations of men.

In this retreat I devoted the morning to labour; but in the evening, when the weather permitted, I walked on the stony beach of the sea, to listen to the waves as they roared, and dashed at my feet. It was a monotonous, yet ever-changing scene. I thought of Switzerland; it was far different from this desolate and appalling landscape. Its hills are covered with vines, and its cottages are scattered thickly in the plains. Its fair lakes reflect a blue and gentle sky; and, when troubled by the winds, their tumult is but as the play of a lively infant, when compared to the roarings of the giant ocean.

In this manner I distributed my occupations when I first arrived; but, as I proceeded in my labour, it became every day more horrible and irksome to me. Sometimes I could not prevail on myself to enter my laboratory for several days; and at other times I toiled day and night in order to complete my work. It was indeed a filthy process in which I was engaged. During my first experiment, a kind of enthusiastic frenzy had blinded me to the horror of my employment; my mind was intently fixed on the sequel of my labour, and my eyes were shut to the horror of my proceedings. But now I went to it in cold blood, and my heart often sickened at the work of my hands.

Thus situated, employed in the most detestable occupation, immersed in a solitude where nothing could for an instant call my attention from the actual scene in which I was engaged, my spirits became unequal; I grew restless and nervous. Every moment I feared to meet my persecutor. Sometimes I sat with my eyes fixed on the ground, fearing to raise them lest they should encounter the object which I so much dreaded to behold. I feared to wander from the sight of my fellow-creatures, lest when alone he should come to claim his companion.

In the mean time I worked on, and my labour was already considerably advanced. I looked towards its completion with a tremulous and eager hope, which I dared not trust myself to question, but which was intermixed with obscure forebodings of evil, that made my heart sicken in my bosom.

CHAPTER III

I sat one evening in my laboratory; the sun had set, and the moon was just rising from the sea; I had not sufficient light for my employment, and I remained idle, in a pause of consideration of whether I should leave my labour for the night, or hasten its conclusion by an unremitting attention to it. As I sat, a train of reflection occurred to me, which led me to consider the effects of what I was now doing. Three years before I was engaged in the same manner, and had created a fiend whose unparalleled barbarity had desolated my heart, and filled it for ever with the bitterest remorse. I was now about to form another being, of whose dispositions I was alike ignorant; she might become ten thousand times more malignant than her mate, and delight, for its own sake, in murder and wretchedness. He had sworn to quit the neighbourhood of man, and hide himself in deserts; but she had not; and she, who in all probability was to become a thinking and reasoning animal, might refuse to comply with a compact made before her creation. They might even hate each other; the creature who already lived loathed his own deformity, and might he not conceive a greater abhorrence for it when it came before his eyes in the female form? She also might turn with disgust from him to the superior beauty of man; she might quit him, and he be again alone, exasperated by the fresh provocation of being deserted by one of his own species.

Even if they were to leave Europe, and inhabit the deserts of the new world, yet one of the first results of those sympathies for which the dæmon thirsted would be children, and a race of devils would be propagated upon the earth, who might make the very existence of the species of man a condition precarious and full of terror. Had I a right, for my own benefit, to inflict this curse upon everlasting generations? I had before been moved by the sophisms of the being I had created; I had been struck senseless by his fiendish threats: but now, for the first time, the wickedness of my promise burst upon me; I shuddered to think that future ages might curse me as their pest, whose selfishness had not hesitated to buy its own peace at the price perhaps of the existence of the whole human race.

I trembled, and my heart failed within me; when, on looking up, I saw, by the light of the moon, the dæmon at the casement. A ghastly grin wrinkled his lips as he gazed on me, where I sat fulfilling the task which he had allotted to me. Yes, he had followed me in my travels; he had loitered in forests, hid himself in caves, or taken refuge in wide and desert heaths; and he now came to mark my progress, and claim the fulfilment of my promise.

As I looked on him, his countenance expressed the utmost extent of malice and treachery. I thought with a sensation of madness on my promise of creating another like to him, and, trembling with passion, tore to pieces the thing on which I was engaged. The wretch saw me destroy the creature on whose future existence he depended for happiness, and, with a howl of devilish despair and revenge, withdrew.

I left the room, and, locking the door, made a solemn vow in my own heart never to resume my labours; and then, with trembling steps, I sought my own apartment. I was alone; none were near me to dissipate the gloom, and relieve me from the sickening oppression of the most terrible reveries.

Several hours passed, and I remained near my window gazing on the sea; it was almost motionless, for the winds were hushed, and all nature reposed under the eye of the quiet moon. A few fishing vessels alone specked the water, and now and then the gentle breeze wafted the sound of voices, as the fishermen called to one another. I felt the silence, although I was hardly conscious of its extreme profundity, until my ear was suddenly arrested by the paddling of oars near the shore, and a person landed close to my house.

In a few minutes after, I heard the creaking of my door, as if some one endeavoured to open it softly. I trembled from head to foot; I felt a presentiment of who it was, and wished to rouse one of the peasants who dwelt in a cottage not far from mine; but I was overcome by the sensation of helplessness, so often felt in frightful dreams, when you in vain endeavour to fly from an impending danger, and was rooted to the spot.

Presently I heard the sound of footsteps along the passage; the door opened, and the wretch whom I dreaded appeared. Shutting the door, he approached me, and said, in a smothered voice—

'You have destroyed the work which you began; what is it that you intend? Do you dare to break your promise? I have endured toil and misery: I left Switzerland with you; I crept along the shores of the Rhine, among its willow islands, and over the summits of its hills. I have dwelt many months in the heaths of England, and among the deserts of Scotland. I have endured incalculable fatigue, and cold, and hunger; do you dare destroy my hopes?'

'Begone! I do break my promise; never will I create another like yourself, equal in deformity and wickedness.'

'Slave, I before reasoned with you, but you have proved yourself unworthy of my condescension. Remember that I have power; you believe yourself miserable, but I can make you so wretched that the light of day will be hateful to you. You are my creator, but I am your master;—obey!'

'The hour of my weakness is past, and the period of your power* is arrived. Your threats cannot move me to do an act of wickedness; but they confirm me in a resolution of not creating you a companion in vice. Shall I, in cool blood, set loose upon the earth a dæmon, whose delight is in death and wretchedness. Begone! I am firm, and your words will only exasperate my rage.'

The monster saw my determination in my face, and gnashed his teeth in the impotence of anger. 'Shall each man,' cried he, 'find a wife for his bosom, and each beast have his mate, and I be alone? I had feelings of affection, and they were requited by detestation and scorn. Man, you may hate; but beware! Your hours will pass in dread and misery, and soon the bolt will fall which must ravish from you your happiness for ever. Are you to be happy, while I grovel in the intensity of my wretchedness? You can blast my other passions; but revenge remains—revenge, henceforth dearer than light or food! I may die; but first you, my tyrant and tormentor, shall curse the sun that gazes on your misery. Beware; for I am fearless, and therefore powerful. I will watch with the wiliness of a snake, that I may sting with its venom. Man, you shall repent of the injuries you inflict.'

'Devil, cease; and do not poison the air with these sounds of malice. I have declared my resolution to you, and I am no coward to bend beneath words. Leave me; I am inexorable.'

'It is well. I go; but remember, I shall be with you on your wedding-night.'

I started forward, and exclaimed, 'Villain! before you sign my death-warrant, be sure that you are yourself safe.'

I would have seized him; but he eluded me, and quitted the house with precipitation: in a few moments I saw him in his boat, which shot across the waters with an arrowy swiftness, and was soon lost amidst the waves.

All was again silent; but his words rung in my ears. I burned with rage to pursue the murderer of my peace, and precipitate him into the ocean. I walked up and down my room hastily and perturbed, while my imagination conjured up a thousand images to torment and sting me. Why had I not followed him, and closed with him in mortal strife? But I had suffered him to depart, and he had directed his course towards the main land. I shuddered to think who might be the next victim sacrificed to his insatiate revenge. And then I thought again of his words—'*I will be with you on your wedding-night.*' That then was the period fixed for the fulfilment of my destiny. In that hour I should die, and at once satisfy and extinguish his malice. The prospect did not move me to fear; yet when I thought of my beloved Elizabeth,—of her tears and endless sorrow, when she should find her lover so barbarously snatched from her,—tears, the first I had shed for many months, streamed from my eyes, and I resolved not to fall before my enemy without a bitter struggle.

The night passed away, and the sun rose from the ocean; my feelings became calmer, if it may be called calmness, when the violence of rage sinks into the depths of despair. I left the house, the horrid scene of the last night's contention, and walked on the beach of the sea, which I almost regarded as an insuperable barrier between me and my fellow-creatures; nay, a wish that such should prove the fact stole across me. I desired that I might pass my life on that barren rock, wearily it is true, but uninterrupted by any sudden shock of misery. If I returned, it was to be sacrificed, or to see those whom I most loved die under the grasp of a dæmon whom I had myself created.

I walked about the isle like a restless spectre, separated from all it loved, and miserable in the separation. When it became noon, and the sun rose higher, I lay down on the grass, and was overpowered by a deep sleep. I had been awake the whole of the preceding night, my nerves were agitated, and my eyes inflamed by watching and misery. The sleep into which I now sunk refreshed me; and when I awoke, I again felt as if I belonged to a race of human beings like myself, and I began to reflect upon what had passed with greater composure; yet still the words of the fiend rung in my ears like a death-knell, they appeared like a dream, yet distinct and oppressive as a reality.

The sun had far descended, and I still sat on the shore, satisfying my appetite, which had become ravenous, with an oaten cake, when I saw a fishing-boat land close to me, and one of the men brought me a packet; it contained letters from Geneva, and one from Clerval, entreating me to join him. He said that nearly a year had elapsed since we had quitted Switzerland, and France was yet unvisited. He entreated me, therefore, to leave my solitary isle, and meet him at Perth, in a week from that time, when we might arrange the plan of our future proceedings. This letter in a degree recalled me to life, and I determined to quit my island at the expiration of two days.

Yet, before I departed, there was a task to perform, on which I shuddered to reflect: I must pack my chemical instruments; and for that purpose I must enter the room which had been the scene of my odious work, and I must handle those utensils, the sight of which was sickening to me. The next morning, at day-break, I summoned sufficient courage, and unlocked the door of my laboratory. The remains of the half-finished creature, whom I had destroyed, lay scattered on the floor, and I almost felt as if I had mangled the living flesh of a human being. I paused to collect myself, and then entered the chamber. With trembling hand I conveyed the instruments out of the room; but I reflected that I ought not to leave the relics of my work to excite the horror and suspicion of the peasants, and I accordingly put them into a basket, with a great quantity of stones, and laying them up, determined to throw them into the sea that very night; and in the mean time I sat upon the beach, employed in cleaning and arranging my chemical apparatus.

Nothing could be more complete than the alteration that had taken place in my feelings since the night of the appearance of the dæmon. I had before regarded my promise with a gloomy despair, as a thing that, with whatever consequences, must be fulfilled; but I now felt as if a film had been taken from before my eyes, and that I, for the first time, saw clearly. The idea of renewing my labours did not for one instant occur to me; the threat I had heard weighed on my thoughts, but I did not reflect that a voluntary act of mine could avert it. I had resolved in my own mind, that to create another like the fiend I had first made would be an act of the basest and most atrocious selfishness; and I banished from my mind every thought that could lead to a different conclusion.

Between two and three in the morning the moon rose; and I then, putting my basket aboard a little skiff, sailed out about four miles from the shore. The scene was perfectly solitary: a few boats were returning towards land, but I sailed away from them. I felt as if I was about the commission of a dreadful crime, and avoided with shuddering anxiety any encounter with my fellow-creatures. At one time the moon, which had before been clear, was suddenly overspread by a thick cloud, and I took advantage of the moment of darkness, and cast my basket into the sea; I listened to the gurgling sound as it sunk, and then sailed away from the spot. The sky became clouded; but the air was pure, although chilled by the north-east breeze that was then rising. But it refreshed me, and filled me with such agreeable sensations, that I resolved to prolong my stay on the water, and fixing the rudder in a direct position, stretched myself at the bottom of the boat. Clouds hid the moon, every thing was obscure, and I heard only the sound of the boat, as its keel cut through the waves; the murmur lulled me, and in a short time I slept soundly.

I do not know how long I remained in this situation, but when I awoke I found that the sun had already mounted considerably. The wind was high, and the waves continually threatened the safety of my little skiff. I found that the wind was north-east, and must have driven me far from the coast from which I had embarked. I endeavoured to change my course, but quickly found that if I again made the attempt the boat would be instantly filled with water. Thus situated, my only resource was to drive before the wind. I confess that I felt a few sensations of terror. I had no compass with me, and was so little acquainted with the geography of this part of the world that the sun was of little benefit to me. I might be driven into the wide Atlantic, and feel all the tortures of starvation, or be swallowed up in the immeasurable waters that roared and buffeted around me. I had already been out many hours, and felt the torment of a burning thirst, a prelude to my other sufferings. I looked on the heavens, which were covered by clouds that flew before the wind only to be replaced by others: I looked upon the sea, it was to be my grave. 'Fiend,' I exclaimed, 'your task is already fulfilled!' I thought of Elizabeth, of my father, and of Clerval; and sunk into a reverie, so despairing and frightful, that even now, when the scene is on the point of closing before me for ever, I shudder to reflect on it.

Some hours passed thus; but by degrees, as the sun declined towards the horizon, the wind died away into a gentle breeze, and the sea became free from breakers. But these gave place to a heavy swell; I felt sick, and hardly able to hold the rudder, when suddenly I saw a line of high land towards the south.

Almost spent, as I was, by fatigue, and the dreadful suspense I endured for several hours, this sudden certainty of life rushed like a flood of warm joy to my heart, and tears gushed from my eyes.

How mutable are our feelings, and how strange is that clinging love we have of life even in the excess of misery! I constructed another sail with a part of my dress, and eagerly steered my course towards the land. It had a wild and rocky appearance; but as I approached nearer, I easily perceived the traces of cultivation. I saw vessels near the shore, and found myself suddenly transported back to the neighbourhood of civilized man. I eagerly traced the windings of the land, and hailed a steeple which I at length saw issuing from behind a small promontory. As I was in a state of extreme debility, I resolved to sail directly towards the town as a place where I could most easily procure nourishment. Fortunately I had money with me. As I turned the promontory, I perceived a small neat town and a good harbour, which I entered, my heart bounding with joy at my unexpected escape.

As I was occupied in fixing the boat and arranging the sails, several people crowded towards the spot. They seemed very much surprised at my appearance; but, instead of offering me any assistance, whispered together with gestures that at any other time might have produced in me a slight sensation of alarm. As it was, I merely remarked that they spoke English; and I therefore addressed them in that language: 'My good friends,' said I, 'will you be so kind as to tell me the name of this town, and inform me where I am?'

'You will know that soon enough,' replied a man with a gruff voice. 'May be you are come to a place that will not prove much to your taste; but you will not be consulted as to your quarters, I promise you.'

I was exceedingly surprised on receiving so rude an answer from a stranger; and I was also disconcerted on perceiving the frowning and angry countenances of his companions. 'Why do you answer me so roughly?' I replied: 'surely it is not the custom of Englishmen to receive strangers so inhospitably.'

'I do not know,' said the man, 'what the custom of the English may be; but it is the custom of the Irish to hate villains.'

While this strange dialogue continued, I perceived the crowd rapidly increase. Their faces expressed a mixture of curiosity and anger, which annoyed, and in some degree alarmed me. I inquired the way to the inn; but no one replied. I then moved foward, and a murmuring sound arose from the crowd as they followed and surrounded me; when an ill-looking man approaching, tapped me on the shoulder, and said, 'Come, Sir, you must follow me to Mr Kirwin's,* to give an account of yourself.'

'Who is Mr Kirwin? Why am I to give an account of myself? Is not this a free country?'

'Aye, Sir, free enough for honest folks. Mr Kirwin is a magistrate; and you are to give an account of the death of a gentleman who was found murdered here last night.'

This answer startled me; but I presently recovered myself. I was innocent; that could easily be proved: accordingly I followed my conductor in silence, and was led to one of the best houses in the town. I was ready to sink from fatigue and hunger; but, being surrounded by a crowd, I thought it politic to rouse all my strength, that no physical debility might be construed into apprehension or conscious guilt. Little did I then expect the calamity that was in a few moments to overwhelm me, and extinguish in horror and despair all fear of ignominy or death.

I must pause here; for it requires all my fortitude to recall the memory of the frightful events which I am about to relate, in proper detail, to my recollection.

CHAPTER IV

I was soon introduced into the presence of the magistrate, an old benevolent man, with calm and mild manners. He looked upon me, however, with some degree of severity; and then, turning towards my conductors, he asked who appeared as witnesses on this occasion.

About half a dozen men came forward; and one being selected by the magistrate, he deposed, that he had been out fishing the night before with his son and brother-in-law, Daniel Nugent, when, about ten o'clock, they observed a strong northerly blast rising, and they accordingly put in for port. It was a very dark night, as the moon had not yet risen; they did not land at the harbour, but, as they had been accustomed, at a creek about two miles below. He walked on first, carrying a part of the fishing tackle, and his companions followed him at some distance. As he was proceeding along the sands, he struck his foot against something, and fell all his length on the ground. His companions came up to assist him; and, by the light of their lantern, they found that he had fallen on the body of a man, who was to all appearance dead. Their first supposition was, that it was the corpse of some person who had been drowned, and was thrown on shore by the waves; but, upon examination, they found that the clothes were not wet, and even that the body was not then cold. They instantly carried it to the cottage of an old woman near the spot, and endeavoured, but in vain, to restore it to life. He appeared to be a handsome young man, about five and twenty years of age. He had apparently been strangled; for there was no sign of any violence, except the black mark of fingers on his neck.

The first part of this deposition did not in the least interest me; but when the mark of the fingers was mentioned, I remembered the murder of my brother, and felt myself extremely agitated; my limbs trembled, and a mist came over my eyes, which obliged me to lean on a chair for support. The magistrate observed me with a keen eye, and of course drew an unfavourable augury from my manner.

The son confirmed his father's account: but when Daniel Nugent was called, he swore positively that, just before the fall of his companion, he saw a boat, with a single man in it, at a short distance from the shore; and, as far as he could judge by the light of a few stars, it was the same boat in which I had just landed.

A woman deposed, that she lived near the beach, and was standing at the door of her cottage, waiting for the return of the fishermen, about an hour before she heard of the discovery of the body, when she saw a boat, with only one man in it, push off from that part of the shore where the corpse was afterwards found.

Another woman confirmed the account of the fishermen having brought the body into her house; it was not cold. They put it into a bed, and rubbed it; and Daniel went to the town for an apothecary, but life was quite gone.

Several other men were examined concerning my landing; and they agreed, that, with the strong north wind that had arisen during the night, it was very probable that I had beaten about for many hours, and had been obliged to return nearly to the same spot from which I had departed. Besides, they observed that it appeared that I had brought the body from another place, and it was likely, that as I did not appear to know the shore, I might have put into the harbour ignorant of the distance of the town of——from the place where I had deposited the corpse.

Mr Kirwin, on hearing this evidence, desired that I should be taken into the room where the body lay for interment, that it might be observed what effect the sight of it would produce upon me. This idea was probably suggested by the extreme agitation I had exhibited when the mode of the murder had been described. I was accordingly conducted, by the magistrate and several other persons, to the inn. I could not help being struck by the strange coincidences that had taken place during this eventful night; but, knowing that I had been conversing with several persons in the island I had inhabited about the time that the body had been found, I was perfectly tranquil as to the consequences of the affair.

I entered the room where the corpse lay, and was led up to the coffin. How can I describe my sensations on beholding it? I feel yet parched with horror, nor can I reflect on that terrible moment without shuddering and agony, that faintly reminds me of the anguish of the recognition. The trial, the presence of the magistrate and witnesses, passed like a dream from my memory, when I saw the lifeless form of Henry Clerval stretched before me. I gasped for breath; and, throwing myself on the body, I exclaimed, 'Have my murderous machinations deprived you also, my dearest Henry, of life? Two I have already destroyed; other victims await their destiny: but you, Clerval, my friend, my benefactor'—

The human frame could no longer support the agonizing suffering that I endured, and I was carried out of the room in strong convulsions.

A fever succeeded to this. I lay for two months on the point of death: my ravings, as I afterwards heard, were frightful; I called myself the murderer of William, of Justine, and of Clerval. Sometimes I entreated my attendants to assist me in the destruction of the fiend by whom I was tormented; and, at others, I felt the fingers of the monster already grasping my neck, and screamed aloud with agony and terror. Fortunately, as I spoke my native language, Mr Kirwin alone understood me; but my gestures and bitter cries were sufficient to affright the other witnesses.

Why did I not die? More miserable than man ever was before, why did I not sink into forgetfulness and rest? Death snatches away many blooming children, the only hopes of their doating parents: how many brides and youthful lovers have been one day in the bloom of health and hope, and the next a prey for worms and the decay of the tomb! Of what materials was I made, that I could thus resist so many shocks, which, like the turning of the wheel, continually renewed the torture.

But I was doomed to live; and, in two months, found myself as awaking from a dream, in a prison, stretched on a wretched bed, surrounded by gaolers, turnkeys, bolts, and all the miserable apparatus of a dungeon. It was morning, I remember, when I thus awoke to understanding: I had forgotten the particulars of what had happened, and only felt as if some great misfortune had suddenly overwhelmed me; but when I looked around, and saw the barred windows, and the squalidness of the room in which I was, all flashed across my memory, and I groaned bitterly.

This sound disturbed an old woman who was sleeping in a chair beside me. She was a hired nurse, the wife of one of the turnkeys, and her countenance expressed all those bad qualities which often characterize that class. The lines of her face were hard and rude, like that of persons accustomed to see without sympathizing in sights of misery. Her tone expressed her entire indifference; she addressed me in English, and the voice struck me as one that I had heard during my sufferings:

'Are you better now, Sir?' said she.

I replied in the same language, with a feeble voice, 'I believe I am; but if it be all true, if indeed I did not dream, I am sorry that I am still alive to feel this misery and horror.'

'For that matter,' replied the old woman, 'if you mean about the gentleman you murdered, I believe that it were better for you if you were dead, for I fancy it will go hard with you; but you will be hung when the next sessions come on. However, that's none of my business, I am sent to nurse you, and get you well; I do my duty with a safe conscience, it were well if every body did the same.'

I turned with loathing from the woman who could utter so unfeeling a speech to a person just saved, on the very edge of death; but I felt languid, and unable to reflect on all that had passed. The whole series of my life appeared to me as a dream; I sometimes doubted if indeed it were all true, for it never presented itself to my mind with the force of reality.

As the images that floated before me became more distinct, I grew feverish; a darkness pressed around me; no one was near me who soothed me with the gentle voice of love; no dear hand supported me. The physician came and prescribed medicines, and the old woman prepared them for me; but utter carelessness was visible in the first, and the expression of brutality was strongly marked in the visage of the second. Who could be interested in the fate of a murderer, but the hangman who would gain his fee?

These were my first reflections; but I soon learned that Mr Kirwin had shewn me extreme kindness. He had caused the best room in the prison to be prepared for me (wretched indeed was the best); and it was he who had provided a physician and a nurse. It is true, he seldom came to see me; for, although he ardently desired to relieve the sufferings of every human creature, he did not wish to be present at the agonies and miserable ravings of a murderer. He came, therefore, sometimes to see that I was not neglected; but his visits were short, and at long intervals.

One day, when I was gradually recovering, I was seated in a chair, my eyes half open, and my cheeks livid like those in death, I was overcome by gloom and misery, and often reflected I had better seek death than remain miserably pent up only to be let loose in a world replete with wretchedness. At one time I considered whether I should not declare myself guilty, and suffer the penalty of the law, less innocent than poor Justine had been. Such were my thoughts, when the door of my apartment was opened, and Mr Kirwin entered. His countenance expressed sympathy and compassion; he drew a chair close to mine, and addressed me in French—

'I fear that this place is very shocking to you; can I do any thing to make you more comfortable?'

'I thank you; but all that you mention is nothing to me: on the whole earth there is no comfort which I am capable of receiving.'

'I know that the sympathy of a stranger can be but of little relief to one borne down as you are by so strange a misfortune. But you will, I hope, soon quit this melancholy abode; for, doubtless, evidence can easily be brought to free you from the criminal charge.'

'That is my least concern: I am, by a course of strange events, become the most miserable of mortals. Persecuted and tortured as I am and have been, can death be any evil to me?'

'Nothing indeed could be more unfortunate and agonizing than the strange chances that have lately occurred. You were thrown, by some surprising accident, on this shore, renowned for its hospitality; seized immediately, and charged with murder. The first sight that was presented to your eyes was the body of your friend, murdered in so unaccountable a manner, and placed, as it were, by some fiend across your path.'

As Mr Kirwin said this, notwithstanding the agitation I endured on this retrospect of my sufferings, I also felt considerable surprise at the knowledge he seemed to possess concerning me. I suppose some astonishment was exhibited in my countenance; for Mr Kirwin hastened to say—

'It was not until a day or two after your illness that I thought of examining your dress, that I might discover some trace by which I could send to your relations an account of your misfortune and illness. I found several letters, and, among others, one which I discovered from its commencement to be from your father. I instantly wrote to Geneva: nearly two months have elapsed since the departure of my letter.—But you are ill; even now you tremble: you are unfit for agitation of any kind.'

'This suspense is a thousand times worse than the most horrible event: tell me what new scene of death has been acted, and whose murder I am now to lament.'

'Your family is perfectly well,' said Mr Kirwin, with gentleness; 'and some one, a friend, is come to visit you.'

I know not by what chain of thought the idea presented itself, but it instantly darted into my mind that the murderer had come to mock at my misery, and taunt me with the death of Clerval, as a new incitement for me to comply with his hellish desires. I put my hand before my eyes, and cried out in agony—

'Oh! take him away! I cannot see him; for God's sake, do not let him enter!'

Mr Kirwin regarded me with a troubled countenance. He could not help regarding my exclamation as a presumption of my guilt, and said, in rather a severe tone—

'I should have thought, young man, that the presence of your father would have been welcome, instead of inspiring such violent repugnance.'

'My father!' cried I, while every feature and every muscle was relaxed from anguish to pleasure. 'Is my father, indeed, come? How kind, how very kind. But where is he, why does he not hasten to me?'

My change of manner surprised and pleased the magistrate; perhaps he thought that my former exclamation was a momentary return of delirium, and now he instantly resumed his former benevolence. He rose, and quitted the room with my nurse, and in a moment my father entered it.

Nothing, at this moment, could have given me greater pleasure than the arrival of my father. I stretched out my hand to him, and cried—

'Are you then safe—and Elizabeth—and Ernest?'

My father calmed me with assurances of their welfare, and endeavoured, by dwelling on these subjects so interesting to my heart, to raise my desponding spirits; but he soon felt that a prison cannot be the abode of cheerfulness. 'What a place is this that you inhabit, my son!' said he, looking mournfully at the barred windows, and wretched appearance of the room. 'You travelled to seek happiness, but a fatality seems to pursue you. And poor Clerval—'

The name of my unfortunate and murdered friend was an agitation too great to be endured in my weak state; I shed tears.

'Alas! yes, my father,' replied I; 'some destiny of the most horrible kind hangs over me, and I must live to fulfil it, or surely I should have died on the coffin of Henry.'

We were not allowed to converse for any length of time, for the precarious state of my health rendered every precaution necessary that could insure tranquillity. Mr Kirwin came in, and insisted that my strength should not be exhausted by too much exertion. But the appearance of my father was to me like that of my good angel, and I gradually recovered my health.

As my sickness quitted me, I was absorbed by a gloomy and black melancholy, that nothing could dissipate. The image of Clerval was for ever before me, ghastly and murdered. More than once the agitation into which these reflections threw me made my friends dread a dangerous relapse. Alas! why did they preserve so miserable and detested a life? It was surely that I might fulfil my destiny, which is now drawing to a close. Soon, oh, very soon, will death extinguish these throbbings, and relieve me from the mighty weight of anguish that bears me to the dust; and, in executing the award of justice, I shall also sink to rest. Then the appearance of death was distant, although the wish was ever present to my thoughts; and I often sat for hours motionless and speechless, wishing for some mighty revolution that might bury me and my destroyer in its ruins.

The season of the assizes approached. I had already been three months in prison; and although I was still weak, and in continual danger of a relapse, I was obliged to travel nearly a hundred miles to the county-town, where the court was held. Mr Kirwin charged himself with every care of collecting witnesses, and arranging my defence. I was spared the disgrace of appearing publicly as a criminal, as the case was not brought before the court that decides on life and death. The grand jury rejected the bill, on its being proved that I was on the Orkney Islands at the hour the body of my friend was found, and a fortnight after my removal I was liberated from prison.

My father was enraptured on finding me freed from the vexations of a criminal charge, that I was again allowed to breathe the fresh atmosphere, and allowed to return to my native country. I did not participate in these feelings; for to me the walls of a dungeon or a palace were alike hateful. The cup of life was poisoned for ever; and although the sun shone upon me, as upon the happy and gay of heart, I saw around me nothing but a dense and frightful darkness, penetrated by no light but the glimmer of two eyes that glared upon me. Sometimes they were the expressive eyes of Henry, languishing in death, the dark orbs nearly covered by the lids, and the long black lashes that fringed them; sometimes it was the watery clouded eyes of the monster, as I first saw them in my chamber at Ingolstadt.

My father tried to awaken in me the feelings of affection. He talked of Geneva, which I should soon visit—of Elizabeth, and Ernest; but these words only drew deep groans from me. Sometimes, indeed, I felt a wish for happiness; and thought, with melancholy delight, of my beloved cousin; or longed, with a devouring *maladie du pays*,* to see once more the blue lake and rapid Rhone, that had been so dear to me in early childhood: but my general state of feeling was a torpor, in which a prison was as welcome a residence as the divinest scene in nature; and these fits were seldom interrupted, but by paroxysms of anguish and despair. At these moments I often endeavoured to put an end to the existence I loathed; and it required unceasing attendance and vigilance to restrain me from committing some dreadful act of violence.

I remember, as I quitted the prison, I heard one of the men say, 'He may be innocent of the murder, but he has certainly a bad conscience.' These words struck me. A bad conscience! yes, surely I had one. William, Justine, and Clerval, had died through my infernal machinations; 'And whose death,' cried I, 'is to finish the tragedy? Ah! my father, do not remain in this wretched country; take me where I may forget myself, my existence, and all the world.'

My father easily acceded to my desire; and, after having taken leave of Mr Kirwin, we hastened to Dublin. I felt as if I was relieved from a heavy weight, when the packet sailed with a fair wind from Ireland, and I had quitted for ever the country which had been to me the scene of so much misery.

It was midnight. My father slept in the cabin; and I lay on the deck, looking at the stars, and listening to the dashing of the waves. I hailed the darkness that shut Ireland from my sight, and my pulse beat with a feverish joy, when I reflected that I should soon see Geneva. The past appeared to me in the light of a frightful dream; yet the vessel in which I was, the wind that blew me from the detested shore of Ireland, and the sea which surrounded me, told me too forcibly that I was deceived by no vision, and that Clerval, my friend and dearest companion, had fallen a victim to me and the monster of my creation. I repassed, in my memory, my whole life; my quiet happiness while residing with my family in Geneva, the death of my mother, and my departure for Ingolstadt. I remembered shuddering at the mad enthusiasm that hurried me on to the creation of my hideous enemy, and I called to mind the night during which he first lived. I was unable to pursue the train of thought; a thousand feelings pressed upon me, and I wept bitterly.

Ever since my recovery from the fever I had been in the custom of taking every night a small quantity of laudanum; for it was by means of this drug only that I was enabled to gain the rest necessary for the preservation of life. Oppressed by the recollection of my various misfortunes, I now took a double dose, and soon slept profoundly. But sleep did not afford me respite from thought and misery; my dreams presented a thousand objects that scared me. Towards morning I was possessed by a kind of night-mare; I felt the fiend's grasp in my neck, and could not free myself from it; groans and cries rung in my ears. My father, who was watching over me, perceiving my restlessness, awoke me, and pointed to the port of Holyhead, which we were now entering.

CHAPTER V

We had resolved not to go to London, but to cross the country to Portsmouth, and thence to embark for Havre. I preferred this plan principally because I dreaded to see again those places in which I had enjoyed a few moments of tranquillity with my beloved Clerval. I thought with horror of seeing again those persons whom we had been accustomed to visit together, and who might make inquiries concerning an event, the very remembrance of which made me again feel the pang I endured when I gazed on his lifeless form in the inn at———.

As for my father, his desires and exertions were bounded to the again seeing me restored to health and peace of mind. His tenderness and attentions were unremitting; my grief and gloom was obstinate, but he would not despair. Sometimes he thought that I felt deeply the degradation of being obliged to answer a charge of murder, and he endeavoured to prove to me the futility of pride.

'Alas! my father,' said I, 'how little do you know me. Human beings, their feelings and passions, would indeed be degraded, if such a wretch as I felt pride. Justine, poor unhappy Justine, was as innocent as I, and she suffered the same charge; she died for it; and I am the cause of this—I murdered her. William, Justine, and Henry—they all died by my hands.'

My father had often, during my imprisonment, heard me make the same assertion; when I thus accused myself, he sometimes seemed to desire an explanation, and at others he appeared to consider it as caused by delirium, and that, during my illness, some idea of this kind had presented itself to my imagination, the remembrance of which I preserved in my convalescence. I avoided explanation, and maintained a continual silence concerning the wretch I had created. I had a feeling that I should be supposed mad, and this for ever chained my tongue, when I would have given the whole world to have confided the fatal secret.

Upon this occasion my father said, with an expression of unbounded wonder, 'What do you mean, Victor? are you mad? My dear son, I entreat you never to make such an assertion again.'

'I am not mad,' I cried energetically; 'the sun and the heavens, who have viewed my operations, can bear witness of my truth. I am the assassin of those most innocent victims; they died by my machinations. A thousand times would I have shed my own blood, drop by drop, to have saved their lives; but I could not, my father, indeed I could not sacrifice the whole human race.'

The conclusion of this speech convinced my father that my ideas were deranged, and he instantly changed the subject of our conversation, and endeavoured to alter the course of my thoughts. He wished as much as possible to obliterate the memory of the scenes that had taken place in Ireland, and never alluded to them, or suffered me to speak of my misfortunes.

As time passed away I became more calm: misery had her dwelling in my heart, but I no longer talked in the same incoherent manner of my own crimes; sufficient for me was the consciousness of them. By the utmost self-violence, I curbed the imperious voice of wretchedness, which some-times desired to declare itself to the whole world; and my manners were calmer and more composed than they had ever been since my journey to the sea of ice.

We arrived at Havre on the 8th of May, and instantly pro-ceeded to Paris, where my father had some business which detained us a few weeks. In this city, I received the following letter from Elizabeth:—

To VICTOR FRANKENSTEIN.

'MY DEAREST FRIEND,

'It gave me the greatest pleasure to receive a letter from my uncle dated at Paris; you are no longer at a formidable dis-tance, and I may hope to see you in less than a fortnight. My poor cousin, how much you must have suffered! I expect to see you looking even more ill than when you quitted Geneva. This winter has been passed most miserably, tortured as I have been by anxious suspense; yet I hope to see peace in your countenance, and to find that your heart is not totally devoid of comfort and tranquillity.

'Yet I fear that the same feelings now exist that made you so miserable a year ago, even perhaps augmented by time. I would not disturb you at this period, when so many misfor-tunes weigh upon you; but a conversation that I had with my uncle previous to his departure renders some explanation necessary before we meet.

'Explanation! you may possibly say; what can Elizabeth have to explain? If you really say this, my questions are answered, and I have no more to do than to sign myself your affectionate cousin. But you are distant from me, and it is possible that you may dread, and yet be pleased with this explanation; and, in a probability of this being the case, I dare not any longer postpone writing what, during your absence, I have often wished to express to you, but have never had the courage to begin.

'You well know, Victor, that our union had been the favourite plan of your parents ever since our infancy. We were told this when young, and taught to look forward to it as an event that would certainly take place. We were affectionate playfellows during childhood, and, I believe, dear and valued friends to one another as we grew older. But as brother and sister often entertain a lively affection towards each other, without desiring a more intimate union, may not such also be our case? Tell me, dearest Victor. Answer me, I conjure you, by our mutual happiness, with simple truth—Do you not love another?

'You have travelled; you have spent several years of your life at Ingolstadt; and I confess to you, my friend, that when I saw you last autumn so unhappy, flying to solitude, from the society of every creature, I could not help supposing that you might regret our connexion, and believe yourself bound in honour to fulfil the wishes of your parents, although they opposed themselves to your inclinations. But this is false reasoning. I confess to you, my cousin, that I love you, and that in my airy dreams of futurity you have been my constant friend and companion. But it is your happiness I desire as well as my own, when I declare to you, that our marriage would render me eternally miserable, unless it were the dictate of your own free choice. Even now I weep to think, that, borne down as you are by the cruelest misfortunes, you may stifle, by the word *honour*, all hope of that love and happiness which would alone restore you to yourself. I, who have so interested an affection for you, may increase your miseries ten-fold, by being an obstacle to your wishes. Ah, Victor, be assured that your cousin and playmate has too sincere a love for you not to be made miserable by this supposition. Be happy, my friend; and if you obey me in this one request, remain satisfied that nothing on earth will have the power to interrupt my tranquillity.

'Do not let this lette disturb you; do not answer it tomorrow, or the next day, or even until you come, if it will give you pain. My uncle will send me news of your health; and if I see but one smile on your lips when we meet, occasioned by this or any other exertion of mine, I shall need no other happiness.

'ELIZABETH LAVENZA.
'Geneva, May 18th, 17—.'

This letter revived in my memory what I had before forgotten, the threat of the fiend—'*I will be with you on your wedding-night!*' Such was my sentence, and on that night would the dæmon employ every art to destroy me, and tear me from the glimpse of happiness which promised partly to console my sufferings. On that night he had determined to consummate his crimes by my death. Well, be it so; a deadly struggle would then assuredly take place, in which if he was victorious, I should be at peace, and his power over me be at an end. If he were vanquished, I should be a free man. Alas! what freedom? such as the peasant enjoys when his family have been massacred before his eyes, his cottage burnt, his lands laid waste, and he is turned adrift, homeless, pennyless, and alone, but free. Such would be my liberty, except that in my Elizabeth I possessed a treasure; alas! balanced by those horrors of remorse and guilt, which would pursue me until death.

Sweet and beloved Elizabeth! I read and re-read her letter, and some softened feelings stole into my heart, and dared to whisper paradisaical dreams of love and joy; but the apple was already eaten, and the angel's arm bared to drive me from all hope. Yet I would die to make her happy. If the monster executed his threat, death was inevitable; yet, again, I considered whether my marriage would hasten my fate. My destruction might indeed arrive a few months sooner; but if my torturer should suspect that I postponed it, influenced by his menaces, he would surely find other, and perhaps more dreadful means of revenge. He had vowed *to be with me on my wedding-night*, yet he did not consider that threat as binding him to peace in the mean time; for, as if to shew me that he was not yet satiated with blood, he had murdered Clerval immediately after the enunciation of his threats. I resolved, therefore, that if my immediate union with my cousin would conduce either to hers or my father's happiness, my adversary's designs against my life should not retard it a single hour.

In this state of mind I wrote to Elizabeth. My letter was calm and affectionate. 'I fear, my beloved girl,' I said, 'little happiness remains for us on earth; yet all that I may one day enjoy is concentered in you. Chase away your idle fears; to you alone do I consecrate my life, and my endeavours for contentment. I have one secret, Elizabeth, a dreadful one; when revealed to you, it will chill your frame with horror, and then, far from being surprised at my misery, you will only wonder that I survive what I have endured. I will confide this tale of misery and terror to you the day after our marriage shall take place; for, my sweet cousin, there must be perfect confidence between us. But until then, I conjure you, do not mention or allude to it. This I most earnestly entreat, and I know you will comply.'

In about a week after the arrival of Elizabeth's letter, we returned to Geneva. My cousin welcomed me with warm affection; yet tears were in her eyes, as she beheld my emaciated frame and feverish cheeks. I saw a change in her also. She was thinner, and had lost much of that heavenly vivacity that had before charmed me; but her gentleness, and soft looks of compassion, made her a more fit companion for one blasted and miserable as I was.

The tranquillity which I now enjoyed did not endure. Memory brought madness with it; and when I thought on what had passed, a real insanity possessed me; sometimes I was furious, and burnt with rage, sometimes low and despondent. I neither spoke or looked, but sat motionless, bewildered by the multitude of miseries that overcame me.

Elizabeth alone had the power to draw me from these fits; her gentle voice would soothe me when transported by passion, and inspire me with human feelings when sunk in torpor. She wept with me, and for me. When reason returned, she would remonstrate, and endeavour to inspire me with resignation. Ah! it is well for the unfortunate to be resigned, but for the guilty there is no peace. The agonies of remorse poison the luxury there is otherwise sometimes found in indulging the excess of grief.

Soon after my arrival my father spoke of my immediate marriage with my cousin. I remained silent.

'Have you, then, some other attachment?'

'None on earth. I love Elizabeth, and look forward to our union with delight. Let the day therefore be fixed; and on it I will consecrate myself, in life or death, to the happiness of my cousin.'

'My dear Victor, do not speak thus. Heavy misfortunes have befallen us; but let us only cling closer to what remains, and transfer our love for those whom we have lost to those who yet live. Our circle will be small, but bound close by the ties of affection and mutual misfortune. And when time shall have softened your despair, new and dear objects of care will be born to replace those of whom we have been so cruelly deprived.'

Such were the lessons of my father. But to me the remembrance of the threat returned: nor can you wonder, that, omnipotent as the fiend had yet been in his deeds of blood, I should almost regard him as invincible; and that when he had pronounced the words, '*I shall be with you on your wedding-night*,' I should regard the threatened fate as unavoidable. But death was no evil to me, if the loss of Elizabeth were balanced with it; and I therefore, with a contented and even cheerful countenance, agreed with my father, that if my cousin would consent, the ceremony should take place in ten days, and thus put, as I imagined, the seal to my fate.

Great God! if for one instant I had thought what might be the hellish intention of my fiendish adversary, I would rather have banished myself for ever from my native country, and wandered a friendless outcast over the earth, than have consented to this miserable marriage. But, as if possessed of magic powers, the monster had blinded me to his real intentions; and when I thought that I prepared only my own death, I hastened that of a far dearer victim.

As the period fixed for our marriage drew nearer, whether from cowardice or a prophetic feeling, I felt my heart sink within me. But I concealed my feelings by an appearance of hilarity, that brought smiles and joy to the countenance of my father, but hardly deceived the ever-watchful and nicer eye of Elizabeth. She looked forward to our union with placid contentment, not unmingled with a little fear, which past misfortunes had impressed, that what now appeared certain and tangible happiness, might soon dissipate into an airy dream, and leave no trace but deep and everlasting regret.

Preparations were made for the event; congratulatory visits were received; and all wore a smiling appearance. I shut up, as well as I could, in my own heart the anxiety that preyed there, and entered with seeming earnestness into the plans of my father, although they might only serve as the decorations of my tragedy. A house was purchased for us near Cologny, by which we should enjoy the pleasures of the country; and yet be so near Geneva as to see my father every day; who would still reside within the walls, for the benefit of Ernest, that he might follow his studies at the schools.

In the mean time I took every precaution to defend my person, in case the fiend should openly attack me. I carried pistols and a dagger constantly about me, and was ever on the watch to prevent artifice; and by these means gained a greater degree of tranquillity. Indeed, as the period approached, the threat appeared more as a delusion, not to be regarded as worthy to disturb my peace, while the happiness I hoped for in my marriage wore a greater appearance of certainty, as the day fixed for its solemnization drew nearer, and I heard it continually spoken of as an occurrence which no accident could possibly prevent.

Elizabeth seemed happy; my tranquil demeanour contributed greatly to calm her mind. But on the day that was to fulfil my wishes and my destiny, she was melancholy, and a presentiment of evil pervaded her; and perhaps also she thought of the dreadful secret, which I had promised to reveal to her the following day. My father was in the mean time overjoyed, and, in the bustle of preparation, only observed in the melancholy of his niece the diffidence of a bride.

After the ceremony was performed, a large party assembled at my father's; but it was agreed that Elizabeth and I should pass the afternoon and night at Evian, and return to Cologny the next morning. As the day was fair, and the wind favourable, we resolved to go by water.

Those were the last moments of my life during which I enjoyed the feeling of happiness. We passed rapidly along: the sun was hot, but we were sheltered from its rays by a kind of canopy, while we enjoyed the beauty of the scene, sometimes on one side of the lake, where we saw Mont Salêve, the pleasant banks of Montalègre, and at a distance, surmounting all, the beautiful Mont Blanc, and the assemblage of snowy mountains that in vain endeavour to emulate her; sometimes coasting the opposite banks, we saw the mighty Jura opposing its dark side to the ambition that would quit its native country,* and an almost insurmountable barrier to the invader who should wish to enslave it.*

I took the hand of Elizabeth: 'You are sorrowful, my love. Ah! if you knew what I have suffered, and what I may yet endure, you would endeavour to let me taste the quiet, and freedom from despair, that this one day at least permits me to enjoy.'

'Be happy, my dear Victor,' replied Elizabeth; 'there is, I hope, nothing to distress you; and be assured that if a lively joy is not painted on my face, my heart is contented. Something whispers to me not to depend too much on the prospect that is opened before us; but I will not listen to such a sinister voice. Observe how fast we move along, and how the clouds which sometimes obscure, and sometimes rise above the dome of Mont Blanc, render this scene of beauty still more interesting. Look also at the innumerable fish that are swimming in the clear waters, where we can distinguish every pebble that lies at the bottom. What a divine day! how happy and serene all nature appears!'

Thus Elizabeth endeavoured to divert her thoughts and mine from all reflection upon melancholy subjects. But her temper was fluctuating; joy for a few instants shone in her eyes, but it continually gave place to distraction and reverie.

The sun sunk lower in the heavens; we passed the river Drance, and observed its path through the chasms of the higher, and the glens of the lower hills. The Alps here come closer to the lake, and we approached the amphitheatre of mountains which forms its eastern boundary. The spire of Evian shone under the woods that surrounded it, and the range of mountain above mountain by which it was overhung.

The wind, which had hitherto carried us along with amazing rapidity, sunk at sunset to a light breeze; the soft air just ruffled the water, and caused a pleasant motion among the trees as we approached the shore, from which it wafted the most delightful scent of flowers and hay. The sun sunk beneath the horizon as we landed; and as I touched the shore, I felt those cares and fears revive, which soon were to clasp me, and cling to me for ever.

CHAPTER VI

It was eight o'clock when we landed; we walked for a short time on the shore, enjoying the transitory light, and then retired to the inn, and contemplated the lovely scene of waters, woods, and mountains, obscured in darkness, yet still displaying their black outlines.

The wind, which had fallen in the south, now rose with great violence in the west. The moon had reached her summit in the heavens, and was beginning to descend; the clouds swept across it swifter than the flight of the vulture, and dimmed her rays, while the lake reflected the scene o. the busy heavens, rendered still busier by the restless waves that were beginning to rise. Suddenly a heavy storm of rain descended.

I had been calm during the day; but so soon as night obscured the shapes of objects, a thousand fears arose in my mind. I was anxious and watchful, while my right hand grasped a pistol which was hidden in my bosom; every sound terrified me; but I resolved that I would sell my life dearly, and not relax the impending conflict until my own life, or that of my adversary, were extinguished.

Elizabeth observed my agitation for some time in timid and fearful silence; at length she said, 'What is it that agitates you, my dear Victor? What is it you fear?'

'Oh! peace, peace, my love,' replied I, 'this night, and all will be safe: but this night is dreadful, very dreadful.'

I passed an hour in this state of mind, when suddenly I reflected how dreadful the combat which I momentarily expected would be to my wife, and I earnestly entreated her to retire, resolving not to join her until I had obtained some knowledge as to the situation of my enemy.

She left me, and I continued some time walking up and down the passages of the house, and inspecting every corner that might afford a retreat to my adversary. But I discovered no trace of him, and was beginning to conjecture that some fortunate chance had intervened to prevent the execution of his menaces; when suddenly I heard a shrill and dreadful scream. It came from the room into which Elizabeth had retired. As I heard it, the whole truth rushed into my mind, my arms dropped, the motion of every muscle and fibre was suspended; I could feel the blood trickling in my veins, and tingling in the extremities of my limbs. This state lasted but for an instant; the scream was repeated, and I rushed into the room.

Great God! why did I not then expire! Why am I here to relate the destruction of the best hope, and the purest creature of earth. She was there, lifeless and inanimate, thrown across the bed, her head hanging down, and her pale and distorted features half covered by her hair. Every where I turn I see the same figure—her bloodless arms and relaxed form flung by the murderer on its bridal bier. Could I behold this, and live? Alas! life is obstinate, and clings closest where it is most hated. For a moment only did I lose recollection; I fainted.

When I recovered, I found myself surrounded by the people of the inn; their countenances expressed a breathless terror: but the horror of others appeared only as a mockery, a shadow of the feelings that oppressed me. I escaped from them to the room where lay the body of Elizabeth, my love, my wife, so lately living, so dear, so worthy. She had been moved from the posture in which I had first beheld her; and now, as she lay, her head upon her arm, and a handkerchief thrown across her face and neck, I might have supposed her asleep. I rushed towards her, and embraced her with ardour; but the deathly languor and coldness of the limbs told me, that what I now held in my arms had ceased to be the Elizabeth whom I had loved and cherished. The murderous mark of the fiend's grasp was on her neck, and the breath had ceased to issue from her lips.

While I still hung over her in the agony of despair, I happened to look up. The windows of the room had before been darkened; and I felt a kind of panic on seeing the pale yellow light of the moon illuminate the chamber. The shutters had been thrown back; and, with a sensation of horror not to be described, I saw at the open window a figure the most hideous and abhorred. A grin was on the face of the monster; he seemed to jeer, as with his fiendish finger he pointed towards the corpse of my wife. I rushed towards the window, and drawing a pistol from my bosom, shot; but he eluded me, leaped from his station, and, running with the swiftness of lightning, plunged into the lake.

The report of the pistol brought a crowd into the room. I pointed to the spot where he had disappeared, and we followed the track with boats; nets were cast, but in vain. After passing several hours, we returned hopeless, most of my companions believing it to have been a form conjured by my fancy. After having landed, they proceeded to search the country, parties going in different directions among the woods and vines.

I did not accompany them; I was exhausted: a film covered my eyes, and my skin was parched with the heat of fever. In this state I lay on a bed, hardly conscious of what had happened; my eyes wandered round the room, as if to seek something that I had lost.

At length I remembered that my father would anxiously expect the return of Elizabeth and myself, and that I must return alone. This reflection brought tears into my eyes, and I wept for a long time; but my thoughts rambled to various subjects, reflecting on my misfortunes, and their cause. I was bewildered in a cloud of wonder and horror. The death of

William, the execution of Justine, the murder of Clerval, and lastly of my wife; even at that moment I knew not that my only remaining friends were safe from the malignity of the fiend; my father even now might be writhing under his grasp, and Ernest might be dead at his feet. This idea made me shudder, and recalled me to action. I started up, and resolved to return to Geneva with all possible speed.

There were no horses to be procured, and I must return by the lake; but the wind was unfavourable, and the rain fell in torrents. However, it was hardly morning, and I might reasonably hope to arrive by night. I hired men to row, and took an oar myself, for I had always experienced relief from mental torment in bodily exercise. But the overflowing misery I now felt, and the excess of agitation that I endured, rendered me incapable of any exertion. I threw down the oar; and, leaning my head upon my hands, gave way to every gloomy idea that arose. If I looked up, I saw the scenes which were familiar to me in my happier time, and which I had contemplated but the day before in the company of her who was now but a shadow and a recollection. Tears streamed from my eyes. The rain had ceased for a moment, and I saw the fish play in the waters as they had done a few hours before; they had then been observed by Elizabeth. Nothing is so painful to the human mind as a great and sudden change. The sun might shine, or the clouds might lour; but nothing could appear to me as it had done the day before. A fiend had snatched from me every hope of future happiness: no creature had ever been so miserable as I was; so frightful an event is single in the history of man.

But why should I dwell upon the incidents that followed this last overwhelming event. Mine has been a tale of horrors; I have reached their *acme*, and what I must now relate can but be tedious to you. Know that, one by one, my friends were snatched away; I was left desolate. My own strength is exhausted; and I must tell, in a few words, what remains of my hideous narration.

I arrived at Geneva. My father and Ernest yet lived; but the former sunk under the tidings that I bore. I see him now, excellent and venerable old man! his eyes wandered in vacancy, for they had lost their charm and their delight—his niece, his more than daughter, whom he doated on with all that affection which a man feels, who, in the decline of life, having few affections, clings more earnestly to those that remain. Cursed, cursed be the fiend that brought misery on his grey hairs, and doomed him to waste in wretchedness! He could not live under the horrors that were accumulated around him; an apoplectic fit was brought on, and in a few days he died in my arms.

What then became of me? I know not; I lost sensation, and chains and darkness were the only objects that pressed upon me. Sometimes, indeed, I dreamt that I wandered in flowery meadows and pleasant vales with the friends of my youth; but awoke, and found myself in a dungeon. Melancholy followed, but by degrees I gained a clear conception of my miseries and situation, and was then released from my prison. For they had called me mad; and during many months, as I understood, a solitary cell had been my habitation.

But liberty had been a useless gift to me had I not, as I awakened to reason, at the same time awakened to revenge. As the memory of past misfortunes pressed upon me, I began to reflect on their cause—the monster whom I had created, the miserable dæmon whom I had sent abroad into the world for my destruction. I was possessed by a maddening rage when I thought of him, and desired and ardently prayed that I might have him within my grasp to wreak a great and signal revenge on his cursed head.

Nor did my hate long confine itself to useless wishes; I began to reflect on the best means of securing him; and for this purpose, about a month after my release, I repaired to a criminal judge in the town, and told him that I had an accusation to make; that I knew the destroyer of my family; and that I required him to exert his whole authority for the apprehension of the murderer.

The magistrate listened to me with attention and kindness: 'Be assured, sir,' said he, 'no pains or exertions on my part shall be spared to discover the villain.'

'I thank you,' replied I; 'listen, therefore, to the deposition that I have to make. It is indeed a tale so strange, that I should fear you would not credit it, were there not something in truth which, however wonderful, forces conviction. The story is too connected to be mistaken for a dream, and I have no motive for falsehood.' My manner, as I thus addressed him, was impressive, but calm; I had formed in my own heart a resolution to pursue my destroyer to death; and this purpose quieted my agony, and provisionally reconciled me to life. I now related my history briefly, but with firmness and precision, marking the dates with accuracy, and never deviating into invective or exclamation.

The magistrate appeared at first perfectly incredulous, but as I continued he became more attentive and interested; I saw him sometimes shudder with horror, at others a lively surprise, unmingled with disbelief, was painted on his countenance.

When I had concluded my narration, I said, 'This is the being whom I accuse, and for whose detection and punishment I call upon you to exert your whole power. It is your duty as a magistrate, and I believe and hope that your feelings as a man will not revolt from the execution of those functions on this occasion.'

This address caused a considerable change in the physiognomy of my auditor. He had heard my story with that half kind of belief that is given to a tale of spirits and supernatural events; but when he was called upon to act officially in consequence, the whole tide of his incredulity returned. He, however, answered mildly, 'I would willingly afford you every aid in your pursuit; but the creature of whom you speak appears to have powers which would put all my exertions to defiance. Who can follow an animal which can traverse the sea of ice, and inhabit caves and dens, where no man would venture to intrude? Besides, some months have elapsed since the commission of his crimes, and no one can conjecture to what place he has wandered, or what region he may now inhabit.'

'I do not doubt that he hovers near the spot which I inhabit; and if he has indeed taken refuge in the Alps, he may be hunted like the chamois, and destroyed as a beast of prey. But I perceive your thoughts: you do not credit my narrative, and do not intend to pursue my enemy with the punishment which is his desert.'

As I spoke, rage sparkled in my eyes; the magistrate was intimidated; 'You are mistaken,' said he, 'I will exert myself; and if it is in my power to seize the monster, be assured that he shall suffer punishment proportionate to his crimes. But I fear, from what you have yourself described to be his properties, that this will prove impracticable, and that, while every proper measure is pursued, you should endeavour to make up your mind to disappointment.'

'That cannot be; but all that I can say will be of little avail. My revenge is of no moment to you; yet, while I allow it to be a vice, I confess that it is the devouring and only passion of my soul. My rage is unspeakable, when I reflect that the murderer, whom I have turned loose upon society, still exists. You refuse my just demand: I have but one resource; and I devote myself, either in my life or death, to his destruction.'

I trembled with excess of agitation as I said this; there was a phrenzy in my manner, and something, I doubt not, of that haughty fierceness, which the martyrs of old are said to have possessed. But to a Genevan magistrate, whose mind was occupied by far other ideas than those of devotion and heroism, this elevation of mind had much the appearance of madness. He endeavoured to soothe me as a nurse does a child, and reverted to my tale as the effects of delirium.

'Man,' I cried, 'how ignorant art thou in thy pride of wisdom! Cease; you know not what it is you say.'

I broke from the house angry and disturbed, and retired to meditate on some other mode of action.

CHAPTER VII

My present situation was one in which all voluntary thought was swallowed up and lost. I was hurried away by fury; revenge alone endowed me with strength and composure; it modelled my feelings, and allowed me to be calculating and calm, at periods when otherwise delirium or death would have been my portion.

My first resolution was to quit Geneva for ever; my country, which, when I was happy and beloved, was dear to me, now, in my adversity, became hateful. I provided myself with a sum of money, together with a few jewels which had belonged to my mother, and departed.

And now my wanderings began, which are to cease but with life. I have traversed a vast portion of the earth, and have endured all the hardships which travellers, in deserts and barbarous countries, are wont to meet. How I have lived I hardly know; many times have I stretched my failing limbs upon the sandy plain, and prayed for death. But revenge kept me alive; I dared not die, and leave my adversary in being.

When I quitted Geneva, my first labour was to gain some clue by which I might trace the steps of my fiendish enemy. But my plan was unsettled; and I wandered many hours around the confines of the town, uncertain what path I should pursue. As night approached, I found myself at the entrance of the cemetery where William, Elizabeth, and my father, reposed. I entered it, and approached the tomb which marked their graves. Every thing was silent, except the leaves of the trees, which were gently agitated by the wind; the night was nearly dark; and the scene would have been solemn and affecting even to an uninterested observer. The spirits of the departed seemed to flit around, and to cast a shadow, which was felt but seen not, around the head of the mourner.

The deep grief which this scene had at first excited quickly gave way to rage and despair. They were dead, and I lived; their murderer also lived, and to destroy him I must drag out my weary existence. I knelt on the grass, and kissed the earth, and with quivering lips exclaimed, 'By the sacred earth on which I kneel, by the shades that wander near me, by the deep and eternal grief that I feel, I swear; and by thee, O Night, and by the spirits that preside over thee, I swear to pursue that dæmon, who caused this misery, until he or I shall perish in mortal conflict. For this purpose I will preserve my life: to execute this dear revenge, will I again behold the sun, and tread the green herbage of earth, which otherwise should vanish from my eyes for ever. And I call on you, spirits of the dead; and on you, wandering ministers of vengeance, to aid and conduct me in my work. Let the cursed and hellish monster drink deep of agony; let him feel the despair that now torments me.'

I had begun my adjuration with solemnity, and an awe which almost assured me that the shades of my murdered friends heard and approved my devotion; but the furies possessed me as I concluded, and rage choaked my utterance.

I was answered through the stillness of night by a loud and fiendish laugh. It rung on my ears long and heavily; the mountains re-echoed it, and I felt as if all hell surrounded me with mockery and laughter. Surely in that moment I should have been possessed by phrenzy, and have destroyed my miserable existence, but that my vow was heard, and that I was reserved for vengeance. The laughter died away; when a well-known and abhorred voice, apparently close to my ear, addressed me in an audible whisper—'I am satisfied: miserable wretch! you have determined to live, and I am satisfied.'

I darted towards the spot from which the sound proceeded; but the devil eluded my grasp. Suddenly the broad disk of the moon arose, and shone full upon his ghastly and distorted shape, as he fled with more than mortal speed.

I pursued him; and for many months this has been my task. Guided by a slight clue, I followed the windings of the Rhone, but vainly. The blue Mediterranean appeared; and, by a strange chance, I saw the fiend enter by night, and hide himself in a vessel bound for the Black Sea. I took my passage in the same ship; but he escaped, I know not how.

Amidst the wilds of Tartary and Russia, although he still evaded me, I have ever followed in his track. Sometimes the peasants, scared by this horrid apparition, informed me of his path; sometimes he himself, who feared that if I lost all trace I should despair and die, often left some mark to guide me. The snows descended on my head, and I saw the print of his huge step on the white plain. To you first entering on life, to whom care is new, and agony unknown, how can you understand what I have felt, and still feel? Cold, want, and fatigue, were the least pains which I was destined to endure; I was cursed by some devil, and carried about with me my eternal hell; yet still a spirit of good followed and directed my steps, and, when I most murmured, would suddenly extricate me from seemingly insurmountable difficulties. Sometimes, when nature, overcome by hunger, sunk under the exhaustion, a repast was prepared for me in the desert, that restored and inspirited me. The fare was indeed coarse, such as the peasants of the country ate; but I may not doubt that it was set there by the spirits that I had invoked to aid me. Often, when all was dry, the heavens cloudless, and I was parched by thirst, a slight cloud would bedim the sky, shed the few drops that revived me, and vanish.

I followed, when I could, the courses of the rivers; but the dæmon generally avoided these, as it was here that the population of the country chiefly collected. In other places human beings were seldom seen; and I generally subsisted on the wild animals that crossed my path. I had money with me, and gained the friendship of the villagers by distributing it, or bringing with me some food that I had killed, which, after taking a small part, I always presented to those who had provided me with fire and utensils for cooking.

My life, as it passed thus, was indeed hateful to me, and it was during sleep alone that I could taste joy. O blessed sleep! often, when most miserable, I sank to repose, and my dreams lulled me even to rapture. The spirits that guarded me had provided these moments, or rather hours, of happiness, that I might retain strength to fulfil my pilgrimage. Deprived of this respite, I should have sunk under my hardships. During the day I was sustained and inspirited by the hope of night: for in sleep I saw my friends, my wife, and my beloved country; again I saw the benevolent countenance of my father, heard the silver tones of my Elizabeth's voice, and beheld Clerval enjoying health and youth. Often, when wearied by a toilsome march, I persuaded myself that I was dreaming until night should come, and that I should then enjoy reality in the arms of my dearest friends. What agonizing fondness did I feel for them! how did I cling to their dear forms, as sometimes they haunted even my waking hours, and persuade myself that they still lived! At such moments vengeance, that burned within me, died in my heart, and I pursued my path towards the destruction of the dæmon, more as a task enjoined by heaven, as the mechanical impulse of some power of which I was unconscious, than as the ardent desire of my soul.

What his feelings were whom I pursued, I cannot know. Sometimes, indeed, he left marks in writing on the barks of the trees, or cut in stone, that guided me, and instigated my fury. 'My reign is not yet over,' (these words were legible in one of these inscriptions); 'you live, and my power is complete. Follow me; I seek the everlasting ices of the north, where you will feel the misery of cold and frost, to which I am impassive. You will find near this place, if you follow not too tardily, a dead hare; eat, and be refreshed. Come on, my enemy; we have yet to wrestle for our lives; but many hard and miserable hours must you endure, until that period shall arrive.'

Scoffing devil! Again do I vow vengeance; again do I devote thee, miserable fiend, to torture and death. Never will I omit my search, until he or I perish; and then with what ecstacy shall I join my Elizabeth, and those who even now prepare for me the reward of my tedious toil and horrible pilgrimage.

As I still pursued my journey to the northward, the snows thickened, and the cold increased in a degree almost too severe to support. The peasants were shut up in their hovels, and only a few of the most hardy ventured forth to seize the animals whom starvation had forced from their hiding-places to seek for prey. The rivers were covered with ice, and no fish could be procured; and thus I was cut off from my chief article of maintenance.

The triumph of my enemy increased with the difficulty of my labours. One inscription that he left was in these words: 'Prepare! your toils only begin: wrap yourself in furs, and provide food, for we shall soon enter upon a journey where your sufferings will satisfy my everlasting hatred.'

My courage and perseverance were invigorated by these scoffing words; I resolved not to fail in my purpose; and, calling on heaven to support me, I continued with unabated fervour to traverse immense deserts, until the ocean appeared at a distance, and formed the utmost boundary of the horizon. Oh! how unlike it was to the blue seas of the south! Covered with ice, it was only to be distinguished from land by its superior wildness and ruggedness. The Greeks wept for joy when they beheld the Mediterranean from the hills of Asia, and hailed with rapture the boundary of their toils. I did not weep; but I knelt down, and, with a full heart, thanked my guiding spirit for conducting me in safety to the place where I hoped, notwithstanding my adversary's gibe, to meet and grapple with him.

Some weeks before this period I had procured a sledge and dogs, and thus traversed the snows with inconceivable speed. I know not whether the fiend possessed the same advantages; but I found that, as before I had daily lost ground in the pursuit, I now gained on him; so much so, that when I first saw the ocean, he was but one day's journey in advance, and I hoped to intercept him before he should reach the beach. With new courage, therefore, I pressed on, and in two days arrived at a wretched hamlet on the seashore. I inquired of the inhabitants concerning the fiend, and gained accurate information. A gigantic monster, they said, had arrived the night before, armed with a gun and many pistols; putting to flight the inhabitants of a solitary cottage, through fear of his terrific appearance. He had carried off their store of winter food, and, placing it in a sledge, to draw which he had seized on a numerous drove of trained dogs, he had harnessed them, and the same night, to the joy of the horror-struck villagers, had pursued his journey across the sea in a direction that led to no land; and they conjectured that he must speedily be destroyed by the breaking of the ice, or frozen by the eternal frosts.

On hearing this information, I suffered a temporary access of despair. He had escaped me; and I must commence a destructive and almost endless journey across the mountainous ices of the ocean,—amidst cold that few of the inhabitants could long endure, and which I, the native of a genial and sunny climate, could not hope to survive. Yet at the idea that the fiend should live and be triumphant, my rage and vengeance returned, and, like a mighty tide, overwhelmed every other feeling. After a slight repose, during which the spirits of the dead hovered round, and instigated me to toil and revenge, I prepared for my journey.

I exchanged my land sledge for one fashioned for the inequalities of the frozen ocean; and, purchasing a plentiful stock of provisions, I departed from land.

I cannot guess how many days have passed since then; but I have endured misery, which nothing but the eternal sentiment of a just retribution burning within my heart could have enabled me to support. Immense and rugged mountains of ice often barred up my passage, and I often heard the thunder of the ground sea, which threatened my destruction. But again the frost came, and made the paths of the sea secure.

By the quantity of provision which I had consumed I should guess that I had passed three weeks in this journey; and the continual protraction of hope, returning back upon the heart, often wrung bitter drops of despondency and grief from my eyes. Despair had indeed almost secured her prey, and I should soon have sunk beneath this misery; when once, after the poor animals that carried me had with incredible toil gained the summit of a sloping ice mountain, and one sinking under his fatigue died, I viewed the expanse before me with anguish, when suddenly my eye caught a dark speck upon the dusky plain. I strained my sight to discover what it could be, and uttered a wild cry of ecstacy when I distinguished a sledge, and the distorted proportions of a well-known form within. Oh! with what a burning gush did hope revisit my heart! warm tears filled my eyes, which I hastily wiped away, that they might not intercept the view I had of the dæmon; but still my sight was dimmed by the burning drops, until, giving way to the emotions that oppressed me, I wept aloud.

But this was not the time for delay; I disencumbered the dogs of their dead companion, gave them a plentiful portion of food; and, after an hour's rest, which was absolutely necessary, and yet which was bitterly irksome to me, I continued my route. The sledge was still visible; nor did I again lose sight of it, except at the moments when for a short time some ice rock concealed it with its intervening crags. I indeed perceptibly gained on it; and when, after nearly two days' journey, I beheld my enemy at no more than a mile distant, my heart bounded within me.

But now, when I appeared almost within grasp of my enemy, my hopes were suddenly extinguished, and I lost all trace of him more utterly than I had ever done before. A ground sea was heard; the thunder of its progress, as the waters rolled and swelled beneath me, became every moment more ominous and terrific. I pressed on, but in vain. The wind arose; the sea roared; and, as with the mighty shock of an earthquake, it split, and cracked with a tremendous and overwhelming sound. The work was soon finished: in a few minutes a tumultuous sea rolled between me and my enemy, and I was left drifting on a scattered piece of ice, that was continually lessening, and thus preparing for me a hideous death.

In this manner many appalling hours passed; several of my dogs died; and I myself was about to sink under the accumulation of distress, when I saw your vessel riding at anchor, and holding forth to me hopes of succour and life. I had no conception that vessels ever came so far north, and was astounded at the sight. I quickly destroyed part of my sledge to construct oars; and by these means was enabled, with infinite fatigue, to move my ice-raft in the direction of your ship. I had determined, if you were going southward, still to trust myself to the mercy of the seas, rather than abandon my purpose. I hoped to induce you to grant me a boat with which I could still pursue my enemy. But your direction was northward. You took me on board when my vigour was exhausted, and I should soon have sunk under my multiplied hardship into a death, which I still dread,—for my task is unfulfilled.

Oh! when will my guiding spirit, in conducting me to the dæmon, allow me the rest I so much desire; or must I die, and he yet live? If I do, swear to me, Walton, that he shall not escape; that you will seek him, and satisfy my vengeance in his death. Yet, do I dare ask you to undertake my pilgrimage, to endure the hardships that I have undergone? No; I am not so selfish. Yet, when I am dead, if he should appear; if the ministers of vengeance should conduct him to you, swear that he shall not live—swear that he shall not triumph over my accumulated woes, and live to make another such a wretch as I am. He is eloquent and persuasive; and once his words had even power over my heart: but trust him not. His soul is as hellish as his form, full of treachery and fiend-like malice. Hear him not; call on the manes* of William, Justine, Clerval, Elizabeth, my father, and of the wretched Victor, and thrust your sword into his heart. I will hover near, and direct the steel aright.

WALTON, *in continuation.*

August 26th, 17—.

You have read this strange and terrific story, Margaret; and do you not feel your blood congealed with horror, like that which even now curdles mine? Sometimes, seized with sudden agony, he could not continue his tale; at others, his voice broken, yet piercing, uttered with difficulty the words so replete with agony. His fine and lovely eyes were now lighted up with indignation, now subdued to downcast sorrow, and quenched in infinite wretchedness. Sometimes he commanded his countenance and tones, and related the most horrible incidents with a tranquil voice, suppressing every mark of agitation; then, like a volcano bursting forth, his face would suddenly change to an expression of the wildest rage, as he shrieked out imprecations on his persecutor.

His tale is connected, and told with an appearance of the simplest truth; yet I own to you that the letters of Felix and Safie, which he shewed me, and the apparition of the monster, seen from our ship, brought to me a greater conviction of the truth of his narrative than his asseverations, however earnest and connected. Such a monster has then really existence; I cannot doubt it; yet I am lost in surprise and admiration. Sometimes I endeavoured to gain from Frankenstein the particulars of his creature's formation; but on this point he was impenetrable.

'Are you mad, my friend?' said he, 'or whither does your senseless curiosity lead you? Would you also create for yourself and the world a demoniacal enemy? Or to what do your questions tend? Peace, peace! learn my miseries, and do not seek to increase your own.'

Frankenstein discovered that I made notes concerning his history: he asked to see them, and then himself corrected and augmented them in many places; but principally in giving the life and spirit to the conversations he held with his enemy. 'Since you have preserved my narration,' said he, 'I would not that a mutilated one should go down to posterity.'

Thus has a week passed away, while I have listened to the strangest tale that ever imagination formed. My thoughts, and every feeling of my soul, have been drunk up by the interest for my guest, which this tale, and his own elevated and gentle manners have created. I wish to soothe him; yet can I counsel one so infinitely miserable, so destitute of every hope of consolation, to live? Oh, no! the only joy that he can now know will be when he composes his shattered feelings to peace and death. Yet he enjoys one comfort, the offspring of solitude and delirium: he believes, that, when in dreams he holds converse with his friends, and derives from that communion consolation for his miseries, or excitements to his vengeance, that they are not the creations of his fancy, but the real beings who visit him from the regions of a remote world. This faith gives a solemnity to his reveries that render them to me almost as imposing and interesting as truth.

Our conversations are not always confined to his own history and misfortunes. On every point of general literature he displays unbounded knowledge, and a quick and piercing apprehension. His eloquence is forcible and touching; nor can I hear him, when he relates a pathetic incident, or endeavours to move the passions of pity or love, without tears. What a glorious creature must he have been in the days of his prosperity, when he is thus noble and godlike in ruin. He seems to feel his own worth, and the greatness of his fall.

'When younger,' said he, 'I felt as if I were destined for some great enterprise. My feelings are profound; but I possessed a coolness of judgment that fitted me for illustrious achievements. This sentiment of the worth of my nature supported me, when others would have been oppressed; for I deemed it criminal to throw away in useless grief those talents that might be useful to my fellow-creatures. When I reflected on the work I had completed, no less a one than the creation

of a sensitive and rational animal, I could not rank myself with
the herd of common projectors. But this feeling, which supported me in the commencement of my career, now serves
only to plunge me lower in the dust. All my speculations and
hopes are as nothing; and, like the archangel who aspired to
omnipotence, I am chained in an eternal hell. My imagination was vivid, yet my powers of analysis and application were
intense; by the union of these qualities I conceived the idea,
and executed the creation of a man. Even now I cannot
recollect, without passion, my reveries while the work was
incomplete. I trod heaven in my thoughts, now exulting in my
powers, now burning with the idea of their effects. From my
infancy I was imbued with high hopes and a lofty ambition;
but how am I sunk! Oh! my friend, if you had known me as I
once was, you would not recognize me in this state of degradation. Despondency rarely visited my heart; a high destiny
seemed to bear me on, until I fell, never, never again to rise.'

Must I then lose this admirable being? I have longed for a
friend; I have sought one who would sympathize with and love
me. Behold, on these desert seas I have found such a one; but,
I fear, I have gained him only to know his value, and lose him.
I would reconcile him to life, but he repulses the idea.

'I thank you, Walton,' he said, 'for your kind intentions
towards so miserable a wretch; but when you speak of new
ties, and fresh affections, think you that any can replace those
who are gone? Can any man be to me as Clerval was; or any
woman another Elizabeth? Even where the affections are not
strongly moved by any superior excellence, the companions
of our childhood always possess a certain power over our
minds, which hardly any later friend can obtain. They know
our infantine dispositions, which, however they may be afterwards modified, are never eradicated; and they can judge of
our actions with more certain conclusions as to the integrity
of our motives. A sister or a brother can never, unless indeed
such symptoms have been shewn early, suspect the other of
fraud or false dealing, when another friend, however strongly
he may be attached, may, in spite of himself, he invaded with
suspicion. But I enjoyed friends, dear not only through habit
and association, but from their own merits; and, wherever I

am, the soothing voice of my Elizabeth, and the conversation of Clerval, will be ever whispered in my ear. They are dead; and but one feeling in such a solitude can persuade me to preserve my life. If I were engaged in any high undertaking or design, fraught with extensive utility to my fellow-creatures, then could I live to fulfil it. But such is not my destiny; I must pursue and destroy the being to whom I gave existence; then my lot on earth will be fulfilled, and I may die.'

September 2d.

MY BELOVED SISTER,

I write to you, encompassed by peril, and ignorant whether I am ever doomed to see again dear England, and the dearer friends that inhabit it. I am surrounded by mountains of ice, which admit of no escape, and threaten every moment to crush my vessel. The brave fellows, whom I have persuaded to be my companions, look towards me for aid; but I have none to bestow. There is something terribly appalling in our situation, yet my courage and hopes do not desert me. We may survive; and if we do not, I will repeat the lessons of my Seneca, and die with a good heart.

Yet what, Margaret, will be the state of your mind? You will not hear of my destruction, and you will anxiously await my return. Years will pass, and you will have visitings of despair, and yet be tortured by hope. Oh! my beloved sister, the sickening failings of your heart-felt expectations are, in prospect, more terrible to me than my own death. But you have a husband, and lovely children; you may be happy: heaven bless you, and make you so!

My unfortunate guest regards me with the tenderest compassion. He endeavours to fill me with hope; and talks as if life were a possession which he valued. He reminds me how often the same accidents have happened to other navigators, who have attempted this sea, and, in spite of myself, he fills me with cheerful auguries. Even the sailors feel the power of his eloquence: when he speaks, they no longer despair; he rouses their energies, and, while they hear his voice, they believe these vast mountains of ice are mole-hills, which will vanish before the resolutions of man. These feelings are transitory;

each day's expectation delayed fills them with fear, and I almost dread a mutiny caused by this despair.

September 5th.

A scene has just passed of such uncommon interest, that although it is highly probable that these papers may never reach you, yet I cannot forbear recording it.

We are still surrounded by mountains of ice, still in imminent danger of being crushed in their conflict. The cold is excessive, and many of my unfortunate comrades have already found a grave amidst this scene of desolation. Frankenstein has daily declined in health: a feverish fire still glimmers in his eyes; but he is exhausted, and, when suddenly roused to any exertion, he speedily sinks again into apparent lifelessness.

I mentioned in my last letter the fears I entertained of a mutiny. This morning, as I sat watching the wan countenance of my friend—his eyes half closed, and his limbs hanging listlessly,—I was roused by half a dozen of the sailors, who desired admission into the cabin. They entered; and their leader addressed me. He told me that he and his companions had been chosen by the other sailors to come in deputation to me, to make me a demand, which, in justice, I could not refuse. We were immured in ice, and should probably never escape; but they feared that if, as was possible, the ice should dissipate, and a free passage be opened, I should be rash enough to continue my voyage, and lead them into fresh dangers, after they might happily have surmounted this. They desired, therefore, that I should engage with a solemn promise, that if the vessel should be freed, I would instantly direct my course southward.

This speech troubled me. I had not despaired; nor had I yet conceived the idea of returning, if set free. Yet could I, in justice, or even in possibility, refuse this demand? I hesitated before I answered; when Frankenstein, who had at first been silent, and, indeed, appeared hardly to have force enough to attend, now roused himself; his eyes sparkled, and his cheeks flushed with momentary vigour. Turning towards the men, he said—

'What do you mean? What do you demand of your captain? Are you then so easily turned from your design? Did you not call this a glorious expedition? and wherefore was it glorious? Not because the way was smooth and placid as a southern sea, but because it was full of dangers and terror; because, at every new incident, your fortitude was to be called forth, and your courage exhibited; because danger and death surrounded, and these dangers you were to brave and overcome. For this was it a glorious, for this was it an honourable undertaking. You were hereafter to be hailed as the benefactors of your species; your name adored, as belonging to brave men who encountered death for honour and the benefit of mankind. And now, behold, with the first imagination of danger, or, if you will, the first mighty and terrific trial of your courage, you shrink away, and are content to be handed down as men who had not strength enough to endure cold and peril; and so, poor souls, they were chilly, and returned to their warm fire-sides. Why, that requires not this preparation; ye need not have come thus far, and dragged your captain to the shame of a defeat, merely to prove yourselves cowards. Oh! be men, or be more than men. Be steady to your purposes, and firm as a rock. This ice is not made of such stuff as your hearts might be; it is mutable, cannot withstand you, if you say that it shall not. Do not return to your families with the stigma of disgrace marked on your brows. Return as heroes who have fought and conquered, and who know not what it is to turn their backs on the foe.'*

He spoke this with a voice so modulated to the different feelings expressed in his speech, with an eye so full of lofty design and heroism, that can you wonder that these men were moved. They looked at one another, and were unable to reply. I spoke; I told them to retire, and consider of what had been said: that I would not lead them further north, if they strenuously desired the contrary; but that I hoped that, with reflection, their courage would return.

They retired, and I turned towards my friend; but he was sunk in languor, and almost deprived of life.

How all this will terminate, I know not; but I had rather die, than return shamefully,—my purpose unfulfilled. Yet I fear such will be my fate; the men, unsupported by ideas of glory and honour, can never willingly continue to endure their present hardships.

September 7th.

The die is cast; I have consented to return, if we are not destroyed. Thus are my hopes blasted by cowardice and indecision; I come back ignorant and disappointed. It requires more philosophy than I possess, to bear this injustice with patience.

September 12th.

It is past; I am returning to England. I have lost my hopes of utility and glory;—I have lost my friend. But I will endeavour to detail these bitter circumstances to you, my dear sister; and, while I am wafted towards England, and towards you, I will not despond.

September 9th,* the ice began to move, and roarings like thunder were heard at a distance, as the islands split and cracked in every direction. We were in the most imminent peril; but, as we could only remain passive, my chief attention was occupied by my unfortunate guest, whose illness increased in such a degree, that he was entirely confined to his bed. The ice cracked behind us, and was driven with force towards the north; a breeze sprung from the west, and on the 11th the passage towards the south became perfectly free. When the sailors saw this, and that their return to their native country was apparently assured, a shout of tumultuous joy broke from them, loud and long-continued. Frankenstein, who was dozing, awoke, and asked the cause of the tumult. 'They shout,' I said, 'because they will soon return to England.'

'Do you then really return?'

'Alas! yes; I cannot withstand their demands. I cannot lead them unwillingly to danger, and I must return.'

'Do so, if you will; but I will not. You may give up your purpose; but mine is assigned to me by heaven, and I dare not. I am weak; but surely the spirits who assist my vengeance will endow me with sufficient strength.' Saying this, he endeavoured to spring from the bed, but the exertion was too great for him; he fell back, and fainted.

It was long before he was restored; and I often thought that life was entirely extinct. At length he opened his eyes, but he breathed with difficulty, and was unable to speak. The surgeon gave him a composing draught, and ordered us to leave him undisturbed. In the mean time he told me, that my friend had certainly not many hours to live.

His sentence was pronounced; and I could only grieve, and be patient. I sat by his bed watching him; his eyes were closed, and I thought he slept; but presently he called to me in a feeble voice, and, bidding me come near, said—'Alas! the strength I relied on is gone; I feel that I shall soon die, and he, my enemy and persecutor, may still be in being. Think not, Walton, that in the last moments of my existence I feel that burning hatred, and ardent desire of revenge, I once expressed, but I feel myself justified in desiring the death of my adversary. During these last days I have been occupied in examining my past conduct; nor do I find it blameable. In a fit of enthusiastic madness I created a rational creature, and was bound towards him, to assure, as far as was in my power, his happiness and well-being. This was my duty; but there was another still paramount to that. My duties towards my fellow-creatures had greater claims to my attention, because they included a greater proportion of happiness or misery. Urged by this view, I refused, and I did right in refusing, to create a companion for the first creature. He shewed unparalleled malignity and selfishness, in evil: he destroyed my friends; he devoted to destruction beings who possessed exquisite sensations, happiness, and wisdom; nor do I know where this thirst for vengeance may end. Miserable himself, that he may render no other wretched, he ought to die. The task of his destruction was mine, but I have failed. When actuated by selfish and vicious motives, I asked you to undertake my unfinished work; and I renew this request now, when I am only induced by reason and virtue.

'Yet I cannot ask you to renounce your country and friends, to fulfil this task; and now, that you are returning to England, you will have little chance of meeting with him. But the consideration of these points, and the well-balancing of what you may esteem your duties, I leave to you; my judgment and ideas are already disturbed by the near approach of death. I dare not ask you to do what I think right, for I may still be misled by passion.

'That he should live to be an instrument of mischief disturbs me; in other respects this hour, when I momentarily expect my release, is the only happy one which I have enjoyed for several years. The forms of the beloved dead flit before me, and I hasten to their arms. Farewell, Walton! Seek happiness in tranquillity, and avoid ambition, even if it be only the apparently innocent one of distinguishing yourself in science and discoveries. Yet why do I say this? I have myself been blasted in these hopes, yet another may succeed.'

His voice became fainter as he spoke; and at length, exhausted by his effort, he sunk into silence. About half an hour afterwards he attempted again to speak, but was unable; he pressed my hand feebly, and his eyes closed for ever, while the irradiation of a gentle smile passed away from his lips.

Margaret, what comment can I make on the untimely extinction of this glorious spirit? What can I say, that will enable you to understand the depth of my sorrow? All that I should express would be inadequate and feeble. My tears flow; my mind is overshadowed by a cloud of disappointment. But I journey towards England, and I may there find consolation.

I am interrupted. What do these sounds portend? It is midnight; the breeze blows fairly, and the watch on deck scarcely stir. Again; there is a sound as of a human voice, but hoarser; it comes from the cabin where the remains of Frankenstein still lie. I must arise, and examine. Good night, my sister.

Great God! what a scene has just taken place! I am yet dizzy with the remembrance of it. I hardly know whether I shall have the power to detail it; yet the tale which I have recorded would be incomplete without this final and wonderful catastrophe.

I entered the cabin, where lay the remains of my ill-fated and admirable friend. Over him hung a form which I cannot find words to describe; gigantic in stature, yet uncouth and distorted in its proportions. As he hung over the coffin, his face was concealed by long locks of ragged hair; but one vast hand was extended, in colour and apparent texture like that of a mummy. When he heard the sound of my approach, he ceased to utter exclamations of grief and horror, and sprung towards the window. Never did I behold a vision so horrible as his face, of such loathsome, yet appalling hideousness. I shut my eyes involuntarily, and endeavoured to recollect what were my duties with regard to this destroyer. I called on him to stay.

He paused, looking on me with wonder; and, again turning towards the lifeless form of his creator, he seemed to forget my presence, and every feature and gesture seemed instigated by the wildest rage of some uncontrollable passion.

'That is also my victim!' he exclaimed; 'in his murder my crimes are consummated; the miserable series of my being is wound to its close! Oh, Frankenstein! generous and self-devoted being! what does it avail that I now ask thee to pardon me? I, who irretrievably destroyed thee by destroying all thou lovedst. Alas! he is cold; he may not answer me.'

His voice seemed suffocated; and my first impulses, which had suggested to me the duty of obeying the dying request of my friend, in destroying his enemy, were now suspended by a mixture of curiosity and compassion. I approached this tre-mendous being; I dared not again raise my looks upon his face, there was something so scaring and unearthly in his ugliness. I attempted to speak, but the words died away on my lips. The monster continued to utter wild and incoherent self-reproaches. At length I gathered resolution to address him, in a pause of the tempest of his passion: 'Your repentance,' I said, 'is now superfluous. If you had listened to the voice of conscience, and heeded the stings of remorse, before you had urged your diabolical vengeance to this extremity, Frankenstein would yet have lived.'

'And do you dream?' said the dæmon; 'do you think that I was then dead to agony and remorse?—He,' he continued, pointing to the corpse, 'he suffered not more in the consum-mation of the deed;—oh! not the ten-thousandth portion of the anguish that was mine during the lingering detail of its execution. A frightful selfishness hurried me on, while my heart was poisoned with remorse. Think ye that the groans of Clerval were music to my ears? My heart was fashioned to be susceptible of love and sympathy; and, when wrenched by misery to vice and hatred, it did not endure the violence of the change without torture, such as you cannot even imagine.

'After the murder of Clerval, I returned to Switzerland, heart-broken and overcome. I pitied Frankenstein; my pity amounted to horror: I abhorred myself. But when I discovered that he, the author at once of my existence and of its unspeakable torments, dared to hope for happiness; that while he accumulated wretchedness and despair upon me, he sought his own enjoyment in feelings and passions from the indulgence of which I was for ever barred, then impotent envy and bitter indignation filled me with an insatiable thirst for vengeance I recollected my threat, and resolved that it should be accomplished. I knew that I was preparing for myself a deadly torture; but I was the slave, not the master of an impulse, which I detested, yet could not disobey. Yet when she died!—nay, then I was not miserable. I had cast off all feeling, subdued all anguish to riot in the excess of my despair. Evil thenceforth became my good. Urged thus far, I had no choice but to adapt my nature to an element which I had willingly chosen. The completion of my demoniacal design became an insatiable passion. And now it is ended; there is my last victim!'

I was at first touched by the expressions of his misery; yet when I called to mind what Frankenstein had said of his powers of eloquence and persuasion, and when I again cast my eyes on the lifeless form of my friend, indignation was rekindled within me. 'Wretch!' I said, 'it is well that you come here to whine over the desolation that you have made. You throw a torch into a pile of buildings, and when they are consumed you sit among the ruins, and lament the fall. Hypocritical fiend! if he whom you mourn still lived, still would he be the object, again would he become the prey of your accursed vengeance. It is not pity that you feel; you lament only because the victim of your malignity is withdrawn from your power.'

'Oh, it is not thus—not thus,' interrupted the being; 'yet such must be the impression conveyed to you by what appears to be the purport of my actions. Yet I seek not a fellow-feeling in my misery. No sympathy may I ever find. When I first sought it, it was the love of virtue, the feelings of happiness and affection with which my whole being overflowed, that I wished to be participated. But now, that virtue has become to me a shadow, and that happiness and affection are turned into bitter and loathing despair, in what should I seek for sympathy? I am content to suffer alone, while my sufferings shall endure: when I die, I am well satisfied that abhorrence and opprobrium should load my memory. Once my fancy was soothed with dreams of virtue, of fame, and of enjoyment. Once I falsely hoped to meet with beings, who, pardoning my outward form, would love me for the excellent qualities which I was capable of bringing forth. I was nourished with high thoughts of honour and devotion. But now vice. has degraded me beneath the meanest animal. No crime, no mischief, no malignity, no misery, can be found comparable to mine. When I call over the frightful catalogue of my deeds, I cannot believe that I am he whose thoughts were once filled with sublime and transcendant visions of the beauty and the majesty of goodness. But it is even so; the fallen angel becomes a malignant devil. Yet even that enemy of God and man had friends and associates in his desolation; I am quite alone.

'You, who call Frankenstein your friend, seem to have a knowledge of my crimes and his misfortunes. But, in the detail which he gave you of them, he could not sum up the hours and months of misery which I endured, wasting in impotent passions. For whilst I destroyed his hopes, I did not satisfy my own desires. They were for ever ardent and craving; still I desired love and fellowship, and I was still spurned. Was there no injustice in this? Am I to be thought the only criminal, when all human kind sinned against me? Why do you not hate Felix, who drove his friend from his door with contumely? Why do you not execrate the rustic who sought to destroy the saviour of his child? Nay, these are are virtuous and immaculate beings? I, the miserable and the abandoned, am an abortion, to be spurned at, and kicked, and trampled on. Even now my blood boils at the recollection of this injustice.

'But it is true that I am a wretch. I have murdered the lovely and the helpless; I have strangled the innocent as they slept, and grasped to death his throat who never injured me or any other living thing. I have devoted my creator, the select specimen of all that is worthy of love and admiration among men, to misery; I have pursued him even to that irremediable ruin. There he lies, white and cold in death. You hate me; but your abhorrence cannot equal that with which I regard myself. I look on the hands which executed the deed; I think on the heart in which the imagination of it was conceived, and long for the moment when they will meet my eyes, when it will haunt my thoughts, no more.

'Fear not that I shall be the instrument of future mischief. My work is nearly complete. Neither yours nor any man's death is needed to consummate the series of my being, and accomplish that which must be done; but it requires my own. Do not think that I shall be slow to perform this sacrifice. I shall quit your vessel on the ice-raft which brought me hither, and shall seek the most northern extremity of the globe; I shall collect my funeral pile, and consume to ashes this miserable frame, that its remains may afford no light to any curious and unhallowed wretch, who would create such another as I have been. I shall die. I shall no longer feel the agonies which now consume me, or be the prey of feelings unsatisfied, yet unquenched. He is dead who called me into being; and when I shall be no more, the very remembrance of us both will speedily vanish. I shall no longer see the sun or stars, or feel the winds play on my cheeks. Light, feeling, and sense, will pass away; and in this condition must I find my happiness. Some years ago, when the images which this world affords first opened upon me, when I felt the cheering warmth of summer, and heard the rustling of the leaves and the chirping of the birds, and these were all to me, I should have wept to die; now it is my only consolation. Polluted by crimes, and torn by the bitterest remorse, where can I find rest but in death?

'Farewell! I leave you, and in you the last of human kind whom these eyes will ever behold. Farewell, Frankenstein! If thou wert yet alive, and yet cherished a desire of revenge against me, it would be better satiated in my life than in my destruction. But it was not so; thou didst seek my extinction, that I might not cause greater wretchedness; and if yet, in some mode unknown to me, thou hast not yet ceased to think and feel, thou desirest not my life for my own misery. Blasted as thou wert, my agony was still superior to thine; for the bitter sting of remorse may not cease to rankle in my wounds until death shall close them for ever.

'But soon,' he cried, with sad and solemn enthusiasm, 'I shall die, and what I now feel be no longer felt. Soon these burning miseries will be extinct. I shall ascend my funeral pile triumphantly, and exult in the agony of the torturing flames. The light of that conflagration will fade away; my ashes will be swept into the sea by the winds. My spirit will sleep in peace; or if it thinks, it will not surely think thus. Farewell.'

He sprung from the cabin-window, as he said this, upon the ice-raft which lay close to the vessel. He was soon borne away by the waves, and lost in darkness and distance.

THE END

APPENDIX A

AUTHOR'S INTRODUCTION
TO THE STANDARD NOVELS EDITION
(1831)

The publishers of the Standard Novels,* in selecting *Frankenstein* for one of their series, expressed a wish that I should furnish them with some account of the origin of the story. I am the more willing to comply, because I shall thus give a general answer to the question, so very frequently asked me —'How I, then a young girl, came to think of and to dilate upon so very hideous an idea?' It is true that I am very averse to bringing myself forward in print; but as my account will only appear as an appendage to a former production, and as it will be confined to such topics as have connexion with my authorship alone, I can scarcely accuse myself of a personal intrusion.

It is not singular that, as the daughter of two persons of distinguished literary celebrity, I should very early in life have thought of writing. As a child I scribbled; and my favourite pastime during the hours given me for recreation was to 'write stories'. Still, I had a dearer pleasure than this, which was the formation of castles in the air—the indulging in waking dreams—the following up trains of thought, which had for their subject the formation of a succession of imaginary incidents. My dreams were at once more fantastic and agreeable than my writings. In the latter I was a close imitator—rather doing as others had done than putting down the suggestions of my own mind. What I wrote was intended at least for one other eye—my childhood's companion and friend,* but my dreams were all my own; I accounted for them to nobody; they were my refuge when annoyed—my dearest pleasure when free.

I lived principally in the country as a girl, and passed a considerable time in Scotland. I made occasional visits to the more picturesque parts; but my habitual residence was on the blank and dreary northern shores of the Tay, near Dundee. Blank and dreary on retrospection I call them; they were not so to me then. They were the eyry* of freedom, and the pleasant region where unheeded I could commune with the creatures of my fancy. I wrote then—but in a most common-place style. It was beneath the trees of the grounds belonging to our house, or on the bleak sides of the woodless mountains near, that my true compositions, the airy flights of my imagination, were born and fostered. I did not make myself the heroine of my tales. Life appeared to me too common-place an affair as regarded myself. I could not figure to myself that romantic woes or wonderful events would ever be my lot; but I was not confined to my own identity, and I could people the hours with creations far more interesting to me at that age than my own sensations.

After this my life became busier, and reality stood in place of fiction. My husband, however, was from the first, very anxious that I should prove myself worthy of my parentage, and enrol myself on the page of fame. He was for ever inciting me to obtain literary reputation, which even on my own part I cared for then, though since I have become infinitely indifferent to it. At this time he desired that I should write, not so much with the idea that I could produce any thing worthy of notice, but, that he might himself judge how far I possessed the promise of better things hereafter. Still I did nothing. Travelling, and the cares of a family, occupied my time; and study, in the way of reading or improving my ideas in communication with his far more cultivated mind, was all of literary employment that engaged my attention.

In the summer of 1816, we visited Switzerland, and became the neighbours of Lord Byron. At first we spent our pleasant hours on the lake, or wandering on its shores; and Lord Byron, who was writing the third canto of *Childe Harold*, was the only one among us who put his thoughts upon paper. These, as he brought them successively to us, clothed in all the light and harmony of poetry, seemed to stamp as divine the glories of heaven and earth, whose influences we partook with him.

But it proved a wet, ungenial summer, and incessant rain often confined us for days to the house. Some volumes of ghost stories, translated from the German into French, fell into our hands. There was the *History of the Inconstant Lover*, who, when he thought to clasp the bride to whom he had pledged his vows, found himself in the arms of the pale ghost of her whom he had deserted. There was the tale of the sinful founder* of his race whose miserable doom it was to bestow the kiss of death on all the younger sons of his fated house, just when they reached the age of promise. His gigantic, shadowy form, clothed like the ghost in *Hamlet*, in complete armour, but with the beaver up, was seen at midnight, by the moon's fitful beams, to advance slowly along the gloomy avenue. The shape was lost beneath the shadow of the castle walls; but soon a gate swung back, a step was heard, the door of the chamber opened, and he advanced to the couch of the blooming youths, cradled in healthy sleep. Eternal sorrow sat upon his face as he bent down and kissed the forehead of the boys, who from that hour withered like flowers snapt upon the stalk. I have not seen these stories since then; but their incidents are as fresh in my mind as if I had read them yesterday.

'We will each write a ghost story', said Lord Byron; and his proposition was acceded to. There were four of us. The noble author began a tale, a fragment of which he printed at the end of his poem of *Mazeppa*.* Shelley, more apt to embody ideas and sentiments in the radiance of brilliant imagery, and in the music of the most melodious verse that adorns our language, than to invent the machinery of a story, commenced one founded on the experiences of his early life. Poor Polidori had some terrible idea about a skull-headed lady who was so punished for peeping through a keyhole—what to see I forget—something very shocking and wrong of course; but when she was reduced to a worse condition than the renowned Tom of Coventry,* he did not know what to do with her and was obliged to dispatch her to the tomb of the Capulets, the only place for which she was fitted. The illustrious poets also, annoyed by the platitude of prose, speedily relinquished their uncongenial task.

I busied myself *to think of a story*,—a story to rival those which had excited us to this task. One which would speak to the mysterious fears of our nature and awaken thrilling horror—one to make the reader dread to look round, to curdle the blood, and quicken the beatings of the heart. If I did not accomplish these things, my ghost story would be unworthy of its name. I thought and pondered—vainly. I felt that blank incapability of invention which is the greatest misery of authorship, when dull Nothing replies to our anxious invocations. 'Have you thought of a story?' I was asked each morning, and each morning I was forced to reply with a mortifying negative.

Every thing must have a beginning, to speak in Sanchean phrase;* and that beginning must be linked to something that went before. The Hindoos give the world an elephant to support it, but they make the elephant stand upon a tortoise. Invention, it must be humbly admitted, does not consist in creating out of void, but out of chaos; the materials must, in the first place, be afforded: it can give form to dark, shapeless substances, but cannot bring into being the substance itself. In all matters of discovery and invention, even of those that appertain to the imagination, we are continually reminded of the story of Columbus and his egg.* Invention consists in the capacity of seizing on the capabilities of a subject: and in the power of moulding and fashioning ideas suggested to it.

Many and long were the conversations between Lord Byron and Shelley, to which I was a devout but nearly silent listener. During one of these, various philosophical doctrines were discussed, and among others the nature of the principle of life, and whether there was any probability of its ever being discovered and communicated.* They talked of the experiments of Dr Darwin (I speak not of what the Doctor really did, or said that he did, but, as more to my purpose, of what was then spoken of as having been done by him), who preserved a piece of vermicelli in a glass case, till by some extraordinary means it began to move with voluntary motion.* Not thus, after all, would life be given. Perhaps a corpse would be reanimated; galvanism* had given token of such things: perhaps the component parts of a creature might be manufactured, brought together, and endued with vital warmth.

Night waned upon this talk, and even the witching hour had gone by, before we retired to rest. When I placed my head on my pillow, I did not sleep, nor could I be said to think. My imagination,* unbidden, possessed and guided me, gifting the successive images that arose in my mind with a vividness far beyond the usual bounds of reverie. I saw—with shut eyes, but acute mental vision—I saw the pale student of unhallowed arts kneeling beside the thing he had put together. I saw the hideous phantasm of a man stretched out, and then, on the working of some powerful engine, show signs of life, and stir with an uneasy, half-vital motion. Frightful must it be; for supremely frightful would be the effect of any human endeavour to mock the stupendous mechanism of the Creator of the world.* His success would terrify the artist; he would rush away from his odious handiwork, horror-stricken. He would hope that, left to itself, the slight spark of life which he had communicated would fade; that this thing, which had received such imperfect animation would subside into dead matter; and he might sleep in the belief that the silence of the grave would quench forever the transient existence of the hideous corpse which he had looked upon as the cradle of life. He sleeps; but he is awakened; he opens his eyes; behold, the horrid thing stands at his bedside, opening his curtains and looking on him with yellow, watery, but speculative eyes.

I opened mine in terror. The idea so possessed my mind, that a thrill of fear ran through me, and I wished to exchange the ghastly image of my fancy for the realities around. I see them still; the very room, the dark *parquet*, the closed shutters, with the moonlight struggling through, and the sense I had that the glassy lake and white high Alps were beyond. I could not so easily get rid of my hideous phantom; still it haunted me. I must try to think of something else. I recurred to my ghost story—my tiresome, unlucky ghost story! O! if I could only contrive one which would frighten my reader as I myself had been frightened that night!

Swift as light and as cheering was the idea that broke in upon me. 'I have found it! What terrified me will terrify others; and I need only describe the spectre which had haunted my midnight pillow.' On the morrow I announced that I had *thought of a story*. I began that day with the words, 'It was on a dreary night of November,'* making only a transcript of the grim terrors of my waking dream.

At first I thought but a few pages—of a short tale; but Shelley urged me to develope the idea at greater length. I certainly did not owe the suggestion of one incident, nor scarcely of one train of feeling, to my husband,* and yet but for his incitement it would never have taken the form in which it was presented to the world. From this declaration I must except the preface. As far as I can recollect, it was entirely written by him.

And now, once again, I bid my hideous progeny go forth and prosper. I have affection for it, for it was the offspring of happy days, when death and grief were but words, which found no true echo in my heart. Its several pages speak of many a walk, many a drive, and many a conversation, when I was not alone; and my companion was one who, in this world, I shall never see more. But this is for myself; my readers have nothing to do with these associations.

I will add but one word as to the alterations I have made. They are principally those of style. I have changed no portion of the story nor introduced any new ideas or circumstances. I have mended the language where it was so bald as to interfere with the interest of the narrative; and these changes occur almost exclusively in the beginning of the first volume. Throughout they are entirely confined to such parts as are mere adjuncts to the story, leaving the core and substance of it untouched.*

M.W.S.

London,
October 15th, 1831.

APPENDIX B

This Appendix first summarizes the types of change made in 1831, before listing them individually.

1. As a more practised, polished writer, MWS regularly amplifies descriptive passages or introduces reflective ones. She gives Frankenstein and to a lesser extent Walton an inner life and a conscience. The most extensive and significant changes occur at the beginning (the most crudely written part of the 1818 text); the first chapter is sufficiently amplified to be divided into two chapters. By the standards of early Victorian literary taste, and still by many standards, these changes enhance the book.

2. The characters of Walton, Frankenstein, and Alphonse Frankenstein are all softened, made more sympathetic and admirable. Walton acquires a gentle, almost feminine character, literariness, and an even greater propensity than in 1818 to hero-worship Frankenstein. Alphonse Frankenstein is still old when he marries, but much haler than before, and his marriage is in 1831 an ideal one. But the most significant changes occur in the narration of Frankenstein, who is partly absolved from blame for his early errors (now put down to bad influences), yet also reproaches himself more than in the first version.

3. Frankenstein's education is heavily rewritten. As before, it is largely scientific. But the family's ignorance of science is now stressed, so that the young boy is left to his own devices, and his involvement with Renaissance science or magic becomes a childish enthusiasm. A stranger teaches him about electricity, not his father (who thus escapes blame too). The first identifiable villains in this version of the story are his teachers at Ingolstadt—a notoriously unorthodox university—who teach him bad knowledge.

4. Partly via Walton, Victor Frankenstein's character is now built up as admirable. His own description of his early craving

for knowledge becomes desire for the ideal—a quintessentially Romantic search for 'the inner spirit of nature and the mysterious soul of man . . . the metaphysical, or, in the highest sense, the physical secrets of the world'. These lines are key ones, for they deny the more consistent links of the original Frankenstein with materialist science. MWS takes other steps to disengage from naturalism, e.g. 'the monstrous Image which I had endued with the mockery of a soul still more monstrous' (III. iv; 1831, xxi). And, lest his antisocial feelings after the Irish expedition should seem to be condoned, 'Oh, not abhorred! they were my brethren, my fellow beings, and I felt attracted even to the most repulsive among them, as to creatures of angelic nature and celestial mechanism' (III. v).

5. Frankenstein is given an explicitly religious consciousness. At the point in his boyhood when he becomes disillusioned with science, he (1831) observes, 'it seems to me as if this almost miraculous change of inclination and will was the immediate suggestion of the guardian angel of my life'; conversely, on arrival at Ingolstadt, it is the angel of destruction that leads him to M. Krempe. And, 'I felt as if my soul were grappling with a palpable enemy' (I. i and ii). Extensive additions to II. i sacralize Nature in a style new to the novel. Almost all the substitute passages in Vol. III soften and Christianize Frankenstein's character, toning down the severity of the portrayal in 1818.

6. A number of scientific passages are either cut, like the seemingly innocuous description of Franklin's famous experiment with electricity (I. i) or transvalued. His youthful flirtation with Renaissance magic becomes equated with 'natural history' generally, now defined pejoratively—'I . . . set down natural history and all its progeny as a deformed and abortive creation.' When he gets to Ingolstadt his reconversion to natural science is represented as regression, 'a resolution to return to my ancient studies'. The 1831 reader is allowed to think that the faculty at Ingolstadt in the 1790s, even the previously sympathetic Waldman (I. ii. 30), were indeed teaching arcane magic under the name of natural science.

7. The family and their blood-ties are carefully revised (I. i). Elizabeth is no longer F's first cousin, but a stranger. A lesser theme hinting at incest is thus removed; even so, a 'dearest' in Elizabeth's letter (III. v) is scaled down to 'dear', and another in her letter of I. v. 48 omitted. The suggestion in 1818 (I. v. 44) that the boy Ernest was sickly as a child has also been dropped. Taken together with the improved health of Alphonse, these changes remove the theme of an aristocratic family's degenerative state which was originally so notable in the first and third volumes.

8. Two emphatic pronouncements by Elizabeth, developing Godwin's critique of the administration of justice (I. v. 48 and I. vii. 67–8) are omitted.

9. Clerval is preparing (1831) to become a colonial administrator (I. v. 49, III. ii. 137 and iii. 147–8); several remarks in 1818, and the Safie theme, imply disapproval of colonialism.

COLLATION OF THE TEXTS OF 1818 AND 1831

The page numbers that introduce each substantive variant refer to the present edition. The 1818 reading is given first and is separated from the 1831 reading by a square bracket (]). The word *omitted* follows the bracket for 1818 readings cancelled without substitution in 1831. As a one-volume edition, 1831 renumbers the chapters in a single series.

VOLUME I

Chapter I

9 He is, indeed . . . moreover, heroically generous.] This circumstance, added to his well known integrity and dauntless courage, made me very desirous to engage him. A youth passed in solitude, my best years spent under your gentle and feminine fosterage, has so refined the groundwork of my character, that I cannot overcome an intense distaste to the usual brutality exercised on board ship: I have never believed it to be necessary; and when I heard of a mariner equally noted

for his kindliness of heart, and the respect and obedience paid to him by his crew, I felt myself peculiarly fortunate in being able to secure his services. I heard of him first in rather a romantic manner, from a lady who owes to him the happiness of her life. This, briefly, is his story.

10 has passed all . . . not suppose that,] is wholly uneducated: he is as silent as a Turk, and a kind of ignorant carelessness attends him, which, while it renders his conduct the more astonishing, detracts from the interest and sympathy which otherwise he would command. Yet do not suppose,

safety.] safety, or if I should come back to you as worn and woful as the 'Ancient Mariner'. You will smile at my allusion; but I will disclose a secret. I have often attributed my attachment to, my passionate enthusiasm for, the dangerous mysteries of ocean, to that production of the most imaginative of modern poets. There is something at work in my soul, which I do not understand. I am practically industrious—pains-taking; a workman to execute with perseverance and labour:—but besides this, there is a love for the marvellous, a belief in the marvellous, intertwined in all my projects, which hurries me out of the common pathways of men, even to the wild sea and unvisited regions I am about to explore.

But to return to dearer considerations.

11 Remember me to . . . Most affectionately yours,] But success *shall* crown my endeavours. Wherefore not? Thus far I have gone, tracing a secure way over the pathless seas: the very stars themselves being witnesses and testimonies of my triumph. Why not still proceed over the untamed yet obedient element? What can stop the determined heart and resolved will of man?

My swelling heart involuntarily pours itself out thus. But I must finish. Heaven bless my beloved sister!

15–16 asked me many . . . a possible acquisition.] frequently conversed with me on mine, which I have communicated to him without disguise. He entered attentively into all my arguments in favour of my eventual success, and into every minute detail of the measures I had taken to secure it. I was easily led by the sympathy which he evinced, to use the language of my heart; to give utterance to the burning ardour of my soul; and to say, with all the fervour that warmed me, how gladly I would sacrifice my fortune, my existence, my every hope, to the furtherance of my enterprise. One man's life or death were but a small price to pay for the acquirement of the knowledge which I sought; for the dominion I should acquire and transmit over the elemental foes of our race. As I spoke, a dark gloom spread over my listener's countenance. At first I perceived that he tried to suppress his emotion; he placed his hands before his eyes; and my voice quivered and failed me, as I beheld tears trickle fast from between his fingers,—a groan burst from his heaving breast. I paused;—at length he spoke, in broken accents:—'Unhappy man! Do you share my madness? Have you drank also of the intoxicating draught? Hear me,—let me reveal my tale, and you will dash the cup from your lips!'

Such words, you may imagine, strongly excited my curiosity; but the paroxysm of grief that had seized the stranger overcame his weakened powers, and many hours of repose and tranquil conversation were necessary to restore his composure.

Having conquered the violence of his feelings, he appeared to despise himself for being the slave of passion; and quelling the dark tyranny of despair, he led me again to converse concerning myself personally. He asked me the history of my earlier years. The tale was quickly told: but it awakened various trains of reflection. I spoke of my desire of finding a friend—of my thirst for a more intimate sympathy with a fellow mind than had ever fallen to my lot; and expressed my conviction that a man could boast of little happiness, who did not enjoy this blessing.

'I agree with you,' replied the stranger; 'we are unfashioned creatures, but half made up, if one wiser, better, dearer than ourselves—such a friend ought to be—do not lend his aid to perfectionate our weak and faulty natures.

17 If you do . . . for repeating them.] You would not, if you saw him. You have been tutored and refined by books and retirement from the world, and you are, therefore, somewhat fastidious; but this only renders you the more fit to appreciate the extraordinary merits of this wonderful man. Sometimes I have endeavoured to discover what quality it is which he possesses, that elevates him so immeasurably above any other person I ever knew. I believe it to be an intuitive discernment; a quick but never-failing power of judgment; a penetration into the causes of things, unequalled for clearness and precision; add to this a facility of expression, and a voice whose varied intonations are soul-subduing music.

if you are . . . do not doubt] when I reflect that you are pursuing the same course, exposing yourself to the same dangers which have rendered me what I am, I imagine that you may deduce an apt moral from my tale; one that may direct you if you succeed in your undertaking, and console you in case of failure. Prepare to hear of occurrences which are usually deemed marvellous. Were we among the tamer scenes of nature, I might fear to encounter your unbelief, perhaps your ridicule; but many things will appear possible in these wild and mysterious regions, which would provoke the laughter of those unacquainted with the ever-varied powers of nature:—nor can I doubt but

18 day!] day! Even now, as I commence my task, his full-toned voice swells in my ears; his lustrous eyes dwell on me with all their melancholy sweetness; I see his thin hand raised in animation, while the lineaments of his face are irradiated by the soul within. Strange and harrowing must be his story; frightful the storm which embraced the gallant vessel on its course, and wrecked it—thus!

18   and it was . . . down to posterity.] a variety of circum-
      stances had prevented his marrying early, nor was it
      until the decline of life that he became a husband and
      the father of a family.

      grieved also for . . . endeavour to persuade] bitterly de-
      plored the false pride which led his friend to a conduct
      so little worthy of the affection that united them. He
      lost no time in endeavouring to seek him out, with the
      hope of persuading

19–22   When my father . . . Clerval was absent.] There was a
      considerable difference between the ages of my par-
      ents, but this circumstance seemed to unite them only
      closer in bonds of devoted affection. There was a sense
      of justice in my father's upright mind, which rendered
      it necessary that he should approve highly to love
      strongly. Perhaps during former years he had suffered
      from the late-discovered unworthiness of one beloved,
      and so was disposed to set a greater value on tried
      worth. There was a show of gratitude and worship in his
      attachment to my mother, differing wholly from the
      doating fondness of age, for it was inspired by reverence
      for her virtues, and a desire to be the means of, in some
      degree, recompensing her for the sorrows she had en-
      dured, but which gave inexpressible grace to his behav-
      iour to her. Every thing was made to yield to her wishes
      and her convenience. He strove to shelter her, as a fair
      exotic is sheltered by the gardener, from every rougher
      wind, and to surround her with all that could tend to
      excite pleasurable emotion in her soft and benevolent
      mind. Her health, and even the tranquillity of her hith-
      erto constant spirit, had been shaken by what she had
      gone through. During the two years that had elapsed
      previous to their marriage my father had gradually re-
      linquished all his public functions; and immediately
      after their union they sought the pleasant climate of
      Italy, and the change of scene and interest attendant on
      a tour through that land of wonders, as a restorative for
      her weakened frame.

From Italy they visited Germany and France. I, their eldest child, was born at Naples, and as an infant accompanied them in their rambles. I remained for several years their only child. Much as they were attached to each other, they seemed to draw inexhaustible stores of affection from a very mine of love to bestow them upon me. My mother's tender caresses, and my father's smile of benevolent pleasure while regarding me, are my first recollections. I was their plaything and their idol, and something better—their child, the innocent and helpless creature bestowed on them by Heaven, whom to bring up to good, and whose future lot it was in their hands to direct to happiness or misery, according as they fulfilled their duties towards me. With this deep consciousness of what they owed towards the being to which they had given life, added to the active spirit of tenderness that animated both, it may be imagined that while during every hour of my infant life I received a lesson of patience, of charity, and of self-control, I was so guided by a silken cord, that all seemed but one train of enjoyment to me.

For a long time I was their only care. My mother had much desired to have a daughter, but I continued their single offspring. When I was about five years old, while making an excursion beyond the frontiers of Italy, they passed a week on the shores of the Lake of Como. Their benevolent disposition often made them enter the cottages of the poor. This, to my mother, was more than a duty; it was a necessity, a passion,—remembering what she had suffered, and how she had been relieved,—for her to act in her turn the guardian angel to the afflicted. During one of their walks a poor cot in the foldings of a vale attracted their notice, as being singularly disconsolate, while the number of half-clothed children gathered about it, spoke of penury in its worst shape. One day, when my father had gone by himself to Milan, my mother, accompanied by me, visited this abode. She found a peasant and his wife, hard working, bent down by care and labour, distributing a scanty

meal to five hungry babes. Among these there was one
which attracted my mother far above all the rest. She
appeared of a different stock. The four others were
dark-eyed, hardy little vagrants; this child was thin, and
very fair. Her hair was the brightest living gold, and,
despite the poverty of her clothing, seemed to set a
crown of distinction on her head. Her brow was clear
and ample, her blue eyes cloudless, and her lips and the
moulding of her face so expressive of sensibility and
sweetness, that none could behold her without looking
on her as of a distinct species, a being heaven-sent, and
bearing a celestial stamp in all her features.

The peasant woman, perceiving that my mother fixed
eyes of wonder and admiration on this lovely girl, eagerly communicated her history. She was not her child,
but the daughter of a Milanese nobleman. Her mother
was a German, and had died on giving birth. The infant
had been placed with these good people to nurse: they
were better off then. They had not been long married,
and their eldest child was but just born. The father of
their charge was one of those Italians nursed in the
memory of the antique glory of Italy,—one among the
schiavi ognor frementi, who exerted himself to obtain
the liberty of his country. He became the victim of its
weakness. Whether he had died, or still lingered in the
dungeons of Austria, was not known. His property was
confiscated, his child became an orphan and a beggar.
She continued with her foster parents, and bloomed in
their rude abode, fairer than a garden rose among dark-
leaved brambles.

When my father returned from Milan, he found playing with me in the hall of our villa, a child fairer than
pictured cherub—a creature who seemed to shed radiance from her looks, and whose form and motions were
lighter than the chamois of the hills. The apparition was
soon explained. With his permission my mother prevailed on her rustic guardians to yield their charge to
her. They were fond of the sweet orphan. Her presence
had seemed a blessing to them; but it would be unfair to

her to keep her in poverty and want, when Providence afforded her such powerful protection. They consulted their village priest, and the result was, that Elizabeth Lavenza became the inmate of my parents' house—my more than sister—the beautiful and adored companion of all my occupations and pleasures.

Every one loved Elizabeth. The passionate and almost reverential attachment with which all regarded her became, while I shared it, my pride and delight. On the evening previous to her being brought to my home, my mother had said playfully,—'I have a pretty present for my Victor—to-morrow he shall have it.' And when, on the morrow, she presented Elizabeth to me as her promised gift, I, with childish seriousness, interpreted her words literally, and looked upon Elizabeth as mine—mine to protect, love, and cherish. All praises bestowed on her, I received as made to a possession of my own. We called each other familiarly by the name of cousin. No word, no expression could body forth the kind of relation in which she stood to me—my more than sister, since till death she was to be mine only.

Chapter II

We were brought up together; there was not quite a year difference in our ages. I need not say that we were strangers to any species of disunion or dispute. Harmony was the soul of our companionship, and the diversity and contrast that subsisted in our characters drew us nearer together. Elizabeth was of a calmer and more concentrated disposition; but, with all my ardour, I was capable of a more intense application, and was more deeply smitten with the thirst for knowledge. She busied herself with following the aerial creations of the poets; and in the majestic and wondrous scenes which surrounded our Swiss home—the sublime shapes of the mountains; the changes of the seasons; tempest and calm; the silence of winter, and the life and turbulence of our Alpine summers,—she found ample scope for

admiration and delight. While my companion contemplated with a serious and satisfied spirit the magnificent
appearances of things, I delighted in investigating their
causes. The world was to me a secret which I desired to
divine. Curiosity, earnest research to learn the hidden
laws of nature, gladness akin to rapture, as they were
unfolded to me, are among the earliest sensations I can
remember.

On the birth of a second son, my junior by seven
years, my parents gave up entirely their wandering life,
and fixed themselves in their native country. We possessed a house in Geneva, and a *campagne* on Belrive,
the eastern shore of the lake, at the distance of rather
more than a league from the city. We resided principally in the latter, and the lives of my parents were
passed in considerable seclusion. It was my temper to
avoid a crowd, and to attach myself fervently to a
few. I was indifferent, therefore, to my schoolfellows in
general; but I united myself in the bonds of the closest
friendship to one among them. Henry Clerval was the
son of a merchant of Geneva. He was a boy of singular
talent and fancy. He loved enterprise, hardship, and
even danger, for its own sake. He was deeply read in
books of chivalry and romance. He composed heroic
songs, and began to write many a tale of enchantment
and knightly adventure. He tried to make us act plays,
and to enter into masquerades, in which the characters
were drawn from the heroes of Roncesvalles, of the
Round Table of King Arthur, and the chivalrous train
who shed their blood to redeem the holy sepulchre
from the hands of the infidels.

No human being could have passed a happier childhood than myself. My parents were possessed by the
very spirit of kindness and indulgence. We felt that they
were not the tyrants to rule our lot according to their
caprice, but the agents and creators of all the many
delights which we enjoyed. When I mingled with other
families, I distinctly discerned how peculiarly fortunate
my lot was, and gratitude assisted the development of
filial love.

My temper was sometimes violent, and my passions vehement; but by some law in my temperature they were turned, not towards childish pursuits, but to an eager desire to learn, and not to learn all things indiscriminately. I confess that neither the structure of languages, nor the code of governments, nor the politics of various states, possessed attractions for me. It was the secrets of heaven and earth that I desired to learn; and whether it was the outward substance of things, or the inner spirit of nature and the mysterious soul of man that occupied me, still my enquiries were directed to the metaphysical, or, in its highest sense, the physical secrets of the world.

Meanwhile Clerval occupied himself, so to speak, with the moral relations of things. The busy stage of life, the virtues of heroes, and the actions of men, were his theme; and his hope and his dream was to become one among those whose names are recorded in story, as the gallant and adventurous benefactors of our species. The saintly soul of Elizabeth shone like a shrine-dedicated lamp in our peaceful home. Her sympathy was ours; her smile, her soft voice, the sweet glance of her celestial eyes, were ever there to bless and animate us. She was the living spirit of love to soften and attract: I might have become sullen in my study, rough through the ardour of my nature, but that she was there to subdue me to a semblance of her own gentleness. And Clerval—could aught ill entrench on the noble spirit of Clerval?—yet he might not have been so perfectly humane, so thoughtful in his generosity—so full of kindness and tenderness amidst his passion for adventurous exploit, had she not unfolded to him the real loveliness of beneficence, and made the doing good the end and aim of his soaring ambition.

with my imagination ... from modern discoveries.] have contented my imagination, warmed as it was, by returning with greater ardour to my former studies.

and although I ... by reality; and] I have described myself as always having been embued with a fervent longing to penetrate the secrets of nature. In spite of the intense labour and wonderful discoveries of modern philosophers, I always came from my studies discontented and unsatisfied. Sir Isaac Newton is said to have avowed that he felt like a child picking up shells beside the great and unexplored ocean of truth. Those of his successors in each branch of natural philosophy with whom I was acquainted, appeared even to my boy's apprehensions, as tyros engaged in the same pursuit.

The untaught peasant beheld the elements around him, and was acquainted with their practical uses. The most learned philosopher knew little more. He had partially unveiled the face of Nature, but her immortal lineaments were still a wonder and a mystery. He might dissect, anatomise, and give names; but, not to speak of a final cause, causes in their secondary and tertiary grades were utterly unknown to him. I had gazed upon the fortifications and impediments that seemed to keep human beings from entering the citadel of nature, and rashly and ignorantly I had repined.

But here were books, and here were men who had penetrated deeper and knew more. I took their word for all that they averred, and I became their disciple. It may appear strange that such should arise in the eighteenth century; but while I followed the routine of education in the schools of Geneva, I was, to a great degree, self taught with regard to my favourite studies. My father was not scientific, and I was left to struggle with a child's blindness, added to a student's thirst for knowledge. Under the guidance of my new preceptors,

24   The natural phænomena . . . in my mind.] And thus for a time I was occupied by exploded systems, mingling, like an unadept, a thousand contradictory theories, and floundering desperately in a very slough of multifarious knowledge, guided by an ardent imagination and childish reasoning, till an accident again changed the current of my ideas.

24-6   The catastrophe of . . . of each other.] Before this I
was not unacquainted with the more obvious laws of
electricity. On this occasion a man of great research in
natural philosophy was with us, and, excited by this
catastrophe, he entered on the explanation of a theory
which he had formed on the subject of electricity and
galvanism, which was at once new and astonishing to
me. All that he said threw greatly into the shade
Cornelius Agrippa, Albertus Magnus, and Paracelsus,
the lords of my imagination; but by some fatality the
overthrow of these men disinclined me to pursue my
accustomed studies. It seemed to me as if nothing
would or could ever be known. All that had so long
engaged my attention suddenly grew despicable. By one
of those caprices of the mind, which we are perhaps
most subject to in early youth, I at once gave up my
former occupations; set down natural history and all
its progeny as a deformed and abortive creation;
and entertained the greatest disdain for a would-be
science, which could never even step within the
threshold of real knowledge. In this mood of mind
I betook myself to the mathematics, and the branches
of study appertaining to that science, as being
built upon secure foundations, and so worthy of my
consideration.

   Thus strangely are our souls constructed, and by such
slight ligaments are we bound to prosperity or ruin.
When I look back, it seems to me as if this almost
miraculous change of inclination and will was the immediate suggestion of the guardian angel of my life—
the last effort made by the spirit of preservation to avert
the storm that was even then hanging in the stars, and
ready to envelope me. Her victory was announced by an
unusual tranquillity and gladness of soul, which followed the relinquishing of my ancient and latterly tormenting studies. It was thus that I was to be taught to
associate evil with their prosecution, happiness with
their disregard.

   It was a strong effort of the spirit of good; but it was

ineffectual. Destiny was too potent, and her immutable laws had decreed my utter and terrible destruction.

Chapter II] Chapter III

26   her favourite was . . . infection was past.] the life of her favourite was menaced, she could no longer control her anxiety. She attended her sick bed,—her watchful attentions triumphed over the malignity of the distemper,—Elizabeth was saved, but

27   This period was . . . forgetful of herself.] It appeared to me sacrilege so soon to leave the repose, akin to death, of the house of mourning, and to rush into the thick of life. I was new to sorrow, but it did not the less alarm me. I was unwilling to quit the sight of those that remained to me; and, above all, I desired to see my sweet Elizabeth in some degree consoled.

She indeed veiled her grief, and strove to act the comforter to us all. She looked steadily on life, and assumed its duties with courage and zeal. She devoted herself to those whom she had been taught to call her uncle and cousins. Never was she so enchanting as at this time, when she recalled the sunshine of her smiles and spent them upon us. She forgot even her own regret in her endeavours to make us forget.

27–8   I had taken . . . have accompanied me.] Clerval spent the last evening with us. He had endeavoured to persuade his father to permit him to accompany me, and to become my fellow student; but in vain. His father was a narrow-minded trader, and saw idleness and ruin in the aspirations and ambition of his son. Henry deeply felt the misfortune of being debarred from a liberal education. He said little; but when he spoke, I read in his kindling eye and in his animated glance a restrained but firm resolve, not to be chained to the miserable details of commerce.

We sat late. We could not tear ourselves away from each other, nor persuade ourselves to say the word 'Farewell!' It was said; and we retired under the pretence of seeking repose, each fancying that the other was deceived: but when at morning's dawn I descended to the carriage which was to convey me away, they were all there—my father again to bless me, Clerval to press my hand once more, my Elizabeth to renew her entreaties that I would write often, and to bestow the last feminine attentions on her playmate and friend.

28–9   professors, and among . . . upon those subjects.] professors. Chance—or rather the evil influence, the Angel of Destruction, which asserted omnipotent sway over me from the moment I turned my reluctant steps from my father's door—led me first to Mr Krempe, professor of natural philosophy. He was an uncouth man, but deeply embued in the secrets of his science. He asked me several questions concerning my progress in the different branches of science appertaining to natural philosophy. I replied carelessly; and, partly in contempt, mentioned the names of my alchymists as the principal authors I had studied.

29   doctrine.] pursuits. In rather a too philosophical and connected a strain, perhaps, I have given an account of the conclusions I had come to concerning them in my early years. As a child, I had not been content with the results promised by the modern professors of natural science. With a confusion of ideas only to be accounted for by my extreme youth, and my want of a guide on such matters, I had retrod the steps of knowledge along the paths of time, and exchanged the discoveries of recent enquirers for the dreams of forgotten alchymists.

31   I departed highly . . . the same evening.] Such were the professor's words—rather let me say such the words of fate, enounced to destroy me. As he went on, I felt as if my soul were grappling with a palpable enemy; one by one the various keys were touched which formed the mechanism of my being: chord after chord was sounded, and soon my mind was filled with one thought, one conception, one purpose. So much has been done, exclaimed the soul of Frankenstein,—more,

far more, will I achieve: treading in the steps already marked, I will pioneer a new way, explore unknown powers, and unfold to the world the deepest mysteries of creation.

I closed not my eyes that night. My internal being was in a state of insurrection and turmoil; I felt that order would thence arise, but I had no power to produce it. By degrees, after the morning's dawn, sleep came. I awoke, and my yesternight's thoughts were as a dream. There only remained a resolution to return to my ancient studies, and to devote myself to a science for which I believed myself to possess a natural talent. On the same day, I paid M. Waldman a visit.

and I, at the same time,] I expressed myself in measured terms, with the modesty and deference due from a youth to his instructor, without letting escape (inexperience in life would have made me ashamed) any of the enthusiasm which stimulated my intended labours. I

Chapter III] Chapter IV

32 It was, perhaps . . . and resolution, now] In a thousand ways he smoothed for me the path of knowledge, and made the most abstruse enquiries clear and facile to my apprehension. My application was at first fluctuating and uncertain; it gained strength as I proceeded, and soon

38 a disease that . . . away such symptoms;] the fall of a leaf startled me, and I shunned my fellow-creatures as if I had been guilty of a crime. Sometimes I grew alarmed at the wreck I perceived that I had become; the energy of my purpose alone sustained me: my labours would soon end, and I believed that exercise and amusement would then drive away incipient disease;

Chapter V] Chapter VI

44-6 'To V. FRANKENSTEIN . . . remember Justine Moritz?] It was from my own Elizabeth:—

'My dearest Cousin,

'You have been ill, very ill, and even the constant letters of dear kind Henry are not sufficient to reassure me on your account. You are forbidden to write—to hold a pen; yet one word from you, dear Victor, is necessary to calm our apprehensions. For a long time I have thought that each post would bring this line, and my persuasions have restrained my uncle from undertaking a journey to Ingolstadt. I have prevented his encountering the inconveniences and perhaps dangers of so long a journey; yet how often have I regretted not being able to perform it myself! I figure to myself that the task of attending on your sick bed has devolved on some mercenary old nurse, who could never guess your wishes, nor minister to them with the care and affection of your poor cousin. Yet that is over now: Clerval writes that indeed you are getting better. I eagerly hope that you will confirm this intelligence soon in your own handwriting.

'Get well—and return to us. You will find a happy, cheerful home, and friends who love you dearly. Your father's health is vigorous, and he asks but to see you,— but to be assured that you are well; and not a care will ever cloud his benevolent countenance. How pleased you would be to remark the improvement of our Ernest! He is now sixteen, and full of activity and spirit. He is desirous to be a true Swiss, and to enter into foreign service; but we cannot part with him, at least until his elder brother return to us. My uncle is not pleased with the idea of a military career in a distant country; but Ernest never had your powers of application. He looks upon study as an odious fetter;—his time is spent in the open air, climbing the hills or rowing on the lake. I fear that he will become an idler, unless we yield the point, and permit him to enter on the profession which he has selected.

'Little alteration, except the growth of our dear children, has taken place since you left us. The blue lake, and snow-clad mountains, they never change;—and I think our placid home, and our contented hearts are regulated by the same immutable laws. My trifling occupations take up my time and amuse me, and I am rewarded for any exertions by seeing none but happy, kind faces around me. Since you left us, but one change has taken place in our little household. Do you remember on what occasion Justine Moritz entered our family?

48   yet I cannot . . . my dearest cousin.] but my anxiety returns upon me as I conclude. Write, dearest Victor,— one line—one word will be a blessing to us. Ten thousand thanks to Henry for his kindness, his affection, and his many letters: we are sincerely grateful. Adieu! my cousin; take care of yourself; and, I entreat you, write!

49–50   was no natural . . . my own part,] had never sympathised in my tastes for natural science; and his literary pursuits differed wholly from those which had occupied me. He came to the university with the design of making himself complete master of the oriental languages, as thus he should open a field for the plan of life he had marked out for himself. Resolved to pursue no inglorious career, he turned his eyes toward the East, as affording scope for his spirit of enterprise. The Persian, Arabic, and Sanscrit languages engaged his attention, and I was easily induced to enter on the same studies.

50   orientalists.] orientalists. I did not, like him, attempt a critical knowledge of their dialects, for I did not contemplate making any other use of them than temporary amusement. I read merely to understand their meaning, and they well repaid my labours.

Chapter VI] Chapter VII

54   raise my spirits . . . his angel mother.] say a few words of consolation; he could only express his heartfelt sympathy. 'Poor William!' said he, 'dear lovely child, he now sleeps with his angel mother! who that had seen him bright and joyous in his young beauty, but must weep

over his untimely loss! To die so miserably; to feel the murderer's grasp! How much more a murderer, that could destroy such radiant innocence! Poor little fellow! one only consolation have we;

58 But we are . . . 'She indeed] You come to us now to share a misery which nothing can alleviate; yet your presence will, I hope, revive our father, who seems sinking under his misfortune; and your persuasions will induce poor Elizabeth to cease her vain and tormenting self-accusations.—Poor William! he was our darling and our pride!'

Tears, unrestrained, fell from my brother's eyes; a sense of mortal agony crept over my frame. Before, I had only imagined the wretchedness of my desolated home; the reality came on me as a new, and a not less terrible, disaster. I tried to calm Ernest; I enquired more minutely concerning my father, and her I named my cousin.

'She most of all,' said Ernest,

60 and, in this . . . an evil result.] My tale was not one to announce publicly; its astounding horror would be looked upon as madness by the vulgar. Did any one indeed exist, except I, the creator, who would believe, unless his senses convinced him, in the existence of the living monument of presumption and rash ignorance which I had let loose upon the world?

made great alterations . . . slight and graceful.] altered her since I last beheld her; it had endowed her with loveliness surpassing the beauty of her childish years. There was the same candour, the same vivacity, but it was allied to an expression more full of sensibility and intellect.

Chapter VII] Chapter VIII

63 Unable to rest or sleep,] Most of the night she spent here watching; towards morning she believed that she slept for a few minutes; some steps disturbed her, and she awoke. It was dawn, and

65 When I returned home,] This was strange and unex-
    pected intelligence; what could it mean? Had my eyes
    deceived me? and was I really as mad as the whole world
    would believe me to be, if I disclosed the object of my
    suspicions? I hastened to return home, and

66 I will every . . . I never can] Do not fear. I will proclaim,
    I will prove your innocence. I will melt the stony hearts
    of your enemies by my tears and prayers. You shall not
    die!—You, my play-fellow, my companion, my sister,
    perish on the scaffold! No! no! I never could

67 'Dear, sweet Elizabeth . . . increase of misery.'] Justine
    shook her head mournfully. 'I do not fear to die,' she
    said; 'that pang is past. God raises my weakness, and
    gives me courage to endure the worst. I leave a sad and
    bitter world; and if you remember me, and think of me
    as of one unjustly condemned, I am resigned to the fate
    awaiting me. Learn from me, dear lady, to submit in
    patience to the will of Heaven!'

68 As we returned . . . I then endured.] And on the mor-
    row Justine died. Elizabeth's heart-rending eloquence
    failed to move the judges from their settled conviction
    in the criminality of the saintly sufferer. My passionate
    and indignant appeals were lost upon them. And when
    I received their cold answers, and heard the harsh un-
    feeling reasoning of these men, my purposed avowal
    died away on my lips. Thus I might proclaim myself a
    madman, but not revoke the sentence passed upon my
    wretched victim. She perished on the scaffold as a mur-
    deress!
        From the tortures of my own heart, I turned to con-
    template the deep and voiceless grief of my Elizabeth.
    This also was my doing! And my father's woe, and the
    desolation of that late so smiling home—all was the
    work of my thrice-accursed hands! Ye weep, unhappy
    ones; but these are not your last tears! Again shall you
    raise the funeral wail, and the sound of your lamenta-
    tions shall again and again be heard! Frankenstein,
    your son, your kinsman, your early, much-loved friend;

he who would spend each vital drop of blood for your sakes—who has no thought nor sense of joy, except as it is mirrored also in your dear countenances—who would fill the air with blessings, and spend his life in serving you—he bids you weep—to shed countless tears; happy beyond his hopes, if thus inexorable fate be satisfied, and if the destruction pause before the peace of the grave have succeeded to your sad torments!

Thus spoke my prophetic soul, as, torn by remorse, horror, and despair, I beheld those I loved spend vain sorrow upon the graves of William and Justine, the first hapless victims to my unhallowed arts.

VOLUME II

Chapter I] Chapter IX

69   to reason with . . . to immoderate grief.] by arguments deduced from the feelings of his serene conscience and guiltless life, to inspire me with fortitude, and awaken in me the courage to dispel the dark cloud which brooded over me.

71   She had become . . . of human life.] The first of those sorrows which are sent to wean us from the earth, had visited her, and its dimming influence quenched her dearest smiles.

72–3   Be calm, my . . . we ascended still] Dear Victor, banish these dark passions. Remember the friends around you, who centre all their hopes in you. Have we lost the power of rendering you happy? Ah! while we love—while we are true to each other, here in this land of peace and beauty, your native country, we may reap every tranquil blessing,—what can disturb our peace?'

And could not such words from her whom I fondly prized before every other gift of fortune, suffice to chase away the fiend that lurked in my heart? Even as she spoke I drew near to her, as if in terror; lest at that very moment the destroyer had been near to rob me of her.

Thus not the tenderness of friendship, nor the beauty of earth, nor of heaven, could redeem my soul from woe: the very accents of love were ineffectual. I was encompassed by a cloud which no beneficial influence could penetrate. The wounded deer dragging its fainting limbs to some untrodden brake, there to gaze upon the arrow which had pierced it, and to die—was but a type of me.

Sometimes I could cope with the sullen despair that overwhelmed me: but sometimes the whirlwind passions of my soul drove me to seek, by bodily exercise and by change of place, some relief from my intolerable sensations. It was during an access of this kind that I suddenly left my home, and bending my steps towards the near Alpine valleys, sought in the magnificence, the eternity of such senses, to forget myself and my ephemeral, because human, sorrows, My wanderings were directed towards the valley of Chamounix. I had visited it frequently during my boyhood. Six years had passed since then: *I* was a wreck—but nought had changed in those savage and enduring scenes.

I performed the first part of my journey on horseback. I afterwards hired a mule, as the more surefooted, and least liable to receive injury on these rugged roads. The weather was fine: it was about the middle of the month of August, nearly two months after the death of Justine; that miserable epoch from which I dated all my woe. The weight upon my spirit was sensibly lightened as I plunged yet deeper in the ravine of Arve. The immense mountains and precipices that overhung me on every side—the sound of the river raging among the rocks, and the dashing of the waterfalls around, spoke of a power mighty as Omnipotence—and I ceased to fear, or to bend before any being less almighty than that which had created and ruled the elements, here displayed in their most terrific guise. Still, as I ascended

73–4 During this journey . . . I did not.] A tingling long-lost sense of pleasure often came across me during this

journey. Some turn in the road, some new object suddenly perceived and recognised, reminded me of days
gone by, and were associated with the light-hearted
gaiety of boyhood. The very winds whispered in soothing accents, and maternal nature bade me weep no
more. Then again the kindly influence ceased to act—
I found myself fettered again to grief, and indulging in
all the misery of reflection. Then I spurred on my animal, striving so to forget the world, my fears, and, more
than all, myself—or, in a more desperate fashion, I
alighted, and threw myself on the grass, weighed down
by horror and despair.

At length I arrived at the village of Chamounix. Exhaustion succeeded to the extreme fatigue both of body
and of mind which I had endured. For a short space of
time

74   ran below my window.] pursued its noisy way beneath.
The same lulling sounds acted as a lullaby to my too
keen sensations: when I placed my head upon my pillow, sleep crept over me; I felt it as it came, and blest the
giver of oblivion.

Chapter II] Chapter X

The next day . . . valley until evening.]   I spent the following day roaming through the valley. I stood beside
the sources of the Arveiron, which take their rise in a
glacier, that with slow pace is advancing down from the
summit of the hills, to barricade the valley. The abrupt
sides of vast mountains were before me; the icy wall of
the glacier overhung me; a few shattered pines were
scattered around; and the solemn silence of this glorious presence-chamber of imperial Nature was broken
only by the brawling waves, or the fall of some vast
fragment, the thunder sound of the avalanche, or the
cracking, reverberated along the mountains of the accumulated ice, which, through the silent working of
immutable laws, was ever and anon rent and torn, as if
it had been but a plaything in their hands.

I returned in . . . rain poured down] I retired to rest at
night; my slumbers, as it were, waited on and ministered
to by the assemblance of grand shapes which I had
contemplated during the day. They congregated round
me; the unstained snowy mountain-top, the glittering
pinnacle, the pine woods, and ragged bare ravine; the
eagle, soaring amidst the clouds—they all gathered
round me, and bade me be at peace.

Where had they fled when the next morning I awoke?
All of soul-inspiriting fled with sleep, and dark melancholy clouded every thought. The rain was pouring

74 I rose early . . . to go alone,] so that I even saw not the
faces of those mighty friends. Still I would penetrate
their misty veil, and seek them in their cloudy retreats.
What were rain and storm to me? My mule was brought
to the door, and I resolved to ascend

Chapter VIII] Chapter XVI

118 when I perceived . . . passing near me.] I entered a
barn which had appeared to me to be empty. A woman
was sleeping on some straw;

She shall not escape:] And then I bent over her, and
whispered "Awake, fairest, thy lover is near—he who
would give his life but to obtain one look of affection
from thine eyes: my beloved, awake!"

'The sleeper stirred; a thrill of terror ran through me.
Should she indeed awake, and see me, and curse me,
and denounce the murderer? Thus would she assuredly
act, if her darkened eyes opened, and she beheld me.
The thought was madness; it stirred the fiend within
me—not I, but she shall suffer: the murder I have
committed because I am for ever robbed of all that she
could give me, she shall atone. The crime had its source
in her: be hers the punishment!

Chapter IX] Chapter XVII

123 but my presence . . . degree of tranquillity.] I took no
rest, but returned immediately to Geneva. Even in my

own heart I could give no expression to my sensations—
they weighed on me with a mountain's weight, and their
excess destroyed my agony beneath them. Thus I returned home, and entering the house, presented myself
to the family. My haggard and wild appearance awoke
intense alarm; but I answered no question, scarcely
did I speak. I felt as if I were placed under a ban—as if
I had no right to claim their sympathies—as if never
more might I enjoy companionship with them. Yet even
thus I loved them to adoration; and to save them,
I resolved to dedicate myself to my most abhorred
task. The prospect of such an occupation made every
other circumstance of existence pass before me like a
dream; and that thought only had to me the reality of
life.

VOLUME III

Chapter I] Chapter XVIII

124 could not resolve . . . returning tranquillity.] shrunk
from taking the first step in an undertaking whose immediate necessity began to appear less absolute to me.
A change indeed had taken place in me:

125 your cousin,] Elizabeth,

cousin] Elizabeth

126 any variation was . . . some accident might] I had an
insurmountable aversion to the idea of engaging myself
in my loathsome task in my father's house, while in
habits of familiar intercourse with those I loved. I knew
that a thousand fearful accidents might occur, the
slightest of which would disclose a tale to thrill all connected with me with horror. I was aware also that I
should often lose all self-command, all capacity of hiding the harrowing sensations that would possess me
during the progress of my unearthly occupation. I must
absent myself from all I loved while thus employed.
Once commenced, it would quickly be achieved, and I
might be restored to my family in peace and happiness.
My promise fulfilled, the monster would depart for

ever. Or (so my fond fancy imaged) some accident
might meanwhile

126–7 the guise of . . . restore my tranquillity.] a guise
which excited no suspicion, while I urged my desire
with an earnestness that easily induced my father to
comply. After so long a period of an absorbing melancholy, that resembled madness in its intensity and effects, he was glad to find that I was capable of taking
pleasure in the idea of such a journey, and he hoped
that change of scene and varied amusement would,
before my return, have restored me entirely to myself.

The duration of my absence was left to my own
choice; a few months, or at most a year, was the period
contemplated. One paternal precaution he had taken
to ensure my having a companion. Without previously communicating with me, he had, in concert with
Elizabeth, arranged that Clerval should join me at
Strasburgh. This interfered with the solitude I coveted
for the prosecution of my task; yet at the commencement of my journey the presence of my friend could in
no way be an impediment, and truly I rejoiced that thus
I should be saved many hours of lonely, maddening
reflection. Nay, Henry might stand between me and the
intrusion of my foe. If I were alone, would he not at
times force his abhorred presence on me, to remind me
of my task, or to contemplate its progress?

To England, therefore, I was bound, and it was understood that my union with Elizabeth should take
place immediately on my return. My father's age rendered him extremely averse to delay. For myself, there
was one reward I promised myself from my detested
toils—one consolation for my unparalleled sufferings;
it was the prospect of that day when, enfranchised from
my miserable slavery, I might claim Elizabeth, and forget the past in my union with her.

127–8 departed, to pass . . . be our feelings?'] again quitted
my native country. My journey had been my own suggestion, and Elizabeth, therefore, acquiesced: but she was

filled with disquiet at the idea of my suffering, away
from her, the inroads of misery and grief. It had been
her care which provided me a companion in Clerval—
and yet a man is blind to a thousand minute circumstances, which call forth a woman's sedulous attention.
She longed to bid me hasten my return,—a thousand
conflicting emotions rendered her mute, as she bade
me a tearful silent farewell.

Chapter II] Chapter XIX

132 amusement.] amusement. He was also pursuing an object he had long had in view. His design was to visit
India, in the belief that he had in his knowledge of its
various languages, and in the views he had taken of its
society, the means of materially assisting the progress of
European colonisation and trade. In Britain only could
he further the execution of his plan.

133 Gower] Goring

Chapter III] Chapter XX

142 nearly a year . . . our future proceedings.] he was wear-
ing away his time fruitlessly where he was; that letters
from the friends he had formed in London desired his
return to complete the negotiation they had entered
into for his Indian enterprise. He could not any longer
delay his departure; but as his journey to London might
be followed, even sooner than he now conjectured, by
his longer voyage, he entreated me to bestow as much
of my society on him as I could spare. He besought me,
therefore, to leave my solitary isle, and to meet him at
Perth, that we might proceed southwards together.

Chapter IV] Chapter XXI

154 I remember, as . . . so much misery.] Yet one duty remained to me, the recollection of which finally triumphed over my selfish despair. It was necessary that I
should return without delay to Geneva, there to watch

over the lives of those I so fondly loved; and to lie in wait for the murderer, that if any chance led me to the place of his concealment, or if he dared again to blast me by his presence, I might, with unfailing aim, put an end to the existence of the monstrous Image which I had endued with the mockery of a soul still more monstrous. My father still desired to delay our departure, fearful that I could not sustain the fatigues of a journey: for I was a shattered wreck,—the shadow of a human being. My strength was gone. I was a mere skeleton; and fever night and day preyed upon my wasted frame.

Still, as I urged our leaving Ireland with such inquietude and impatience, my father thought it best to yield. We took our passage on board a vessel bound for Havre-de-Grace, and sailed with a fair wind from the Irish shores.

155   and pointed to . . . were now entering.] the dashing waves were around: the cloudy sky above; the fiend was not here: a sense of security, a feeling that a truce was established between the present hour and the irresistible, disastrous future, imparted to me a kind of calm forgetfulness, of which the human mind is by its structure peculiarly susceptible.

Chapter V] Chapter XXII

155–6   We had resolved . . . he would not] The voyage came to an end. We landed, and proceeded to Paris. I soon found that I had overtaxed my strength, and that I must repose before I could continue my journey. My father's care and attentions were indefatigable; but he did not know the origin of my sufferings, and sought erroneous methods to remedy the incurable ill. He wished me to seek amusement in society. I abhorred the face of man. Oh, not abhorred! they were my brethren, my fellow beings, and I felt attracted even to the most repulsive among them, as to creatures of an angelic nature and celestial mechanism. But I felt that I had no right to share their intercourse. I had unchained an enemy among them, whose joy it was to shed their blood, and to revel in their groans. How they would, each and all, abhor me, and hunt me from the world, did they know my unhallowed acts, and the crimes which had their source in me!

My father yielded at length to my desire to avoid society, and strove by various arguments to banish my

156 for ever chained my tongue,] in itself would for ever have chained my tongue. But, besides, I could not bring myself to disclose a secret which would fill my hearer with consternation, and make fear and unnatural horror the inmates of his breast. I checked, therefore, my impatient thirst for sympathy, and was silent

secret.] secret. Yet still words like those I have recorded, would burst uncontrollably from me. I could offer no explanation of them; but their truth in part relieved the burden of my mysterious woe.

157 DEAREST] dear

158 and I have ... your affectionate cousin.] and all my doubts satisfied.

cousin,] friend,

160 My cousin] The sweet girl

161 my cousin.] Elizabeth.

162 A house was ... at the schools.] Through my father's exertions, a part of the inheritance of Elizabeth had been restored to her by the Austrian government. A small possession on the shores of Como belonged to her. It was agreed that, immediately after our union, we should proceed to Villa Lavenza, and spend our first days of happiness beside the beautiful lake near which it stood.

163 pass the afternoon ... go by water.] commence our journey by water, sleeping that night at Evian, and continuing our voyage on the following day. The day was fair, the wind favourable, all smiled on our nuptial embarkation.

Chapter VI] Chapter XXIII

166 did not accompany them; I was exhausted:] attempted
to accompany them, and proceeded a short distance
from the house; but my head whirled round, my steps
were like those of a drunken man, I fell at last in a state
of utter exhaustion;

166 At length I . . . a long time;] After an interval, I arose,
and, as if by instinct, crawled into the room where the
corpse of my beloved lay. There were women weeping
around—I hung over it, and joined my sad tears to
theirs—all this time no distinct idea presented itself to
my mind;

168 niece,] Elizabeth,

Chapter VII] Chapter XXIII

181 We may survive . . . good heart. Yet] Yet it is terrible to
reflect that the lives of all these men are endangered
through me. If we are lost, my mad schemes are the
cause.
And

APPENDIX C

In its opening article in the number for November 1819, the *Quarterly Review* gave unusually full, retrospective attention to an issue rather than individual publications—the debate on vitalism, or the principle of life, conducted in eight books, pamphlets and lectures between 1814 and 1819. Though William Lawrence is certainly the principal target, the discursive review is able to incorporate other bogeys, such as the British apostle of French natural science T. C. Morgan, the phrenologists Gall and Spurzheim, and populist, irreverent reinterpretations of Scripture, represented here by the new translation by John Bellamy. Between 1817 and 1822 the *Quarterly* kept up a consistent, orchestrated campaign against cultural subversion, concentrating on books, journals, pamphlets and even caricatures produced for the mass market. Its most distinguished and, for most modern critics, its most visible target was Byron, as author of *Don Juan* (1819–   ). Equally representative was the long article by Southey with which the campaign began, against Spenceanism, i.e. agrarian communism, and Cobbett's broadside reprinting of the rousing leader-articles of his *Political Register* for only two pence (*QR* 16 (Oct. 1816), 225–80). A year later the typical target was religious—William Hone, tried and acquitted in December 1817 on three counts of blasphemy, for publishing parodies of the Prayer Book and Scripture, Bellamy (*QR* 19, both April and July numbers) and in the latter half of 1819 Richard Carlile, convicted of blasphemy for publishing Paine's *Age of Reason*. The article below follows the pattern of most of these articles, in being primarily concerned with a religious offence (which is, however, considered politically subversive), and in ending with a demand for suppression.

Divided among our specialisms, we miss the coherence of a campaign spread across disciplines, but identifying a common theme, irreligion. The quite excellent articles by histori-

ans of science on the reception of Lawrence and the significance of the vitalist episode (see Bibliography for Goodfield·
Toulmin, Jacyna₂ Temkin, and Wells) all underplay the
cultural prestige and influence of the *Quarterly Review*. Until a
new crop of journals appeared with the ending of the war, it
had shared with the *Edinburgh Review* a hegemonic role, selecting the important books across what was claimed to be all
fields, interpreting them for the public with semi-academic
authority, legislating culture with different nuances (the typical *Quarterly* reviewer was an Anglican, perhaps a clergyman,
the typical *Edinburgh* reviewer a lawyer or Scottish academic),
but within the orderly parameters of a two-party system. The
Quarterly was now fighting, like the *Edinburgh Review*, to
maintain its cultural dominance, and the *Quarterly* was making the better job of it. By grouping disparate radical elements into a single materialist phalanx, it made them
dangerous and also recognizable, so that they could be tar-
geted for destruction. Lawrence could not have been so easily
quelled, London radical science would not have experienced
this damaging defeat, had not the witty, gifted Lawrence deliberately chosen a style and mode of publication that allowed
purposeful press campaigning—in the right place at the right
time—to earmark him for elimination. Within a year a notable pamphlet followed the *Quarterly*'s lead, its title indicating
that Lawrence had suddenly acquired a household name. By
someone who identified himself as 'Oxonian', it was called
'The Radical Triumvirate; or, Infidel Paine, Lord Byron and
Surgeon Lawrence, colleaguing with the Patriotic Radicals
to emancipate mankind from all laws, human and divine'
(1820).

Frankenstein is not mentioned here, as it well might have
been. Nevertheless the *Quarterly*'s own reviewer the previous
year did summarize the experiment scenes in the novel with
a distaste that plainly stemmed from a religious frame of mind
(see Introduction, p. xlvi). Now that the vitalist issue as a
whole had been so prominently aired, and the naturalist
vocabulary so firmly demonized as irreligious, anti-social, and
immoral, the pro-religious, anti-scientific interpretation of
the novel was in effect in place. The anonymous novel was still

at this point relatively little known. It is a case where a book's reception-history begins with a pause —for the book to circulate, become familiar, attach to itself meanings the public wants expressed. By this process *Frankenstein* was detached from its source, and reconstituted as a parable of the retribution for which the *Quarterly* journalist called.

THE *QUARTERLY REVIEW*
vol. XXII (1820), 1–34

ART. I.   1. *An Enquiry into the Probability and Rationality of Mr Hunter's Theory of Life, being the Subject of the first two Anatomical Lectures delivered before the Royal College of Surgeons of London.* By John Abernethy, F.R.S. &c. Professor of Anatomy and Surgery to the College. 1814.

2. *An Introduction to Comparative Anatomy and Physiology, being the two Introductory Lectures delivered at the Royal College of Surgeons on the 21st and 25th of March,* 1816. By William Lawrence, F.R.S. &c.

3. *Physiological Lectures, exhibiting a General View, &c. delivered before the Royal College of Surgeons,* 1817. By John Abernethy, F.R.S.

4. *Lectures on Physiology, Zoology, and the Natural History of Man, delivered at the Royal College of Surgeons.* By William Lawrence, F.R.S. 1819.

5. *Sketches on the Philosophy of Life.* By Sir T. C. Morgan. 1819.

6. *Remarks on Scepticism, being an Answer to the Views of Bichat, Sir T. C. Morgan, and Mr Lawrence.* By the Rev. Thomas Rennell, A.M. Christian Advocate in the University of Cambridge. 1819.

7. *Cursory Observations upon the Lectures, &c.* By one of the People called Christians. 1819.

8. *A Letter to the Rev. Thomas Rennell.* From a Graduate in Medicine. 1819.

We find our attention called by the pamphlets before us to a subject of no ordinary importance, the discussion of the doctrine of materialism: an open avowal of which has been made in the metropolis of the British empire, in lectures delivered under public authority, by Mr Lawrence, Professor of Anatomy and Surgery, in the Royal College of Surgeons.

In the year 1814, Mr Abernethy, who has long been known as a medical gentleman of the highest eminence, and one of the professors of that college, delivered two lectures on the Probability and Rationality of Mr Hunter's Theory of Life. It can scarcely be necessary to remind our readers, *in limine*, that the nature of the living principle is among the subjects which are manifestly beyond the reach of human investigation. The effects and the properties of life are indeed obvious to our senses, through the whole range of organized creation; but, on what they depend, and how they are produced, never has been discovered, and, probably, never will. Mr Abernethy, however, following the steps of the celebrated J. Hunter, elucidates his views on the subject, which have the high merit of attempting to explain but little, but which seem fairly derived from the most probable conclusions to which our reason can carry us; viz. that life, in general, is *some* principle of activity added by the will of Omnipotence to organized structure,—and that, in man, who is endowed with an intelligent faculty in addition to this vital principle possessed by other organized beings, to life and structure an immaterial soul is superadded.

'We perceive,' he says, 'an exact correspondence between those opinions which result from physiological researches, and those which so naturally arise from the suggestions of reason that some have considered them as intuitive. For most reflecting persons in all ages have believed, and indeed it seems natural to believe, what modern physiology also appears to teach, that in the human body there exists an assemblage of organs, formed of common inert matter, such as we see after death, a principle of life and action, and a sentient and rational faculty, all intimately connected, yet each apparently distinct from the other . . .' *Enquiry*, p. 77.

He thus concludes:

'Thus my mind rests at peace in thinking on the subject of life, as it has been taught by Mr Hunter; and I am visionary enough to imagine, that if these opinions should become so established as to be generally admitted by philosophers, that if they once saw reason to

believe that life was something of an invisible and active nature
superadded to organization; they would then see equal reason to
believe that mind might be superadded to life, as life is to stucture.
They would then indeed still farther perceive how mind and matter
might reciprocally operate on each other by means of an intervening
substance. Thus even physiological researchers enforce the belief
which I may say is natural to man; that in addition to his bodily frame,
he possesses a sensitive, intelligent, and independent mind: an opinion which tends in an eminent degree to produce virtuous, honourable, and useful actions.'—pp. 94, 95.

Two years after the appearance of these lectures, Mr Lawrence, who had recently been elected to the situation of
colleague to Mr Abernethy, delivered at the college his two
introductory lectures on Comparative Anatomy and Physiology. Mr Lawrence is, we understand, a young surgeon, who
has acquired considerable reputation in his profession, and
particularly by a diligent study of comparative anatomy,
through the medium of foreign, for the most part German,
writers and professors. He had been the pupil of Mr Abernethy, and had lived for many years under his roof; and he
speaks, in the warmest terms, of the invariable kindness and
disinterested friendship with which that gentleman directed
his early studies.

After giving, in his first lecture, an excellent sketch of the
objects and the history of comparative anatomy, he proceeds,
in the second, to develope his ideas concerning the principle
of life. Here he assumes a very different character. Forgetting
the encomiums which he had just passed on his benefactor
and instructor, the respect which he owed to his professional
situation and character, and, we hesitate not to add, the direct
object of the professional station he was then filling, (a station
expressly founded for displaying Mr Hunter's noble Museum,
purchased by Parliament for the use of the College, and of
illustrating his physiological investigations,) he indulges in
taunts and sarcasms, not of the modest, or mild description,
against Mr Hunter's theory as maintained by Mr Abernethy in
the former year, and the manner in which he illustrated and
supported it. In explaining his own opinions, Mr Lawrence
involves himself in much perplexity and confusion; but still

he inculcates, in terms too plain to be misunderstood, the portentous doctrine that the principle of life, whether sentient or intelligent, is in all organized beings the same; that, whether we look to man, the highest of the animal creation, with all his faculties of invention, memory, imagination, or to an oyster or a cabbage, the vital properties are all derived from their organic structure, and that the difference of this structure constitutes the only difference in their faculties and powers. He mentions, p. 144, as if it were a known and acknowledged truth, that '*medullary substance* is capable of sensation and of thought.' And at p. 155, favours us with the following notable passage:

'The *cerebral functions*, which are much more numerous and diversified in the higher orders of the mammalia, than in any of the preceding divisions of the animal kingdom, receive their last development in man; where they produce all the phenomena of intellect, all those wonderful processes of thought, known under the names of memory, reflection, association, judgment, reasoning, imagination, which so far transcend any analogous appearance in animals, that we *almost* feel a repugnance to refer them to the same principle.—If therefore we were to follow strictly the great series of living bodies through its whole extent, we should see the vital properties gradually encreased in number and energy from the last of plants, the mosses or the algæ, to the first of animals, man!'

Mr Lawrence, it will be instantly recollected by every reader, whatever other merit may belong to him, has not that of being the inventor of these doctrines. They are as old as any on record, and have been advanced and confuted, and revived and driven into obscurity again and again. In the present instance, Mr Lawrence has copied them, and even the terms in which he has expressed them, from the school of modern French philosophy. Indeed, this is not the first occasion on which he has consented to become a mere copyist, and for the purpose of propagating these worn-out but mischievous opinions: he is understood to be the writer of several articles on life, and other subjects connected with it, in the interminable Encyclopædia of Dr Rees, in which the same principles are maintained, and in which Mr Rennell has discovered, that he has translated whole sections from M. Bichat, without the slightest acknowledgment; and we have traced him, in like manner, still more frequently transcribing into his own pages materials of the same description from the free-thinking physiologists of Germany.

In 1817, Mr Abernethy delivered another course of 'Physiological Lectures, exhibiting a general view of Mr Hunter's physiology, and of his researches into comparative anatomy,' in which he affords an interesting detail of the course of study of that distinguished naturalist, of the additions which he made to our stock of useful knowledge in these departments, and of the valuable ends to which he directed his pursuits. At the same time, he took occasion to defend the theory which he had previously explained, from the miserable ribaldry with which it had been assailed, and to guard his hearers from the mischief of the sceptical principles promulgated in that lecture-room in the preceding year. With that view, he made some very just observations on the general tone and method of proceeding of persons professing these principles, on the evil consequences arising to society from the unguarded adoption of them, and on the imputations which must attach to the medical profession, if a firm stand were not made against the conversion of the lecture-room of students in surgery into a school of infidelity. Exhibiting too the pious feeling of a well principled mind, he strove to elevate, as Hunter had ever done, the thoughts of the student from the contemplation of nature, to nature's God.

[Quotation follows from *Physiological Lectures*, pp. 331, 332.]

Mr Lawrence sufficiently understood that these observations, though delivered in general terms, applied directly to himself; but, instead of taking the reproof in good part, expressed as it was without harshness or severity, he was unfortunately excited by it to a high pitch of angry feeling, and to a determination to shew his contempt for it by redoubling the offence. Accordingly, in his lectures, delivered in the ensuing year, (1818) under the pretence of defending himself, he indulges in the most coarse and virulent invective against his former patron. He talks, among other things, of being attacked with the *odium theologicum*, which he describes as 'the most concentrated essence of animosity, and rancour.' p. 10. However this be, Mr Lawrence evinces, by his own example, that the *odium anti-theologicum* is of a far more dark and deadly character:—and if we are ever called upon to say where we should expect to find 'the most concentrated essence of animosity and rancour,' we shall answer without hesitation, in a sceptic, who found himself thwarted and exposed by one who felt the full force and value of sound religious principles, especially if such a person had once been his especial friend and benefactor. Mr Lawrence, as if determined to endure no longer the imputation of delivering his opinions with some degree of mysticism and obscurity, now affirms, in language which none can misunderstand, that all the phenomena of life and of mind result entirely from the bodily structure, and consequently that death, which destroys the bodily structure, destroys the whole of man! Nor is he content merely to announce these opinions, and to leave them to their natural effect on the reader's mind, but he recurs to them again and again with an earnestness which seems to result more from passion and irritation, than from any motive intelligible even to himself; or, if he has such a motive, it must arise from conceiving that the maintenance of every thing valuable to the happiness of man depends on his success in establishing and propagating the belief of such opinions.

Unsatisfied with converting the lecture-room of the College into a school of materialism, Mr Lawrence travels out of his course whenever it suits his purpose, and indulges his hearers with his opinions on various subjects of politics, religion, education, &c. In one place, he introduces a long diatribe on the controversies which have taken place among Christians, and facetiously compares religious discussions with the quarrels of the fair sex; in another, he rails at what he calls the vain attempts of persons in power to make men act or think alike. We find him, at one time, venting his mawkish lamentations over the human propensities to war, and passing high encomiums on the Quakers for the *rationality* of their creed; and, at another, bursting forth with all the fury of a disappointed sportsman, against 'the *oppressive cruelty* and *intolerable abuses* of that iniquitous and execrable code, the game laws.' p. 40.

Nor does he conceal his political prepossessions. The governments of the old world he is pleased to inform us, in one line, are 'worn out despotisms;' and in the next, that Europe is likely to be converted, by 'the conspiracies of the mighty,' (those *worn out* despots) into 'one great state prison.' p. 37. But it is in America that all which is great and good is to be found; there, exclaims this enraptured seer, there is 'the animating spectacle of a country sacred to civil liberty,'—a country which has 'established itself out of the prejudices of the old world—where *religion is in all its fervour* without needing an alliance with the state to maintain it—where the law commands by the respect which it inspires, without being enforced by any military power.' Whether this eulogium on America be poured forth in the design of transferring at some future time to that land of 'liberty and religious fervour' his own acquirements, and opinions, in case they should not be sufficiently appreciated in this country, we venture not to conjecture. Certain we are, that, if such an event should take place, he would meet with persons there, whose *fervour* in religion is nearly on a par with his own.

While doctrines of such a fearful nature were maintained by a professor acting under public authority, and, what is not a little singular, without discountenance by the Collegiate body by which he was appointed, it could not be supposed that they would be suffered to pass without any animadversion whatever; or that no stand would be made against the diffusion of principles so revolting to the feelings of mankind, and so destructive of all that tends to advance their happiness and to ennoble their nature. Our readers will hear with great pleasure that many of the most eminent members of the Lecturer's profession are anxious to rescue their community from the disgrace which would deservedly attach to it, if the taint of such principles should be supposed to be deep or extensive. Two pamphlets on the subject have also appeared from other quarters, the one by the Rev. Thomas Rennell, Christian Advocate in the University of Cambridge; the other, entitled Cursory Observations on Mr Lawrence's Lectures by one of the people called Christians; to which we must now turn our attention.

It may not be generally known, that the person holding the office of Christian Advocate in the University of Cambridge is required by the founder to answer any cavils or objections which may be brought against rational or revealed religion. Mr Rennell, therefore, was peculiarly called upon to come forward on the occasion. His pamphlet was published before Mr Lawrence's second work had issued from the press, and when it was only known from the evidence of his two intro-ductory lectures, and from general rumour, in how deter-mined and persevering a manner he was endeavouring to subvert the principles of the medical students. Mr Rennell has performed his task with equal spirit and ability. By applying the touchstone of close examination to the notions of Mr Lawrence and some others who agree with him, he has shewn, to the satisfaction we apprehend of every reader, the endless perplexity and confusion of their ideas, the miserable incon-sistencies with which their writings abound, and the gross improbability or positive falsehood of many of their asser-tions. He has entered into an investigation of the doctrine of vitality, and shewn, by clear and powerful reasoning, and aptness of illustration, how much more consonant it is with the best conclusions of our reason, to believe that life, through the whole range of organized beings, consists in some principle of inherent activity superadded to the mate-rial structure, while in man, who lives in a state of reflection as well as sensation, an immaterial and immortal soul is added to the living principle which he possesses in common with other animals. Mr Rennell concludes with some excellent remarks on the general character of modern scepticism, a severe and solemn reproof of those who are guilty of endeavouring to pervert the religious tenets of the young and inexperienced; and a suitable and impressive caution to those who are likely to be exposed to such seductions. The anonymous author of the 'Cursory Observations' has exclusively directed his atten-tion to Mr Lawrence's second work, his Lectures on Physi-ology, &c. He has remonstrated with him in terms of well-deserved severity on their general tone and character, and pointed out with great success the errors and inconsisten-cies into which he has been betrayed, errors which are truly astonishing in a man of his abilities, but still are naturally to be expected in one who undertakes to maintain a cause so radically unsound.

There remain to be mentioned two other works which stand at the head of this article. The one, 'A Letter to the Rev. Thomas Rennell concerning his remarks on scepticism,' by a Graduate of Medicine. The other, 'Sketches on (of) the Philosophy of Life,' by a fit auxiliary to Mr Lawrence in the cause of scepticism and materialism, Sir T. C. Morgan.[1] The Graduate professes himself friendly to the cause which Mr Rennell supports, but objects to several parts of his reasoning. . . . The Knight is a prodigious quoter of Greek and other outlandish tongues, of which he understands nothing, and trusts to his reader's understanding as little. He appears to be a true disciple of the French physiologico-sceptical school; and has a number of favourite terms, taken from it, such as, functions, tissues, reaction, &c. on which he rings perpetual changes, to the utter confusion of all sense. The following is a specimen (casually taken) of his jargon;—language it is not.

'Essentially linked with the power of loco-motion, relative sensibility is distributed to the different animals in an exact proportion to the wants of their organization, being resident in a tissue, whose development is regulated in the various species, by the sphere of activity necessary to their preservation.'—p. 276.

According to this great philosopher, 'there is in all individuals a preponderance of some viscus (in the brain) which gives it a lead in the organization.' p. 365. In another place he informs us, that 'the distinction between material and spiritual beings is made a watch-word for fanaticism and persecution:' and that 'the proposition of a Deity without parts or dimensions approaches to absolute atheism.' *ib.* But it is

[1] Sir Thomas Charles Morgan (1783–1843), MD, Fellow of the Royal College of Physicians, physiologist, was an active liberal, a Francophile, and an interpreter to the British public of the ideologue scientific views expounded by Cabanis and Destutt de Tracy. His wife was Lady Morgan, the former Sydney Owenson, well-known Irish writer. Her widely reviewed and reviled pro-French travel-book, *France* (1817) (see *QR* 17 (1817), 260–90), contains T. C. Morgan's Appendices, which give an enthusiastic account of the state of medicine in France. See Bibliography, L. S. Jacyna (1983), 314–15 and O. Temkin (1977), 351–2.

needless to multiply quotations from a work, of which the mischievous tendency is wholly blunted by the unutterable dullness and puzzle-headedness of the writer.

We now return to Mr Lawrence.

'In accepting,' says the author of the "Cursory Observations," 'the office of a Professor at the Royal College of Surgeons, you were not indeed bound to accede to the creed of the Established Church, nor compelled to express your admiration of the civil institutions of the English nation. You were still at liberty to enjoy your opinions in private, nay, to publish them to the world in any separate and independent form. But, I appeal to your sense of decorum and propriety, whether it be fair or expedient to transform the professor's chair into the seat of the scorner and the sceptic? Suppose, Sir, that I had sent my son to attend upon your Lectures, that your fame and reputation as Anatomical and Surgical Professor had determined him to give you the preference above all your brethren; should not I be shocked, on his return, to find that his religious principles were destroyed, and his moral principles corrupted; that he had ceased to admire the constitution of his country; and that he had gained his professional knowledge at the expense of all dignified and elevated moral sentiment? . . .

'Instead of contemplating physiology, in its reference to surgery and medicine, you have exhibited it as the road to materialism in metaphysics, to faction in politics, and to infidelity in religion. . . . If, in the following Letters, it shall be proved that these are the natural consequences of your speculations, then, as a man of honour, you will feel yourself driven to the following dilemma: either you will, for the future, refrain from expressing such opinions in your character as Royal Professor, or, you will renounce a situation so totally incompatible with the display of these sentiments in politics and religion.'—p. 8.

Nothing can be more just than the language of this remonstrance. Mr Lawrence, at the close of his lectures, (p. 573) says, 'I have now performed the task assigned to me by the Board of Curators.' We beg leave to ask *what* was the task assigned to him by that Board? . . . Can any one doubt that its sole object was to improve the means of education for students and practitioners in surgery and medicine?—not to form a nursery for scepticism in religion, or republicanism in politics. . .

Amongst the subjects to which Mr Lawrence directs the attention of his pupils in lectures founded expressly for their improvement in the science and practice of surgery, is (strange as it may appear) the Mosaic account of the creation and of the early history of the world! He seems very properly to conclude that his work would be imperfect, if he were not to level a blow at the records of Revelation, at the same time that he proves from physiological principles that men have no souls; accordingly he devotes several pages to an 'attempt' to shake the confidence of his hearers in the truths of them. 'The entire or even partial inspiration of these writings (he says) has been and is doubted by many persons, including learned divines, and distinguished oriental and biblical scholars;' (p. 248) and he kindly proceeds to inform us, that 'the account of the creation and subsequent events has the allegorical figurative character common to eastern compositions.' To what 'distinguished biblical scholars' he alludes, he does not condescend to explain, and we are unable to conjecture. In vain have we taxed our memory; two only (notwithstanding the *many* of which he boasts) occur to us, of sufficient eminence to deserve to be quoted as authorities: these are Sir William Drummond[2] and Mr John Bellamy,[3] persons known to all the world for their boundless proficiency in oriental literature, and their matchless judgment in applying it; and who, though they certainly differ in their views of the sense of Scripture from a large body of divines, still, as far as their opinions of their own talents and attain-

[2] Sir William Drummond (?1770–1828), sceptical writer, was much admired by Shelley and Peacock for his Socratic *Academical Questions* (1805), and for his unorthodox *Oedipus Judaicus* (1811), which explained Old Testament stories as astronomical allegories.

[3] John Bellamy's new translation of the Bible, with critical and explanatory notes (1818), represented the same kind of challenge to the Authorized Version as Alexander Geddes' Old Testament in Blake's heyday (1792). It was awkwardly timed because it followed William Hone's sensational trials for blasphemy for parodying Scripture, Dec. 1817. The prosecution claimed that Scripture as it stood was 'parcel' of the law of England; Hone, conducting his own case, that it was and always had been common property. The dispute is reworked in the *Quarterly's* reviews of Bellamy's Bible (19 (1818), 250–82 and 446–60), which turn on the sacrosanct words and their role in maintaining moral and legal authority.

ments go, are highly deserving of the entire confidence of Mr Lawrence. . . .

But Mr Lawrence's most formidable objections are to the scriptural account of the various animals being brought to Adam to receive their names, and to their being collected in the ark at the time of the deluge. 'I have only to add,' he says, 'that the representations of all the animals being brought before Adam in the first instance, and, subsequently, of their being all collected in the ark, if we are to understand them as applied to the living inhabitants of the whole world, is *zoologically impossible.*' He goes on to state that we have abundant proofs of animals being so completely adapted by their structure, functions and habits to the local peculiarities of temperature, soil and food, that they cannot subsist where these are no longer found. How, then, he shrewdly asks, could all the living beings have been assembled in one climate, while some are adapted to hot climates, others to cold? how could the polar bear have traversed the torrid zone, &c.? To all these questions (and a thousand might be put, involving equal '*zoological impossibilities*') the answer is very short and very simple. The narrative implies that these transactions took place under the control of an extraordinary Providence; which was, no doubt, extended to the subduing of the natural habits of the animals, and to the sustentation of their lives, in circumstances not adapted to their natures, as far as was necessary for the end proposed. This is the clear sense of Scripture, and in this sense it has ever been understood by all who have not been desirous of casting ridicule upon it. As to animals adapted to cold climates, *polar* bears, &c. how does he know that there existed, at that time, any animals adapted to cold climates? or any such animal as the 'polar' bear? It is sufficient for the reasonable view of the subject that some of every species should then have existed; the distinction into varieties being for the most part the result, subsequently to their dispersion, of their adaptation to particular soils, climates and modes of life.

We must now enter a little more particularly into Mr Lawrence's notions of life and organization. Before we proceed, however, we entreat the reader to call to mind, what it is that the materialist, who is generally in the habit of smiling at the credulity of the world at large, modestly requires him to believe? It is, that there is no other difference between a man and an oyster, than that one possesses bodily organs more fully developed than the other; that all the eminent powers which we know to exist in man, the powers of reason, reflexion, imagination, memory, the powers which distinguish a Milton, a Newton, and a Locke, are merely the functions of a few ounces of organized matter called the brain; and that, as soon as this is dissolved, the being which possessed those powers, perishes altogether! Even in this view of the subject, there is nothing new—nothing but the stale repetition of older sceptics, which has been discussed and disproved a thousand times. Dr Darwin, indeed, carried the hypothesis still farther—for it was a favourite part of his creed that man, when he first sprang by chance into being, *was* an *oyster*, and nothing more; and that by time alone, (a lapse of some chiliads or myriads of ages, for he has not given his chronology very particularly,) and the perfectibility of his ostraceous nature, he became first an amphibious, and then a terrestrial animal! . . .

Let us inquire what direct proof Mr Lawrence's work affords, that the material brain is the source of thought and of all other faculties. He deals mainly in hardy asseverations, which seem intended to supply the want of regular reasoning; and scatters his opinions, without pointing out the grounds on which they rest: we find him, however, insisting on the close connexion between the mind and body as evincing in his judgment that there is no immaterial principle in man.

'Where (he says) shall we find proofs of the mind's *independence* of the bodily structure, of that mind, which, like the corporeal frame, is infantile in the child, manly in the adult, sick and debilitated in disease, phrenzied or melancholy in the madman, enfeebled in the decline of life, doting in decrepitude, and *annihilated by death*?'— *Phys. Lect.* p. 7. Again, 'Where is the mind of the fetus, where that of the child just born? Do we not see it *built up* before our eyes by the actions of the five external senses, and of the gradually developed internal faculties?'

The reader will at once perceive that most of this is gratui-
tous. Mr Lawrence assumes that the mind is *built up* by the
external senses, by which, we suppose, he means that no mind
exists at first, and that all which we call mind is formed by the
action of the external senses. Now whether it be harder to
believe this, or that an immaterial mind is an original part of
the human being, and—not that it is built up by, but—that it
derives its ideas through the external senses, let the reader
judge.—But what proof is afforded of the non-existence of an
immaterial soul distinct from the material body, from the fact
of the mental and corporeal faculties beginning to act together, of their growing together to maturity, of their being
(often) strengthened and enfeebled together, and (generally) decaying together in the decline of life? . . .

Mr Lawrence, who, like all other persons of the same
school, is fond of drawing comparisons between brute animals and man, says, (p. 110) 'If the intellectual phenomena
of man require an immaterial principle superadded to the
brain, we must equally concede it to those more rational
animals which exhibit manifestations differing only in a degree from some of the human. If we grant it to these, we
cannot refuse it to the next in order, and so on to the oyster,
the polypus, &c. Is any one prepared to admit the existence of
immaterial principles in all these cases? if not, he must
equally reject it in man.' The insidious design with which
these observations are made, is easily discerned, but that they
are availing to establish the point proposed, will not be so
readily allowed. What, if it be granted that the principle of life
in brute animals, the principle of inherent activity and voli-
tion, and, in some, of a certain share of sagacity, is an immaterial adjunct to the organic structure? This has been granted
by many able and philosophical inquirers into the subject,
and it is perhaps the best conclusion we can come to, on a
matter which is placed so far beyond the range of our knowledge. But is this to allow to brute animals any thing like the
understanding soul of man? Surely not. Immateriality does
not *necessarily* imply *immortality*. They are not convertible
terms; nor does it follow that, because the Almighty has con-

ferred the gift of immortality on the soul of man, he has therefore necessarily conceded it to the soul of brutes. The distinction between the condition of the brute and that of man, as to faculties and capacities of acquirement, is marked by lines too broad and deep to be overlooked. The brute, above all, is not a responsible being, subject to moral discipline, or susceptible of moral amelioration. 'The greatest part of the animal creation,' says Mr Rennell, (p. 116) 'is capable of no sort of improvement whatever; and with the very few, in whom education and discipline have any effect, the improvement is merely mechanical. A dog may hunt this year better than he did last, but it is not therefore in any degree the better adapted for a spiritual and a future world. If the habits of an animal are changed for the better, it is in reference only to sensible objects and to its present sphere of action.' On the other hand, man lives the life of understanding: his soul is a reasoning soul, which not only receives ideas through the senses, but alters them at will, abstracts them from the sensible objects with which they were connected, forms them into new combinations of an endless variety, and thus opens a field of immeasurable extent for the exercise of its powers. Man too has a feeling, of which he cannot by any reasoning divest himself, of the moral responsibility which he incurs for the quality of his actions; he feels that, by care and self-controul, he may discipline himself to gradually encreasing habits of moral goodness: he feels too that he is susceptible of continual improvement, as well in knowledge as in virtue, and that scarcely any point can be assigned in the scale of attainment beyond which he may not aspire to advance. . . .

Mr Lawrence comes upon us with a pair of scales, speaks of the number of ounces' weight of the human brain, and of 'the prodigious development of the cerebral hemispheres, to which no animal, *whatever ratio its whole encephalon bear to its body*, has any parallel;' (p. 195) and, in conclusion, tells us, that 'it is strongly suspected that a Newton or a Shakespeare excels other mortals only by a more ample development of the anterior cerebral lobes, by having an extra inch of brain in the right place.' p. 110. Suspected! by whom? by Gall and

Spurzheim?[4] by himself?—Mr Lawrence must pardon us; but in truth we cannot avoid 'strongly suspecting,' in our turn, that he is impelled to these speculations by having some extra inch of brain in the *wrong* place, or some exterior, or, peradventure, posterior lobe twisted into some strange convolution.—In another place he says that, 'unless we allow thought to be an act of the brain and not of an immaterial substance residing within it, this large and curious structure which receives one fifth of the blood sent from the heart, has the easiest lot in the whole animal economy; it is better fed, clothed and lodged than any other part, yet has less to do.' p. 106. Is it possible he can suppose that in all this there is a particle of serious argument in favour of his position? It is fully allowed that the brain is *the seat* of thought and intelligence, the centre in which the nervous system terminates, and the instrument by which the soul performs its functions during its union with the body. When it is considered how very high and important these functions are, it surely cannot be maintained, that the human brain has any inferior office allotted to it, or one which is ill suited to its ample bulk, its curious structure, and the supplies which it derives from the animal system. . . .

[A more technical disussion of the brain follows.]

We have seen with what earnestness Mr Lawrence contends that man is only a superior kind of brute as to intellectual endowments, possessing them in common with animals of every description, and differing only in degree; the distinction mainly consisting in two or three additional anterior or posterior lobes of brain, or in the relative number and depth of the convolutions in the medullary matter. Consistently with these ideas it might be expected that he would have placed

---

[4] F. J. Gall (1758–1828) and J. H. Spurzheim (1776–1832), German phrenologists, were authors of an empirical system of psychology, further promoted and developed in Britain by their admirer George Combe (1788–1858), author of *The Constitution of Man* (1858). Phrenology had a considerable radical following in Britain throughout the 1820s and 1830s, notably in the town but not the university of Edinburgh, because it implied that abilities were randomly distributed and moreover could be improved. See A. Desmond (1989), under Phrenology and Combe.

him, as to corporeal qualifications, in the rank of a better sort of baboon or monkey. It happens, however, that he is very indignant at this opinion, though maintained by Monboddo and Rousseau. According to these great philosophers, (who yet must yield to Dr Darwin,) man, in his natural and proper state, loses the os sublime, goes on all fours, is covered with a clothing of hair, and furnished with a tail (whether prehensile or not has never been stated). It may still be doubted whether the species will be very highly flattered by the generic and specific characters which Mr Lawrence, under the auspices of Blumenbach, has substituted in the place of these at which he is so much offended—

'Order, bimanum (two-handed); genus, homo; the species, single, with several varieties: characters, erect stature; two hands, teeth approximated and of equal length; the inferior incisors perpendicular; prominent chin; rational, endowed with speech, unarmed, defenceless.'—p. 133.

—In which it is manifest that he deems the perpendicularity of the inferior incisors and the prominence of the chin quite as important characteristic marks of man, as his powers of reason and his intellectual faculties. He proceeds, however, with no inconsiderable degree of anatomical knowledge, to prove that man is evidently formed to bear an erect attitude, and that he is clearly distinguished in his corporeal structure from every other living creature. He observes, among other proofs of his being designed for erectness of attitude, that the length and strength of the lower limbs are peculiar to man; and, that all the monkey tribe, even those which are thought to approach him most nearly, fall very short in this respect, their lower limbs being short and weak, and manifestly inadequate to sustain the body in an erect posture. He notices the disproportion in the respective lengths of our upper and lower limbs, as clearly pointing out the different offices they are intended to execute; the superior length and power of the latter making us totally unfit to go on all fours. To the long and powerful femur, he says, to the strong tibia, to the broad articular surfaces which join these at the knee, no parallel can be met with in any animal. . . .

Mr Lawrence instances many other peculiarities of the human structure, in the form of the pelvis; the distribution, size, and offices of the muscles; the shape of the breast and thorax, and peculiar formation of the spine, as clearly shewing that man is destined to be erect, and that he is most clearly distinguished by essential characters from all the brute creation.— pp. 146–54. He afterwards considers more particularly the upper extremities of the human frame, shewing that, while they are entirely unsuited to the office of supporting the body, they are admirably adapted to the uses to which we put them, that of seizing and holding objects, and thereby executing, besides all the processes of the arts, many minute but most serviceable actions of constant recurrence. Comparing, too, the structure of those animals which approach nearest to the human form, with that of man, he shews that they are as ill suited to the erect attitude as man is perfectly adapted for it. As the result of his inquiry, he states 'that the erect stature is not only a necessary result of the human structure, but that it is peculiar to man; and that the differences in the form and arrangement of parts, derived from this source only, are abundantly sufficient to distinguish man by a wide interval from all other animals.'—p. 165.

From the forms of the limbs, and the general structure of the frame, Mr Lawrence proceeds to the head, and the moral and intellectual qualities; and here he reverts to his former speculations, considering that in these most important characteristics of his nature, man is nothing more than an orangoutang or ape, with more 'ample cerebral hemispheres,' in whom the rotundity of the skull gives room for 'the more exquisite, complicated, and perfectly developed structure of the brain, and in consequence, for superiority in propensities, feelings and intellectual faculties.'—p. 237. In consistency with these ideas, he maintains that, in those varieties of the human species which have a retreating forehead and depressed vertex, there is a natural inferiority in intellectual capacity; and that it is as unreasonable to expect that the Americans or Africans can be raised by any culture to an equal height in moral sentiments and intellectual energy with Europeans, as to hope that the bulldog may be made to equal the greyhound in speed, or the mastiff taught to rival in talents and acquirements the sagacious and docile poodle.'— p. 501. We might, and perhaps ought, to reply to this argument, by physiological facts derived from other animals whose percipient powers are not varied by greater changes in the form of the brain in individuals of the same species inhabiting different parts of the globe; and by historical facts repecting various tribes of man himself, experiencing as little change of faculty under like changes of the sensorium: but we are hastening to a conclusion, and cannot therefore stop to inquire the precise degree in which Mr Lawrence is borne out in this assertion, or to consider how far it is consistent with what he allows in other passages respecting some of the savage tribes of North America, that they are intrepid, ardent, generous and humane; faithful to engagements; 'that their lofty sentiments of independence, ardent courage, and devoted friendship would sustain a comparison with the most splendid similar examples in the more highly gifted races.' We content ourselves with remarking that this warm friend of civil liberty and the rights of man supplies the best apology for those who would repress the benevolent attempts to raise the poor African in the scale of civilization; and that if at any time a slave-driver in the West Indies should feel some qualms of conscience for treating the blacks under his care as a herd of oxen, he would have only to imbibe Mr Lawrence's idea respecting their being as inferior to himself in mental faculties as the mastiff is to the greyhound in swiftness, and his mind would at once be set at ease on the subject.

To return, however, to the important subject of Mr Lawrence's doctrine of materialism. It is not certainly to physiology that we look for the main proofs of the immateriality of the soul, and its continuance after death—we only ask that this valuable science may not be enlisted into the service of infidelity; that, by disguising or concealing its facts, or misrepresenting the inferences to which they justly lead, it may not be brought to invalidate those other proofs of the immaterial and immortal nature of the soul, which, in reality, it is calculated to support. Mr Lawrence has the confidence to tell his readers, while he is striving with all his power to prove that men have no souls, and that the medullary matter of their brains thinks, that he is only speaking physiologically, and that 'the theological doctrine of the soul and its separate existence has nothing to do with this physiological question.'—p. 8. Nothing to do with it! Is he in his senses, or is he insulting the understandings of his readers? He endeavours to demonstrate from physiological principles, that what he calls the theological doctrine of the soul is *totally false*, and then says that this doctrine has nothing to do with the 'physiological question'! Why will he not be content with endeavouring to rob men of their religious hopes, and to degrade them to the brute creation, without expecting to impose on their simplicity by such assertions! . . .

[The reviewer turns to the grounds supplied by reason and Revelation for belief in a Supreme Being.]

One word more, and we have done. Mr Lawrence contends (p. 106) that the doctrines which he promulgates are true, and that truth ought always to be spoken. We beg leave to remind him that, when he affirms the doctrines to be true, the most he can possibly mean is that he *believes* them to be so; and it is not to be justified, we must inform him, on any sound principle, that a man should, at all times and under all circumstances, give currency to opinions of every description, on the mere ground that, in his private judgment, he believes them to be true. A considerate person will always feel a certain distrust of his own opinions, when he finds them opposed to those maintained by the generality of mankind, including the wisest and the best; and above all, he will most seriously weigh the tendency and the probable consequences of their general reception. Apply this to the opinions maintained by Mr Lawrence. Their tendency to impair the welfare of society, to break down the best and holiest sanctions of moral obligation, and to give a free rein to the worst passions of the human heart, is fully admitted even by those who embrace them. Voltaire, it is well known, checked his company from repeating blasphemous impieties before the servants, 'lest,' said he, 'they should cut all our throats;' and Mr Lawrence, we apprehend, would much sooner entrust his life and property to a person who believed that he had an immortal and accountable soul, than to one who believed, with him, that medullary matter thinks, and that the whole human being perishes with the dissolution of the body. What advantage then can he propose to himself, by endeavouring to promote the general reception of his opinions? Is it possible that he can desire to increase human vice and misery, to degrade his species by sowing the seeds of more sensuality, impiety, profligacy and worldly-mindedness than he actually finds among them? Or, when he knows that such is the tendency of his conduct, is it possible that his fancied love of truth, or the indulgence of his vanity can outweigh the feeling of what he owes to the welfare of his fellow-creatures?

We are by no means surprized to hear that Mr Lawrence has seriously injured himself in the opinion of the more respectable part of his profession by his late proceedings; and that he has already experienced from the public some of those consequences which he might have foreseen as the natural result. It has sometimes been said that sceptical opinions are prevalent to a considerable extent in the profession to which he belongs. We hope, and we believe, that this is not the case. Certain we are, that while Mr Lawrence is an almost solitary instance of a person of any consideration in that profession who has publicly maintained opinions hostile to religion, very many of the most eminent individuals in it have been distinguished for the firmness and the soundness of their religious principles; and, on the present occasion, the stand which many of them have made against his pernicious and degrading doctrines has been such as do them infinite credit.

But something more is necessary for the satisfaction of the public and the credit of the institution. It appears to us imperative on those who have the superintendence of the Royal College of Surgeons, to make it an indispensable condition of the continuance of Mr Lawrence in the office of lecturer, not only that he should strictly abstain from propagating any similar opinions in future, but that he should expunge from his lectures already published all those obnoxious passages which have given such deserved offence, and which are now circulating under the sanction of the College.

EXPLANATORY NOTES

Preface

3 The unsigned Preface was written by Percy Shelley, as though author of the novel. See MWS, Introduction to 3rd edition, Appendix A: 'As far as I can recollect, it was entirely written by him.' In 1831 the Preface is dated 'Marlow, September 1817'.

Dr Darwin: See Erasmus Darwin, *The Temple of Nature* (1803), especially i. 247–8 and Add. Note I, 'Spontaneous Vitality of Microscopic Animals'. Also relevant to the question of spontaneous generation are Darwin's footnotes to i. 235 on heat, attraction, chemical affinity, and contraction, and his long Add. Note XII, 'Chemical Theory of Electricity and Magnetism.' An outstanding popular writer on science in his annotated poem *The Botanic Garden* (1791) and above all his medical-physiological treatise *Zoonomia* (1794–6), Darwin's proto-evolutionary outlook has illuminated much of the natural science in *Frankenstein*, e.g. the development of the Creature in Vol. II, and hereditary disease in Vol. III (for the latter, see Add. Note XI).

physiological writers of Germany: Mary and Percy Shelley would have been aware of the distinction of current German physiologists from their friend William Lawrence, professor at the Royal College of Surgeons and since 1814 Percy Shelley's doctor. Lawrence translated Blumenbach's *Comparative Anatomy* (1807), and gave an account of 'Recent German Zoologists', including Blumenbach, Rudolphi, and Tiedemann, in his Introductory Lecture to his course on Comparative Anatomy (1817), published as Lecture I in his *Lectures on Physiology, Zoology and The Natural History of Man* (1819). See Introduction.

yet . . . terrors: Shelley cautiously draws attention to the paradox on which the novel rests: its use of the fashionable medieval tale of the supernatural to tell a present-day or futuristic narrative grounded in real-life modern science.

casual conversation: for this conversation, see MWS's Introduction (1831) in Appendix A, pp. 195–6. MWS's account does not fully accord with Polidori's contemporaneous *Diary*. See Introduction, pp. xxi–xxiv and James Rieger (ed), *Frankenstein*, p. xvii.

4 *of whatever kind*: another coded reference, presumably to the likelihood that the book would be read as an attack on Christianity.

stories of ghosts: *Fantasmagoriana, ou Recueil d'Histories d'Apparitions de Spectres, Revenans, Fantomes, etc; traduit de l'allemand, par un Amateur*, 2 vols. (Paris, 1812). The translator was Jean Baptiste Benoit Eyriès (1767–1846).

to write each a story: This number is incorrect. Of the five adults in the party staying near Geneva, only Claire Clairmont seems to have expressed no interest in taking part. Percy Shelley, already the author of the two short Gothic novels, *St Irvyne* and *Zastrozzi*, did join in, Mary Shelley later recalled, though he produced almost nothing. She also remembered an elaborate tale from Polidori, about a woman whose head was turned into a skull because she saw something forbidden through a key-hole. (See MWS's Introduction in Appendix A, p. 194.) For Polidori's *The Vampyre* and Byron's vampirish 'A Fragment', see Introduction, p. xxiii.

Frankenstein; or, The Modern Prometheus

6 *I may discover . . . for ever*: Walton's hopes of the Arctic are based on the speculative science of the day. Electricity and magnetism were provisionally thought of as 'ethereal', i.e. invisible fluids, as yet imperfectly understood, but dependent, like the motions of the sun and planets, air and ocean, on attraction and repulsion. These fluids, surrounding individual bodies and the planets, were connected with heat and light, and might therefore be an essentially material source and precondition of life. Walton may, in short, be looking (like Frankenstein) for the source of life. See Introduction, pp. xvii–xviii, xxxiv–xxxvi.

9 *keeping*: in drawing, proper relations between nearer and more distant objects, i.e. perspective, harmony.

10 *the land of mist and snow*: Coleridge, *Ancient Mariner* (1798), l. 403.

12 *ground sea*: a heavy sea with large waves.

18   *syndics*: legislators of Geneva, chosen out of the small group of
      élite families of this aristocratic republic.

21   *Orlando . . St George*: Ariosto's *Orlando Furioso* was favourite
      reading for quite young English children following its blank
      verse translation by Hoole, 1774. Joseph Ritson made tradi-
      tional Robin Hood ballads available in his popular collection,
      1795. *Amadis de Gaul*, a traditional Spanish and Portuguese
      romance, was first translated into English from Garcia de
      Montalvo's Spanish version by Southey in 1803. There is noth-
      ing Genevan about this list.

22   *Natural philosophy*: common eighteenth-century term for the
      physical sciences, especially physics.

      Cornelius Agrippa: of Nettesheim (1486–1535), German cab-
      balist and author of *De Occulta Philosophia Libri Tres* (1529).
      Perhaps the most sinister of the trio of Renaissance scientists
      studied by Frankenstein, since he was popularly remembered
      by the story of his disobedient apprentice, who on peeping
      into his master's books accidentally conjured up the Devil,
      with fatal results. For the ballad about him see Introduction,
      pp. xxvii–xxviii.

23   *Paracelsus and Abertus Magnus*: Paracelsus, born Theophrastus
      Bombastus von Hohenheim (1493?–1541), Swiss doctor,
      chemist and mystic, whose interests spanned medieval al-
      chemy and early modern empirical medicine. Enlighten-
      ment historians of science recognised the contribution of
      Paracelsus's experimentalism and holism; the different evalua-
      tions by Krempe and Waldman reflect arguments Percy
      Shelley heard in his schooldays, on which Frankenstein's scien-
      tific education is largely based. Frankenstein's career is also
      modelled on that of the hero of Godwin's novel *St Leon*, who
      meets a man resembling Paracelsus: see Introduction, p. xiv.
      Albertus Magnus (1193?–1280), Dominican theologian, Aris-
      totelian and teacher, who studied plant life and the brain. He
      is associated with the device of a brazen head, illusion or
      mechanical device, that could answer questions.

24   *The raising of ghosts or devils*: eighteenth-century Illuminists,
      including the Order of that name established by Weishaupt at
      Ingolstadt in 1775, but also including Cagliostrans, Martinists,
      and others, searched for a knowledge whereby the initiated
      might communicate with supernatural beings. Members of
      such groups were often, though not always, revolutionary sym-
      pathizers. P. B. Shelley seems to acknowledge his own experi-

ments of this kind in *Alastor* (ll. 26–9) and 'Hymn to Intellectual Beauty' (1816), 'While yet a boy I sought for ghosts . . . I . . with fearful steps pursuing I Hopes of high talk with the departed dead.I I called on poisonous names with which our youth is fed; I I was not heard—I saw them not.' (ll. 49, 51–4).

24 *fluid from the clouds*: an allusion to the famous experiment conducted by Benjamin Franklin, who did most to launch the intense public interest in electricity both as a source of power and as the key to some of science's theoretical riddles.

25 *Pliny and Buffon*: Caius Plinius Secundus or Pliny (AD 23–79), Roman naturalist, was the author of *Natural History*, which helped convince Percy Shelley of the case for vegetarianism. Buffon (1707–88), French naturalist and author of the monumental *Histoire naturelle*, 44 vols. (1749–1804), was still the inescapable point of reference; see e.g. the Creature's carefully drawn learning-process in Vol. II.

26 *university of Ingolstadt*: Bavarian university, 1472–1800, notorious in the French Revolution period as the home of the feared sect of conspirators and unorthodox religionists, the Illuminati. See above, n. 24 on *the raising of ghosts or devils*.

28 *old familiar faces*: title of popular sentimental poem (1798) by Charles Lamb.

35 *seemingly ineffectual light*: see *Thousand and One Nights*, Sinbad's Fourth Voyage.

36 *if I could bestow . . . corruption*: a number of well-known attempts had been made to induce life, whether by animating single-cell creatures, such as body-parasites, or by reviving dead bodies, including executed criminals. Some of the best-known were associated with Luigi Galvani (1737–98), who was testing the functions of electricity: see Bibliography for the book by Galvani's nephew, John Aldini. For allusions to contemporary experiments in the novel, see Introduction, pp. xxix–xxx.

38 *instruments of life*: Galvani's experiments explored the role of 'animal electricity' in the nerves and muscles of small creatures such as frogs. To animate a much larger animal (such as the eight-foot Creature) Frankenstein may have calculated he needed a gigantic Voltaic battery. It is at this point in the story, at the culmination of the experiment, with the sentence 'It was on a dreary night . . ', that the original tale began.

41   *close behind him tread*: Coleridge's 'Ancient Mariner' (MWS's note), ll. 446–51.

       diligence: a stagecoach.

       Dutch schoolmaster in 'The Vicar of Wakefield': Goldsmith, *The Vicar of Wakefield*, ch. 20.

46   *the beauty of Angelica*: Angelica is the heroine of Ariosto's *Orlando Furioso* (1516).

54   *cabriole*: a small two-wheeled horse-drawn carriage.

55   *palaces of nature*: Byron, *Childe Harold's Pilgrimage*, III (1816), lxii. 2.

70   *Belrive*: the Frankensteins' country home is on the south shore of Lac Léman, some four miles beyond Cologny, where the Byron–Shelley party stayed in 1816. From this direction Geneva is entered via the park at Plainpalais, outside the city wall, where William was murdered. The river Arve, flowing down from the Mont Blanc range through the Val de Chamonix, enters Lac Léman through Plainpalais. The Shelleys took the expedition to Chamonix and its glacier, or river of ice, in July 1816, recording it in their letters and journals and in P. B. Shelley's 'Mont Blanc.'

73   *aiguilles*: peaks.

75   *necessary*: Enlightenment materialist and sceptical thinkers (such as Godwin) saw a multigeneity of causes, predisposing indivduals to certain attitudes, subjecting them to their environment, and drastically curtailing their power to act freely. This is the 'law' of science and nature, which implicitly challenges Divine Law. Tactfully worded, this passage nevertheless appears to accept such a law and to imply that Frankenstein's unhappiness comes from his inability to do so, i.e. his alienation from the natural.

76   *. . . mutability*: from P. B. Shelley, 'On Mutability', published in *Alastor: or the Spirit of Solitude* (Jan. 1816).

83   *lake of fire*: Milton, *Paradise Lost*, i. 670 ff.

92   *the ass and the lapdog*: see La Fontaine, *Fables*, the fable of the Ass and the Lapdog. Seeing that the Lapdog is fondled when he rubs against his master, the Ass tries this, but is shouted at and beaten.

95   *Ruins of Empires*: Constantin François Chassebœuf, comte de Volney, *Les Ruines, ou meditation sur les révolutions des empires*

(Paris, 1791; English trans., 1792), a powerful polemic on the government of ancient and modern empires, and particularly on the role of religion in sustaining them. Volney's *Ruins* remained a force in English radicalism throughout the first half of the nineteenth century. The Eastern style and range of reference to which Felix alludes arises from Volney's experience as a scholarly travel-writer in the Middle East; this dimension gives the Creature a world rather than a European perspective.

103 *Paradise Lost . . . Werter*: Milton's *Paradise Lost*, 1667; Plutarch's *Parallel Lives* (*c.* AD 100); Johann von Goethe's *Sorrows of Young Werther* (1774), three books presumably intended to complement the political and historical sweep of Volney through their focus on individuals and their concern with morality, both public and private.

104 *The path . . . was free*: Shelley, 'On Mutability'. See n. 76 above on *mutability*.

Numa . . . Theseus: Numa Pompilius, early king of Rome, and Lycurgus, Spartan lawgiver, are legendary, like the soldier-heroes Romulus (Rome) and Theseus (Athens). Solon, Athenian lawgiver, is a historical figure.

107 *De Lacy*: De Lacey in Ch. VI. Rieger speculates that it was at this point in the text that MWS on 24 Sept. 1817 handed over a new packet of proofs to P. B. Shelley, giving him carte blanche to make changes. Alternatively the 1818 typesetter sometimes misread MWS's handwriting. 1823 has De Lacey throughout.

111 *bore a hell within me*: cf. Satan, envious in the Garden, *Paradise Lost*, iv. 75 ff.

113 *Whither . . . bend my steps*: cf. the expulsion of Adam and Eve from Eden, 'The world was all before them, where to choose | Their place of rest.' *Paradise Lost*, xii. 646–7.

123 *dull ugly siroc on its way to consume me*: the sirocco, an unpleasant hot wind from N. Africa that blows into S. Europe and is sometimes considered poisonous.

hellish hypocrites: Dante, *Inferno*, xxiii. 58 ff.

130 *very poetry of nature*: MWS's note: 'Leigh Hunt's "Rimini" ', i.e. his narrative poem on the love affair of Paolo and Francesca, *The Story of Rimini* (1816).

Unborrowed from the eye: MWS's note: 'Wordsworth's "Tintern Abbey" ', 77–83.

133   *Falkland*: Lucius Cary, 2nd Viscount Falkland (1610?–43), writer, courtier, statesman and reluctant participant in the Civil War. He deliberately rode into enemy gunfire and was killed at the Battle of Newbury, 20 Sept. 1643. As the model Cavalier hero he is a prototype for Godwin's character Falkland in *Caleb Williams* (1794).

Gower: a mistake for Goring; corrected 1831. George Goring, Baron Goring (1608–57), was another Royalist courtier, but by reputation Falkland's antitype—ambitious, dissolute, treacherous and unprincipled.

Isis: the name given to the river Thames as it flows through Oxford.

ennui: French for boredom and lassitude, but at this time a term with specific medical connotations as a symptom of *hypochondria*: i.e. chronic depression, considered an occupational disease of the well-off modern leisured male, while *hysteria* was the affliction of the female of the same class. In her admired short novel *Ennui* (*Tales of Fashionable Life*, 1st series, 1809), Maria Edgeworth depicts an English nobleman suffering from the same complaint, documenting her account from a current medical treatise, William Cullen's *First lines of the practice of physic*, new edn. (Edinburgh, 1796) iii. 299. The depressive heroes of Godwin's *Fleetwood* (1805) and *Mandeville* (1817) also seem to suffer from a malady at least in part socially induced.

patriot fell: John Hampden (1594–1643), statesman and Parliamentarian leader, was killed at Chalgrove Field, Buckinghamshire, twelve miles east of Oxford. In 1809 Godwin wrote an *Essay on Sepulchres*, which reacted against official monuments preponderantly to royalty, politicians, and military men: Godwin demanded plain wooden crosses for Opposition heroes, of whom Hampden was still one of the most admired.

134   *Servox and Chamounix*: in July 1816 the Shelleys visited the Swiss village of Servox, where there were lead and copper mines, and a small exhibition reminding Shelley of similar 'cabinets' he had seen at Keswick and Bethgelert. PBS to T. L. Peacock, 22 July 1816.

cheat me into happiness: a tentative compliment to the Lake poets, Wordsworth and Southey. Percy Shelley visited Southey in 1812 and sent him a copy of *Alastor* (1816), though it contained criticism of the Lake group. The work of both

Shelleys, 1816–18, remains full of echoes of Southey, Coleridge, and Wordsworth.

135 *friend expected us*: from June to November 1812, and June 1813 to March 1814, Mary Shelley stayed in the region north of Edinburgh, with her friends the Baxters at Dundee.

140 *period of your power*: i.e. termination of your power.

145 *Kirwin*: one of MWS's two named Irish characters shares a name, perhaps coincidentally, with the leading Irish chemist of the day, Richard Kirwan (1733–1812), described in DNB as 'the Nestor of English chemistry'.

154 *maladie du pays*: homesickness.

163 *quit its native country*: able Swiss leaving for France included Rousseau, Necker (Louis XVI's Minister), and Necker's daughter Germaine, afterwards de Staël, who in 1816 still lived across Lac Leman at Coppet.

invader who should wish to enslave it: another patriotic and topical reference. French republican generals did indeed invade and 'enslave' the Swiss republics in 1797–8, to the dismay of many British liberals. Like the persistent dating of the novel's letters 17—, these hints encourage the reader to put the action in or shortly before the 1790s. One political interpretation of the plot is that it re-enacts the dying stages of the Genevan republic, its death unwittingly brought on by the intellectual over-reaching, selfishness, and exclusivity of its ruling order.

178 *manes*: spirits of family dead.

183 *turn their backs on the foe*: Rieger points out that Frankenstein's last speech echoes one in which Dante's Ulysses persuades his sailors to join him in a fatal voyage of discovery 'to pursue power and knowledge'. Dante finds Ulysses consigned to the ditch reserved in Hell for evil counsellors. *Inferno*, xxvi. 118–20.

184 *September 9th*: this date was corrected in 1823, from 19th September

Appendix A

192 *Standard Novels*: i.e., Henry Colburn and Richard Bentley, the publishers of the new Standard Novels series, a much cheaper format in a single volume than the customary 2–5 volumes.

192 *companion and friend*: perhaps Isabel Baxter of Dundee, with whom MWS stayed for much of 1812 and 1813–14. But MWS hardly 'lived principally in the country as a girl'.

193 *eyry*: or eyrie, (remote) nest of a bird of prey.

194 *tale of the sinful founder*: The second, unnamed story, about a vampire, appears to have partly prompted both Byron and MWS. See Introduction, pp. xxiv–xxv. Rieger comments that MWS does not recollect the two stories accurately.

Mazeppa: see Introduction, pp. xxiii and xxvi.

[*Peeping*] *Tom of Coventry*: spied on Lady Godiva, and is supposed to have been struck blind. But Polidori claims that the story he really told at Cologny was a first attempt at his novel *Ernestus Berchtold: or the Modern Oedipus* (1819).

195 *Sanchean phrase*: Sancho Panza, in Cervantes' *Don Quixote*, II. xxiii.

Columbus and his egg: when Columbus was told by a courtier that anyone might have discovered the Indies, he allegedly challenged all present to stand an egg on end. After everyone failed, he did it himself by crushing the end.

Many and long . . . communicated: MWS remembers only Byron and Shelley in one conversation, but Polidori's *Diary* indicates a conversation at which he was himself present. For 'the principle of life', see Introduction, pp. xviii–xxi, and Appendix C.

move with voluntary motion: Darwin discusses the principle rather than a particular experiment in *Temple of Nature*, Add. Note 1. For experiments, see Introduction, pp. xviii–xxi, and note to p. 36, *if I could bestow . . . corruption*.

galvanism: see Bibliography, Aldini.

196 *My imagination . . .* : MWS mystifies the train of ideas that led from the conversation to the story, omitting both literary and scientific sources.

Creator of the world: the first passage by MWS reinterpreting her own plot in a religious style that a reader of post-1831 editions encountered. For the authorial reinterpretation, see Appendix B.

197 *It was on a dreary night of November*: i.e., the opening lines of Vol. I, Ch. III.

husband: the MS of *Frankenstein* shows minor corrections only by P. B. Shelley, and tends to confirm MWS's claim that his contributions were minor. See Bibliography, E. B. Murray, and A. Mellor (1988), appendix, pp. 219–24.

197   *untouched*: but cf. Appendix B. What MWS says is strictly truthful, but also in Burke's phrase 'economical of the truth': it leaves out her consistently religious reworking of (e.g.) the inward discourse of Frankenstein.

The Oxford World's Classics Website

www.worldsclassics.co.uk

- Information about new titles
- Explore the full range of Oxford World's Classics
- Links to other literary sites and the main OUP webpage
- Imaginative competitions, with bookish prizes
- Peruse the Oxford World's Classics Magazine
- Articles by editors
- Extracts from Introductions
- A forum for discussion and feedback on the series
- Special information for teachers and lecturers

www.worldsclassics.co.uk

American Literature

British and Irish Literature

Children's Literature

Classics and Ancient Literature

Colonial Literature

Eastern Literature

European Literature

History

Medieval Literature

Oxford English Drama

Poetry

Philosophy

Politics

Religion

The Oxford Shakespeare

A complete list of Oxford Paperbacks, including Oxford World's Classics, Oxford Shakespeare, Oxford Drama, and Oxford Paperback Reference, is available in the UK from the Academic Division Publicity Department, Oxford University Press, Great Clarendon Street, Oxford OX2 6DP.

In the USA, complete lists are available from the Paperbacks Marketing Manager, Oxford University Press, 198 Madison Avenue, New York, NY 10016.

Oxford Paperbacks are available from all good bookshops. In case of difficulty, customers in the UK can order direct from Oxford University Press Bookshop, Freepost, 116 High Street, Oxford OX1 4BR, enclosing full payment. Please add 10 per cent of published price for postage and packing.